CONFESSIONS

CONFESSIONS

Diana Silber

BANTAM BOOKS
NEW YORK · TORONTO · LONDON · SYDNEY · AUCKLAND

CONFESSIONS

A Bantam Book / March 1990

Library of Congress Cataloging-in-Publication Data

Silber, Diana.
   Confessions / Diana Silber.
     p. cm.
   ISBN 0-553-05745-6
   I. Title
PS3569.I413C6   1990
813'.54—dc20   89-17853
                                         CIP

Published simultaneously in the United States and Canada

Bantam Books are published by Bantam Books, a division of Bantam
Doubleday Dell Publishing Group, Inc. Its trademark, consisting of the
words "Bantam Books" and the portrayal of a rooster, is Registered in
U.S. Patent and Trademark Office and in other countries. Marca
Registrada. Bantam Books, 666 Fifth Avenue, New York, New York 10103.

PRINTED IN THE UNITED STATES OF AMERICA

BG   0 9 8 7 6 5 4 3 2 1

To my mother, Doreen Henstell

"Between friends there is no need of justice."
　　　　　　　　　　—Aristotle *Nichomachean Ethics*

"Love can die of a truth, as friendship of a lie."
　　　　　　　　　　—Abel Bonnard *The Art of Friendship*

"The past is in its grave,
Though its ghost haunts us."
　　　　　　　　　　—Robert Browning *Pauline*

PROLOGUE

The chapel, actually a self-contained building, a church with a steeple and a bell tower, a small, whitewashed structure at the top of the senior quadrangle, was filled with students, faculty members, and the town's curious. Bodies of all shapes and sizes and in various dress crowded the straight, uncomfortable benches from the plain walls to the center aisle, and those who arrived late massed in the rear under the jutting choir loft. The chapel had never held so many, not at graduation services when even nonchurchgoers attended the morning prayer ceremony, or at historic moments, the nation's as well as the college's, when some sort of religious gesture seemed in order. William Jennings Bryant once spoke from behind the very same pulpit the Reverend Shay leaned against now, and earlier William Lloyd Garrison roared his anathemas down on that "divine institution" slavery, as did Frederick Douglass, so tall and handsome, in his sweet tones like a lion's purr, and they all drew crowds. But no one brought out so many as did Lily Vaughan, dead and in the mahogany coffin—closed, of course—displayed at the front of the church.

Dead, Lily Vaughan commanded far more interest than she ever had alive, and students who wouldn't have recognized her crossing the campus, or had never even heard her name, turned out for her final rites. Cabot's president, a shrewd woman who understood the allure and seduction of fame, or, more accurately, infamy, canceled classes for the morning. But few Cabot girls slept in. Most came to the chapel instead to stare at the coffin—so large for such a small girl!—at Newbury, Vermont's paunchy, slow-moving, but sharp-eyed police chief, at the state trooper in a neatly pressed uniform and black sunglasses that masked the top of his face, at Lily's mother, a brittle woman accompanied by a recent husband, almost as young as her dead daughter. But most of all, people came to stare at the four girls who sat together on the east side of the chapel, midway down, looking neither right nor

1

left, but straight at the Reverend Shay in his raven's robes, and at President Wellsberg, dark suited as a nun, to his side. The girls, all seniors, and far better known to their fellow students than Lily Vaughan, had celebrity status now. In the midst of the maelstrom, rumors eddied about them, fast, faster, as furious as the winter's storm in which Lily Vaughan had been stabbed to death.

One of the fanciful stories had the girls stabbing Lily together, four hands on the handle of the ice pick; but it hadn't been an ice pick that drove through Lily's heart, just an ordinary kitchen knife, and it would have taken a handle four times the size for all those hands to fit.

Then there was the story that one girl killed her but the others swore silence in a satanic ritual performed on the snow in moonlight. There was even the silly notion passed about Cabot that Lily died by her own efforts, that her hand forced the knife into her own heart.

The truth, chilling though it was, failed to satisfy those who enjoyed their mysteries neat and tidied up, the perpetrator tried and locked away. The truth failed to pin the label "murderer" on anyone. The truth was that the girls, awakening on the third morning of midsemester k in the ski house belonging to Quinn Webster's uncle, discovered Lily Vaughan gone.

The snow, falling steadily most of the day, stopped around midnight, long after the girls had gone to bed and slept, all but obviously Lily. For some reason nobody was able to explain, when the clouds crumbled into wisps of tissuey light, as the icy wedge of the moon appeared against the velvet sky, Lily Vaughan went outside without boots or a jacket.

On the long slope of white between the house, an angular building of new bleached wood, and the cluttered blackness of the flanking trees, Lily Vaughan waged a struggle not to die, if the churned-up snow, the bright blood-red poinsettias were evidence.

When dawn came, morning with its brilliant light, Lily, sculpted out of ice, frozen in a sea of red, lay lifeless, the wooden handle like some peculiar ornament in one breast. An awkward tangle of arms and legs, Lily might have been seeking rest, shelter, or entombment, in the snow. All about the landscape, from the house to Lily, from Lily down the short drive to the secondary two-lane road, the flat, unblemished white had been trampled. And nearby was Susie Bannon's undigested breakfast, which she'd thrown up.

Lisbeth Ross had been the one who phoned the police, or rather the operator who sent out the state troopers. Dinah Esterman, bundled in parka, scarf, woolly hat and matching gloves, waited by the turn in the road, for the house, which Quinn's playboy uncle had won in a poker game, was difficult to see beyond the trees, and besides, it had started to snow again.

The four girls who'd gone out together to stare at Lily dead, in her mummy's wrapping of navy slacks and heavy sweater with prancing reindeers in friezes at neck and waist, stood stupefied, surprised by death. Yet in that just-above-zero cold, on the scuffed snow, they refused to look at one another. It was only hours later, returning in Lisbeth's jeep to Cabot, that each swore: "Not me." The girls singly and collectively claimed innocence. Eventually the troopers and Newbury's police chief decided to believe them, as did President Wellsberg, the Cabot administration, and after a time, the other students. It was much more reassuring to think of some stranger, a wandering drugged-out hippie, committing such a crime. And the girls, the best of friends since freshman orientation, clung together, bound even tighter by dead Lily Vaughan, bound as if in chains by the dead girl whom they had all hated alive. They promised themselves when the funeral service ended, and after the burial in Newbury's old cemetery, which they chose not to attend, not to think about "this," or talk about it more than they had already, and they didn't really, not for years anyway, until it seemed that Lily Vaughan had risen from the dead.

1

The rain clinked against the roof of The Home of The Good Shepherd in an insistent metallic clatter, the rhythm never varying. Susie's screams were drowned out by the deluge of the September storm. In the third-floor linen closet, large as a small office, the shelves stacked with old sheets, patched and washed so often they had thinned to webbing in spots, gray military blankets, frayed towels cut skimpily and rough against the skin, Susie's cries struck the walls, the ceiling, with less impact than puffs of dust.

His raspy, excited breathing was louder than her small panicky screams. Terrified and disbelieving, she watched the cracked hands with hair that ran in a wiry pelt along the backs and the fingers to the ragged nails black with half moons of dirt. They darted about with the frenzy of small, rapacious animals, sought some purchase, as if she were a slippery slab of mountain rock that the man meant to climb, and they scrambled at her small breasts beneath the soft cashmere sweater-vest and silk shirt, rousing in her a breathless, watery fear.

Oh God, help, please! Susie begged voicelessly as even through her clothing she felt the stab of those cruel fingers. But that pain was nothing to the battering of his bony knee against her thigh. Her legs were forced apart as though he had hammered a clear passage with a blunt instrument. In his urgency the parts of his body, legs, hands, arms, feet, even his mouth, were weapons, and the man, so much larger than Susie's slight five feet two, one hundred pounds, became deadly. His breath blew in a fetid stream along her cheek and his tongue darted lizardlike between her lips.

The shirt ripped loose from the waistband of her skirt and his hand plunged at her, the scaly touch of rough skin unmooring a wave of disgust and nausea. The lacy bra tore in his grasp and when he grabbed one of her breasts, squeezing the nipple like a grape until it seemed it

4

had to burst, the pain overrode everything and Susie screamed again. The man smacked her then, a full slap to the side of her mouth, and blood spurted over her tongue. The taste of her blood started to choke her and she gagged, but the big man paid no attention to anything but his own wild need.

His other hand sped beneath her skirt and Susie's struggles increased, frenzy escalating beyond the panic that constricted her throat and changed the cries to moans of despair and terror so deep she thought she was drowning. Her heart hammered and the rapid punching under her ribs hurt.

Her panty hose tore, and with her skirt rucked up to her waist, a cold draft swept over her, and then she felt the nudge of his swollen penis, hot as a flame, and she bucked up, crazed, to force him off. For a second, desire made him weak, and Susie loosened his hold, twisting backwards and to the side. In that moment she saw his face for the first time. A hard-ridged scar snaked across his forehead and between busy caterpillar brows, striking the bridge of a shark's nose like a jagged bolt of lightning. With his wild, coal-dark eyes, he seemed to be the storm itself beating on the old warehouse building. His lips—all but hidden in the unkempt thicket of beard which gave him the maniacal appearance of a raving prophet—parted. She saw the gleam of his rat's teeth.

Her hand grasped frantically for a weapon, anything to flail away at him. She discovered nothing but the bedding, neatly stacked, and she pulled blankets and sheets down on them, which he shrugged off as if they were nothing more than the thin wetness of the rain. There really was no weapon lethal enough to counter his need. He was the first man at the beginning of time, crawling up from the slime, and Susie, expensively dressed, coiffed, and made up, Susie, schooled and knowledgeable, Susie, a high-bred, finely boned creature of culture and civilization, now, on the dusty closet floor, blood spurting from the tear in her bottom lip, breath discordant and desperate, had become nothing but woman with that dark, hidden cove in which he struggled to spend himself.

Susie had been dragged to the edge of a towering cliff in the worst of nightmares, and now, like death itself, the inevitable rushed over her, and she flew in a tumbling drop without any hope of being saved. *I'm dying,* she thought, terrified as he rammed himself in her, pummeling the unyielding flesh, fighting the lack of desire and her last violent, futile effort to eject him.

Darkness and pain firing beyond the borders of any known previous pain spread through Susie as he pounded her flesh like dead meat,

5

lifting her up in his paws and thumping her down again. Her head slammed the floor and her heels thumped in muffled drum rolls. The fragile vertebrae of her spine felt as if they were snapping like walnut shells.

In the second when he galloped, crazy for that spurt of pleasure, just before he arched and whimpered the bleating cry of relief, Susie prayed not to die but to be already dead, to be anywhere, even in hell, rather than in the boiling sea of pain. And she did, just that instant, rise up and fly off in terror so complete it could have been death itself, death erasing the last shimmering flicker of consciousness with a heavy black wave.

"Soooosssseeee! Soooosssseeee!" Her mother's voice, thin and far away at the bottom of the Baltimore stairs, calling her to breakfast, trying to disinter her from the snug clasp of sleep, to get her moving, dressed, on the path to school. She would hear that call, her own name elongated, all her life, heard it still. No firm nudge of imagination was needed to jettison Susie Bannon Lamton into the calm waters of long ago, to glide her gently along a river of memory. Only it wasn't Ivy Bannon in her daily attempt to pry her daughter free from sleep who spoke her name in the distance, the sound slowly floating nearer and nearer in a feeble smudge of light, a faltering of darkness like the sky at the rim of early dawn. No, it wasn't her mother at all, and she didn't lie warm, drowsy, still tingly with sleep, wisps of some dream lingering, in her sixteen-year-old's bed, fine lisle curtains at the window billowing lazily in the faint spring breeze.

I hurt, she thought, pain in tiny spurts licking her back, her legs, rippling down her arms, and a deeper well of pain inside, *there. That secret place,* they used to call it back in Baltimore, the girls whispering conspiratorially, mystery and longing mixed in hushed nighttime voices. Her breasts hurt too, though less than *there,* and her face. Her tongue felt raw and swollen.

"Susie! Oh dear Jesus! Mother of God! Susie, speak to me!"

In the grayness heavier shadows coalesced. "Father Simon?" Her whisper had the cramped sound to it of a voice long silenced, fragile from disuse. Her throat was dry and it hurt to swallow. "Father Simon," she wheezed again, "is that you?"

"Thank God! You're alive!"

Arms reached down, hands, slender with finely tapered fingers and not hairy, blunt, tearing, ripping, but still she squeezed herself in sudden panic, shivering as she was raised off her back into a sitting position. Gently placed, she leaned against the wall. Then the dizziness drained away so that she saw Father Simon squatting in front of her. His face hung, close up like a medallion, shaded pools in his eye sockets, black declensions along the sides of his straight nose and streaming from the corners of his mouth. It seemed, for a moment, more a spider's web than a face, but then he moved and the light blanched the shadows. She recognized his face, and her hand crept toward his gratefully. They clung to each other through the fragile entwining of fingers. He seemed as relieved as she was.

"What happened?" he asked minutes later, when her breathing had calmed and her heart regained its steady pace.

Susie licked her lips and got the salty taste of blood. *My face!* She feared some terrible destruction, but would not reach up to investigate. Her thoughts came clear all at once. Just knowing she survived, the mists dissipated. What visible damage there was she'd have to cover up somehow and was grateful Greg had gone to Chicago on business. The girls, as she often said, wouldn't notice an elephant in the bathtub. As for Mrs. Sloan, whatever she suspected she'd never say. The housekeeper's talents, beside cooking and keeping the apartment in perfect shape, included discretion and silence.

"Susie?"

He'd asked her a question, she remembered suddenly, as if that had been yesterday. Time played funny tricks in her head and she wondered how long she had lain half dead, her consciousness closed to pain and the assault on her body. All at once she realized *I've been raped!* That was what the pain meant, that aching scream she couldn't free herself from. And the blood. Slowly the big man with his tangle of hair and his filthy breath crept back into memory, and her hand squeezed the priest's until her nails dug into his palm. Gently he loosened her grasp and stroked her hair, the side of her face, went pat-pat on her shoulder the way an old man, a grandfather or an honorary uncle, would do, though he was approximately her own age. Strange, but she'd never considered his age before, or his humanness, his individual self, that part of him that was man and had been before he'd been consecrated.

"Susie?"

Seen through the tears in her eyes his face was indistinct, his plaid flannel shirt a blur of shifting colors. She blinked and cried, soft as a bird (though she didn't know that), "I was raped."

"Oh sweet Jesus!" he breathed, in pain himself. She felt his tension run through his hand like a low sizzle of electricity. She turned away, afraid he found her loathsome. But that fear no sooner rose inside her strong as the pain itself than she pushed it down. He wasn't that sort of man or priest. Father Simon had seen every degradation man was capable of; nothing in the slums of Manhattan or the jungles and villages of Vietnam before that could surprise him anymore. Once he'd bled raw from each individual suffering, he had told her, until the world's agony almost washed him away. Like a physician in the midst of a plague, he had learned to harden himself in order to help. Sympathy made him useless.

Susie wanted to tell him she was sorry, that she'd caused trouble by coming to the shelter to help, to offer something. Now she would be taking more away than she gave: Father Simon's time and concern when there were those needier who deserved them. He was saying something to her, and she had to concentrate to understand him. How odd! The pain made her sleepy. She wanted to burrow down right here, in this corner *where it happened* and just drift off. Maybe, if luck were with her, she'd wake up in Baltimore. It would be 1957 and she'd be ten years old. That was when she'd gotten her first two-wheeler, a red and white Schwinn. Oh, how jealous her sister Jody, only eight, had been!

"Come on, Susie. Let me get you into my room. You can wash up and then we'll go downstairs and call the police."

He lifted her up, and the motion felt like a whirl on a carousel, the world a blur, the air throbbing with music! From the long-ago Baltimore past the sounds of "Daisy" caroled and Father Simon spun upside down in her vision.

He walked her out of the closet into the empty third-floor corridor. The overnighters weren't upstairs yet in the two big dormitories, women on the east side of the building, men to the west. He said it again. *Police!*

"No!" she cried, dragging him to a stop. "No police!"

"Susie, we have to. You were attacked. Assaulted," he said, avoiding the word *rape*. As always, in the worst of times he sounded reasonable. Hearing Father Simon say mass downstairs at the small portable altar made Susie believe in God, so this time how could she not, in the horrible real world, follow where he led? But she couldn't.

A tall man, easily six feet, he didn't seem as big to her now as she usually felt him to be. He loomed over her, a blur except for his blue eyes, the shade of the nighttime sky, so dark the pupils were difficult to distinguish. She imagined herself reflected in those eyes.

They began to move again in a motion stately and deliberate as a minuet, and she tried to explain how the police were out of the question. The publicity. Greg. The girls. Her mother and father home in Baltimore. Even her best friends. Not one of the three of them knew of the shelter. My secret, she struggled to tell the priest, but the words got lost somewhere. She drooped, sleepy again, and when he laid her carefully on the frayed white chenille spread of his bed in the tiny cubbyhole he kept for himself, she slipped off. In the misty distance she heard him ask, "Who, Susie? Who did this to you?"

She meant to answer she didn't know. A stranger in the darkness, jumping out at her. A man lurking in the dormitory where he shouldn't have been. Only a face, pocked and rough as the surface of the moon, and those hands. Gone now, she thought she said, like the rain that had ceased its clattering at last. But her lips remained motionless as her eyes closed.

He let her sleep. She had no idea how long she'd been gone, but awakening she found him on a straight-back chair at the side of the bed keeping a vigil. From beyond the door she heard the shuffling bodies like cattle in a truck moving themselves along the floor, squeaking the springs of the iron cots. She heard murmuring. She thought of birds beating their wings to take flight.

She came out of sleep with a clear head and an aching body. The pain had diminished to a throbbing soreness. *I've been raped,* she told herself. She saw it completely, immediate as a Technicolor movie splashed on a large screen, replaying inside her head. Even the spidery hairs on his hands came back to her.

"How do you feel?" Father Simon asked, bending over her. Above him she saw the naked bulb hanging on a long cord from the ceiling. This bulb was like a small sun, not like the one in the closet.

"Better," she replied, and wanted to grope for his hand to latch onto. She felt shamed once again, as though the attack had been her fault, as though the violation made it painfully plain she was a woman. Well, that was true. At the shelter she meant not to be female and financially comfortable, privileged, an alien from a far-off planet. Susie sensed that Mars was closer than her apartment on Central Park West, which took up a whole floor and had wraparound windows.

"I think I should get you over to St. Vincent's." He had found her hand all by himself and warmed the fingers cold as icicles, as though the blood had ceased to circulate. She supposed she was in shock, her body and mind malfunctioning. "The doctors will check you over. There are procedures for this, Susie," he coaxed.

She moved her head sideways on the pillow, away from him. "No. Just let me clean up and then, if you could find me a taxi, I'll go home."

"Susie. . . ."

"Father, I'll take a hot bath and I have some antibiotics. I'll swallow a handful of those. And don't worry about my getting pregnant."

"You don't know . . ." he tried again.

She almost smiled. "Birth control pills, Father. One a day, regular as clockwork." Something broke loose inside her chest like a wall of earth shifting, and she found herself wanting to comfort him more than she wanted his consolation. "I'll be okay," she whispered, as if women got raped every day. *Well, they do, only not me, never me.* "Time," she added, and curled her hand into a fist. Now she felt safe . . . but later? She wondered how she'd feel then, high up in her aerie. She lived nearer the sky than the ground, and had less substance in that rarefied atmosphere. Wife and mother on the thirtieth floor. Where was Susie?

Sitting up cautiously, she pulled loose from the priest and raked her hands through her hair, touched her face like a blind person and felt the swelling on her lip, the crust of dried blood. "I must look a sight." She laughed brittly, not meeting his eyes. "May I use your bathroom?" She knew he had a small private bathroom behind this room somewhere that he shared with Jose and Sven, the shelter's two paid helpers who also had rooms on the third floor.

"Of course!" He came off his chair and stood away from the bed so she could swing her legs over the side. She started to rise in the funnel of a tornado and had quickly to sit again until the storm in her head cleared. He darted forward to help her but she waved him away.

"I'm fine," she whispered after a moment. This time when she stood the room remained in place, the furniture held to its usual location. But as she followed him a painful grinding began between her legs, spiraling up inside her like a riptide. That will go away, if not tonight, tomorrow, she forced herself to believe; the body heals. The mind was another matter. Her bravado wouldn't last much beyond the taxi ride, and once she returned to her own world, the enormity of what had happened would sweep over her.

I have survived worse than this; I'll survive this too, she repeated over and over in her head, in a litany, as if it were a prayer.

The narrow hands of her Cartier tank watch met at twelve midnight, Susie saw in the lights along Eighth Avenue as the taxi squealed to a stop at a signal. She tried to tell the driver to slow down, that the springless cab and the split, saggy leather seat were causing unbearable pain, but he replied with a snarl and she felt herself tighten with fear.

In his shadowed face she saw the attacker in the third-floor closet and shrank childlike into a knot in the corner of the seat.

Finally the taxi careened in a wide U-turn to the front of a large gray apartment building. The relief doorman, Tim she thought his name was, held the taxi door for her as she dropped a ten-dollar bill over the front seat, not waiting for change. She lowered her head and angled past the heavyset man dressed like a Romanov general in his uniform. Luckily it wasn't John, the regular night man, who'd been with the building when the Lamtons moved in. John, a chatty, street-smart Irishman, would never miss the swollen lip, even heavily smeared with pink lipstick, or the purpling bruise on her cheek. He'd be able to tell from her slow shuffle, one step sliding warily after the other, that she'd been injured. Furthermore, John gossiped. She could hear his whisper like the hiss of a pneumatic door, *Something bad happened to Mrs. Lamton up on thirty.* He'd even ask Greg on his return, she fantasized, *Is the missus better now?* But it wasn't John at the door, and the elevators went automatic after eleven P.M., so she escaped being trapped under the watchful scrutiny of either Will or Kurt.

Upstairs the girls slept in their twin beds, whiffles of breath flutter-ing out to Susie when she cracked their doors, and Mrs. Sloan must be sleeping too for no sliver of light oozed out into the back hall from her narrow room off the kitchen.

She was grateful as she slipped through the silent apartment that she needn't tell one more lie, create yet another fantasy which she'd have to remember. The underbelly of her entire life trembled in a spidery web of lies, a fragile aerialist's net that wouldn't hold her if she fell.

Mrs. Sloan had turned the bed down, left the small lamp on the night table lit, and filled the crystal carafe with fresh water. Susie stripped off her clothes, dropping skirt and shirt, ripped panty hose and lacy pants, the wisp of brassiere, on her way into the bathroom. Except for her shoes and leather jacket, she'd wad up the soiled clothing and stuff everything into the garbage. Nothing should remain of this night, yet no matter how much she threw away, everything would. When she least expected it, some fragment would rise up out of darkness to confront her. Wasn't it always like that with what one ardently longed to forget?

She ran herself a tub as hot as she could tolerate, adding bath oil, and a steamy perfumed cloud rose up to envelop her when she lowered her abused body into the water. It took a moment before she could relax and lean back to let the heat work at the disgust that filled her. The pain had already softened, losing its sharp edges, becoming a dull ache. How tired she felt, as though she'd traveled nonstop halfway around the world and then some. It would be so easy to fall asleep in the tub, lulled by the warmth, the soothing caress of the water. But finally Susie forced herself up and out, toweling, patting her skin with a fragrant dusting powder.

Mirrors covered one wall of the bathroom, permitting no escape. Small, sleek, with no fat on her bones, her short hair slicked back like an otter's on a perfectly shaped skull, her big eyes round as silver dollars, the green dark as a midnight forest, she seemed a shy, delicate animal under the gun. She couldn't look at herself, not now, not yet. But the wall threw back too many Susies for her to avoid the reflection entirely, and before she could stop, she found herself confronting the woman in the glass, inspecting her as, wincing, she searched for visible signs, for some damage others might glimpse, Greg especially, though her husband preferred loving her with the lights doused. Even as she investigated her image, Susie knew the worst marks were inside.

Slipping on an old nightgown that covered her from neck to toes, the sleeves down to her fingertips, she approached the bed, thinking, *I won't sleep.* She saw Father Simon with his gaunt medieval face, and his eyes leaking tears of blood, and she wanted to reach out with some relief for him, but his suffering wasn't for her alone, rather for all the cruelty humans wreaked on one another. *I'm only one more,* she thought, *nothing else,* and wished she might find some solace in that. *I'm not the first woman in the world to be raped and won't be the last.*

Lying uneasily in the kingsize bed, she couldn't sleep, and after a while ceased trying. She pulled on a robe and went into the kitchen, moving in a trancelike state, having to remind herself with each step, *This is me, Susie Lamton.* She considered calling Lisbeth on the phone, for Lis had a no-nonsense approach to experience, even the worst, the most wrenching events. *You'll learn, you'll carry it away with you, transform the exactness of it into something beneficial,* but no, Lis wrote, and everything was sucked into a maw that churned and churned until it got rewritten and thrown out to the world up on the screen in a movie or, as now, a play.

As she poured milk into a saucepan, Susie thought she could call Quinn too, that Quinn was more likely than Lisbeth, and certainly Dinah asleep up in Westport, Quinn who had a medical degree though she never practiced her profession on people. The diploma hung framed in the office of her lab like a piece of wallpaper. Quinn knew more of the body and the mind than the rest of them did; Quinn was both physician and friend.

But, of course, Susie wouldn't say a word to any one of the three friends, for her secret had other secrets honeycombed through it.

The milk began to froth and she lowered the flame and crossed the kitchen with its oblong center island and high chairs for a ceramic mug. It was then that she saw the large tissue-wrapped package beside the sink. Mrs. Sloan had propped a note up against it. *Arrived by messenger, 5:10 p.m.* It contained flowers certainly, and Susie wondered who had sent them. Not that flowers were at all unusual, but no recent event prompted them, and Greg had been working in Chicago all week. She thought for a single crazy moment of the bearded man with the heavy rough hands, the rapist of the stinking breath and no name. *Thank you, Darling, for a swell time!* Greg, before their marriage, often sent roses from Harvard to Cabot and once a sprig of orchids with just such a note, and she'd thought then how thrilling, how chic, how debonair. That younger Susie had read too many books, talked more nights than she should have of dreams, of desires, and of fantasy supermen whom she'd love, who'd love her, which all of Susie's men did. Why not the rapist then?

She trembled so violently that she bit into her puffy lower lip, tasting again the salty tang of blood. She gagged, disgusted with her foolish imagination. The flowers had an innocuous origin, one of her committees, a thank-you for a dinner party, an admirer among Greg's many friends or clients. *Open it, for God's sake!* she screamed silently at her frozen hands. She tore at the paper, ripping it away until the large bouquet in a glass vase was revealed. *Lilies-of-the-valley!* Susie sucked in her breath, blundering away from the counter.

The milk boiled over, the flame hissing angrily, and she rushed to switch off the gas. She had to hold on to the edge of the stove, shaking, before she was able to move back, stumbling across her kitchen, *my kitchen!* she reminded herself. *Safe here!* But she wasn't safe anywhere, and Susie saw for a second the shelves and the cracked ceiling of the shelter closet. She touched the flowers then, the delicate bells, so white, and the long, skinny green stems. So many, hundreds it seemed, bunched tightly together as they soared up from the vase. She eased them loose from one another, and her fingers slid into the dense thicket.

"Oh!" she cried out as something pierced her finger. Blood twined down her knuckle in crimson streams to her palm. When she pulled loose from the flowers an untidy trickle of blood splashed onto the quarry-tile floor, another stained the silk of her robe when she raised the finger to suck it. This final, unexpected pain added to all the others, much worse and more enduring. But she had no idea what had caused this slashing. She pulled the flowers from the vase by their heads, bloodying their whiteness as she threw them into the double sink until, deep down, embedded in the center of the lovely lilies, she found the razor blade. Its deadly edge glistened red.

Who sent them? Who? What malevolent person and why? Lilies-of-the-valley couldn't be accidental. But there was no card. Susie searched carefully, wary of other boobytraps, but couldn't find a florist's card with the name of the shop. The flowers came out of nowhere as had that man when she climbed alone to the third floor. Out of the unknown, the blackness, leaping like a wild animal from the brush, bringing her down, his hand over her mouth to choke off any exploding scream. She had been so unsuspecting, as now when she'd touched the flowers.

She leaned over the sink, feeling faint and sick; but below her face in a carpet on the bottom of the sink lay the lilies-of-the-valley. She must throw them in the trash just like the clothes that retained the invisible imprint of that man's hands, his body; yet she couldn't bring herself to touch the flowers again.

Susie gathered a handful of paper towels, and making several trips from the sink to the garbage can, finally scooped up all the lilies. She even threw the vase away.

She wanted so very much to forget the flowers altogether as she climbed into her bed, swallowing a sleeping pill instead of the warm milk still in the kitchen. But she wouldn't. The flowers with their razor blade were as deliberate as the rape. Tightness cincturing her chest like a chain, Susie knew there had been no mistake.

2

Dinah had been in the middle of making a cake when Susie called not sounding like Susie at all. Her voice dragged, with a husky cadence to it, and twice Dinah suggested she might be coming down with a cold, but Susie said no, her health was just fine thank you, nice of Dinah to be concerned. Susie being southern with her Scarlett O'Hara mannerisms that drove them all nuts at Cabot and that she only dropped into on rare occasions since graduation set Dinah to wondering so much that she left the bowl with the hand beater sitting in it and called Lisbeth. But Lisbeth had problems of her own, with the play and its producer. She ran on about some actress in the nude, though she promised to call Susie and decide for herself if Suz was bothered by anything real or just being premenstrual or what.

Actually, having a conversation with Susie in which Susie failed to bubble over with laughter and wasn't full of a first-class trip to some exotic locale, or a new fur coat, or a posh charity dinner that meant her picture the next day in the *Times*, wasn't, Dinah thought, such a bellyache. Dinah, who'd never admit such a feeling, occasionally pulsed with jealousy of her old college friend Susie Lamton, nee Bannon, just as she did now and then of her two other Cabot friends and roommates, Lisbeth and Quinn.

Dinah carefully poured the batter into the two round cake tins that she'd greased and floured beforehand, then twice made wary journeys across the kitchen to the oven, intently watching Rebecca, who lay poised on her rag rug in her corner, ready to pounce at the slightest spill. Hope shimmered eternally in Rebecca's Airedale brain that Dinah might drop some morsel on the floor. Usually when Dinah cooked, the dog wasn't disappointed.

"Forget it, Becky!" said Dinah when the tins rested safely inside the oven. She whispered a silent prayer that this time the layers would rise evenly rather than like ski slopes, also that the double chocolate would be moist with no charcoal edges. Baking wasn't Dinah's particular talent, and Rebecca, more often than Hatch or Mikey, was the happy recipient of Dinah's efforts. Actually all her culinary skills were below par, but on Saturday night she and Hatch went to a dinner party at the Petersons on Old Shore Road, and Mary Lou had capped an incredible beef Wellington with a coconut custard pie that, as Dinah told Susie earlier on the phone, was to die. Dinah ate every morsel and would have taken seconds, but when Mary Lou reached for her plate Hatch gave her one of his dirtiest looks, and she demurely, if unhappily, declined. Hatch was right, of course, for Dinah had twenty-five pounds distributed over her thighs and stomach, with a good cushion of padding on her behind, twenty-five pounds, she joked, that didn't belong to her. Dinah said, "I'm only renting them." Hatch, however, failed to find her plumpness amusing and called her fatty and chubby and the blimp last week when they had a fight.

Well, she couldn't take the extra poundage off one, two, three; slimming down took time. As she announced to Hatch on Sunday morning after the Petersons' lavish dinner, she had gone, officially, on a diet. He greeted this announcement with a sour look and said he'd heard that the week before, never mind the week before that. Her dieting seemed to be a matter of several starts but no middle or end. Dinah had been wounded by Hatch's skepticism and tried twice as hard these past few days, which left her doubly depressed when she found an Entenmann's chocolate chip cookie in her hand and one in her mouth, or the remnants of a hot pastrami on the plate at the counter of the deli into which she seemed to have wandered somnolently, like someone in a deep trance. Her intentions, however, were pure gold, and until they actually resulted in her old, girlish figure emerging like one of Rodin's women out of solid rock, Dinah decided to calm Hatch's impatience with upgraded meals. Hatch could eat his way through the refrigerator, shelf by shelf, without gaining an ounce. He had a whippet's leanness and would, Dinah sighed sadly, if he ate nothing but ice-cream sundaes and Godiva truffles. In fact, Hatch loved good food. His days in Manhattan centered around some fabulous meal at an East Side restaurant. No wonder she'd gotten so heavy, Dinah sometimes thought. It was Hatch's loving description of lunch over dinner—when he was home for dinner, which he wasn't often lately— that excited her salivary glands so she grabbed anything within reach to shove into her mouth. Having a teenager in the house meant much of that consisted of pure calories. Twinkies and Devil Dogs, soda, Dove bars, potato chips, plus other favorites of Mikey's like frozen pizza and chocolate donuts.

Hatch had gone on and on about Mary Lou's Saturday night sit-down for twelve, so when Dinah called to thank her, she got recipes. Just writing them down convinced Dinah she'd never survive the beef Wellington or the pie. Over the years she had dropped more crumbly messes of what should have been piecrust but wasn't into the trash than she could count. No matter which recipe she followed, Fanny Farmer's or Julia Child's, she always came out with hard impossible lumps or flaky pieces like week-old Play-Doh. Years before, Dinah had faced one of those immutable facts of life: she was never going to make it with piecrust.

Cakes, however, were easy, or should have been with packaged mixes and icing you spread straight from the can. Her stove was the culprit, she decided, since everything burnt to a crisp at least fifteen minutes before the cookbook or the package said to remove it. The oven also caused one side of the cake batter to swell up and the other to droop like a sagging slip. She thought once, but only fleetingly, of buying a new stove. The old, unreliable monster always gave her something to blame.

Dinah set the timer ten minutes earlier than the directions on the box instructed and synchronized her watch with the moonface clock set into the back of the stove. Then she started for the studio followed by the click-click of Rebecca's nails on the hardwood floors. She kept her head turned and eyes averted from the vacuum in the middle of the living room and the can of Pledge on the coffee table. Cleaning bored her, bored her profoundly this afternoon, though she hadn't done a lick around the house for several days. The previous night Hatch had run an accusatory finger along one of the bookshelves and it came away black. That and his arched brows, like storm signal flags on the Sound, fueled her guilt so that after lunch she finally began a whirlwind of cleaning during which she decided she owed Hatch something special, a deli-cacy to satisfy his gourmet's stomach. Thus the cake in the oven. Of course the cake wouldn't take that long to bake, not long enough for Dinah really to get into dusting and polishing, so it seemed silly not to wait. After the cake baked and cooled and she iced it, she'd attend to the living room. Meanwhile she might as well work on a painting.

At the turn of the second-floor hall hung a full-length mirror in an ornately carved frame from Hatch's grandparents' house in Stonington. It was a genuine antique and quite handsome except for the waddling figure in sloppy jeans and an overly large work shirt that filled it, together with the furry, red-haired dog in desperate need of a trim. She couldn't ignore the size sixteen who had to be Dinah no matter how much she wished it wasn't, but she resolutely kept her gaze above the

17

neck at the pleasant, youthful face that had changed almost not at all since Cabot. ''Your face is your fortune, kiddo!'' She laughed, snapping a salute on the right turn out of the mirror's grasp and up the narrow steps to the studio, a large, open space under the eaves which Hatch— and Mikey, following his father's lead—insisted on referring to as the attic.

Studio or attic, this top story of the colonial contained a surplus of broken, outworn furniture, Mikey's crib and changing table, his potty chair and tyke bike draped with plastic sheeting, these relics waiting ghostlike for another baby who for some mysterious reason never arrived. Crammed into corners were boxes of old books held for a charity sale, winter clothing in long anonymous garment bags stowed during the summer months, and summer clothes hidden away for the endless winter, stacks of magazines along the walls, a wheelless bicy- cle, several hockey sticks, a box of dull ice skates, Hatch's notebooks from college, Dinah's too, a set of outdated medical books some peculiar uncle of Hatch's left him in his will, which made no sense because Hatch practiced law, and sundry other debris that had escaped the garbage heap for one obscure reason or another.

At the southern edge of the attic a space had been swept clear of junk, though a broken chair, a tilting floor lamp, and a rusty metal roadster Mikey had once been small enough to pedal, stood at the edges threatening to invade. On sunny days light streamed in through the twin windows before which Dinah positioned her easel, but today was overcast, gray as a soiled sheet. Dinah switched on the long bracket of round hundred-watt globes along the outmost side of the center beam and blasted the attic with a golden glow. She hated painting under artificial light, which seemed to infuse her canvases with a copperish tinge like the dull patina of time flattening out old works.

Dinah had just turned the easel, righting it for the best fall of light, when she glanced out the window down onto the side yard of their house, to the hedge which separated the Johnsons from the property to the north on Delphinium Lane. The privets, like Rebecca's coat, were overgrown. Dog and hedges definitely needed a good clipping, as Hatch reminded her at least once a day. He nagged at her about the privets anyway, but Becky could stay shaggy for all he cared. Hatch failed to appreciate the family dog. Dinah and Mikey, on the other hand, treasured the lovable Airedale who pranced when she walked, all four feet miraculously leaving the ground in unison, and curled into a big fur ball on your lap if you happened to sit on the floor. True, she adored presenting those she liked, which meant everyone who came into her orbit, with wet slobbering kisses, and true too, as Hatch claimed, she smelled. But Becky possessed the personality of an archangel and had liquid brown eyes that stared at humans with an excess of love. Dinah thought it a lack in Hatch that he hated the dog and was hopeful that in time he'd change his mind. But Rebecca had celebrated her fifth birthday just the other day and Hatch disliked her more than ever.

Dinah cast a last glance down at the hedges and beyond to the Berger house, up for sale because first Missus dropped dead of heart failure, then, two weeks later, so did Mister. Sixty years of marriage, but still, that was a kind of awesome togetherness. She wondered if such would be her fate with Hatch. Dinah was also curious about who would finally buy the Berger place, large as the ark and in need of interior reconstruction. A *For Sale* sign decorated the shaggy front lawn now that the estate was settled.

The half-finished painting waited on the easel. While Rebecca curled herself into an overstuffed, sagging armchair, Dinah took up her palette and began squeezing out dollops of bright oil paint, trying not to remember that Hatch at breakfast had given her firm instructions to call, "today and no stalling," the Perfecto Gardening Group, a highly touted Westport firm with its own green trucks like large slugs. She was, Hatch insisted, not to rehire poor Mr. Alonzo.

Mr. Alonzo, far more overweight than Dinah, and with high blood pressure that flushed his face cherry red whenever he exerted himself, which was any time he climbed his ladder, inevitably left sprigs jutting off the sides of the privets like unruly children breaking line, and couldn't give the hedges level flattops no matter how he struggled. The tops rolled and dipped like a slowly incoming wave and made Hatch frantic. Each time Mr. Alonzo trimmed, Hatch gritted his teeth and said, "This is it! From now on we get a professional!"

Dinah didn't hire Mr. Alonzo because he worked on the cheap. In fact, when she checked around she found he was the most expensive gardener in town. Still, she hadn't the heart to fire him and contract with Perfecto because Mr. Alonzo pushed himself so. One day, Dinah feared, he'd collapse on her lawn. Yet even this constant worry failed to motivate her to send him walking. She kept him on for the same reasons she had employed him years ago. He had brown eyes exactly like Becky's and a houseful of children always needing operations or glasses or special built-up shoes.

Dinah had been painting only a few years, starting cautiously with pastels, then gradually moving into the tricky medium of watercolors, but really working up steam with oils and canvas after having taken an

19

adult education course at the local high school during that fuzzy period of her life when she searched frantically for some skill, talent, or profession to make her own. At Cabot she had studied English, that catchall major for those liberal arts students who liked to read and who turned out passable term papers, twenty-year-olds undecided about what they wanted or what to do with their lives. Of course there were some English students like Lisbeth who burned with a hot white flame to write and knew so from the crib. Some too, again like Lis, possessed that unbuyable gift, talent. But Dinah was what Quinn called an academic butterfly. She breezed through a catalog of subjects, always with good grades, for lack of intelligence wasn't her problem, rather a lost or unfound intent, the churning motivation that would shove her in the small of the back. For a brief moment in her junior year, she thought of teaching as a career; but she'd heard too often that those who can, do and those who can't, teach. This inane slogan struck her with the fearsomeness of divine writ, pinching her insecurity like a tight shoe and sending her scurrying off to take a course in advertising.

Advertising never made Dinah's heart pound faster; she didn't even particularly like commercials or print ads, but she discovered that her caustic wit sprang from an ability to say the right, the punchy thing, very quickly. So, for a while, during the years between Cabot and her marriage, she fudged around in the lower depths of several New York agencies waiting for the right break, the toothpaste or hair spray ad that would vault her into the prestigious position of account executive. She wasn't actually unhappy working in a tiny cubicle with partitions that ended only a few inches beyond her head and lacked a door, for she loved living in Manhattan, though a fifth-floor walk-up with the tub in the kitchen on a dark East Village street wasn't exactly living well. She supposed in time her career would take off like a moon shot, but after she met and married Hatch—a good catch whom she delighted in parading before her three friends like a prize moose—the only place she took off for was Connecticut. Hatch dreamed of a big white house set back on the lawn of green velvet to go with his wife and eventually his child, and Dinah, making only fifteen thousand a year, had no reasonable excuse not to quit her job and move.

But she hadn't counted on having even less talent for housewifery than other better-paying careers she had once considered. While she and Hatch comfortably cramped themselves into his one-bedroom on West End Avenue, it was all fun, doing the vacuuming each weekend along with the dusting and the wash. Since they seldom ate in, and since in the flush of those early marriage days, Hatch enjoyed puttering along with his bride in the kitchen, meals weren't a problem. Westport was a different matter and the woman's world of cooking, cleaning, and running innumerable errands expanded until these chores occupied Dinah's entire life. Especially after Mikey was born, Dinah found herself spending hours and days keeping their ship shipshape as Hatch would say, and afloat. But only barely. As time passed, as Mikey grew, became less of a daily burden, then toddled off on his chubby little legs to school, Dinah's skills should have improved, for practice surely signified something, but she simply became more inept at everything.

Ironing a shirt or polishing the silverware meant nothing in the real world, and though there was Susie, Mrs. *Ladies' Home Journal,* exemplifying the happy housewife, Susie really slaved at her unpaid career of charity volunteer and partygoer, not at keeping up her apartment. Susie never waxed the floor or changed the sheets or scoured a toilet; Susie made quite sure when she married Greg that he intended to provide her with household help. Greg, of course, had money, and though Hatch finally earned more than a living wage, that hadn't happened until a few years ago. He'd already spent most of their marriage enjoying the services of a free maid, meaning Dinah, who fought an uphill battle to induce Hatch into paying for a once-a-week cleaning lady. That was Mae, a genteel black woman who never cooked and, of course, refused to do windows. Dinah finally refused to do them too, and they had to hire a professional firm four times a year. After the first bill from Spotless Panes, Hatch came right out and asked her face to face, "Exactly what is it you do, Dinah? All day I mean, when I'm in the office?"

Luckily Dinah had already taken up art.

She dabbed away at the canvas, explosive with blasts of vermillion in mushroom-shaped clouds—she planned to call it *Apocalypse*—and stroked in with the narrow point of her smallest brush stick figures such as a child might draw, then stepped back squinting, letting the picture flow to the perimeters of her vision, deciding. . . .

"No," Dinah said aloud. Rebecca raised her shaggy head, ears perked, waiting to see if some call was about to be given. Dinah, oblivious to the dog, chose a wider brush from a jar on the table and carefully built up, with blocks of color rather than dark lines, a large figure sprawled in the foreground of this holocaust nightmare she was creating, this colorful, quite cheery end of the world.

Only at the last, the figure prone on its back, in an attitude so flat and lifeless it could be nothing but dead, did she add with a dab here, another there, a tad of brownish twist for hair, the vaguest of details that defined it as a female. Then she moved off again, cocked her head

21

and stared, breath caught and held while she moved a critical eye across the canvas. She'd done too much, for the woman's body sucked one's attention away from the clouds, the slapped strokes of black depicting a city's slide and collapse, the flaming sky all cinnamon and orange.

Dinah wandered back behind Rebecca's chair for a longer, a better look. The dog again lifted her head, searching blindly for a human hand to slither under, bumping insistently at Dinah's left until the fingers automatically scratched behind the ears and along the firm slope of the jaw. Ah! Rebecca sighed in a swoon of pleasure while Dinah stared, thinking, there's something familiar about her. The woman, drawn bigger, made more prominent to give depth, a sense of distance to the world's final moment, stirred the sludge of memory, but recognition wouldn't come.

Eeeeee! Becky screeched suddenly, bolting, throwing herself in a floppy scurry of red fur off the chair, over the side, almost tipping it. Dinah had unintentionally gripped a silky ear and yanked.

The dog crawled under a card table and worked at the sore ear with a wet paw, regarding Dinah balefully. "Oh Beck!" Dinah cried, dropping to her knees. "I'm sorry! I didn't mean it, honestly!" In penance Dinah hugged her even though she smelled like dirty socks, and kissed the moist black nose. The dog, sorrowing, remained unconvinced.

Dinah crept in beside Rebecca, who, ignoring her offended ear, curled up on Dinah's ample leg. Dinah thought, *How nice it is in here under the card table, secreted in the middle of all the junk, how cozy and nestlike*. Rebecca's fishy breath blew down her neck in a warm sirocco as she cradled the Airedale, rocking ever so slightly, just a slow back and forth, feeling a warm, drowsy happiness like a child.

Events forever conspired against Dinah's creating a delicious meal, something wonderful to set out before Hatch and Mikey, that would have Hatch nearly swoon as he did over Mary Lou's beef Wellington. Not that she intended any dish so elaborate, but just one lip-smacking treat. Tonight, it was to be chocolate cake with sugary white icing. Only up in the studio she completely lost track of time, and the two layers baking away, rising, browning, went black and charred like kindling in the fireplace. Even as she trimmed off the burnt edges, she knew no cake could withstand an hour and a half in the oven. It was hard as a rock when Dinah finally remembered, hurtling down two floors to the kitchen, hearing the shrill of the timer all the way.

Dinah popped each layer out of its tin into the garbage can and heard her mother's recorded announcement, played at every meal Dinah had eaten in Hanover, Nebraska: *Don't waste your food. Think of the starving children all over the world who'd be happy to eat what you don't want.*

It would have to be canned peaches and vanilla Häagen-Dazs for dessert again, for Dinah was too debilitated even to attempt another cake. There was nothing wrong with peaches and ice cream after meatloaf and packaged au gratin potatoes, with a salad. Meatloaf was a dish Dinah really made quite well. The secret lay in the canned tomato sauce stirred into the meat.

The phone rang while Dinah's hands were deep in the mush of ground beef and bread crumbs, minced garlic and chopped onions, raw egg plus the tomato sauce. She gingerly picked the receiver off the wall phone with two sticky fingers and held it near her ear, careful not to get meat in the hair that, since early morning, had little by little been escaping the rubber band that held it in a draggy ponytail.

"It's me, Mom," Mikey said at the other end. "I'm in school and there's swim practice till six. Then Shane's asked me to go home for supper with him. Okay?"

Mikey even at fourteen did everything he could to avoid one of Dinah's meals.

"Sure," she agreed, and hanging up, thought it would be nice for a change, she and Hatch alone at the dining room table with candlelight. Yes, definitely candles. Hatch could select a good bottle of red wine from the cache in the cellar. His newest interest was wine, and he had collected almost fifty bottles, keeping them in specially constructed racks. He'd allow them to drink only the almost good, while he let the best of his cellar ripen and mature. In the year two thousand, Dinah kidded him, we're going to have one drunken blast.

The meatloaf was baking in the oven, the salad made and sitting on the counter, the packaged potatoes laid in their casserole ready to be cooked, when Dinah, changed to a clean sweater, a boatneck of olive green, and a floppy pair of harem pants that hid most of her bulges, heard the door.

"Is that you?" she called out, running a brush one last time through the tangles of thick hair and ignoring the ripples of gray.

"Who else, the iceman?" Hatch's voice floated up from the bottom of the stairs.

She muttered, hurrying down, "Funny, funny," at his literary allusion. He liked, even in minor moments and with Dinah who knew him well, too well sometimes, to have himself considered learned, cultured, a man who had read and seen and done. In fact, in most subjects he was an ice skater rather than a deep-sea diver. He skimmed

23

fast as an arctic wind over the surface of most intellectual matters, and was good for the occasional quote or pun, the one-line review, but a dead loss, Dinah sometimes thought guiltily, in serious conversations.

"Dinner will be ready in about twenty minutes," she said as she came off the steps ready to offer her rouged cheek up for his kiss. But Hatch was already in the dining room at the sideboard where they kept the bar, pouring scotch.

"No ice," he said, holding up the empty bucket accusingly.

"I'll get it." She stretched out her hand, but he swung right by her through the door into the kitchen. "The potatoes have to cook, then we're ready," she offered as she shoved the casserole in the oven on the shelf over the happily bubbling meatloaf. The cake seemed less of a loss to Dinah now.

Hatch was saying something behind her she couldn't hear, or rather heard but didn't process. She turned, her cheeks rosy from the heat of the stove and asked, "What did you just say?"

He held the glass in two hands against his shirt and Dinah noticed he hadn't removed his suit jacket, hadn't even unbuttoned it. For a moment she imagined this wasn't Hatch Johnson, her husband of fifteen years, the father of her son, the provider of sustenance and mortgage payments, the lover she'd once happily welcomed into her bed, but a stranger, a salesman of encyclopedias who'd finagled his way into the kitchen, or maybe a police detective who'd arrived with bad news gumming up his mouth.

Hatch didn't repeat whatever it was he'd said, just raised the scotch, again two-handedly, to his lips. His hands held steady on the trip up and when he drank and back down to chest level. Well, why shouldn't they? Dinah wondered. Except that he was staring at her in that way characters in horror movies do. Horror movies were a secret vice of Dinah's, which she satisfied by watching videos or in empty theaters on afternoons while Hatch was at the office.

"You said something, Tehachapi," she reminded him, using his old lover's name that hadn't passed her lips in a decade. He winced.

"I said, I don't want dinner."

"Oh." That wasn't so bad. She expected worse for some reason, maybe because she knew there had been something worse. "Well, all right." She certainly wouldn't force him, or even sigh plaintively on the word "meatloaf," and an inner, early-warning device kept her from asking the ordinary *Why not?*

She was about to shut off the gas and retrieve the uncooked potatoes, the almost-baked meatloaf, but after all she had to eat. Besides, conscience kept her from depositing still more food in the trash.

"I think I'll have a drink too," she decided, heading back into the dining room, Hatch close on her heels. "I thought," she flung over her shoulder, "you'd open some wine, maybe a Beaujolais, but since we're not eating, or you're not anyway, I'll have—" She swung back the doors of the liquor cabinet and inspected the various intoxicating possibilities. The bottles of varying shapes and sizes reminded Dinah of the barbershop back in Nebraska where her father got his hair cut once a month. Rows of different bottles with little metal spouts instead of caps standing on a ledge by the big front window and filtering the sun in a riotous confusion of colors. "Amaretto, I think," she said, suddenly swooping the long-necked bottle with its bright red label off the shelf, not because she actually liked the sweetish liqueur but because, as Hillary said of Everest, it was there.

"Amaretto's an after-dinner drink," Hatch reminded her punctiliously as if she didn't know that.

"Who said I was going to eat dinner by myself?" she replied, forgetting her decision of a minute before to eat despite him.

Something was definitely wrong. Dinah felt it in her bones, a chill that, even if she pushed up the thermostat, wouldn't disappear. *Goose walking over my grave,* she thought, and regretted allowing Mikey to eat dinner at Shane's. She wanted company, someone to partially fill up the big colonial that suddenly seemed as vacant as the Berger house next door.

Hatch had thrown down his scotch and was pouring himself another. Dinah perched at the edge of the couch, ready to leap. The coffee table had gray smudges on it, and she made a silent promise to clean it with Windex tomorrow. No, tomorrow Mae came; she'd let her do it.

Hatch took his drink and crossed the room. Dinah thought he intended to sit on the couch next to her, but he trotted right by. Wanting to keep him in sight, she twisted about. "Where are you going?"

"Upstairs. I have things to do."

"Things? What things?"

Hatch wasn't a person with things to do; he had his specifics, such as the wine in the cellar or the small sailboat docked on the Sound. *Things* had a heavy sound, a foreign ring to it. Dinah remembered reading that if you heard the whiz of a bomb falling that meant it wouldn't fall on you, but if you didn't . . .

She slammed the glass down on the coffee table, the amaretto sloshing over the rim, and hurried up the stairs after him. She could hear him moving about in their bedroom, slinking like a cat burglar, and as she rounded the corner she decided to feel his head for a fever.

Hatch had finally taken off his jacket, unbuttoned the top button of his shirt, and loosened his tie. He looked like a harried politician. Somehow his hair, fine dirty blond strands that normally fell straight over his brow, had gotten mussed and stood up in tiny peaks like well-beaten meringue. Under the harsh glare of the overhead light elaborate shadows draped his face, ruffled in the wells beneath his eyes, and erased his thin, pinched lips altogether. He became an old man, older than he appeared downstairs drinking his scotch with two hands, as he packed things in the large suitcase spread open on their king-size bed. *Suitcase?* All at once Dinah wished she'd kept the amaretto, for she needed a drink, something to fling down her throat and unfreeze the arctic ice blocks cramped in her stomach.

If she asked, What are you doing? he'd tell her. He'd say, packing my suitcase; worse, he'd explain why. She no more wanted to hear that than she wanted to watch his shirts in their plastic bags straight from the Chinese laundry pile up in the suitcase alongside his underwear, and now his sweaters.

The tumbler stood on top of his dresser still filled with scotch, and Dinah, her tongue swollen in her mouth like a piece of meat from the butcher's, circled around to get it, being careful not to cross in front of this alien male person she was married to. He'd run her over, she knew, with the disregard and finality of a speeding tractor trailer.

It came immediately after her second swallow of scotch, which she loathed, Hatch's flat, unemphatic announcement like a replaying of the weather, "I'm leaving, Dinah." She had to put the glass down to cover her ears, but she couldn't avoid "I'm moving into Manhattan and filing for divorce so I can marry—"

She blotted out the name, which fell between them like a dead bird. Then Hatch shouted, "God damn it! Listen to me!"

"No!" she yelled back. "Why should I when you're talking nonsense! Words, just words!"

"Dinah . . ." He lowered his voice to the danger point and gritted his teeth so her name came out in a growl. And she heard him plainly enough because it wouldn't work, shutting Hatch out with her hands, so she dropped them from her ears and shoved them in the voluminous harem pants pockets.

Hatch continued his packing, moving faster now, speeded up like a character in a silent movie, except that he said, "When's Mikey coming home? I want to tell him myself. God knows what you'll say." He glowered at her over a handful of socks as if she were the one walking out on him, as if he had some right to be mad at her.

"There's some mistake" was all Dinah could think to say, and it did feel wrong, terribly wrong, Hatch packing, Hatch going away not on a business trip but into Manhattan permanently. Didn't it have to be some gross error, a marital computer screwup? She simply couldn't conjure up even the facsimile of a life. The kind and substance, the feel of it and the structure, after Hatch went out the door. She imagined time would end, like a theater's curtain dropping on the final scene, when he stepped off the porch.

No, no! She shook her head as if she had water in her ears; this was ridiculous! Hatch meant something other than what he said, though he'd said it plain enough. In spite of a strong instinct to keep her mouth shut, she blurted out in a loud bleat, "It's just ridiculous!"

Hatch stopped. He jerked his tie, pulling it out from under his collar; then he grabbed the scotch, which Dinah had put back on the dresser, and drank until he reached the bottom and the scanty remains of the ice. *See!* she told herself, *We use the same glass, drink the same scotch,* and she remembered how, before they were married, when she'd sleep over at Hatch's they'd share his toothbrush in the morning until he bought her one of her own. A man and a woman who used the same toothbrush surely don't, years later, after having a son and owning a Westport colonial plus two cars, get a divorce and become nothing more important than a statistic.

"Dinah," he said slowly, slurring, which made her suspect this scotch wasn't merely the second he'd had tonight, "pay attention." He actually moved nearer to her, clamped his hands on the olive-green boatneck, gazed down into her eyes from only the slightest angle since they were approximately the same height, and said, "I'm leaving. I'm moving out. You and I are going to get a divorce. And when we do, I will marry Stacy Delmonico."

She thought of going limp and falling to the floor, dragging him down with her, but her curiosity kept her upright and forced her to say, "Who's Stacy Delmonico?"

"A fantastic woman who I'm in love with!" he practically crooned.

Why had she asked? She should have known that this Stacy Delmonico person wasn't a hunchbacked dwarf with acne and the personality of a cobra.

"An associate in the office," he went on. "Just brilliant. Harvard undergrad and Harvard Law. Law review. The works. Stace has got a big future. Who knows, she might even make the bench. Women are hot right now. Just give her time. She's only twenty-eight."

And she has AIDS, that was what Dinah hoped he'd say, tacking it on at the end. But apparently this paragon's health was perfect too, just like everything else about her. Oh Christ, why had Stacy Delmonico ever been born!

27

Dinah clenched her jaws as she sucked in a deep breath of air, wishing with the intensity of an eight-year-old, *Make her dead!*

In the same second a voice screamed in Dinah's head, *No!* and she pulled back from Hatch, slipping free of his hands. Dinah had sworn never ever to think, to wish, such an awfulness again, no matter what, for God might hear and make the impossible happen.

Time began to fly as if the hands of the clock on her night table were in a furious race with each other. Hatch's suitcase got packed, and then he filled another one, found a cardboard box in the utility room and stuffed that too. As he went along he became less discriminating, and anything his restless eye lighted on he snatched for Manhattan. She had actually to scream at him before he'd relinquish the latest John Updike novel she'd bought herself the other day and was reading in snatches to induce sleep at night.

Finally this frenzy slowed and Hatch, like a mechanical toy winding down, took several deep breaths, slapped his hands on his thighs, and tried to smile for Mikey who popped up in the doorway, moving silently as always in his sneakers. The boy offered a quick, "Hi, I'm home," before taking a long step down the hall.

"Mikey!" Hatch yelled, and Dinah raised her hands again, halfway to her ears as *Don't!* snagged in her throat like a fish bone. If he said it one more time—leaving, divorce, Manhattan, Stacy Delmonico—she'd be less able to cling to the hope that this scene was, to use that overworked expression, a bad dream. If Hatch told Mikey, it would no longer be Hatch just having a snit, mad at her for being a lousy cook, a mediocre housekeeper, the unhappy temporary owner of twenty-five spongy extra pounds, the staunch defender of a shaggy, odoriferous Airedale who at that moment slunk into the bedroom and nuzzled at Dinah's leg. "Get out of here, you flea-bitten hound!" Hatch shouted.

"Mikey . . ." Hatch began as Rebecca fled the scene. He paused, obviously finding it harder to inform his son of the gross treachery he was about to indulge in than his wife. This hiatus allowed Dinah to rush forward with, "Don't listen to your father, he's not well, having a hard night after a worse—"

Hatch took three giant steps to the other side of the room and closed her mouth with the palm of his hand.

Mikey hiked himself up on the balls of his feet and tilted his head curiously like a long-legged, skinny wading bird. The boy seemed better built for basketball than swimming, his arms hanging down to his knees. He might have been readying to leap for a dunk shot, watching his parents. Though he'd witnessed fights between them before, overheard other squabbles, somehow his father clamping his mother's mouth shut was extreme. The question, Should I do something? passed across his innocent face, and then relief slipped from forehead to chin as Hatch let Dinah loose.

"See you guys." Mikey waved at them, lurching sideways in an attempt to disappear again. Once more Hatch summoned him back.

"I've got to talk to you, Mike," he said to his son in a man-to-man tone of voice.

"Yeah, about what?" Mikey sounded truculent, but it was more that jolting drop in his voice which he couldn't control. He sounded as though he was falling down a well.

"Your mother and I have something to tell you!" Hatch had the nerve to say, even smiling at Dinah, casting out his net to drag her in as an accomplice.

"No way, Jose!" she screamed at Hatch, and crouching crablike on the side of the bed, his side as it happened, the muscles in her face and neck shrieking from the effort of holding back the tears, she let go, crying. Still she growled through her tears, baring her teeth, "The nerve, the absolute nerve!"

"Now look, Di, let's be civilized about this!"

"Civilized. I haven't done a damn thing and already you're trying to put me in the wrong. You're the one breaking up a home and family out of . . . of *angst* and some midlife shit! Just so you can rut like a barnyard animal with some teenybopper lawyer!"

"Listen, I've got homework to do and tomorrow we're having a quiz in American history, so . . ." But neither would let Mikey go, both yelling at him, at one another, until it seemed the walls might balloon out any minute. Yet, snatching a word here and there, sifting their anger like a prospector panning for gold, Mikey got the message. He said, in the one moment both his parents paused, "I guess what you're trying to say is you're getting a divorce."

"That's right!"

"No! Never!"

They both replied at the same time, and Mikey's glance shifted from one to the other. "Don't worry about me," he offered, "I was about the only kid in my class whose parents were still married anyway. Now I won't feel like such an oddball."

He was lying, only Dinah wouldn't realize it until much later, weeks after this moment of Hatch's betrayal. *Betrayal.* She used that word with Hatch as she watched him finish his packing, making damn sure he took only what was his. "You betrayed me," she accused him.

Hatch's retort rebounded like a tennis ball off Ivan Lendl's racket. "For Christ's sake, Di, I'm not defecting to the Russians!" He arched his brows and kinked his arms, elbows in chickeny points. He looked faggy, thin as he was, and Dinah wondered if she'd feel any less grievously used if he had deserted her for a man rather than a woman.

At some moment weariness overtook Dinah, coming down heavily as the lead covering the dentist's technician draped her with during X rays. She moved lethargically, a land creature underwater, and would have fallen asleep if she hadn't summoned the energy to stay awake. This could be the final conversation she and Hatch would ever have without some lawyer buddies of his present, certainly the last in their Westport bedroom, now hers.

Hatch's earlier discomfort had passed, and as he meticulously finished his packing, he talked at her, full of instructions. He might as well have been heading off on a business trip to Boston or Chicago instead of an uncoupling. Their life together was crashing about her, but Hatch's concern was for mail, his other possessions to be picked up by truck, time and places for Mikey's visiting, the temporary alimony he most generously—his word—would provide Dinah with, the cars—he'd take the Volvo and she'd get the Chevy station wagon—his wine, his eventual decision whether to sell the house or not. He'd obviously been thinking of walking out on her and up the aisle with Stacy Delmonico for some time. Even eating Mary Lou Peterson's beef Wellington and custard pie on Saturday night, he'd known about this, Dinah thought, shocked. Winding up with what she would afterwards describe as his KO punch, he said, "And get the God damn hedges trimmed by somebody reliable. Perfecto and not that blind butterfingers Alonzo!"

"Fuck you! Mr. Alonzo will cut my hedges until hell freezes over!" she screamed. Leaping up like Rebecca, both feet practically off the ground at the same time, and throwing the first thing her hand encountered, which happened to be a pillow, Dinah exploded. She called Hatch every damnable name she could think of, cursed him, then cursed him some more, swore not to take this defection, this cruel and inhuman marital treatment, lying down or even sitting, yelled that she'd be on her feet in a court of law bleeding him dry!

Though Mikey emerged from his room and came down the hall to peer in on his mother at tornado force, then silently padded off, Hatch merely shrugged as though to say, You're not going to change my mind. And it was true. For all the good her tantrum did she might as well have developed laryngitis. Hatch wasn't to be deflected. The whole structure called marriage, called Hatch and Dinah, slowly crumbled into ash and blew off in the wind as she watched.

When Hatch left at last, shuttling back and forth with his suitcases and boxes, it was anticlimactic. Dinah heard the Volvo cough into life, that weird kicky sound the ignition made when starting, and crawled out of the bedroom like a survivor from a crash site, descending the stairs with creaky, groaning joints. Once on ground level she wondered why she'd made the effort, and supposed she should climb up again to console Mikey. He, too, had been cast adrift for all of Hatch's big promises about weekends and trips to Aspen and Acapulco (pie in the sky, Dinah thought). But she wasn't ready for Mikey yet, to shoulder his burdens and cope with his distress. She had her own misery and despair to grapple with first, and if she was able, to survive. How, for instance, would she ever be able to relate this tragic news to her friends, and then to withstand their sympathy? She cringed thinking of Quinn patting her shoulder, while from Lisbeth she'd receive a tight hug, and Susie would break down and cry. Dinah hoped for invisibility as she saw the only thing that she possessed to distinguish her, meaning Hatch, vanish. She'd lost him. The house felt as empty as though she'd lived here all these years alone.

Oh, she thought, finding her way as if by Geiger counter to the liquor, why hadn't Hatch dropped dead from a coronary or a cerebral aneurysm! There was, after all, some cachet in being a widow; besides, black, with her superfluous poundage, was a good color for her.

The Stolichnaya in one hand, a tumbler in the other, Dinah wandered into the living room. She sat on the couch peering through the glass table at Becky, who mournfully stared back at her like a trapped aquarium creature. "Good girl!" she said, and banged the vodka bottle down so sharply the dog surged from under the table in fright. "Good girl," she muttered again, meaning herself, weeping.

Tomorrow she'd get on the phone and call around, announcing the Johnsons were no longer a couple, but tonight Dinah planned a good drunk, a first-class binge to drown her misery.

Maybe she could think of a way to slant her announcement without actually lying so various recipients of the news would believe she'd left Hatch and not vice versa. *I've got to work on this,* she thought, curled into the cushions, lowering the level of the vodka as fast as she could swallow. All about her she viewed rubble. She might have been in a bomb crater rather than her large, nicely furnished colonial. Eventually she hoped to float into unconsciousness, but nothing happened. Another glass, half full, usually a lethal dose, and still the vodka disappointed, no magical daze of feathery inebriation ensued. Only a leaden feeling in her stomach and an agitated surge of nausea rising up her throat.

Hatch going, Hatch gone, Hatch already in Manhattan. Dinah imagined *her* husband and the exemplary Stacy Delmonico. She saw them cuddling, hugging and kissing, even making love in a soft, downy bed, and wished she wouldn't. It wasn't right, some strange woman with Hatch, Hatch having another lover, never mind preparing to marry her. That struck her with the whooshing force of a punch to the stomach. She doubled over with as severe a pain as any she had suffered in childbirth.

Dinah barely made it to the downstairs bathroom, dropping with a groan to her knees by the toilet bowl into which she regurgitated the vodka and the amaretto and that drink of scotch from Hatch's glass. Bits and pieces of her nibbling throughout the day floated in the sour mash, none of which she remembered but all of which smelt foul. *God!* she thought, rinsing out her mouth with tepid sink water and trying to align the two faces in the mirror above, *I'll never drink again.* A lie, but she believed it as she staggered out to the hall. Her body empty as a sieve, her mind drifting to multiplied images of Hatch now and long ago, she struggled, wretched and full of misery, in a wavering trail to the foot of the steps. Bed was the last desire she had left, but in a sudden burst of clarity she saw it before her, kingsize, hers and Hatch's, the polka-dotted ruffled spread rucked about from the suitcase, the debris Hatch decided not to take tossed on it—old shoelaces, a particularly garish tie Mikey gave him for a birthday once, a pair of plaid Bermudas, a torn Yogi Bear sweatshirt—and realized she could never bed down there, not to sleep, or if she slept, to endure a parade of nightmares.

The loss of Hatch's lean smoothness and warmth next to her throughout the night caused tears to seep from Dinah's eyes. Oh, how she loved, she had to admit it, to curl next to her husband. They were alone together, two travelers on the sea of sleep. And when they did join themselves—not as often as Dinah might have liked, but such she stoically realized was marriage—pleasure arrived, or at least some of the time.

With her foot on the first step, poised to go up and face the silence of being alone, Dinah felt her solitude and would have given years of her life right then to have Hatch back. Then, the phone rang. Her heart soared. God, for the first time in Dinah's forty years, answered her prayers, and instantaneously no less.

No doubt about it, she decided as she rushed for the phone, Hatch had come to his senses and reconsidered his foolishness. He couldn't give up his love, wife, friend, the mother of his son, the one person who knew his habits, foibles, the good with the bad.

No way, the restrained, sober part of Dinah's mind cautioned as she snatched the receiver from the cradle and cried, "Hatch, I love you!"

A faint crackling was the only reply.

"Hello!" Dinah yelled down the wires. "Hatch, where are you?"

No Hatch shouted from Manhattan, *I'm coming back!* No one broke through the silence with a word, just the static sizzling.

Disappointment made Dinah sag.

"Dinah . . . Dinah . . . Dinah . . ." Her name came vaguely from the receiver, barely audible, just as she was deciding to hang up. Whoever it was—it was impossible to tell male or female—sounded halfway around the world, on another continent, one signal beamed out in space and lost in a meteor shower.

"Who is this?"

"Dinah . . ." The spectral voice, so eerie, sent shivers in a chilly current down Dinah's backbone. Why? It was simply her name blurred by a bad connection, eroded over too many miles.

"What do you want?" she whispered, too softly to be heard, and at the same time she realized Becky was crooning a terrible sound, half pliant, half a whinny of mortal terror. She yanked the phone on its long cord around to the living room archway and saw the Airedale still beneath the coffee table, but cowering now. Becky had rolled into a fur ball, head and legs and paws a confusion of ruddy curls.

"Cold . . ." the distant voice said, and Becky howled. Dinah knew *that* voice from horror movies. It was the true, bottomless cry of dread.

The familiar room, through which she could pick her way sightlessly, became alien, unknown, and without thinking about it, trying once more to make sense of the voice, she heaved the phone. It crashed into the wall, the cord snapping loose from the socket. As if she had gone into a trance, Becky ceased her crying and slowly unwrapped herself.

Dinah stood, feet firmly planted on the wall-to-wall carpet, breathing deeply, as if she'd just run for miles. Something . . . something . . . She knew she should remember that something, but didn't want to.

When her heart ceased its frantic thumping, she called to the dog, "C'mon, Beck, let's go upstairs." With the Airedale's head on the other pillow, maybe she'd sleep, Dinah thought, and then, in the morning, with a clear head, she'd return to the awfulness of Hatch's leaving and what it meant.

3

"Oh Gilly, *think*! It will be Minsky's burlesque!" Lisbeth Ross's husky voice carried through the small theater though she and Gilford Aronberg stood in the lobby unseen by the cast clustered onstage attempting to rehearse the third act of Lisbeth's play. The director, Corbert Fleis, a youngish man with several off-Broadway successes securely under his belt, kept turning a head of golden curls, obviously undecided: go on with the rehearsal, or trudge up the long sloping center aisle to the rear of the theater into the lobby, and join the fray.

No one enjoyed arguing with Lisbeth Ross, who had the dazzle of a sunset and the sharp intelligence to turn words upside down. She tangled people up in their own explanations until they were held hostage by what had seemed, only moments before, sound reasoning. That she was a beautiful woman with a classy sexiness contributed to Lisbeth's skill in getting her way. Then too, like any good highwire artist, she walked where the proverbial angels had sense not to.

Now, after a successful screenwriting career, Lisbeth had written a play. She behaved like a new mother with an only child. Playwrights usually did, Gilly Aronberg knew, which was why he slouched, hands in pants pockets, head bowed, saying not a word.

Though Lisbeth secretly called Gilly "the pear," with his fat broad bottom, skinny arms, and narrow chest, his tiny bald head, part of her felt sorry for the homely little man. Gilly's brows, so blond as to be almost invisible, and dove-gray eyes made him seem underdone, a practice person improvised by its creator before he got on to the real thing. Even Gilly's voice, soft and embroidered with esses, lacked authority. Lisbeth wondered for the hundredth time what she was doing with such a producer, why he'd chosen her play to mount and why she allowed him. Not that he was a novice, for he'd been on the theater scene for decades, riding the tide with musicals once, then flying high with British imports. Now he was in his middle late period, or late middle period, Lisbeth never remembered which, when he thought only off-Broadway mattered. He had done one O'Neill, two Shakespeares, a Pinter, a Beckett, and a Garcia Lorca, he often reminded people, so he wasn't either a fly-by-night or a Philistine. Which was why Lisbeth couldn't understand this need he had for a nude scene in the second act.

"Gilly, darling, explain it to me, *please!*" She moved in on him, bending—for Gilly reached only five feet three inches—so close she felt the windy little draft of his breath wash her cheek. Gilly smelled of cloves, like a baking ham.

"I have explained it, Lisbeth, until I am limp with weariness."

She sighed. "I'm sorry for being difficult."

He stared at her plaintively though she knew he saw only a grainy blur; at fifty-four he needed bifocals but was too vain to wear them. "Don't be upset, Lisbeth! You're so talented and I adore you." They both understood that he lied. Lisbeth the writer was simply necessary to Gilly the producer. Such was the business of the theater. But the theater also demanded postures of affection as well as declarations of eternal devotion.

Lisbeth stepped back. "I won't try and kid you, Gilly. I am upset. Very. Just think about how I must feel, how trivialized. It's humiliating to have a naked female behind in the middle of my second act."

"It's good box office," he whispered, as if telling a secret.

"Why?"

Yet she did actually understand, for ever since they'd signed the contracts she'd been hearing endlessly about that pivotal scene. When Gilly brought Corbert in to direct and they began to cast, she'd asked him right away, "What do you think?" But Gilly had coached him well. Fleis, widening his china-blue eyes and ruffling his curls, replied innocently as any cherub that he didn't know. He'd have to see how it played. Now, apparently he had, for he and Gilly ganged up on her a week ago, sprang the naked Tilda Moran, a curvaceous ingenue, on her, and asked her to do the requisite rewrites. Tilda's body was magnificent even in clothes, usually jeans and a tee shirt, and her flashing would be worth the price of admission. Lisbeth had answered laughingly that they'd get the entire Eighth Avenue crowd. But she didn't think it was funny, not at all, and had yet to put an additional word on paper.

A success, Lisbeth believed, based on a piece of fluffery, a dirty theatrical trick, instead of on what she'd written, would be no success at all.

"It's a tough season. Ticket prices are in the next galaxy, and the critics must work for the KGB. At least they seem hell-bent on the demise of the capitalistic theater," Gilly told her, then repeated variations on the same themes over and over. None of which Lisbeth cared about. Compromises with *Silver Street* didn't fit into her scheme of things, not now, not after so many years in California. Whoring seemed banal compared with writing for the movies, she explained to her friends. Sometimes, when she'd finally see what she had crafted splashed on the big screen, she wouldn't recognize her vision, the characters, and the words they spoke. Movies had come to have as little sex appeal to her as a gang bang and were just as unsatisfying.

Gilly unglued himself from the lobby wall and said, "Let's get a drink at the White Horse and think on this, Lizzy-bet." He used his pet name for her shyly, as if some intimacy yoked them together rather than need, hers to wrench the flattened vision off the page and give it dimension, and his to supply artificial respiration to a moribund bank account. He patted her arm with his short, pudgy fingers in a mothlike caress.

Lisbeth shook her flaming red hair and it whipped about her face in a curtain of fire. She presented Gilly with the saddest of expressions, though she struggled inwardly to tamp down her rising anger. Lisbeth had been worked over by experts, by Hollywood pros who made Gilly look like an eagle scout, and she realized that losing her temper wouldn't help matters.

"No, Gilly, I'm too depressed." She did not add that she had to meet Charlie Morgan over on Bank Street.

Gilly bobbed his head. "I swear, Lisbeth, the play will be marvelous!" He raised his hand on making this promise. Earnestness made sweat pop out along the receding hairline.

The little girl in Lisbeth who believed the impossible wanted to trust Gilly Aronberg, but the residue of that long-ago self had dwindled to ash.

She refused. "Just swear you'll cover Tilda's bare ass, that you won't undrape it in my play!"

Gilly winced. "It's only a little oomph, something to grab the hicks from Nowheresville by the nuts, along with all those Hadassah groups. Nothing serious, Lizzy-bet."

"No, Gilly, *no*," she said, softly now.

"Oh, you're breaking my heart!" he cried as if they were lovers, as if he really cared how Lisbeth felt. But Lisbeth had seen his performances often. Besides, she was made of sterner stuff than his prior opponents.

When Lisbeth didn't answer, Gilly said, "It's very simple. If you want *Silver Street* put on by me in this theater, and directed by Corbert who agrees *completely,* Tilda will strut her pretty bare buns in the second act. And if you don't, we'll just part friends, sad but wiser. Finito.''

Gilly was playing hardball now, and Lisbeth saw he meant what he said. She clenched her fists as the dizzying anger, coiled dangerously as a sleeping cobra, stirred. Through a spill of red like a sheet of cellophane overlaid on her vision, she saw Gilly glare and she knew he'd hang tough no matter how she swore or threatened. She was the one who would need to back off, and Lisbeth felt ready to throw up.

The curtain swayed as Corbert slipped out into the lobby, ducking his head, skinny bird shoulders up about his ears. Though in his midthirties, Corbert hunched his more than six feet of bones and very little flesh, a convex chest and a rounded hump on his back like Quasimodo. He was painfully shy and continually embarrassed by life, and Lisbeth thought no actor would respond to his direction. He rarely uttered a word, indicating his criticisms with feints and shrugs. When he spoke it was hesitantly and in whispers. Yet the cast of *Silver Street* lay worshipfully at his feet and he had his directorial way with them.

"Tell her, Fleis," Gilly ordered, curling a lip, his doughy baby face suddenly riven with creases, but the harsh lobby lights dimmed and for a moment the power seemed slammed off at the source. Blackness filled up the screen in Lisbeth's head. *No!* she thought, and held her breath, frightened that she would have one of her episodes, that she'd pass through time oblivious, a lost wanderer, to wake up with the pain diminished but the immediate past amputated from memory like a useless limb.

"Lisbeth?" Gilly's hand found its way once again to her arm. A frame was sliced from reality in a quick cut and Lisbeth saw the hand moving in crabby jerks on her sleeve. "Are you okay?"

Lisbeth flung herself out of the Majestic onto Barrow Street and fled east from habit. On automatic pilot, the blood drumming in her ears, a headache drilling through bone, she ran.

The day had died while Lisbeth argued with Gilly, and an early darkness weighted down the city now, falling blackly between the buildings, into the cramped side streets where the metallic glow of the neon signs and traffic signals barely shimmered. Her boots clicked sharply on the pavement as she fled across the Village, failing to outstep the anger or the pain of the increasingly throbbing headache. She extended her arms under her black cape like wings and became a dark, fleeing shadow. In the uncertain light solid objects around her seemed unmoored, watery, escaping their perimeters.

She knew the Village, had always known it well, came here as a teenager on weekends and afternoons stolen from school. She had paraded the length and breadth of it in short skirts and pointy-toed three-inch heels, in fishnet stockings, her eyes outlined with kohl like an Egyptian princess. But now, on cobbled sidewalks with narrow houses tilting close as lovers in an embrace, she had no firm idea where she was. Cracked stoops led to hidden entranceways where doors hung crippled on one hinge. A lighted window stared down at her like a half-blinded man. Suddenly, Lisbeth walked faster, for no reason afraid. It was the headache that made the houses on the opposite side of the street shimmer. She swung around and crashed into a Volkswagen half parked on the sidewalk.

She turned hurriedly, regaining her balance, and strode toward a brighter cross street in the distance. *I should remember where I am . . . should. I will if I only concentrate.* But the pain blurred her vision. She was afraid of blacking out as she almost had at the theater. Stopping, she fumbled in the pocket of the cape for the vial of pills. Her hands shook as she popped the lid. She swallowed the Percodan dry, then put one foot cautiously in front of the other. Only a little while, a few minutes, she told herself, until the narcotic dimmed the terrible thundering, reduced it to a hum.

She thought as she went on, *I won't think of* Silver Street *or of Gilly, I'll think of something wonderful,* and she imagined as she hadn't in a long, long while, that up ahead her father, Ferris Rosenthal, would magically reappear. He'd arrive out of nowhere, just come walking along, one singular man on the street.

A small park bloomed in the vee formed by two narrow streets like a dark flower from the city's cracks. Inside the iron railing she could see that bodies claimed most of the benches, sprawled in drugged stupor or in slumbering escape from insanity. She stepped through the park around the human flotsam and thought herself invisible. She might have been miles away wielding a long, powerful telescope, a Palomar contrivance homing in on city space, picking up the matted hair and rotted teeth, even the fleas in the layers of clothing. But all her senses were acute at moments like these and she smelled the decay on the sudden, ruffling breeze.

She imagined the flesh when life left it, and wept. She shivered and for an instant was eleven, then sixteen on her knees in the Long Island cemetery.

Ferris Rosenthal died on the back seat of a taxi on the way from Fifth Avenue to his office in the financial district. Though her mother, Anne, would not sugarcoat Ferris's death and told her, "Elizabeth, your father died,'' Lisbeth refused to believe her. There had to be some awful mix-up.

Lisbeth at eleven knew, of course, that death was a reality, a vast nothing. Death meant never again, but she could not relate it to her father. She tried to believe that Ferris Rosenthal had left to travel. She saw him on a train, an exact replica of the one the three of them sometimes took out to their summer home on a South Shore beach, or on an airplane. He might even have driven, just taken off for some mysterious business. Some nights, when she lay in her bed and couldn't sleep, she fantasized that Ferris Rosenthal was like one of King Arthur's knights gone on a quest. He'd return home at some point in the future laden with gifts, bursting with tales of his adventures. Yet even half asleep, Lisbeth (who was Elizabeth then) knew she was being foolish.

A car passed, then two, headlights blazing, horns punching quick one-two shrieks. A Mustang roared by. Through its open windows laughter floated.

The wind mixed with The Grateful Dead and the music, along with the headache that still held steady in its intensity, wiped away the memory of her father and brought instead the Porsche doing a hundred, a hundred and ten, flying in exhilarating motion along the San Diego Freeway. The Porsche, a spaceship in orbit down the middle lane, could outrace any car on the freeway. Now the 944 was a wreck, its shiny black skin crushed, its precision, jewellike engine destroyed. She hadn't recognized it when, after her recovery from the coma the crash had thrown her into, the police showed her pictures of what the car had become.

Lisbeth came to a stop in front of a clock store. *Horologes* was scripted in rolling letters across the window. In the dim light inside, on shelves, along the counters, she could see every variety of timepiece, each set to a different hour and minute.

She felt the impact of the Porsche smashing into the back of a panel truck which had swung out into her lane without signaling. That was the last moment she remembered until waking, weeks later, in the ICU of Cedars Sinai. How strange that such a great block of time weighed heavy and impenetrable as cement in her head while the hour or so before the crash was as vivid as a sharply focused film, so perfect in its clarity it would rise up in memory to blind her.

Restless, she had started out from her house in the hills of West Hollywood, gliding, wandering, as nomadic as a Bedouin across the sands. She had finished the first draft of *Silver Street* and no one had offered her a script to do. Drifting, she thought of herself then, unanchored, forty, which was a treacherous age for a woman (she would turn forty-one while in that deep underwater sleep). So Lisbeth had taken to driving, at home in the Porsche that fitted her as superbly as a wet suit.

She had stopped for gas just off Santa Monica. That was when she saw the nursery sign. What had made her go in, down a long walk between tubs of azaleas? It was as though a debt long unpaid, a bill not forgotten—no, *never* forgotten—but put long out of mind in a secret and cobwebbed corner—had abruptly come due without explanation. The past rushed up to claim her that early afternoon when she saw the profusion of flowers, the lilies-of-the-valley not growing but cut, already dying in their large metal vases. She bought every last sprig of the delicate flowers. Wrapped, they filled the passenger bucket seat of the Porsche, and as she swung up on the San Diego Freeway it seemed as if Lily Vaughan herself, a ghostly shimmer, sat next to Lisbeth as she pressed down on the gas. The past was suddenly flung back upon her, lethal as poison gas. She remembered Lily with her sly little laugh, the pinched face, button eyes set too close together, and felt a sadness deep as the twenty years that had passed, a sorrow for the hateful creature that she'd never been capable of feeling before. Poor hopeless Lily, so angry, so hurt, she could only be cruel. With shaky fingers Lisbeth reached over and touched the jiggling little bells, her gaze averted momentarily from the road ahead. When she looked back a second later, there was the van swinging imperiously out ahead of her.

The Percodan was finally taking effect. The penetrating pain eased, and the shadowy forms took shape at last. She knew where she was now and hurried left toward Bank Street, to Charlie Morgan.

Charlie Morgan was substantial, real, his bulk like a wall she could lean against. Charlie was the best thing that had happened to Lisbeth in a longer period of time than she could calculate. A decent, intelligent man whose inclination was to be happy. I believe in that trite saying, he once told her with a wide smile, that it's better to view the glass half full rather than half empty. A Columbia professor of sociology, he read, wrote, and taught of a world less than perfect, a world crowded with the maimed and deprived, and had at some moment made a conscious decision not to be dragged down by what he knew of the human condition. At first Lisbeth had been suspicious of Charlie's buoyancy, leery of his apparent strength, even caustic in the face of such unfailing good humor. She knew many men who were tough as storm troopers but each of those steely creatures had jagged cracks in his armor, deep chasms in the heart. Charlie was different.

Lisbeth bumped into Charlie at the big B. Dalton's on Fifth Avenue. Literally. She was working her way along the shelves of paperback novels and slammed into him. Even before she turned she could tell Charlie was a big man, well over six feet, broad, too, with linebacker shoulders and a massive chest. To Lis who stood five seven he seemed immense. More than his size, however, it was his eyes, a shade of aquamarine she'd never seen before, certainly not in a man, and which quite captivated her when she spun around. Darkly fringed, womanish eyes, they regarded her with an avid curiosity that wasn't lustful but *human*. Right then she'd have given anything to see the Lisbeth Ross Charlie Morgan saw.

The affair with Charlie began slowly, rather awkwardly, like a bus lumbering in rush-hour traffic, which definitely wasn't California minimalist style. Lisbeth liked Charlie's old-fashioned drawl—he originally came from North Carolina—and the easy, shambling way he moved whether walking or playing tennis in the East Side bubble or on the park court, and how he trawled her so smoothly into his life. He worked neatly, but in a steady, purposeful fashion. When Lis told Susie about Charlie, Susie was impressed. Different, she said, more right for you. How do you know? Lisbeth asked. But it was simply a feeling Susie had.

Strappado's, the bar Lisbeth was heading for, came up on her left. It had latticed windows, a heavy oak door with iron studs in it, and an aged wooden facade like a fifteenth-century Italian tavern. Inside it was warm, with a large stone fireplace at one end in which artificial flames flickered merrily, polished brass lanterns, and a long, curving bar at which Charlie Morgan waited, one cowboy boot up on the railing. He wore his usual beige corduroy jacket with leather patches on the elbows, a white shirt open at the neck, and he looked, she thought, moving toward him, healthy. Yes, that was it. Charlie Morgan was a fine specimen. Decidedly American with a straightforward, ruddy face, shortish blond hair cropped above his ears, and an open, unsecretive expression. Charlie's smile blossomed when he saw her.

I'm safe with him as I once was with my father, she realized, knowing all at once that if Charlie had been in the black Porsche with her on the San Diego Freeway she'd never have been speeding. Charlie never went too fast, he obeyed all the rules and limits. Probably the riskiest thing he'd ever done in his life was fall in love with Lisbeth. For in love he surely was, his feelings, which he couldn't mask if he'd wanted to, shining out of his eyes.

Charlie had been married once before, to a thin, frail female with enormous black pupils who gazed blankly out of the one picture Charlie kept on his bookshelves, looking like one of the daunted

41

women, too weary to be even hungry, that Walker Evans photographed in Appalachia. Lisbeth wondered, though didn't ask, why Charlie hadn't hidden the picture in a desk drawer or thrown it out with the trash, for the woman—Joelle—an assistant professor in Victorian literature at Marymount, had run off to England with a visiting Oxford scholar. A Joycean, he told her, almost laughing, shaking his head, when explaining it to Lisbeth. It was the Englishman's specialty more than the loss of Joelle that seemed to upset him. Irrelevant in this day and age, he'd sighed, and Lisbeth often wondered if he would have felt better if his ex-wife had decamped with a physicist or a psychologist. She never asked him that either. She buried Charlie's past in mothballs.

He was much more curious about the events in Lisbeth's life and he asked her endless questions. He probed and prodded, wanting to know every minute, and Lisbeth, backed against an emotional wall, lied. Or committed innumerable sins of omission. One of the sore places in their relationship was the fact that Lisbeth never introduced him to her three best friends, the girls from Cabot. She didn't know exactly why, and it wasn't that she felt any need to keep Charlie secret. He wasn't, after all, an egregious mistake as most of the other men in her life had been. She had revealed the existence of her own ex-husband, Billy Reynolds, but even with Billy Lisbeth glossed over the details.

"Lisbeth!" Charlie cried, and opened his arms to embrace her. Warmth moved from Charlie right through her when he held her against his chest. How secure and safe it was within the closed circle Charlie created, and how too soon Lisbeth felt suffocated and drew away. That was when she noticed the other man.

"Meet Neff," Charlie said.

Neff was a different fish altogether, as opposite from Charlie as dusk from dawn. He stared at her, and Lisbeth, meeting this Neff's eyes, felt cornered. His face sloped, the skin an olive color, dark with the shadow of a beard. He needed a shave. His eyes, the corners tugging downward, were like burned-out cigarettes, and a finely etched scar ran like a pen stroke diagonally along his left cheek to the hard edge of his jaw. He was attractive—that scar, the jut of his cheekbones, the sleepy dead look he had. Brown hair slicked back from his brow. He looked like a dangerous animal. He looked like a tango dancer. She had written a script about one of those men, a mean script set in the twenties, with violence and cruel sex. The studio decided not to film it, but in her imagination Lisbeth had cast it with somebody not dissimilar to this man and her mouth went dry.

"Neff's a cop, a homicide detective. He was lecturing at my four o'clock and we just kept going. I won't say we stopped in every bar from a Hundred and Sixteenth Street down to here, but we managed to hit a hell of a lot of them.'' Charlie laughed.

Lisbeth saw he was slightly drunk, though Neff was clearly stone cold sober. Nothing would have much of an impact on Neff, not alcohol, not women, not even death. She *recognized* him in a way she never had Charlie, and her understanding set a lightning flash of pain in a ring of fire around her head. She kept from wincing but barely. Then the familiar throbbing settled in again and she knew she shouldn't drink the vodka tonic Charlie handed her.

"To all the dead bodies,'' Lisbeth said, and clinked her glass to Neff's, then to Charlie's.

"Hell of a toast.'' Neff shrugged, but he drank anyway.

Lisbeth had a surge of desire to run her fingertips along the scar, her tongue too. She wondered how the ridge of flesh tasted.

"How did you get it?'' she asked.

Automatically his hand rose to his face. "This?'' When he touched himself Lisbeth held her breath.

From behind her she heard Charlie say, "Where're we going for dinner?'' But he sounded at the other end of a long tunnel.

"From a crazie over in the East Village when I walked a beat. You might say we had something of an argument.''

"What happened to him?''

Neff smiled, if the movement on his face could be called that. His heavy upper lip inched up just enough so Lisbeth noticed one of his front teeth was slightly crooked. "The usual,'' Neff replied.

"What's that?''

"Let's just say that right now he's being eaten by maggots.''

"That's disgusting,'' Lisbeth said. Yet the bland manner in which he announced the death excited her, sparked the pain a notch higher.

Lisbeth wanted to turn her back on Neff, ignore him for Charlie, but something in the cop pushed at her, some essential darkness that was heart-stoppingly exciting. *He can't touch me,* she swore silently, not Lisbeth Ross who had been Elizabeth Rosenthal until she took the bus her freshman year up to Cabot and on the way changed her name, thereby reinventing herself.

"There's disgusting and disgusting,'' Neff said, refusing to be insulted.

"Come on,'' Charlie said, "I'm starving.'' His hand lighted on Lisbeth's shoulder.

She left Neff finally and looked at Charlie. "Let's go to O. Henry's and have a steak.''

Charlie paid the bar bill and went to the men's room. When he did Neff said, "The professor mentioned you were beautiful, but that's not the half of it."

Lisbeth ignored the compliment. "Charlie and I plan to have dinner by ourselves." She wanted Neff gone. His siren's song was too insistent.

Neff smiled as though they already shared secrets. "Until next time."

"There won't be a next time," Lisbeth whispered, knowing even as she said the words she was wrong. But Neff was already off the stool and moving away from the crowded bar. She expected him to look back when he reached the door, but she was wrong about that too.

All during dinner Lisbeth tried to pay attention to Charlie Morgan, but he kept slipping in and out of focus. In the ladies' room she swallowed another Percodan and hoped it would anesthetize the pain as effectively as the first. At the perimeters of her vision the blackness lapped like nighttime water. Quinn would advise her to see other doctors, but Lisbeth knew what they would say: time, rest. Or they'd subject her to more tests until she felt like a laboratory animal. She had come to hate hospitals, the clear crisp whiteness of them, the harsh, medicinal smells, the hushed flapping of voices, the possibility of death hovering ghostlike in the air.

Lisbeth picked at her food, moving it around the plate rather than eating, and Charlie noticed. Not much missed his scrutiny. Loving her had given him a laser eye.

"What's the matter? Don't you like the steak?"

"It's fine," she said.

"You've barely had a mouthful. Lisbeth?"

"Yes?"

"Is something wrong?" Concern made him lean forward.

But she could tell him nothing. The headaches, like beasts refusing to be placated, and those frightening moments of darkness in time, weren't to be shared. They were secrets and she'd bury them.

After the lackluster meal Charlie expected to go home with Lisbeth but she put him off. She mentioned the second act, how she had to rethink it. Of course she'd do no such thing. Let Gilly sweat.

Out on Sixth Avenue the wind had died down and an unusual silence hung suspended over the Village. Lisbeth coaxed Charlie into a taxi and said she had to walk, that walking stirred up the words, set new ideas clashing against each other.

As she reached Eighth Street a clattering metallic racket swept away the quiet. Underneath the sidewalk the subway rumbled, leaving a seismic quiver as a train fled downtown. She had a momentary desire to be on it, looping around the lower end of Manhattan to ricochet up to the Bronx.

As she walked north Lisbeth rubbed her temples, but no touch could ease the pain now. That last trip in the Porsche filled her mind again, and after, what she couldn't remember, the days when she'd lain unconscious, a slab of useless meat attached by wires to machinery, a lifeless thing. Then, for some unknown reason she came back. Quinn, Susie, and Dinah had flown out, and Quinn, her doctor's antennae sharp, had been the first one to see Lisbeth's lashes flutter on the pale plane of her cheek.

Why? Lisbeth asked later, and Quinn, like the Cedars physicians, could only offer: because. There's a time, Susie suggested, and this wasn't yours. Lisbeth loved Susie as much as the others, more even, Susie her sister, but often she sounded foolish. Time? *Horologes.* She thought of the clock store as she walked, slowing, running down.

In the middle of tree-lined Tenth Street, Lisbeth climbed a flight of high, wide front steps to the glass doors of a townhouse. Her apartment filled the entire first floor except for the communal foyer and the stairs.

She unlocked the door and felt reflexively for the wall switch. When the chandelier exploded with light, flooding the high-ceilinged living room, Lisbeth gasped. A tornado might have swept through, for the damage was everywhere. Chairs were overturned, cushions tossed about, books tumbled from the shelves. A large abstract oil hanging above the fireplace was ripped half out of its frame. A Philip Pearlstein nude was slashed from throat to groin. The glass doors of her ornate Victorian breakfront were shattered and the crystal on its shelves lay in glittering shards. A Steuben vase that had been filled with roses lay cracked on the floor, the red flowers ruffled across the white carpet like a necklace of blood.

Shakily, Lisbeth wandered through the apartment viewing the senseless destruction, but as far as she could tell nothing had been taken, only destroyed.

In the bedroom her clothes hung draped from those drawers that hadn't been pulled right out of the dresser. Dresses hung limply on the closet rod, scissored into streamers. Papers lay across the carpet like confetti.

In the kitchen dishes were broken, plates cracked in two. Not even the food in the refrigerator had escaped. Cartons of milk and orange juice were crushed and dripping and eggs had been smashed and smeared over the shelves.

45

Lisbeth sat shivering and made no effort to try and clean up. In the morning she'd call the service and have them put the apartment to rights again. Then she'd phone the decorator to replace what couldn't be repaired. She never considered calling the police, though the violation brought a taste of vomit into her mouth. *Don't tell, not anything, ever!* The admonition rose in her mind like an old, half-remembered prayer.

The pain fired across her brow and she groped to the bed. Even before she fell onto the tangle of quilt and satin sheets the tide of blackness seeped in from the edges of her vision. She saw nothing at all and her last thought was only a whisper.

4

The piercing scream, screechy as the highest note of a damaged flute, sliced through the early morning silence, an airborne sliver of glass, and spun Quinn Webster around outside the door of her private office in Stanton Hall. She stumbled against the wall and her hands rose protectingly to her ears. A knife might have flashed into Quinn's heart, the cry struck inside her with such force.

She had just come off the elevator and down the corridor of the north wing, thinking the fourth floor empty except maybe for Verensky, who had the south end and who was also an insomniac, ever since the gulag, he said. Quinn had a long adversarial relationship with sleep and came often to the lab before eight. She didn't expect anyone else to be there. Most of the assistants and graduate students arrived around eight-thirty at the earliest unless they had experiments running that needed close monitoring.

It was a living thing that made such a frightful sound, but Quinn couldn't tell if it was animal or human. Whichever, it was a creature in terrible anguish, and she bounded away from the wall and rushed into the largest of the labs.

Far off, at the opposite end near the high bank of windows, a white-coated figure was bent over one of the long tables.

"Derek?"

"Jesus, Dr. Webster, you scared me!" He jumped and flung about, pushing a hand through the white hair that hung limply over his colorless albino face. Thick, tinted glasses masked the pink eyes that looked to Quinn to have no life in them, to be a dead man's eyes. Now, as she maneuvered across the lab, Derek Sonderson shielded his eyes further, as if the fluorescent tubes high above still cast too strong a glare.

"What was that horrible cry? My God, it was awful!"

47

"Cry?" He shifted so that as Quinn came toward him he faced her head-on.

"Surely you heard it! You'd have had to be deaf not to." Derek shifted again. He was a small man; Quinn topped him by three or four inches. Still, he held his body at such an angle that Quinn couldn't see exactly what he'd been working on at the table. "What are you doing here so early anyway?"

"I wanted to double check the latest results from number twenty-five."

"Twenty-five is Stevie's project."

He turned yet again; this time Quinn knew it was to hide something.

"I don't see why it should be strictly hers," Derek was saying as Quinn quickly swung around to the other side of the table.

There was nothing he could do to hide what lay in the tray. Quinn's cry was almost as anguished as the rabbit's had been. The small mound of soft golden-brown fur lay sprawled on its side, stretched out, front and back paws reaching, in midstride, as if death had caught it leaping over a field.

"How . . . ?" Quinn whispered, her hands hovering above the syringe, which was stuck the entire length of the needle into the center of one wide, staring dark eye.

"I was trying to inject some of the new extract and he jumped, that's all," Derek said, shrugging. "I didn't lose any, don't worry. It's still in the syringe." He spoke cautiously as he leaned over and withdrew the needle from the dead rabbit's eye, because Quinn's concern for animals was notorious. She wouldn't have used them at all if it were possible to test results in some other manner.

The rabbit, a lop-eared Netherland's dwarf, had lifted up slightly when Derek pulled the syringe free, and now it softly thumped back in the metal tray. The sound was such a dead one Quinn felt sick.

"No one mistreats animals in this lab!" she cried, and before she could think or stop herself, she slapped Derek Sonderson's face. Her palm left a blood-red welt on the white, white skin. "Get out, you're fired!" she snapped.

"*Fired?* Dr. Webster, you're kidding! Over a rabbit?" Tentatively he touched the livid blotch on his cheek. "That's crazy, you know that? To fire me over an accident with a rabbit! Jesus, everybody will laugh themselves silly when they hear this." His own pink leporine eyes gleamed with ridicule and—she saw with a shock—fierce dislike. He hated her, she realized, forget she had just slapped and fired him. Her rage surged. No one should hurt or strike out at the weak. Such cruelty was morally wrong.

"Furthermore," she told him through clenched teeth, "I'll do my best to see you have a hard time, a very hard time, finding another job."

Derek laid down the syringe and took a macho stance, his hands curled to fists on his hips, but with tears trickling along his cheeks, he merely looked pathetic. Working with Quinn was prestigious, being fired by her was a black mark indeed, and if she half tried she could very well ruin his career in research.

"You wouldn't do that," he croaked.

"The cat two weeks ago. Both legs broken. Those clamps were too tight. I know it. And you never checked. Then sneakily, like a thief in the night, you disposed of it before I read your report. I thought then—"

"Nothing gets done in research if you keep thinking animals are the same as people," he protested, as if he hoped to sway her from both her anger and beliefs.

"Get out. I don't want to see your face around this building ever. And no reference, I promise you. Just the opposite. I'll write everyone I can think of to warn them about you. You're going to learn, Derek, never to make a living creature suffer." She spoke quickly, on her way out of the lab.

"You bitch!" he shouted at Quinn, but the curse hit only her back.

Just coming in the door, Stevie Carmichael, her chief lab assistant, stopped short at the sight of Quinn's angry face. "Clean up in here, Stevie. Take care of the poor rabbit. And get rid of *him*." She nodded her head at Derek, standing stunned, as if he were as disposable as the dead animal. "Get his keys and ID. I'll be in my office."

"Why . . . ?" Stevie's ferret's face, usually expressionless, was startled as she stood there, hunched in one of her enormous sweatshirts— this one with THE NEW YORK METS stretched across her generous breasts. But Quinn strode right by her and slammed the door.

Later, when Stevie went into Quinn's office to say Derek was in his cubicle weeping that his life was destroyed and that she, Quinn, had done it, Quinn told Stevie either to get Derek out or security would do it. The rabbit was dead, that cat too, and who'd ever know how many other poor dumb beasts.

Edmund Terhune was a serious man and looked it, from his navy-blue suit and gleaming black shoes, to the gold wire-rim glasses firm on a long, haughty, aristocratic nose. His profile reminded Quinn of a Roman stamped on a coin. Behind his glasses, his eyes were a lackluster brown and small as baby buttons. He never seemed to blink and as the limousine crept along in the midday traffic, Terhune turned toward her from his corner in the back seat and tried to stare her down. All through lunch at Périgord East, he had kept his eyes fastened on her as if through the sights of a high-powered rifle, and now in the car as well.

Quinn had known Terhune since she'd been a girl, when her father hired him right out of law school to be one more hired gun in the legal pool of Webster, Inc. Somehow, over the years, he had managed to eliminate the competition—ruthlessly, Quinn assumed—and to emerge as her father's right hand, to be, in fact, president of the company though George Webster remained as chairman of the board, the reins gripped tightly as ever.

Now, however, her father was seventy-five and ailing. Soon, he must have known, he'd die.

"Things change, people too," Terhune had reminded her over his spartan lunch at their secluded corner table. He ate sparingly, only a paillard of veal, a few steamed green beans, drinking Vichy water. Quinn had kept her face rigid, intent on discovering what Terhune wanted. Now she knew and regretted wasting so much time. Two hours for lunch, two hours away from her lab, was extravagant.

She sat, in stony silence; she had nothing to say to him that hadn't been said already. Still, the oppressive weight of his presence forced her into repeating, "I won't go back to Boston. I won't involve myself in the company."

"You don't care then, if he sells it, the whole thing?"

"Why should I," she replied, knowing Terhune cared a great deal. Cared enough to convince her father to lend him Earl and the limousine for this trip down to New York and an effort at talking her around.

"The company financed your research, for one thing," he said, steepling his fingers.

"Part of my research. Most of the money comes from foundations and government grants. I'll survive without Webster money, Edmund, don't worry." She'd get along without her father, Quinn meant. Neither needed reminding that Quinn was privately wealthy, having inherited millions from her mother and her uncles.

"I wouldn't dream of worrying about you, Quinn. That would be an effrontery. You're one of the strongest women . . . people . . . I've ever met." A quiver of movement stirred his lips like a ripple of palsy. Edmund Terhune had actually smiled at Quinn.

Quinn never considered returning the gesture. She didn't like Terhune any more than she cared for her father's other minions. What she meant, of course, was that she really disliked her father. Now she held Terhune's gaze and replied, "Strong? Because I survived and George, Junior, and Will didn't?"

"That *is* quite an accomplishment, Quinn. You can be proud of yourself," he intoned.

She was, but she'd never admit as much to Terhune. Terhune was the enemy. Instead, she went on the offensive. "You've lasted yourself, Edmund, more than lasted," Quinn said. Which was true, and oh, how furious he must be under that icy demeanor, that steely centurion face, to know that George Webster was about to sell one of the country's largest privately held conglomerates right out from under Edmund Terhune's skinny shanks. Unless, that was, she, Quinn Webster, only surviving offspring of the great man, promised to involve herself one way or another. Terhune hinted that what George Webster meant was her assuming the chairmanship. As a figurehead presumably, with Terhune actually in charge when her father was dead.

The tall iron fence surrounding the south side of the university came into view. Over the clusters of people and the cars, the thick hedges like a bulwark, Quinn saw the familiar gray towers and slipped one glove on. "Thank you for lunch, Edmund," she said as Earl guided the long car with its darkened windows between the gates and onto the circular drive. The limo crawled because of the meandering pedestrians who ambled along the drive as if the automobile had yet to be invented. This afternoon seemed worse than usual, and Earl had to stop the car and wait a distance from Stanton Hall, the cumbersome, ugly building built like a bunker that housed most of the medical research facilities.

Terhune repeated what he'd said earlier, over espresso at the end of lunch. "You should come up to Boston and talk to George yourself, Quinn. As his daughter you have both rights and obligations."

Quinn hadn't answered then, but now she said, almost sweetly, "Such bullshit, Edmund." Then she swung her head to glance out the window and up the road to Stanton. "I'd better walk from here," she decided, and tapped on the glass partition. The chauffeur slid the panel aside and Quinn said, "Earl, no need to go on. I'll walk. You can back out the drive."

"Yes, Miss Quinn," he replied, and knuckled the brim of his hat. "Good seeing you again too, I might add. Don't be such a stranger. Come up to visit. Your father's lonely since your mother passed on."

Behind her Quinn could have sworn she heard Edmund Terhune laugh quietly. "It was nice seeing you too, Earl, and I hope your arthritis doesn't act up too badly this winter." She'd known Earl even longer than Terhune and more intimately. When Quinn was younger, and when her mother had been alive, her older brother George, too, and before Will, who was in the middle, had run away, Earl spent most of his time driving the family. Now there remained only her father and Earl. She realized with a shock that Earl must be at least seventy. Too old to make a long trip like this one in a day. Quinn pursed his lips. Terhune should have taken the shuttle.

Earl creaked forward, about to get out of the limousine and open the rear door for her, but she waved him back. "Don't bother, Earl."

Before Quinn could say good-bye to Terhune, he snatched her ungloved hand, holding her off balance. His cool, dry skin felt reptilian and quite unpleasant. Besides, Quinn loathed the touch of another person. But to pull away would be rude, not that it would matter to Terhune. He was single-minded if anything.

Now that he held her, Terhune bent nearer and said, "He's going to die, you know." Something sweetish perfumed the air between them, and it surprised Quinn that Terhune used cologne. "Your father, Quinn," he said in case she doubted whom he meant.

Quinn raised her voice, hoping fruitlessly to scare him off. "We're all dying, Edmund, and have been since birth."

"That's not what I mean," he replied dryly, refusing to be baited. "The cancer is in an advanced state and his heart is unreliable."

"Whose isn't?" she said with a shrug, and tugged until he loosened his grip. Quickly she gloved the bare hand.

The limousine, insulated, was a vacuum, another country, separated from the noisy outer world. But now, the door ajar, loud cranky sounds swept in on them. As she eased out onto the sidewalk Quinn thought Terhune said, "Don't make a mistake," although she might have misheard him. Moored in his shadowy corner, he could have said something quite different.

She glanced back as she headed toward Stanton.

At the bend in the walk Stevie Carmichael poised on one foot, looking as though she wanted to bolt. Quinn beckoned, however, and Stevie reluctantly came. Quinn, watching the girl, thought, *How homely she is.* Stevie moved about uneasily in her skin, as she always seemed to do if she carried bad news, or news Quinn wouldn't like to hear.

"Did you get Derek out of the lab?" Quinn asked.

"He was pretty upset," Stevie answered. "Distraught, really. So I told him it was okay if he stayed until lunchtime, but then, absolutely, he had to leave."

"When I say *now,* Stevie, you know I mean *now.* And *now* was before nine o'clock if my watch is correct." Quinn walked rapidly toward the double front doors of Stanton, Stevie beside her. Tufts of Stevie's dirty-blond hair poked up like a bird's plumage right at Quinn's shoulder.

"I'm sorry, Dr. Webster, but I'm not good with people," Stevie said miserably, bringing the words up from a deep well of distress.

She surprised Quinn, who studied the girl, slumped unhappily with her hands jammed in the pockets of her slacks, as they waited together for the elevator.

A hurricane of laughter roared up behind them and neither needed to be told that the university's star turn, Verensky, the Russian emigré, was approaching. Unkempt, a Kodiak bear of a man in his "American" clothes—plaid shirt, jeans, and Tony Lama cowboy boots—Verensky had an arm around the shoulder of his leggy, platinum-blond secretary, Jessica, an ex-surfer from La Jolla. A large paw lay a bare inch of decency from the girl's breast.

Stevie blushed and shuffled about, but Quinn stared straight at the Russian and said, "Good afternoon, Verensky."

"Quinn, my dear friend! How are you today?" he bellowed.

Quinn disliked his using her first name. She felt neither dear nor a friend to Verensky and was in a touchy enough mood to say so, but the elevator doors parted and they all stepped inside. He stood nuzzling Jessica's ear and murmuring nothings in his mother tongue until the fourth floor, when the lovers, still entwined, shuffled out together. They stopped so quickly that Quinn bumped into Verensky. At the same moment Jessica screamed.

Faster than Quinn would have thought it possible for the bulky man to move, Verensky flung himself and Jessica to the side. As they fell her scream turned into a series of mewling cries. He slapped a hand over her full pink lips. "Enough!" he ordered.

Verensky's quickness left Quinn just outside the elevator with Stevie hidden at her back whispering "Oh, oh, oh" over and over again and Derek Sonderson in front of her holding a revolver.

Later Quinn would wonder why Verensky had taken such defensive action, for the gun was pointing not straight out but to the side, the muzzle tight against Derek's right temple. But then she lacked time to think decisively or even be frightened. There was simply one frozen moment when Quinn confronted those tinted glasses and was unable to make any connection with the pink eyes behind them. Then Derek's finger squeezed the trigger.

"It was impossible to stop him. The whole thing happened in seconds," Quinn said later to the detective, Field or Feld, she wasn't sure of his name. Quinn and the lopsided man in a wrinkled gray suit stood over a dead Derek Sonderson, shrunken to almost child size in death, the white skin so bleached it became no-color but still clung tenaciously to bone. On the floor, with the sheet that had been draped over him pulled back, he seemed younger, more a boy, though Quinn knew he'd been over thirty.

Good riddance, Quinn thought, fighting even the notion of remorse, which would swamp her if she allowed it. The detective dropped the sheet back over Derek with professional indifference. Around them several uniformed men took measurements, cleaned up, put bits and dabs of brain and skull into plastic containers.

With Stevie, greenish and slicked in a nervous, shiny sweat, they retreated to the lab. Stevie was sent to wait in the records room with the filing cabinets and one lone desk, its glass wall looking out onto the main lab. Quinn led the policeman into her private office. She took the leather chair behind the broad, neatly organized desk and let him perch uncomfortably upon a wooden one like the intruder he was.

Field or Feld scowled just as Edmund Terhune had only minutes that seemed hours before. What would Terhune think if he knew what she had come back to? Would he see Derek's suicide as proof that she should give up research for Webster, Inc.? Abandon the time she spent in repetitive tasks, performing the same experiment over and over until even her sleep contained parts of the intricate tinkering with genes? Or would he say, *Again, Quinn?* For she remembered all at once that it had been Terhune whom her father sent up to Newbury all those years before, to protect her interests if need be. She almost wanted her father then, and had had to settle instead for Edmund, monkish in the extreme and more stressed than she was. Quinn learned during that awful time never to want her father again, not for anything.

The detective asked Quinn, "Why'd he shoot himself up here, on the same floor as your lab?"

While Quinn told about firing Derek, the detective took a pack of Marlboros from his shirt pocket. Fishing out a cigarette, he shoved it in the corner of his mouth and let it hang there unlit. Quinn continued her account of what Derek had done, her eyes fixed on the white cylinder. The cigarette bobbing up and down was her reference point.

"Derek was getting even, I suppose," she ended sourly, unable, finally, to think of anything else to say.

The detective snorted, "Some getting even! To blow a wind tunnel through his brain! Je-sus! He must of been nuts!" The cigarette came away and like a magician's prop disappeared back down the shirt pocket. He stood up saying, "That's about it then. There'll be a coroner's inquest, but it's nothing much. A formality. You'll get a notice, whenever." He didn't offer to shake hands, for which Quinn was grateful, and she walked him to the hall door, though not down to the elevator where she saw one of the janitorial staff swabbing the floor.

Quinn detoured through the two large labs at the end of the corridor, moving among the students and research assistants, none of whom breathed a word. They all avoided her eyes. Probably they blamed her for Derek's suicide, not that she intended to shirk accountability. It might be true that in Derek's twisted, obviously deranged mind she loomed monsterlike, the authoritative end to his career, at least in this university. But Quinn considered the fault Derek's. She hadn't pulled the trigger, after all. Even in death people shouldn't be excused.

Stevie waited, crouched on her chair in the records room. Quinn had almost forgotten the girl.

"He's gone," Quinn said, sticking her head in the door. "It's over."

Stevie was still the color of cold oatmeal and Quinn half expected her to crumple, but Stevie rose and shuffled about, then throwing her shoulders back, sniffed, "He didn't have to keep me sitting here. I want to separate that latest blood sample for twenty-five."

"Why don't you take the rest of the day off?" Quinn asked sympathetically. She felt a faint worry over Stevie. Bright though she might be, her center was soft as cream caramel.

"Are you?"

"What for? I can't bring Derek back to life. As for seeing him shoot himself, I'll think about it less if I keep busy with something to occupy my thoughts."

"I probably will too." She shuddered. "It was just so awful."

Quinn started away. She wanted to forget about Derek Sonderson, to push the memory of him alive as well as dead into her subconscious.

"Oh, Dr. Webster," Stevie called before Quinn reached the door, "this came for you when you were with the cop."

"What is it?" Quinn asked as Stevie handed her a package the shape of a shoe box, wrapped in plain brown paper and secured with twine. Nothing was written on it except Quinn's name in bold block letters.

"They sent it up from downstairs." Quinn flipped the package over curiously as Stevie tensed. "You know, they always say if you get something anonymously never open it."

"Why?"

Stevie licked her lips. "Bombs."

"A bomb? For me?" Quinn laughed, so amused she almost tossed the oblong package at Stevie in fun, but poor Stevie, horrified enough for one day, leaped behind the chair. "Stevie, what can I say, except I'm neither an Israeli nor an Arab nor a member of the IRA. So I doubt it's a bomb." But Stevie wasn't totally convinced, and in recognition of the girl's unraveled nerves, Quinn took the box to her office before opening it.

Putting it down on the edge of her desk, Quinn, still smiling, thought that if it were a bomb it would blow a hole in the floor and take her crashing down into the lab below where a team of behaviorists constantly performed experiments on stress and how to lessen it.

After reading over the reports in her in-basket, Quinn took a scissors from her middle drawer and cut the twine. She ripped off the paper on what was indeed a shoe box with the Italian designer name Bruno Magli inscribed on it in elegant script—someone certainly had expensive taste—and raised the lid. Nothing exploded and whatever the box contained lay shrouded in tissue paper. Some delicate and fragile object, she supposed, her curiosity sharpened. She parted the tissues, rather childishly pleased at the idea of an unexpected present, and saw the small white, pathetic corpse of a mouse. Its tiny limbs rigid in death, its beadlike eyes no bigger than pencil points sightlessly staring up at her, the mouse was punctured in its middle, held to the tissues with the smallest of paring knives. Even so, the knife, so grotesque in conjunction with its poor victim, resembled a fence post.

As with the rabbit, whose dead image flashed in her memory, Quinn's gorge rose up her throat as though she'd been punched under the heart. She shoved the box across the desk. Sweat broke out in a frill above her upper lip, and she turned to the window, resting her cheek against the pane. Below, a tide of people passed along the paths and walks.

She could call the precinct and ask for Feld, yes, Feld, that was his name—and say . . . Say what? Someone sent her a dead mouse in a Bruno Magli shoe box? Derek Sonderson before he shot himself; that would be Feld's explanation. And maybe, maybe, Quinn hoped, he'd be right.

She drew in her breath, steadying the frantic beating of her heart, thinking for an instant of what her father's fright must be when that sturdy engine, unreliable after all these years, broke into a rapid tap dance and threatened to swerve loose in his chest.

A mistake's been made, she decided, forcing herself to return to the desk. Then, before she stopped to consider further, Quinn smashed the lid back down on the box. Scooping up paper and string, she shoved all of this horrible gift down into the metal trash basket and carried it out to the incinerator. She threw the box, the mouse with the knife jammed in its belly, down to the roaring blaze below. She hadn't looked, so she couldn't know, that under the tiny corpse was a little sprig of lovely white bell-shaped flowers.

5

Their dinners were almost always planned in advance. Though they had no fixed date they managed to meet one night during the last week of the month. Dinah would drive or take the train down from Westport and Susie would find a time in a busy schedule of charity events, business dinners, cocktail parties. Quinn more often than her friends could come at a moment's notice. Her social contacts were minimal compared to the other Cabot women's. "I spend all day surrounded by people. At night I like to relax, read, listen to music," she'd explain. She was especially partial to Mahler. Also, with one of those unexplainable peculiarities often found in particularly intelligent people, Quinn had a lowbrow appetite for the television program *Dallas*. Then too she enjoyed spending time with her dogs. Actually, as the others knew, most humans bored Quinn, their everyday conversations about ordinary events as strange and unappealing as punk rock. Her tolerance for stupidity had never been high and grew less the older she became.

When Lisbeth first moved back to New York, she spent endless hours with Susie when Suz was free, with Quinn too. Dinah not as often, but then Westport was a trek and Lisbeth liked suburbia even less now than California. But when Lis met Charlie everything changed. They went to the theater, toured the museums like tourists, attended most of the major gallery openings, and devoted much time to dinners all over Manhattan. Still, Lisbeth never let Charlie intrude on her nights with the women.

Dinner this Friday night wasn't arranged a week or two ahead of time. Dinah needed them and when she called each of the friends, crying, "I have to see you!" they all agreed immediately. Susie canceled a foursome at Lutèce with one of Greg's partners and his wife, and Lisbeth told Charlie he'd have to wait until Saturday night to see her. Quinn had had no plans.

They all sensed Dinah's panic at being set adrift in the Westport colonial. Through the endless calls they heard her careen like a car out of control and closer to the cliff of hysteria. They hoped she could hang, at least by her fingertips, until Friday night. She did, but barely. Her edges were unraveled and her clothes might have been slept in. The makeup she had applied in Westport was badly smeared by the time she reached the Village. When she rang Lisbeth's doorbell, Susie cried, "Oh dear!" and enfolded her in a tight hug.

Some essential part of Dinah had been sliced off and disposed of, or that at least was how she felt. As the train pulled into Grand Central she decided to put a good face on—to lie outright, she meant. Of course, with the friends, no bold fabrication could hold for a minute even if she hadn't already told them most of the outrageous news on the telephone. Besides, she looked terrible. Without pause she blurted out everything she hadn't already revealed.

"I've ended up sleeping in the living room. With all the lights blazing no less. Mikey finds me there the next morning, still dressed, Becky scrunched up under my arm. You know, he doesn't say a damn thing about it," Dinah said.

"He's upset and confused," Susie said. "Don't think, no matter how sophisticated they all appear, that they can just take divorce in their stride. You've got some rough weather ahead with Mikey, Di."

Susie was at her most earnest, which stabbed Dinah's wounds like a sharp stick. "Well, thanks a bunch, Suz. It's great to know I've got a future of shit swamps!"

Lisbeth threw up her hands. "Better to know the worst and try to avoid it, than to fall in up to your neck."

"Oh!" Dinah flapped about on Lisbeth's couch as if she might levitate. "I'm not made for divorce. I'll turn into a spongy mess."

"Do tell," Quinn muttered under her breath, annoyed with Dinah's self-pity. Dinah must have heard, however, for she swung round on Quinn, who rushed on hastily, "You'll get along just fine, Di, wait and see if you don't. Under everything you're strong, steel, like the rest of us. Believe me, you will survive." Quinn worked to calm Dinah's temper, uncomfortable to find herself arguing with these friends. They'd been through too much with one another, but more important, they centered her life. Molded together, they created a sturdy breakwater to which Quinn, in one of her few imaginative moments, saw herself as clinging in a boiling, treacherous sea.

"I don't understand any . . . of this." Susie sighed, staring down into the amber pool of brandy that she swirled right and left, then spun around in the glass.

"Of what?" Lisbeth asked.

"Of the lives we've come to since Cabot. They're all such foreign countries." She laughed.

Quinn shrugged. "You brood too much, the three of you. Life is doing. Action. Work."

"As a housewife in a nonproductive vineyard, i.e., a busted marriage, that makes me feel great, Quinn," Dinah cried, and threw a cushion across the room, hitting Quinn's knees.

The remains of a takeout dinner from the Chinese restaurant around the corner on Sixth Avenue were still scattered about the table in the dining alcove. Lisbeth, restless, moved on bare feet, gathering the cartons together. "We didn't have our fortune cookies." She held up the small plastic bag. "Anybody game?"

"You're kidding!" Dinah cried, flopping back on the couch and lighting a cigarette. Quinn wrinkled her nose, but she wasn't about to tell Dinah, not now, that smoking would kill her, kill the rest of them too just from breathing the fumes.

Lisbeth tossed the fortune cookies into the remains of the pork lo mein, and stacking plates on a tray, carried a load into the kitchen. Susie got up to help, but Lisbeth, nudging the door with a shoulder, waved her off. "I'll just do this stuff and then come back."

At the sink Lisbeth took some Percodan, swallowing the pills in a mouthful of cold tea. Her eyes felt hot and heavy. Through the rear window the bottom edge of the fire escape glowed luminously, outlined in an orangish-yellow neonlike light that emanated from nowhere. She imagined silent traffic padding up and down the metal steps, boots and clumsy brogues, high-heeled sandals with rhinestone straps, and they gleamed, the shoes, the legs, of those wanderers on the iron stairs. She watched through the glass of the kitchen window.

There were worlds within worlds, other existences, folded into what was known like a collapsing Japanese fan. She'd read that six other dimensions could possibly be rolled up in their mathematical space, so infinitesimal they'd be dwarfed by neutrinos. Lisbeth liked the physicists' fanciful notion and believed if she listened attentively she could hear the vibrations.

If she ever gained exactly the right speed in the Porsche, would she have looped around on one of those spatial tangents and entered somewhere else? *Is that what happens in the darkness I can't remember?* She wondered and shuddered.

Quinn was saying from where she crouched in an Eames chair by the fireplace, "He blew his brains out right in front of us."

"Ugh! Why did you look?" Dinah asked, her disordered hair standing on end, the image of someone who'd had too much to drink.

In fact, she had downed four beers with dinner. Now she sipped coffee, hot and black, but with a generous dash of brandy. Maybe she'd really sleep tonight, and in a bed.

The coffee cup rattled when Dinah lifted it. She said, "Sometimes you see things you shouldn't, that you never wanted to, and that are hard to forget. Damn!" The liquid splashed over the cup's edge to the saucer.

"It happened too fast," Quinn said.

Lisbeth, coming back, asked, "What did?"

Susie, pale, explained. Quinn closed her eyes as if she might will the memory into oblivion. She hadn't realized how awful the experience was until she repeated it to the friends. Somehow Derek's splattered brains were more horrifying in the retelling.

Lisbeth glided about the room, swaying side to side, dancing to a soundless tune. She heard herself saying what she hadn't meant to, "We do have a way with violent death, don't we? Look at Lily." She stopped midstep.

"Oh God!" Susie said, covering her mouth in a childish gesture, as if she'd been the one who blurted out Lily's name instead of Lisbeth.

"You're crazy!" Dinah yelled, jumping up and upending her coffee cup. A brown puddle eddied across the table. Susie threw a handful of napkins on it. Dinah never noticed as she windmilled her arms and cried, "What's the matter with you, bringing up Lily?"

Quinn, expressionless as a blank slate, came out of the chair and grabbed Dinah's elbow. "Calm down, Di!" she ordered.

Quinn's voice hit Dinah with the chilling splash of cold water. She collapsed on the sofa. "I hate bringing *that* up," she said, then added defiantly, "not that I know anything because I was asleep!" None of the others even looked at her, and she snatched Susie's brandy, downing it in one swallow.

Quinn sat, staring into the small blaze that crisped what remained of the logs, which emitted a miserly draft of warm air.

Susie moved nearer Dinah and tried soothing her as Dinah poured another brandy, in a hurry, it seemed, to get drunk. Lisbeth had yet to stop the dancing, the watching. Quinn couldn't keep still and again was on her feet, leaning against the mantel. Her father filled her mind, north in Boston, secreted like an extravagant and sacred old Buddha in the big empty house. Not even the ghosts of her mother and brothers wandered the halls or lingered in the cold rooms with her wheezing father, never mind her younger self—so clumsy yet so sure of the future, that promising tomorrow time which all too quickly came to be now and meant nothing. Except for Earl and the housekeeper, Selma, who slept in a nun's cell behind the kitchen, her father lived alone. But hadn't he always, even with wife and children? And what about you, Quinn? a nagging voice asked before she could quiet it.

The brandy sent Dinah, already on the edge of dislocation, right over, and she tore at her hair as if she intended to rip it loose from her scalp. "Oh, how could Hatch just throw away his life, my life too, over some tight-ass female lawyer! Hatch, oh Hatch! I love him! I need him!"

"Forget Hatch," Lisbeth said, ending the slow dancing at last.

Susie could roll back the years and see Lisbeth dancing in exactly the same way, a younger Lis who looked as long and lean and sinuous as this one. She turned her eyes away, and took a rare cigarette from Dinah's pack, holding the Marlboro with the same awkwardness she had as a girl. Smoking was the only clumsy thing Susie Lamton ever did.

"Let him go," Lis continued, tossing her hair, playing with the strands. She sank effortlessly to the floor. "We always expect too much from other people, expect them to push the darkness aside. And they can't."

"Stop it, Lis!" cried Dinah.

Quinn struck a pose stern as one of her Puritan ancestors behind the pulpit in the whitewashed severity of an early church. "You're going to have to pull yourself together and go on, Dinah, and not rant and rave because things haven't gone your way."

"You're being too harsh, Quinn," Susie said quickly before Dinah could scream or Lisbeth laugh. "After a while, Di will be just fine, but it takes time. She has to adjust and we have to be kind, which is why we're here."

And Lisbeth did laugh, clap her hands, hooting gleefully, "Saint Susie!"

"That's not funny, Lisbeth," Susie said harshly, for the name had been flung at her before.

In the Philippines with Greg, after days of seeing things she never wanted to, dead dogs, one half eviscerated in a gutter, skeletal children scattered everywhere, withered old people humped and broken who were probably not so old in actual years; after so many wounds and dead eyes and limbs like twigs, she cried at the sight of a group of ancient women under a thatched roof weaving baskets with rapid fingers. Barely clothed, in bits and ragged scraps, sprouts of lank lichen hair, toothless, eyes filmed white as sea foam, they squatted like monkeys, no differently than monkeys. They had passed backwards on the chain of evolution. Hopeless, the guide had shrugged, and Susie wept for all her privileges. Saint Susie, Greg called her then, amused, charmed by what he thought of as her innocence. A rather sweet bloom, if unrealistic, he teased.

It is human, Susie tried to explain, but Greg laughed and swept her off to buy something wonderful, something lovely and expensive.

"Of course we're here to help, Di," Quinn protested. "Haven't we always stayed together since Cabot? Isn't that what we *do*?"

"You came for my accident," Lisbeth said as though the crack-up in the Porsche had been a celebration, a wedding for example. Lisbeth cross-legged on the dhurrie, mussed and devoid of makeup, shone and Quinn covered her eyes. Lisbeth, despite all that had happened in the intervening years, was still the girl from Cabot days.

Susie slipped to the floor opposite Lisbeth and sat in the lotus position just as she used to in the living room of the Cabot suite they shared. "Of course we did, darling. We were there for as long as you needed us, right at your bedside. Just as Di needs us now."

"Obligations," Lisbeth said, though she smiled.

"Not obligations, love," Susie insisted.

"I seem to remember that you were always the one exhorting us to live in the here and now," Quinn said to Lisbeth.

Lisbeth laughed, flung out her arms and bent back from the waist like a stalk in the wind. Then she whispered, "Someone vandalized my apartment the other night. Skewered, sliced, ripped it, and tossed it from stem to stern."

"What?" Quinn cried.

"This apartment?" Susie asked, looking around. "I don't understand. Nothing's different."

"The cleaning service. An industrious pack of out-of-work actors. And blue-haired Emma, the decorator. Fastest fingers through the Yellow Pages you ever saw. Presto and gobs of money," Lisbeth said.

"I'm going to be sick," Dinah said and rushed into the bathroom.

Susie started to go after her but Quinn said, "Leave her alone. Let her get all that alcohol out of her system."

Sitting down stiffly on the edge of the couch, Susie asked Lisbeth, "Did you call the police?"

"What for?"

"To find out who did it," Susie replied. Even as the words left her mouth she thought, *How ridiculous. We never want to know, or not too much.* She hadn't cared at all about catching the man who raped her in the shelter closet. Just let him disappear, fall down a sewer. More important, let me simply forget him, it, the outrage.

Dinah, colorless, returned finally and poured more brandy. When

Quinn repeated the story of Lisbeth's break-in Dinah asked in a shrill voice, "Why are these things happening to us? We were the golden ones." At Cabot, she meant. It surprised Dinah even now, her inclusion, that elevation which resulted from the girls' friendship, their love and communion, the hub of her life that let her ascend to some higher level, beyond anything she thought she might reach, such a funny girl from Hanover, Nebraska.

Conversation stalled as midnight came. The women had worn themselves out, as they often did with one another, and sat now, fatigued, a little drunk, or in Dinah's case—the new brandy setting her off again— not the least bit sober.

Dinah pulled loose from the couch's embrace after she emptied the glass. "Gotta go. Last train. Miss it." She swayed, unsure of the floor and her own feet, eyes opaque as aspic.

Quinn said, "You can't get there under your own steam, Di. I'll take you and see you safely on the train. Come on." She stood.

Dinah slurred, "No way. A little bit of air . . . Have to learn to do things by myself. Isn't that what you've all been saying? Stand up, Di, on your own big feet!" She giggled and looked at her shoes. "Not so big, just sixes."

Quinn took her in hand. Susie asked, "Want me to go with you?"

"No, it's okay. I'll hand her over to the conductor. He'll see she gets off at Westport. By that time she'll be semisober."

Dinah kissed Susie and hung for a second in Lisbeth's arms. They thought she'd start crying again and patted her affectionately. "Old dog, that's me. Just like Becky," Dinah sniffed, pushing them off. "But I did nothing wrong, not a damn bloody thing. I was a good wife, would have been even better. I was planning on improvement," she insisted, straightening her shoulders. "You just remember, okay?"

"Poor Dinah," Susie sighed when the door closed.

"Stop feeling sorry for her," said Lisbeth. "You can't weep for everyone."

Susie protested. "This isn't *everyone,* it's Dinah."

"Go on then, but it won't help Di one bit." Besides, there was something dangerous about pity and sorrow, about regret. The thought was startling and Lisbeth pushed it away. "Oh, let's not fight." She leaned against Susie, holding her.

Susie stood motionless. "I was raped." The whisper fluttered against Lisbeth's neck. Breath and words mixed, stirring old feelings so that Lisbeth doubted she heard Susie correctly. She stepped back, holding Susie at arm's length. Susie, so close, waited at the end of a long corridor. Suddenly miniaturized, she pulsed darkly, cast in cobwebbed shadows.

"What did you say?"

Tears ran then, spring rain falling, and they carried her again into Lisbeth's arms. She'd cried so much already though she tried to be strong. It was over with, a past event, merely a statistic now, nothing more. The rape was yesterday's news. But despite her struggling she experienced the pain once more and, worse in a way, the humiliation of that forced intrusion into her body. "I was raped," she said again, pulling free. She rubbed her arms, chilled, and began roaming the room nervously, pausing at the window to glimpse the street, a stream of silver under the lights.

"Who? Where?"

A half smile kissed Susie's lips. "What difference does it make?" She picked up a snifter with some brandy left in it and drained it, leaving the glass on the mantel as she passed. The room was a mess, ashtrays, empty glasses, and cups scattered everywhere. "I'll help you clean up," Susie said, unable to stay still.

Lisbeth yelled just like the Lisbeth Susie recalled from school, and stamped a bare foot soundlessly on the rug. She'd always gone without shoes at Cabot until the coldest day, then took them off again in the early spring.

Susie waited patiently, as she always had with Lis, for the yell to change into words. "Damn, what a thing to say! Raped, and isn't that just fabulous, now let's clean up and not mention it again. Oh, Miss Cool, you are a complete revelation."

"You're acting the same about your apartment."

"My apartment isn't your body!"

"Okay, Lis, what do you want? It wasn't the big treat. Okay? It was awful. I felt dirty and humiliated. Unclean. And . . . and I hurt, all over, inside and out. But it's over. I'm fine now. Semi anyway. No use, as we always say, crying over what's already down the toilet." But Susie's tears ran down her cheeks in channels. She dabbed at them with a napkin.

"All night we've been talking about Dinah and her divorce, and Quinn's seeing her assistant blow his brains into oatmeal, while you . . ."

"*Stop!* There's not a damn thing anyone can do, hear?" She wept like a lost child.

"Susie." Lisbeth said her name dangerously, but Susie shook her head, then shook it again more violently when Lis demanded, "Tell me."

"I just did. I had to tell somebody, and I probably, no, I do, you know that, Lis, love you more than anyone I can think of. I had to let some other person know. As if I had cancer. Just telling you stirs the blackness a little." She smiled more authentically now, the tears glimmering on her cheeks. "Really, I'll be fine, or better. But don't say a word to the others, please. I don't know why, just that Quinn would be offended and a tiny bit disgusted. Dinah, well, with Hatch leaving, Dinah's unreliable. Look how much she drank, getting drunk, without our noticing."

"Slyly, that's always Di's style. If we know too much we'll push her out, which is what she's thought from forever. She told me that once, in her cups, very vague about it, then later swore up and down she hadn't. When she sobered up, that was. In L.A., that time she came with Hatch. When he left her at my house for a day and a half."

"I remember."

"He wasn't in San Jose on some legal business. He was shacked up in the Beverly Wilshire with a soap opera writer, the sister of some sleazy producer whose divorce Hatch was handling back here."

"Oh God! Did Di find out?"

"From me?" Lisbeth laughed sourly. She never told secrets. Susie should know that. The question, or something else, a vague stirring memory she couldn't quite grasp, caused a sudden spurt of anger with Susie. Susie. Susie always understood . . . everything. She loved Susie. Susie loved her.

Pain cut a chasm across Lisbeth's brow. She forced herself to walk carefully into the kitchen.

"What's the matter?" Susie asked, following her to the sink where Lis swallowed another pill, washing it down with water drunk right from the tap. When she looked up she saw that the fire escape had changed its psychedelic color from orangish yellow to a violent shade of green.

"Lis?" Susie touched her arm.

"Nothing. Headache."

"You better go to bed."

"I suppose so. But, Suz, this—" She embraced Susie once more. "Please, tell me. I'll try and help. No more smart-ass remarks or yelling." She pressed her body tightly against Susie's, remembering. A moment later they parted and Susie wouldn't look into Lisbeth's eyes.

"I should get home," Susie said. Yet she paused for an instant as Lisbeth's arm went out, her hand dangling, the fingers groping. Then Susie swept back into the living room, almost running, gathering her coat and bag, hurrying for the front door. There she hesitated.

Lisbeth came only half the distance. "Don't be mad. Don't be sad."

"Remember the night we climbed to the top of the Cabot tower singing 'The Bear Went Over the Mountain'?"

Lisbeth laughed. "Sure I do."

"We had such fun!" Susie's eyes glistened. "Shit, I really better get out of here, or I'll stay the whole night and wail and weep."

"Anytime."

"I'm sorry, for everything. I really am," Susie cried as she rushed out the door. But her voice came floating back, "No, not for some things."

6

Quinn lived mostly by habit, her life compartmentalized. Work. The Cabot friends. Yin and Yang, the corgis. Her days formed patterns, here at a certain time, there at another, meals, sleep, awakening. She walked the dogs early in the morning, then around five or five-thirty when she arrived home from the lab, and again, though briefly, before bed. These outings occurred along East End Avenue and in Carl Schurz Park, though on weekends when the weather was good, she'd taxi over to Central Park.

This afternoon Central Park was already crowded when Quinn arrived. For a moment, checking that the leashes were securely fastened to the corgis' collars, she wondered if there mightn't be too many people for an enjoyable walk. But the dogs strained, eager to get started, and she allowed their enthusiasm to sway her.

Voices, the hum of traffic out on Fifth Avenue, the cries of children, barking dogs, runners' pounding steps, bike tires crunching over gravel, noises of every kind swirled into the cloudless sky and fell over the crowds. The dogs, social creatures that they were, loved not only the park, the grass and dirt, the click-click of their nails on the pavement, but all the tumult. They lurched toward other dogs, big or little, and more than once gazed back happily at Quinn as if to say *Isn't this wonderful!* And she'd smile, forever amused at such exuberance, at the almost-humanness. People might say to Quinn—if courageous enough in the face of her stony reserve—they're not children. But to her they were and she spoiled them, devotedly and with pleasure.

Skirting the playground, the dogs barking through the fence at a horde of children swarming about the jungle gym, Quinn climbed a steep slope into a quieter, shadowy section of the park. The crowds were thinner here, a trickle of strollers, some graceful roller skaters, lovers of every combination arm-in-arm, teenagers—boys mostly—jiving with headsets attached to their ears, and the usual lone wanderers. One, a man, in jeans and a windbreaker, scuffed boots, idled, hanging back, then suddenly decisive. He wound through the park on the same paths as Quinn but some distance behind; as her pace increased he walked faster, as she slowed, he shuffled his feet. Quinn, who seldom looked over her shoulder, never noticed him. When she stopped at the crest of a small hill, the man was sitting on a flat outcropping of rock smoking a cigarette. He blended into the scenery, another detail, a single impressionistic brushstroke.

One of the dogs yapped, the other joined in. They'd gotten themselves twisted. "Oh really!" Quinn scolded them lightly, squatting. Yin leaped into her lap when freed and Yang licked her cheek. Smiling, she continued on, leading them out of the shade into the sunlight.

That was a Saturday. On Sunday it rained and Quinn stayed in except for quick necessary walks along her block of East End Avenue. On Monday the drizzly clouds blew out into the Atlantic and after work Quinn took the corgis over to Carl Schurz for a short run just inside the park. They didn't linger, for dusk this time of year was only a momentary shift of light, and darkness came abruptly.

Quinn was just cutting across the sidewalk when the signal blinked from green to red. A tall, broad-shouldered man, starting to cross, stopped as she passed with the dogs.

"Quinn? *Quinn?*"

She hesitated. The dogs almost tugged her off balance.

"Quinn? Jesus! Is that you?"

They met face to face, their eyes locked, breathless as old lovers.

Oh no! Thoughts stormed in her mind like agitated birds in flight. *A mistake* was the only one Quinn could keep hold of. *Mistake, mistake, mistake,* she repeated silently. It wasn't Will at all, oh no, only a quirky resemblance, she insisted as the man approached. The dogs barked, but for once Quinn ignored them.

"Will—" Quinn didn't know what to say. In the realm of make-believe meeting a lost brother after so many years would be conceivable, but Quinn was a realist. She clung to facts, to the reassurance of black and white, disbelieving in gray areas. Only some things were possible.

"A shocker, that's for sure," he said with shaky laughter, as he stood with legs spread, fists curled on his hips. She remembered him posing that exact way in his youth, in hers.

"Yes," she replied, stunned by the sight of this big man, her brother, who when she thought of him Quinn supposed lived far, far away from New York, never mind Boston. In Alaska maybe, or at least California. Yet he materialized *here,* much the same at forty-five, no, forty-six, though the years had left their imprinting in crow tracks on his ruddy skin. But his eyes were that remembered pale blue, icy as crystals; his chin retained its hard edge. His curly brown hair, however, had gone gray among the ringlets which he now wore long, about his ears. Her beautiful brother looked like an aging angel, and despite herself, Quinn found tears blurred her vision. Impulsively she reached up and haltingly kissed him. She loved Will as though it hadn't been more than twenty years since she'd seen him last, on the dock off the house in the Vineyard before she left for Cabot.

Time ran aground, stuck on the rocky shoals, swallowed in deep sinkholes so that past and present purled together, whirling in a high tide.

"How have you been?" he asked Quinn.

"All right. Fine. You?" Shyness gripped her. She might have been that young gawky girl again, but Will, serious in the almost sullen way she recalled, tried smiling. He looked as though his face ached. "Oh, Will, I'm sorry," she blurted. "I mean . . ." She wanted to say she regretted this miraculous encounter if it brought him pain, if, after so long, he still shunned it.

"For what? For falling over me accidentally? Hey, Quinn, come on, it's chance. I'm never in this neighborhood. But tonight"—he shrugged with that easy lift of his shoulder—"I had to see some people over here. Business."

She ran a tentative hand down the sleeve of his windbreaker. "It's so strange."

"Fate." Will laughed. "It could have happened before, or if not tonight, tomorrow. Brooklyn isn't in outer space."

"You live in Brooklyn?"

Will's laugh escalated to a roar, and for a second, regaining his Boston face, he was that young boy who taught her to roller-skate on the Commons. "Brooklyn's not such a bad place. It's not back of Mongolia." Only he couldn't help but know what she meant. The Websters weren't people who ever even left those approved locations in New England, that restricted geography, except for Quinn, who did the unthinkable by moving to Manhattan. But Brooklyn! Despite herself Quinn wondered what their father would say.

"We have a pretty nice house. A yard. The usual."

"We? You have a family?"

"Oh, Quinn." Will took her in his arms then, and tall as she stood, he seemed to envelop her. She had no space, but never thought about the touching, relishing the sturdiness of her brother, the male smell coming off his jacket. Something broke inside her, an ice floe dissolving, splintering as it cracked and melted.

Yin and Yang had tangled their leashes, winding about her ankles. They barked and Quinn stepped away from Will.

"How have you been?" he asked in a moment of embarrassment.

"Grown old and fat," she said.

He laughed and Quinn saw that one of his front teeth had a tiny chip out of it and that there was a dark space toward the back where one of the molars had been. But for all of that his smile was boyish, and a pang nudged her heart.

"Not old at all. Younger than me. And not fat," he said.

She never considered herself an attractive woman, not beautiful certainly, never even pretty when younger, so she didn't expect to see admiration cross Will's face. "Big," she said. "As mother would promise, I've grown into my bones."

Again embarrassment overtook them. Quinn had questions, hundreds of them, and there were things to tell Will too, details of the family, about their mother certainly, and the old man. But the wind began to stretch and shiver in off the river, and in the sliding shadows, they were such strangers.

Quinn walked a little ahead and Will went beside her. "I just live up here," she said.

"Not in Boston?"

"Not for a long time. My lab is here."

"Lab?"

"I'm a doctor, Will. I do research in genetics."

He stopped and in a raised voice of surprise, cried, "A doctor! Oh my God, Quinnie. When I left home you were just a kid."

"That was over twenty years ago, remember?" How could he forget, how could she? So much time, so much of life happened. A lingering resentment made her walk faster. At the curb, she seized the light and almost rushed the corgis off their feet. Will easily kept pace.

At the other side Quinn stopped abruptly and took a good look at her brother's face, trying to sort out the love from the anger, the resentment. He'd gone away, and never sent a word back. Not alive or dead, happy or sad . . . nothing. Their mother cried; their mother, in more ways than Quinn suspected she knew, never recovered. She hadn't herself, for Quinn loved her brother, loved him or had more than anyone but her Cabot friends, loved him certainly more than their older brother, poor dead George.

"Mama's dead," she said without thinking whether she should tell him here and now. "She died six years ago."

"I know. Believe it or not, whenever I could find one I read *The Boston Globe,* and it was one of those times, sheer coincidence, when I saw her obituary. A long illness it said, but not what."

"Cancer of the liver, and it wasn't so long, less than a year from start to finish. Mama and her stomach, always so delicate. Well, eventually she ended up in Peter Bent Brigham. When they opened her up they took one look, then stitched her closed. We tried the usual, of course, chemotherapy, radiation, even whatever experimental treatment seemed sensible. Nothing helped, but then it never does, just adds a day or two, maybe a week or a month. In the end she slipped away, but not before she'd lost thirty pounds and her hair fell out. You wouldn't have known her. She looked like one of those awful pictures from the concentration camps."

Will winced. Quinn, who'd been there at the end of their mother's long dying, at the beginning too, thought she'd forgiven him long before for disappearing. The Websters were the kind of family you ran away from if you could. But when their mother's cheeks caved in and her eyes, the same exact shade as Will's, protruded, when her breath smelled of rot and her fingers scrabbled on the sheets in a relentless spastic motion like sand crabs, she hated them all, her father who kept to the office or his own room, and Will, and George Junior too, dead though he was.

"I couldn't come back."

"You never wrote or called." Will turned to her carefully, waiting. The dogs pulled, barked, eager for home and their dinner, but Quinn held her ground. "Just like George, you could have died."

"I probably would have if I stayed as he did. The poor sod." He shook his head in sorrow as the ghost of their older sibling slouched through their memories. George Junior had gone even a longer distance than Will, and forever, out the high window of the little cubicle office he'd been allotted at Webster, Inc., with the ironic gold lettering of *Vice President* on the door. George had swan-dived twenty-two floors to Storrow Drive in the early morning when the traffic was at its heaviest, adding to the rush-hour chaos though he'd landed on a narrow walkway. For a moment her other, more recent suicide came to mind, Derek Sonderson, who was neither grieved for nor lamented over, despite the blood and brains and chips of bone he left on the tile floor. George, Jr., had claims of family and a shared childhood though he'd already been old when Quinn was young, his hair beginning to recede before his twenty-first birthday. By the time George crashed into the hereafter with his broken bones and pulpy flesh, he'd been nearly bald.

They'd reached the awning of Quinn's building. The doorman held the door open and the corgis strained for the lobby. "I live here. Can you come up for a while?"

"Sorry, no, I have to get home to Maria and the kids."

"A family," Quinn said finally, stooping to scoop up Yin and Yang, holding one in each arm.

"Yes. Two girls and a son."

"Children." Quinn paused. Her head drooped. Will tentatively touched her shoulder, and though the dogs squirmed, she didn't shrug him off. "I'd like to meet them. Yes, I'd like to meet them very much. Bring them . . ." She stopped. "I mean, can you come for dinner?"

"Why not . . . ?"

Will never mentioned that his wife was Mexican, and when Quinn opened the apartment door he watched cautiously over Maria's jet-black hair. What, Quinn wondered, did he expect, that she'd throw up her hands and shriek, or that their Mayflower ancestors would tumble about in their graves? She was annoyed with Will, but then he smiled and introduced the children. Isobel and Carlos, thirteen and fourteen, both with licorice hair and almond eyes, but ten-year-old Sarah was fairer, with mahogany-brown curls and those familiar china-blue irises. Sarah strongly resembled Quinn's mother.

Quinn possessed no household skills, nor did she care to. The few times she had people to dinner the meal was catered, with someone to serve and someone else to clean up. Tonight was no exception, and a tuxedoed waiter slipped about the living room with drinks and hors d'oeuvres.

The children, regarding the young man who offered them caviar on rounds of toast as an apparition, inched close to their mother. Maria sat uneasily on the edge of a chair, still as a frightened bird, expecting at any moment to be startled into motion. She couldn't relax with this large, assured woman, hair tucked back behind her ears and pinned with little barrettes. *This sister,* Quinn almost heard Maria thinking, *is the past, she blows in from those choppy seas of New England, a storm out of memory.*

Quinn struggled with clumsy attempts at reassurance. She repeated stories of their childhood, hers and Will's.

"Even when he was Carlos's age, Will was the best sailor. He'd go out anytime, clear skies or in the rain. Our mother would worry so, standing at her bedroom window until she'd see him coming into the dock. He loved the sea, didn't you, Will?''

"Back in the days of the dinosaurs," Will said, rubbing his chin.

He wandered about the apartment perfectly at home. Except for the cheap pants and the worn tweed jacket, he might live here. "This was mother's," he said, pointing to a small Dürer etching of a hanged man.

"You remember," Quinn said.

"I wouldn't so easily forget something like that, for Christ's sake. It must be worth a fortune now. You should be careful."

"Careful?" She wasn't sure what he meant.

Will moved on to the Rouault—an elongated Christ, anguished as death—which had also been their mother's. "This hung in the small parlor off her bedroom." His voice had a tight, hard edge to it. He picked up a cloisonné box and put it back on the end table. Looking around he said, "Nice, Quinn. All in the usual Webster good taste."

Quinn was kneeling and calming the dogs, who were frenzied, unused to so many people. When she glanced up Will had sat down and was absentmindedly turning in his hands a Steuben bird Quinn had bought one day on a whim.

"Can I pet them?" Sarah asked, slipping to the floor beside Quinn.

"Of course."

The corgis yelped delightedly. They swooned with pleasure when Sarah lay flat on the rug and pressed her small nose to their wet ones. Then Maria uttered a machine-gun rush of Spanish and Sarah quickly sat up.

At the table Will's family was still subdued, speaking when spoken to, letting Will bridge the distance with Quinn. Not that he revealed much, only bits and pieces, such as that he made a living doing carpentry and that they'd come north from Cuernavaca three years earlier. What he had done before or where he never said. He was, she realized later, miserly with details.

The evening stirred uneasily, rushing one moment, dragging the next. Maria couldn't relax, nervous fingers pinching at a sleeve or wandering over a child's hair. And the children, they were so timid, though after dinner Carlos did take down a book from a shelf and Isobel helped herself to a second mint without first glancing at her mother.

Sarah, however, captured Quinn's attention and she had the entirely unfamiliar desire of wanting to touch the child. Sarah stirred up a feeling Quinn didn't recognize.

At the door when they were leaving Will said, "Well, Quinn, this has been very nice."

Maria, her elbow held tightly by her husband, nodded, *"Sí. Muchas gracias.* Yes, many thank-yous, *Señora."*

"No, not *Señora.* Quinn. Quinn, Maria." She hunched forward, almost threatening it seemed, for the smaller woman drew back.

"Yes, Quinn."

Quinn looked up at her brother, satisfied and eager. "We'll have to do this again."

She was about to ask them for another night, ready to set the day and the time, when Will said, "Why don't you come out to Brooklyn on Sunday afternoon?" The pleasure Will's invitation gave Quinn surprised her and she agreed at once.

Finally alone in the apartment she wandered from room to room, unable to settle down. She saw again her own hand, with its short-cropped, unpolished nails and thick veins, stroke a caress on Sarah's cheek just as the family was about to step into the hall. The child had smiled and she clutched Sarah in a hug. Maria spat some Spanish admonition as Sarah squirmed, but Will smiled broadly.

Quinn slid a CD of Mahler's Second Symphony into the stereo, and as the first faint strain whispered through the speakers, she felt again the warm glow holding the child had roused in her. How much, she thought, sinking down on the couch, both dogs jumping up beside her, she looked forward to the weekend.

She considered taking Yin and Yang, but then decided, no, that would be presumptuous. Wine, of course, was proper, and Quinn chose an excellent rosé, but then worried if that was what one drank with the Mexican food she supposed Maria would make. In case she erred, she returned to the liquor store and bought a bottle of cabernet sauvignon and a very good California chablis. One of the three should do.

The children required something more suitable, but she couldn't think what that might be. Candy was all her imagination conjured up, and she taxied down to Godiva for a large assortment of chocolates. Still dissatisfied, she stopped in the florist at the Waldorf and bought a bouquet of white roses for Maria. Then, overflowing with packages, she hailed another cab and drove to Brooklyn.

The light was ebbing as she arrived, dropping a pink wash over the white house, the minuscule front yard with its metal fence and gate of entwining leaves, the lattice against the porch to one side with its darkly climbing vine. The house squatted between its identical neighbors, small and insignificant. Quinn saw her apartment, filling an entire

75

floor, and the baronial stone mansion in Boston with many more rooms than people, and the big Victorian house on the Vineyard, sprawled like a dowager queen on three manicured acres at the water's edge. This small square box could have fitted into the Vineyard boat house. It was not at all where she imagined her brother. But there stood Will behind the screen, laughing. "What in the world have you got?" He took the wine from her arms and the candy. Quinn carried the roses into the house and handed them to Maria.

"Gracias," Will's wife said softly, burying her face in the profusion of whiteness, but when she glanced up, her eyes were still uneasy. Her tension seemed to charge the air around her.

The children loved the candy, however, though their mother slapped someone's hand gently and ordered, "Not for now. Later."

The meal, served almost immediately, was spread across a colorful embroidered cloth, but it wasn't Mexican at all. Maria served, with pursed lips and heat-reddened cheeks, a traditional North American Sunday dinner of roast chicken, mashed potatoes, string beans, and salad. For dessert she presented golden pies, one peach, the other apple.

The conversation as they ate was as strained as it had been at Quinn's though the children were more relaxed and spoke to her directly. Sarah sat on Quinn's right and she and Isobel talked of school. When she passed Quinn the vegetables, there was the clear, pure scent of soap and little girl, and for a second Quinn felt her heart stand still.

Dinner over, Will took Quinn out to the glider on the front porch. They creaked back and forth in a lazy, indolent motion, watching the occasional blurred figure drift past the fence, the lone car purr softly along the sleepy neighborhood street. The night rustled with mysterious sounds; the air was tart and crisp. The environment felt alien and Quinn remembered with difficulty that she was still in New York City, though she couldn't precisely pinpoint the locale more than *Brooklyn*. If asked to guess from only what she viewed and what she sensed about her, Quinn would have hazarded the Middle West, in the center of the continent rather than here on the eastern edge.

They swung slowly back and forth on the glider, not talking as Quinn thought of what she had yet to share with Will, their father's illness, Edmund Terhune and the corporation, Earl's advancing age.

Finally she did. But Will asked few questions, and answered only a handful until he was driving Quinn back into Manhattan. Then, as they drove along the long, lonely streets, he began to talk.

"When I left, I'd only been at the office, what, five or six months, but it felt like a lifetime. No way could I stay and climb up the corporate ladder, not with the old man knocking it out from under me again and again. And watching me, betting I'd break. Hoping."

In the worst times, such as their mother's funeral, Quinn hated the old man with a deep abiding passion; at other moments she was ambivalent, for she remembered his touch when she was a child, his smile, how he'd swing her up and say that if she tried, she'd reach the sky. Most often she simply refused to think of him, whether dying or as he had been in more robust days, and silently damned Edmund Terhune for forcing her to. Yet for all her confusion over the old man, she disputed Will.

"Oh, surely not. Why would he? George was already dead. He needed the business handed on."

"Now you say he does, but that was then. Remember 'the king is dead, long live the king'? He wasn't going to allow me to kill him, not even to elbow myself a space on his mountaintop. And I had a whole life ahead with all sorts of possibilities." He paused, hunched over the wheel. They rode through Brooklyn, separated from her world as surely as though it was another galaxy.

Will continued, "I hated the office, the old man's style of doing business, the way he stuck his tentacles into everything, and how he berated the employees. Me too. No one was safe from his tirades, that wrath I used to think of as Godlike. It fell in a hailstorm. Damn, he was a vicious son of a bitch, still is, I suppose. I hated him, for myself, for Mother, for you and especially George, and for the shakes and stutters of that slavey secretary he had. What was her name? Never mind, it doesn't matter. He seemed to have it in for the world, and yet he made so much money. If he touched it, like magic it became gold." He sighed and slipped into a thoughtful silence, driving one-handed, a man now, someone, Quinn supposed, who fought battles she could know nothing of. Winning some and losing too.

"Where did you go?" she asked at last.

"Where didn't I is more the question," he said with a bark of laughter, baring his teeth. But Quinn, recalling their mother's pain, saw for a moment Will's smile as a wolfish grin. He had been a determined boy, this man, and had gone off not concerned about the ones he left behind. Quinn supposed, trying to be fair to her newly discovered brother, that that was what survival meant.

As they approached the bridge Will described his travels, working his way across the country, going north for a while to Canada, then climbing further up the continent to Alaska. "I worked on the pipeline, and finally had enough money to fly over to Europe. I stayed two or three years bumming around, seeing the sights, living the good life. Eventually I ran out of dough, so back I came and ended up in St. Louis. Not a bad town. I stayed, even got married, to a girl named Alice, but she died in a helicopter crash.'' He hunched his shoulders as they rattled on the metal floor over the river to the shoreline of Manhattan. ''I was at the controls,'' he explained. ''Yeah, I have, or had, a pilot's license and was cleared for most kinds of birds except the big ones, but after that crash I never took a plane up myself. Oh, I'll ride as a passenger, but I won't be responsible for anyone's life, not like that, not after Alice.

''So,'' he continued, ''when I was more or less patched back together, I left St. Louis and wandered around, ending up in Mexico after about a year and a half. That's where I met Maria. I had a couple of jobs, one bartending in an out-of-the-way saloon that the Brits were all crazy about, and crazy about me too. They liked having their gin fizzes served with a Boston accent,'' he said, though Quinn couldn't hear much of Boston in him now. ''And I gave some English lessons to well-heeled Mexicans, one of whom was Jorge, a doctor and Maria's father. The rest, as they say, is history.''

''How did you get to Brooklyn? And a carpenter? You, Will? I don't understand.''

''Jorge bought it in the hospital, in the operating room no less, while performing an appendectomy. A massive coronary blew a hole clear through his heart. After the funeral we might have stayed, but Maria's got a rat pack of relatives and it was just such a hassle. None of them are nuts about gringos, and with Jorge dead things got difficult. Besides, I missed the U.S., and I wanted my children to grow up here. As for Brooklyn, well, New York, the whole city's, a great place and this is the best I can afford. The neighborhood's quiet, not too much crime, and the schools are okay.''

''Couldn't you do something, I don't know, more—''

Will interrupted her, laughing, ''More white collar, more Websterish, more in line with all that crap I had stuffed in my skull at Harvard, relevant stuff like the symbolism in Henry James?'' They sped along the East River Drive, lights twinkling on the waterfront like dying stars as Will spun his story and Quinn listened. It reminded her of the adventure tales read by Nanny when they were children.

''In my travels,'' Will went on, ''I picked up the right way to bang a nail with a hammer, and I like the smell of new wood. I also enjoy working with my hands, believe it or not, and the satisfaction that comes from building something that will be used. And it sure as hell beats fiddling with the stock market or writing corporate reports. So there, baby sister, you have William Adolphus Webster's life, more or less, to the forty-sixth year.''

They came off the highway and threaded a steady course through the East Side streets, hitting most of the green lights. Will pulled the Toyota up in front of a yellowish river of light flowing out of Quinn's lobby, and the burly doorman came off his chair by the intercom. When he got near enough to the car to see Quinn framed in the window, he hurried to open the door. ''Good evening, Dr. Webster,'' he said.

Quinn waved him off.

Will said, ''So now that you've been exposed to your poor relations, good old Will and his half-breed brood, are we going to see you again?''

Quinn was furious. ''How dare you!'' she cried. ''I never did or said—''

''No, of course not, Quinn. Sorry.'' It didn't sound as though he were sorry at all.

They sat in an uncomfortable silence until Quinn said, ''You were never good old Will!''

''God, that's true!'' He laughed, seeming to regain some kind of balance.

''Of course I want to see you all, Maria and the children also. You're family, Will.''

''Family.'' The word when he said it had a ponderous weight, and she wondered, finally leaving the car, if she'd ever know more about her brother than she did this very moment. But had she ever actually known him at all?

7

The mirrored wall of the Park Avenue living room reflected the women in their attentive poses as they sat on the two paisley-printed couches, on the green velvet settee, on an assortment of spindly-legged chairs carefully placed to hear the tall, lanky man, a wave of dark hair falling over his brow as he leaned against the desk. Wearing a corduroy sports jacket, an open-neck shirt, and a pair of navy slacks, his casualness was a contrast to the women in their designer suits and their hand-knit sweaters and beautifully cut skirts.

"So handsome! Would you believe he's a priest?" Alex Harding, whose husband engaged in complicated financial transactions, leaned over and, practically licking her burgundy lips, whispered in Susie's ear.

Susie ignored Alex and snatched a cigarette from the crumpled pack in her purse, lighting it off the flame of a match. She now smoked like an addict, with no excuses and few regrets. Cigarettes kept the gnawing of her insides from getting worse.

Someone passed Susie a delicate ormulu ashtray, and she heard a hiss of annoyance. Cigarettes were out now, not that Susie cared, watching Father Simon through the drifting curl of smoke. As he talked to the women about the shelter, his blue eyes, so dark and sooty, shifted restlessly back and forth, his gaze stopping momentarily on each face. If he lingered a few seconds longer on Susie, no one noticed.

They had yet to acknowledge each other, Susie and Father Simon. When Claire McGrath, the wife of Greg's senior partner and the recognized social doyenne of the firm, called to announce there was a special charity she was considering sponsoring with a select group of people, she never mentioned the shelter. Later when the women gathered and Claire magically produced the priest from the back of the large apartment like a rabbit from a hat, Susie froze though her cheeks

80

burned. Claire, smugly smiling, explained that Father Simon was a childhood friend of her brother's.

Susie couldn't have said no to Claire even if she'd known about Father Simon; that wasn't done in the complicated world of wives maneuvering for their husbands' benefit. Chesspieces on a corporate game board, the women exercised their power in a practiced pattern, and while a wife's inadequacies might not get her husband fired, they could certainly keep him from advancement. Susie had learned all this palace politicking from her mother, who had craftily manipulated her father into a position as chief of staff at the hospital and president of the medical society.

The women, handpicked by Claire, listened quietly to Father Simon's mellifluous voice, for it was a time when those who slept in beds, who enjoyed comfortable roofs snug over their heads, viewed the plight of the homeless sympathetically. Those in Susie's circle considered the shabby wrecks curled in city doorways or lined up in front of church soup kitchens not exactly as brothers and sisters, as Father Simon suggested, but as human jetsam whom it was their *duty* to bring in from the cold, especially during the winter when the temperature could drop so low many of these lost souls froze as they slept. Yet Susie resented Claire's commandeering the shelter as her "special charity" because of her familial connections, and making plans for a fund-raiser to support Father Simon's "good works." Susie had found the shelter and the priest by accident. She now had a history with its constantly changing inhabitants, with Jose and Sven, and considered the shelter hers alone, a personal haven if a different kind of one, even though she hadn't returned since the rape.

Father Simon had never known Susie's last name. Whenever he hinted questioningly, she skittered away from his probings. Why she didn't want the priest to learn anything about her, and why she kept the shelter secret from family and friends, Susie couldn't say. Except that the shelter was a place of her own. She helped out there as a stranger, ladling up soup or making beds, doing hands-on labor directly for the poor souls who viewed her so dubiously. Yet at the shelter Susie didn't feel distanced from the neediness of the recipients, as she did when working on a charity dance or an art auction, but at the same level, aware to her bones that there but for God's grace she could be. Nothing at the shelter separated her from them; in that reclaimed warehouse the self and the other merged to become one. Now Claire wanted to snatch The Home of The Good Shepherd away from her, to make it public, and though money would be raised, Father Simon's daily struggle

81

made easier, and the homeless benefited, anger spread like a tide pool in Susie's chest.

How can I be so selfish? she asked herself, knowing that what she did downtown during those hours when she slipped away from her organized life was minuscule compared to the thousands of dollars Claire's effort would bring in. And she hadn't been at the shelter in weeks, though she meant to go each day. She knew she had not only to set foot in the place, make sandwiches, hand out towels, change the linens, and sweep the common halls along with Jose, but return to the third-floor closet and face the terrible memories. Her body would continue to be a violated vessel, her mind a cache of dark terrors, if she refused to deal with those long minutes in which she had been overpowered and made into a thing rather than a person. But her skin turned icy, her heart slowed, and her breath grew shallow when she tried to force herself to travel down to the shelter.

She thought of Father Simon often, of the thin netting of grace his presence had dropped over her that terrible night. In some mysterious fashion, he had given Susie his hand in the dark and brought her up from the abyss. If he couldn't alleviate the pain, emotional as well as physical, that wasn't his fault. The rape wounded him too, and if he could not know the horror of that dank breath and the pressure of ruthless, frantic hands, it wasn't because he wouldn't have switched places with Susie, gladly taken the outrage as his own. Susie understood this, and was grateful for the depth of his concern and his attempt to share her pain. But it wasn't enough. That she actually bled and that the priest bled spiritually weren't at all the same.

The meeting lasted longer than the two hours planned. The women, though experienced volunteers, were reluctant to part from the priest, because, Susie suspected, of the brown hair threaded with gray that he kept combing through his fingers, the shy tug at the corner of his lips and his blue-black eyes. If he had worn his collar instead of the casual jacket and pants, Claire McGrath would never have been able to remove the women from the apartment. Father Simon was an attractive man, which should help generate money for his haven. Susie realized she'd known just how attractive he was all the time, but never until now allowed herself to think so. As she had so many other things connected to this small secret side of her life, the *way* Father Simon looked was kept hidden. She hadn't, she realized with a small shock like a surge of electricity along her spine, wanted the priest to be such a man. She'd have preferred a Barry Fitzgerald kind of cleric, short, chubby, and balding, one whose masculinity was cloaked by a black uniform, his sex lost in religious commitments.

The priest wasn't the least disconcerted by the women's attention, not even after Claire called the meeting officially closed, announcing that she'd plan a series of intimate little dinners to start the ball rolling for a large-scale bash. Her lieutenants surged across the living room from their cushiony perches to encircle him. Susie, hanging back, lost sight of Father Simon amid the women.

"Quite impressive, don't you think?" Claire McGrath came aground at Susie's elbow. She was a much larger woman than Susie, built along the utilitarian lines of a battleship. Susie sensed that Claire disliked her, that the disparity in their sizes caused Claire to stiffen her majestic dimensions and beam formidable glances at her from a distance. If it weren't that Greg was the most profitable younger partner in the firm, and Susie respected by various important organizations for her devotion, Claire might have avoided her altogether. They looked so ridiculous next to one another, after all, that even Susie couldn't ignore how she outshone the awkward Claire, how her beauty flared beside such a dowdy companion. Claire made her, she often thought, more than she was, as she made Claire less. It was an unfortunate combination considering how often they were thrown together on social-cum-business occasions.

"His shelter seems to be quite a help to the homeless," Susie said.

"Oh that!" Claire shrugged. "I mean Simon himself."

"He's probably a very good priest," Susie offered carefully.

Claire laughed. "There aren't any others. Or there aren't supposed to be. But then you wouldn't understand about that, not being Catholic."

"My father is."

That brought an even chillier frost down from Claire, icing Susie's cheeks. "I didn't know." Claire sounded as if Dr. Bannon were a turncoat, and Susie had a swiftly repressed urge to tell her about the Irish aunts, the cousin in a Carmelite nunnery, the old uncle for the last twenty years entombed in some Vatican research. But such protests would only freeze Claire more, making Susie's paternal relations seem like bragging, and she wasn't prepared for any further hostility with this dangerous woman. Though it was only noon, the meeting a breakfast gathering, Susie sagged wearily. Holding herself so cautiously throughout Father Simon's talk had exhausted her.

"Donnie and Simon were such good friends, clamming on the South Shore, biking out to Montauk, sailing their boats. Well, for years he practically lived in our house. Of course once he went into the seminary all that changed. They quite lost touch. My brother"—Claire smiled, rather proudly—"is such a playboy. And now, living in Frankfurt running the German branch of the company, well, they're even more of a lamb and lion. I can't for the life of me imagine Simon going about armed with a forty-five or a thirty-eight or some such revolver, and having bodyguards with machine guns which is what one does if you're anyone in Germany these days. Say what you will about Hitler, awful he might have been, but back then people never got kidnapped right off the street and held for impossible ransoms.''

"Only if they disagreed with the Reich or were Jewish!'' Susie snapped, furious, as much at herself for always forgetting this streak of bigotry in Claire McGrath as at Claire.

Claire rolled her eyes and started to move off, the circle about Father Simon finally fragmenting. "Spare me, Susie, from your usual armchair liberalism.''

Afterwards Susie would say to the priest, "I really think at times that Claire is overly convinced of her own divinity.''

Susie slipped out while Claire and the last few women still held Father Simon captive. Up close there'd be no hiding that they knew each other rather better than they should have, certainly not from Claire's X-ray eyes.

Susie crossed Park Avenue to the stone pile of a church on the corner and waited in the recessed doorway next to a sculpted angel for the priest. How did she know he'd emerge from Claire's building searching for her? But he did, stepping from under the caterpillar-green canopy into the coppery autumn sunlight, his hands hanging loosely, as if, she thought, gazing at him obliquely, the nape of her neck prickling, he only waited to reach and touch her. Susie remained motionless until his glance found her and he started across the street against the light. Only then did she descend from her doorway.

"Susie Lamton. I never knew your last name until this morning,'' he said, as if she hadn't deliberately hidden it from him. "I would have called you, Susie, to see how you are.''

"I'm fine.'' She shrugged, acting as if she were indifferent. Dressed and made up, she would appear foreign to him, not at all the woman in a plain sweater and slacks, with only a hint of mascara to darken her spidery lashes, who scrubbed the stove in the shelter kitchen. But if he noticed the incongruity between the two Susies, he never mentioned it.

Slowly they began walking west, Father Simon so close the breeze he stirred up ruffled her skirt. Their hands almost touched.

Susie was so conscious of the priest she dared not look at his face. When they neared the Madison Avenue corner she said, "I'm surprised you're a friend of Claire's.'' She spoke angrily of Claire's intolerance and of her bigotry.

Father Simon laughed. "Some people never change. I seem to

remember the McGraths were always like that. But I never knew Claire well. Her brother, Donnie, and I hung out together as kids. Haven't seen him in years. Hadn't honestly thought of him in years until I recognized Claire's picture in the *Times*.''

Susie said, ''And you decided Claire was good for a few charitable dollars.''

She felt him staring at her when he said, ''That's right. I'm a real beggar when it comes to The Good Shepherd. We get almost nothing from the diocese, and we're constantly short of cash. Some days I feel more like a hustler than a priest.''

''Well, Claire will put you on easy street.''

''No such place for the homeless. The poor are like a bottomless pit. Jesus said they are always with us and he never knew about New York.''

Central Park lay ahead of them, visible at the end of the street in a knot of trees, leaves burnt orange along the sagging branches and drooping over the stone wall. When they reached Fifth Avenue they saw the brilliant foliage sweeping like a fire up and down the street. They entered the park as if with a destination, as if they weren't simply strolling alongside each other, not ready to part.

''I supposed you'd stay away after that night,'' he admitted on the curving path, ''but I was disappointed when you did.''

''I always meant to return. I will,'' she said, turning with him up a short incline that led deeper into the park, to its heart from where the city was only partially visible, the towering buildings like guarding Visigoths. ''I wanted to come back before now,'' she added, as if he'd doubt her.

Beyond the walls and the thick growth the city hummed its music. Few people ventured this far into the park in the middle of a weekday, and except for an occasional jogger, they were alone. A stray brown mongrel trotted with them for a few moments, his nails clicking on the walk before he veered off into a bosky clump of greenery on a tantalizing scent.

''You'll let Claire help you?'' Susie asked after a while.

He was surprised. ''It's not me, Susie, it's the shelter. How could I in all good conscience say no?''

How could he? He was right, yet Susie wanted to keep that place, no matter if she suffered so cruelly there, for her own. The Good Shepherd existed as both a hell into which, trailing the faint scent of Joy, she descended, and a place where she could atone and be redeemed. In the hush of Central Park, branches scraping against one another like tuning violins, Susie refused to retrieve from memory

85

those stark wintry images, those remembrances that damned her. Once she might have been able to confess to the priest, to receive his forgiveness and blessing, once perhaps that had been the reason she sought, though subconsciously, such a haven as the shelter, but now so much had changed. Fear broke in from the streets with the homeless and their tattered rags, their shopping-bag souls, and fear stalked the halls like an avenging ghost. Climbing up another short path into a burnished flank of autumn trees with Father Simon, who in civilian dress resembled no priest, no man of God but a man only, Susie entered the shelter where the light misted dimly and the shadow of the rapist became a chimera.

The priest had taken Susie's hand to help her around a muddy sinkhole of stagnant water left over from the last rain, and he kept it. A shiver winged up her arm and the silk blouse stuck to her skin in the sudden river of sweat along her spine.

Any fool would have run back the way she came, but not Susie. She moved on, oblivious to the danger, never thinking to ask, *Why am I doing this?* She focused on Simon's warm hand, fingers entwined with hers, his palm slightly moist. She sensed his fear, much deeper than her own. She wanted to say, *My heart is black.*

At last they sat on a bench beneath a canopy of branches, and he lifted her right hand with both of his. He brought her fingers to his cheek and she traced circles in the hollows beneath the bones. All breath left her, and she was curiously light, a paper person, delicate as a cobweb, fluttering with the quivers of desire she tried to but couldn't suppress.

"I have no words," he said, sounding so sad, so lost, as if no path trailed out of this leafy enclave in which they sat, as if, in fact, they'd forgotten to mark the way back.

Susie brought her hand around to Simon's mouth and his lips brushed gently against the soft palm and his tongue in a silky touch licked a burning circle for only an instant, but long enough so an echo spurted fire between her legs.

The shuddering spasm of pleasure lifted her off the bench, though once on her feet she could barely stand. If Simon hadn't still been grasping her hand she would have fallen.

"It's late. I should go," Susie whispered, and slowly, as though their entire bodies were uncoupling, their hands detached. Right away she wanted his touch again and almost reached out greedily for Simon, who now rose too. She was a young girl here and now, with a girl's desires even as she stepped to the side, thinking, *I must be mad.* She imagined herself on the bank of a river whose waters churned and whose far shore lay burdened in a fog.

"I know," he sighed, yet neither of them moved off from the other, not for a while.

Susie was almost an hour late for her conference with Miss Allen, the headmistress of the Adams Day School for Girls, and the upper form secretary was fluttering about wildly when she finally arrived in the outer office.

"Oh, dear, Mrs. Lamton, we thought you must have gotten the time wrong. We knew, naturally, you being such a concerned parent, that you'd never just forget."

The conference had, in fact, completely vanished from Susie's mind. Halfway up Central Park West in a taxi, she suddenly remembered and had the cabby swing around in a U turn to cross back to the East Side.

Simon had walked her all the way through the park, from the light in pools to the shadows, the two of them seemingly on separate paths though their arms swung so close their sleeves brushed. The city's sounds crescendoed as they neared the street, and whatever words they might have said, if they'd spoken at all, were crushed beneath the bleating horns, the screech of brakes, the rumble of tires over pavement, the bass groan of the thundering buses.

Susie supposed that anyone observing them as they came out onto the sidewalk would have thought they had quarreled, for Simon appeared both abstracted and agonized, and her own face hung in an unyielding mask. Yet no argument had flowered between them. If anything they were conspiratorially silent, trying to decipher their feelings. An autumn stroll under the fiery trees, a few sentences and those brief touches. Yet it so unnerved them that at the curb, when Simon put Susie into the cab, they could only stare hopelessly at one another in confusion.

"Well, Mrs. Lamton, I'm certainly glad you could find time to drop in for a chat." Miss Allen swept into the doorway and ushered Susie into the spare office, closing the door with a funereal hush. When she confronted Susie over the clear, uncluttered desk, she sighed long and exhaustedly.

"I thought this was Betts's semester conference," Susie said when the older, gray-haired woman, as primly clothed as a mourner, remained silent.

"No, not at all."

"I see." Which she didn't. All at once, with a sinking feeling as if she had fallen too rapidly in a plummeting elevator, she wanted to get up and rush out. Something was about to be said that Susie knew she'd rather not hear.

"Betts is an interesting girl, quite bright, as I'm sure you and Mr. Lamton recognize, with an unusual mind. But so often children like Betts, those select few who always are out ahead of the pack, become the ones most likely to flounder and go astray." The headmistress paused for breath or for Susie to nod her head, then sat still a moment longer, hands knotted in a small hummock on top of the desk. The polished wood glowed and Susie was certain she'd be able to see her reflection in it. How often did the headmistress chart her own expressions in the gleam?

"It is my duty, and that of our Adams staff," Miss Allen went on, "to notice immediately the slightest variation in a girl's behavior. To be forewarned is to be forearmed."

Susie found her voice at last. "What's wrong with Betts?"

The headmistress's brow crinkled like crushed paper. "Wrong? Well, I don't know what's wrong. Not for certain. No, not definitely at all. I can only point to certain disquieting, ah, symptoms." She sounded as though Betts, fifteen, and already with the incandescent beauty of a pre-Raphaelite, all long curly black hair and milky skin, was succumbing to some foreign disease.

The temperature in the headmistress's sanctuary dropped steadily, a chill breeze seeping beneath the closed door and along the unsealed edges of the window. Under the sleeves of her wool suit jacket and silk blouse, the pale golden hairs rose stiffly on Susie's arms. It was no part of the unwritten contract that governed Susie's marriage to Greg Lamton that he should join in these meetings. Greg, though loving and concerned, let her handle the children as he handled business, turning up at Adams only on special occasions such as the Christmas pageant and the yearly parents' night. Right now, however, Susie would have given anything to have him in the other, the father's, chair to her right. Greg would cut with surgical precision through Miss Allen's array of vague statements and reach the heart of her discomfort with Betts. But Susie could always wait for bad news or to face the inevitable. She remembered all too vividly how the inevitable rushed up to assault you.

"Her marks, for one thing," Miss Allen was saying finally, settling down to specifics. "We expect the very best from Betts, and, unfortunately, Mrs. Lamton, her grades are falling. Not that Betts is in any danger of not completing the term, but much less satisfactorily than last year. From A's, with an occasional B in advanced-placement math, she now more often gets merely C's.''

"Do you think she needs tutoring?" Susie asked, leaning forward, her instinct, as always, to repair the damage, to smooth over any roughness.

Miss Allen shook her head. "It's not that Betts doesn't understand what's happening in class, or that her courses on the fast track have reached a level of difficulty beyond her. No, it is more that she isn't paying attention. She has, quite simply, lost interest. Vague, rather dreamy, she's floating through the term. Her feet, Mrs. Lamton, must be returned to the proper path."

"Oh, it's probably her age," Susie said, wishing.

"Every age produces problems, believe me," Miss Allen countered. "But girls no longer lose their heads over the normal biological course of nature as in my day."

"Then what is it?" Susie asked, having been skillfully led by the headmistress to that question.

Only Miss Allen wasn't ready yet to jump the hurdle with a student's mother. Her eyes remained muddy. "That's what we're here to talk about now, isn't it?" Her hands parted like wings, then quickly jammed together. Susie, her gaze caught by the temporarily fluttering fingers, recalled with a rushing sensation Simon's hands.

"It could be one of several possibilities, or some combination," Miss Allen stated. "However, in this complicated age of ours, we have to make some harsh guesses."

"What exactly does that mean?"

"Well, I can assume, can't I, that there are no unfortunate disturbances at home?" she asked to Susie's instant agreement. "I didn't think so, because Tia is the same darling girl we've known since she started Adams, and family troubles are never confined to one sibling."

Miss Allen's long, exclamation-point nose twitched and Susie almost broke into hysterical laughter, but fear gripped her. Problems with her daughters, who from the day each of them was born, had never given her a moment's worry, were new to Susie. Even Ivy Bannon, Susie's mother, said she was both lucky and blessed.

"I don't understand what's happened to Betts that she's not doing well in school all of a sudden." Susie, flustered, managed to force out the words, shifting distractedly to the very edge of the chair. Even here behind the shut door of the closed-in office, Susie smelled those school aromas, odors of childhood, of long ago, which brought back Baltimore memories and consoled her. What could be so terrible that she floundered, unable to change it? But almost as soon as she thought this,

89

the memory of an awfulness that no one was ever magician enough to fix floated up through the debris of time into the light of the present.

"Perhaps she's been experimenting with some foreign substance as so many, too many, teenagers do," Miss Allen said, so rapidly that it took Susie a moment to process the sentence. The headmistress might have been announcing a death, for in her white-faced distress she appeared as unhappy as Susie.

"You mean *drugs*? You think Betts has been taking *dope*?" Susie's voice dropped a full octave and a knife's blade of disbelief sliced through her chest.

"It's been known to happen, Mrs. Lamton," Miss Allen said, gaining courage. "I have no proof, of course, but given the signs, it's possible. Unfortunately we've encountered the dilemma of drugs before, even here in Adams. It's a disease, an epidemic, in this city."

"Not Betts!" Susie swung her head frantically from side to side in adamant denial. *Not my daughter! No, not mine!* The outside world, held firmly at bay like a warring army, breached the walls of Susie's careful life and invaded. She saw herself, Greg and both girls, swept up in a tornado, saw them ground into the dust of bones under the impossible weight of this disaster.

I refuse to accept this! She didn't know if she thought those words or spoke them aloud to the now impassive headmistress, wooden as a cigar-store Indian. Miss Allen's silence announced as plainly as anything she might say that she'd seen this identical reaction before, that she did not expect Susie to remain silent against such a charge.

Before Susie even realized it, she burst into motion and ran from the office, past the secretary who sat with averted gaze, for she too had witnessed just such a scene in the past, down the school's second floor and through the wide red doors. Susie flung out of the school like a survivor from a burning building, the blaze licking at her shoulder blades, ready to reach out in flaming arms to claim her and draw her back.

Susie's first thought when, gasping for air, she leaned against the brick face of a bank on Lexington Avenue was to flag a cab and speed home. But the apartment across the park was empty as a ship in dry dock, silent except for the quickening rattle of the high wind against the windowpanes. Even Mrs. Sloan wasn't there today, moving through her rigid schedule as she cleaned and created order, but off with her sister in Bayonne. She wouldn't return until after dinner.

As for the girls, they were still at Adams, in their classrooms, Tia intent, Betts dreaming. . . . *Drugs? No!* Such violations were alien to the Lamtons; they belonged in other people's lives. So Susie tried to assure herself, but Miss Allen wasn't given to waving false flags, to crying wolf when no danger existed. She was too canny an administrator, too careful with her girls and her school.

Susie didn't know what to do, or if, indeed, she should do anything. Talk to Betts, yes, and tell Greg too; but such confrontations lay hours away, and the rest of the afternoon waited to be gotten through. She wandered south, past stores that on another day when depressed and moody she'd have browsed in, spending money to soothe some uncoiling snake. Life had shifted suddenly into another gear and Susie was being sped rapidly away from what she knew, from the expected. And yet . . .

Who am I? What's happened? Questions boiled up in her mind as they hadn't since Cabot and the early years of her marriage. And even that wasn't *quite* true, she admitted, sunk in thought, as she wandered along the avenue, into the crowds about Bloomingdale's.

Simon moved through her in memory. She watched him again navigating beside her in the park, both of them without compass or map, charting this alien territory by some inner astral chart. She sensed the priest's fear and awe as powerfully as her own. *I won't think about this either,* Susie decided firmly, lost in the hordes spilling over the sidewalks, and on she walked, with no conscious intention or destination, further south.

Susie unlocked the apartment door and it brushed open with a hushed sigh. The doorman said neither girl was home from school yet, and all that space spreading out from the foyer was filled with silence, a turgid quiet, it seemed to Susie, once she put down keys and purse and took off her jacket.

What had earlier been a sunny day had gone gray and a grizzled light clung at the windows. Like a stranger, tentatively, Susie came to the bedroom hallway with the line of closed doors. She walked softly, making no noise on the oriental runner, a sensation of dread at the base of her spine. *This is my home!* she insisted against the sudden, unexplained fear that stirred in her as she walked along the darkening corridor. *No sense, no sense at all thinking someone's up here.* The Lamtons lived in a secure building, protected and insulated on all sides. Nothing, no one, could approach without some announcement. But it was a day of upheavals, of sudden quakes, of cracks breaking through the crust

91

of Susie's life, and now, as she passed the girls' bedrooms, listening, straining to hear the sounds that shouldn't, that couldn't be there beyond the doors, she thought, *Anything's possible*. Her world had been upended.

Unsuspectingly, she'd gone to the shelter closet just as innocently as she entered her own apartment. Her arm had stretched out to the string hanging from the bulb, and when the light came on *that man*, dark as any nightmare, crashed upon her. She could feel the horrifying weight of him still. Time stopped in that one unbelievable moment, as in a car crash or a plane exploding in the sky.

Not me. Oh no. Never me!

Betts, her marks, the grim specter of drugs. This terror too came out of nowhere and was rejected as rigorously as the suspicion of a lurker inside Susie's bedroom. *No! I won't have it!* And, her throat closed tight, her mouth dry, she flung the door aside, crying, "Who's there? Who's in here?"

Silence echoed, but still she fantasized the unknown, a threatening figure cloaked beyond the draperies or in the double closet standing stiff as a mannequin. Or maybe he hid behind the bathroom door. Or in the shower, unseeable through the opaque pebbled glass.

After "the first time" everyone said life would never be the same, but life, inexorably, continued on as before, the experience pale beside the fantasies. But this, this violation, this crime against her, this horrible act in which she had been only an object, changed the whole landscape. Of course Betts could be taking drugs if Susie, the untouchable one, the golden girl, had been thrown down on the floor and raped.

Don't be foolish and dwell on what's better put aside, Ivy Bannon said loud and clear in her daughter's head; but still Susie called out, "Is anybody here? Come out or I'll call for help." And with that, moving lightning fast, she rushed to the bathroom and shoved the door back so hard it cracked against the wall.

No one.

Susie stretched out her hand as far as she could and yanked the shower doors open. Just as the white tile walls slid into view a voice asked, "What's the matter?"

Susie screamed as terror exploded in her insides with the kick of a gun blast. She remembered suddenly the horrible flowers and the razor blade. *My God! Was nothing safe anymore, not me or mine?* she thought, still screaming as she spun around.

Tia stood in the doorway. "Mommy, are you okay?"

———

"I don't see what the big deal is." Leaning against the chopping block, Tia chewed a carrot. She grabbed for another one just as Susie brought the knife down and sheared off the top.

"Watch out!" Susie snapped as the blade dug into the wood an inch from Tia's fingers.

Tia grabbed the second carrot and continued, "John was off getting a taxi for Mrs. Maxwell so he didn't see me come in. You can ask Mrs. Maxwell if you want, Mommy. And then I was in my bathroom. I heard you anyway, so I don't know why you didn't hear me." Tia gazed up at her speculatively. "Did you think I was hiding in your shower?"

Susie's hands still shook as she shredded the lettuce. "Where's your sister?"

"I don't know. She never tells me anything. Ever since she got to take the public bus instead of that old Leary's, ugh! I feel like a child. Ever since, Mommy, she's Miss Snooty Puss with her big nose in the air."

"Your sister doesn't have a big nose."

"She might as well have. When can I come home myself, Mommy, huh?"

"When you're as old as Betts," Susie said, though thinking it had been a mistake to give in to Betts's persistent nagging, for surely in that unregulated hour or two between home and school lay a battlefield, a city as treacherous as war-torn Beirut. Betts could be off with any stranger doing God knew what, and who'd ever find out? Not Miss Allen or Susie herself.

Susie imagined her daughter in a greasy little candy store on a side street still waiting for redevelopment where the buildings were sagging tenements and far too many of Father Simon's homeless crouched in doorways. She saw Betts back behind the comic books, beyond the tall, white refrigerator illuminated like a space capsule, filled with sodas and beers, in a storage room maybe, buying a small cellophane bag of grass, then rolling a joint and lighting up. Susie could even smell the sweet unmistakable aroma.

Well, what's so bad? Grass doesn't kill anyone or send you into orbit. Grass is no worse than an occasional beer. But, wait, didn't some new study just come out which proved that marijuana was addictive? So what? Susie asked in this silent dialogue she was conducting with herself as she set the breakfast nook table. The Lamtons always ate in the kitchen on Mrs. Sloan's days off.

Susie lit a Marlboro and thought *So what?* again, for hadn't she smoked grass in her day, Greg too, all of them?—meaning the educated eastern adult world—and not one person in Susie's wide acquaintance ended in Bellevue or short-circuited her wires. *That's not the same*, she thought, *and besides, I gave it up*. It had, in fact, been so long since Susie smoked a joint that she couldn't remember when.

No, grass wasn't the end of the world, if that's all it was. But coke! Susie shivered, and that terrifying stuff all over the papers and television, crack, that's definitely something to be frightened of.

Susie's head ached and she wished she could just leave dinner half prepared, leave the apartment and maybe go out for something to eat with Lisbeth. She could tell Lisbeth about the meeting at school, and though Lisbeth had no children she'd surely know what to do. She'd give Susie advice so that she might act intelligently. For so many years Susie relied on Lisbeth, more so than Quinn or certainly Dinah, taking her problems to Lis over the long-distance lines like a penitent with sins, so often that Greg finally became annoyed. You're married to me, not Lisbeth Ross, he complained, his mouth pulled down in a characteristic gesture of unhappiness, when Susie announced she was going to California. Greg liked Lisbeth, but he assumed marriage put Susie on the far side of a high wall, separated her from the outer world, from her friends. To Greg, marriage and family excluded other people as effectively as an orthodox religious sect.

Susie, therefore, behaved deviously, collecting quantities of coins and calling not from the apartment but from a booth. Usually she walked down Central Park West to the Mayflower Hotel and called from the lobby where people seldom, for some reason, used the pay phones. Nobody ever hurried her out of the glass enclosure. After the call Susie could stop for a drink in the dim bar, which even on sunny days was clotted with shadows like a murky aquarium. Calling Lisbeth long distance came to be one of Susie's favorite outings.

Funny, but she was less in contact with Lisbeth now that she had moved to New York than she'd been when Lis lived high up in the hills of Hollywood. Susie stubbed out the butt of the cigarette and immediately lit another, picturing Lisbeth down in Greenwich Village.

Lis was different these days, out of focus. Susie couldn't pinpoint when the change began, but it was some time after the accident, the freeway smack-up that almost killed her. During any one of those days when Lisbeth lay comatose, on life-support systems, she might have died. Skinny wires kept Lisbeth attached to the here and now, but as Susie and Quinn and Dinah huddled by her bed, she looked good as dead. Only her chest rose and fell carefully, stirring the sheet, lifting it just a millimeter.

Different after that rebound from death, yes, but how? Susie had difficulty describing it. Was there something less in Lis than there had been before? Or something more?

The table set, dinner ready to be started, Susie shook herself nervously as if to shuck her skin. And then she picked up the receiver off the wall phone, dialed Lisbeth's number, and rushed breathlessly when she heard the husky hello that even so many years after Cabot came to Susie as a promise, "Let's have lunch tomorrow. I'll come down to you. And next week we have to plan a dinner for all of us. *Please!*" Right that second, as Lisbeth agreed, Susie wanted her three friends gathered around her in a protective circle. She had always been closer to them than anyone, these women who were girls with her at Cabot, and with whom, for a little while, she shared a certain innocence for all their smoking grass, their sexual fumbles, an innocence she suspected Betts had lost while Susie wasn't paying attention.

There was no way to watch her daughter surreptitiously, Susie discovered, realizing for the first time how little time Betts spent with the family. Of course she surfaced for meals, but excused herself as soon as she'd eaten the minimum, and escaped to her room. Did she lock the door, Susie wondered, when she knocked and a muffled voice asked, "Who is it?"

"Me, darling," Susie said in her mother voice.

"Come in."

Betts and her books, a white paper sea, stuffed animals in a zoo, a box of Ritz crackers, several unidentifiable articles of clothing, and a Walkman were all jumbled together on the single childhood bed with its Laura Ashley sheets and quilt.

"That bed is a real rummage sale," Susie remarked as Betts let her hair slide down the slope of a marble cheek to drape over one violet eye identical to Susie's.

Betts stared at her mother steadily, full lips, a shade of tangerine, closed tightly together. How long had it been since Betts had taken to silence, tense as a cat? "Doing your homework?" Susie asked for something to say if she wasn't to blurt out, most probably in a soprano scream, *Are you on drugs?* Foreign substances, Miss Allen called them in her schoolmistressish fashion.

Betts lifted up a sheet of paper down which Susie glimpsed a scaffolding of numbers and waved it. "Math," she said.

"Hmmm," Susie replied as she and her daughter focused on each other, Betts enigmatic as a sphinx. It was Susie who finally shifted, ducking her head. Where had Betts gotten such composure? The child who wasn't a child set off tiny detonations of worry, and Susie, wanting her baby back, felt near tears. Time was a third presence in Betts's room.

Quickly Susie said, "Don't stay up too late, honey."

"I won't," Betts said.

Susie retreated, pulling the door shut. She paused and listened. The bedsprings squeaked and she sensed Betts's presence through the wood. The lock snapped loudly, bolting her out, her daughter in. *That's not safe,* Susie fretted, continuing along the hall. She stopped for a long, loving glance at Tia bedded in sleep before she went into the master bedroom.

Greg sat spine straight under the sheet, only barely in contact with the upholstered headboard as he read the latest *Newsweek.* His navy blue pajamas with the white piping were crisp and wrinkleless, and he had shaved. His cheeks were a baby pink. Such primping meant he wanted to make love.

"The merger with Clayton went through this afternoon," Greg said, smiling.

"It did? Well, congratulations, darling. But why didn't you tell me the minute you got home?"

"Because I wanted to share it when we were alone. It's been a long road and a tricky business. Everyone's been crazy worrying over mergers and inside trading accusations, and I only pulled it together by a hair." He shrugged modestly. Greg always worked hard and never took his successes for granted. "It's been a tough sleigh ride, really touch and go." He smiled at her as the girls used to when they were small and came home with gold stars on their papers.

What a handsome boy he'd been when Susie first met him at a Cabot mixer! He had dimpled cheeks and a cleft in his chin, clusters of thick dark curls almost to his collar. *Well,* she thought, watching this man she'd married so long ago and with such expectations watch her, *he's still handsome.* And he was, though his hair had grayed and lines now crosshatched beneath his lower lids and ran in channels along his mouth. He never really changed with the years and remained the optimistic, buoyant person she remembered. Greg had determined all those years before to be happy, each day and moment, with the zeal of a fundamentalist hell-bent on keeping the faith.

Now as Susie unbuttoned her blouse, slipped off the soft wool skirt, she saw in her husband's eyes not love, which was there, but an unformed accusation, which wasn't. She had to turn her back because, once again, as with Betts, she was frightened she'd burst into tears.

"I had a meeting with Miss Allen this afternoon," she said, kicking the black pumps into the closet's darkness. She thought, *Oh, what a reward I'm about to hand him for his victory.*

"Is it that time of year already?" Greg's attention settled on her in a warm mist. She felt the silky caress of his desire as she undressed and it made her edgy.

"No, actually not." She pulled down her panty hose and unhooked her bra, keeping most of her nakedness hidden. Always she obligingly stretched and pivoted about in a graceful sexual dance for Greg's pleasure. But the idea of his touching her now, of running his fingers over her skin with the practice that came from habit, professionally, like a skilled musician, depressed rather than excited Susie. Desire was banked or left in Central Park. It came as no great shock that if it were Simon who wanted her there would be a pitched fire, followed by a dislocation of her parts, then a decided harmony. Passion would sing throughout her body as though along high-tension wires.

"Betts or Tia?" Greg asked, having no idea what Susie was thinking. He'd be aghast if he learned her thoughts were on another man, devastated over the infidelity that, though desired, hadn't taken place. Bewilderment would join anguish if he discovered Simon was a priest. Greg, the most liberal of men, prided himself on his tolerance. He treated Jews and blacks with equanimity, but Catholics—though he wasn't conscious of this—roused his suspicions. Susie's aunts, when they talked of masses and novenas, of the sodality and the Church, the Pope, Rome, made him prickle uncomfortably.

"Betts," Susie replied, tugging a long-sleeved nightgown over her head, a signal she didn't care especially to have sex.

"Yes?"

Susie kept her revelation a moment longer as she went into the bathroom, brushed her teeth, creamed her skin until she glowed, young as a bride. People were often surprised that she was old enough to be Betts's mother, or even ten-year-old Tia's. But the reflection confronting Susie tonight wore webby wrinkles in plummy crepe and creases like secondary highways. There, so well imagined that it actually appeared for the fraction of a moment in the glass, was her future face. Soon she'd be old and look like that, and in no time at all she'd die. They'd take her home to Baltimore so she could rest in southern ground, a fancy of Susie's.

Why am I standing here in my bathroom brooding about dying? Susie wondered, annoyed with herself. Ivy Bannon, Susie's ideal for life as well as marriage and motherhood, wouldn't ever do such a foolish thing. But the apple, contrary to expectations, does most often fall some miles from the tree, and though Susie labored she couldn't transform herself into her mother. *Well, I'm no worse than Jody,* Susie supposed, though there was little satisfaction in that thought. Her rebellious sister lived on a commune near Schenectady and two years ago had married, in a quaint, incomprehensible ceremony, an elderly Indian guru.

Susie was procrastinating, putting off the instant when she would say to Greg, as she suddenly did from the bathroom, wringing her hands like Lady Macbeth, though she hadn't done anything wrong, "Miss Allen thinks it's possible that Betts is taking dope."

"What?"

Greg had already dropped the magazine on the floor, switched off his lamp, and slipped down flat on his back. Susie's bald statement dragged him back up on his elbows.

"Betts's marks are lousy this term, and Miss Allen, assuring me she's had experience in these matters, suspects dope. Well, not addiction, but experimentation, or enough anyway to make Betts function on no more than automatic pilot scholastically. Maybe. I mean drugs aren't certain, but they could be," Susie fumbled, trying to repeat the speech she thought she had memorized so carefully.

"No! There's some mistake!" Greg's face squeezed with pain. Susie hated to see her husband like this; despite his abilities as a hard-driving business trader, his emotions were too near the surface. As from an underground spring, fear burst out in a geyser as he cried, "Not Betts!"

"How can we be so sure?" Susie asked, turning off her lamp as if the question of Betts and dope might disappear in the dark. But Greg snapped his on immediately, plunging Susie into a lighted world when she much preferred the night.

"Betts is our daughter, brought up properly, just like we were, and besides, she'd no more take dope than . . . than . . ." Greg searched for some suitable comparison and came up with, "J. Edgar Hoover. Betts is no more a dope addict than Hoover would have been." The boy buried in Greg the man, the law student who used to laugh and roll on the floor over his own jokes, which often were quite funny, juggle five oranges at a time, send Susie teddy bears and oversized valentines, pushed up to the surface looking as though he'd been in a train wreck.

"She's fifteen" was all Susie could think to reply. She had exhausted her own indignation during the endless day.

Greg stared down at her as if on a disaster site. Disbelief clouded his eyes, and it seemed possible that he would cry, but then he whispered, horrified, "You think it's true!" Betrayal threw him back against the pillow.

Susie felt like Benedict Arnold. Now that she had laid the headmistress's accusation on Greg, some relief should have arrived, at least enough for the tension in her muscles to ease, but none did.

"We have to be realistic," she offered, rubbing Greg's shoulder. "It doesn't really help to pretend. It never helps."

"Susie, listen to me," Greg said. "Your vision is faulty. You're not seeing this whole business from the proper perspective." Unaware of what he was doing, Greg cracked his knuckles, an old nervous habit. "We're a family, a single unit distinct from any other, from all those hordes out there." She felt he was shaking a finger disapprovingly at her. "Haven't we worked *diligently* to see to that?"

"Which doesn't mean, darling, that we're to be spared our share of woes." She struggled with a sad, weary smile. How could she argue with Greg when she thought much the same. *I and mine, an island in a storm-tossed sea.* But islands, she remembered, were often struck by hurricanes.

"Oh, Susie!" He scrambled out of bed. "I'm going to call Miss Allen myself. Right now. She'll elucidate for me. Then you'll see that you got it all wrong. She only mentioned drugs in passing."

Greg didn't want simply to believe the best of people and of life—he wasn't naive—but here, at home, with his family, he had a need for a glossy perfection, for them to be authentic. Nothing ruffled, smiles and warmth and love—he sought them all like a hungry dog. And time hadn't hardened him, rather the reverse, enfeebling him inside as it softened his muscles on the outside.

Susie soothed him as she had learned to do over the years. "Of course, you're probably right. There's no reason to call Miss Allen so late at night though. I'm dizzy from this, and worse even than at the meeting. I've spent the whole afternoon working my way from under the wall that crashed on my head. But still"—she ran her tongue along her bottom lip—"maybe we should take her to Dr. Berger and have him drug-test her."

"Never!" he shot, abruptly stopping his pacing on the bedroom rug. "Berger's account, Susie, is with the firm. It would be . . . *humiliating*," he cried angrily, seeing the walls of his separate worlds bulge and crack, "to take Betts over to the university and say she might be a dope addict." He flung himself on his side of the bed and stared up at the ceiling as if there were someone invisible above who could hear him.

99

"Greg . . ." But her husband no longer listened. He sped on recklessly, a runaway car.

"I really think this is a wait-and-see situation, not something we should just gallop into, all hysterical. Remember, if we cry wolf, our, well, our disloyalty might push Betts into something potentially dangerous. She could get involved with drugs because we tell her we think she is. God knows, I'd get angry if I were falsely accused of some malfeasance, wouldn't you?"

Susie's head ached. Greg, up again and wandering around the bedroom—thinking in motion was his style—still had to come up with a plan of action. Discussing it with Betts, he decided, was definitely out.

"If we ask, are you smoking grass or sniffing coke, what do you think she'll say? Oh, certainly, every Saturday and Wednesday after school. She'd never tell us in a million years. Children aren't supposed to tell their parents anything," he said as if she should know that.

"Maybe she wants us to ask, to show we're concerned. Maybe she can't help herself until we get involved."

Stricken, Greg sank to his knees at Susie's side. "Do you honestly think I'm not concerned about this, that there isn't a terrible pain stabbing me straight in the heart?" His carefully arranged hair was mussed. Pouches hung under his eyes. Forty-five, he seemed sixty now, aging right before Susie. His unhappiness stung, and pity pushed her into opening her arms. Greg fell against his wife with a strangled cry.

"Come on, darling, get back into bed. And let's turn off the lights. Wait, in the morning, you'll see, everything will look better."

"Don't humor me!" he snapped, half under the covers. He levered himself up and leaned over Susie, trapping her between his arms.

"I'm not," she countered untruthfully. A lie was a lie even when told in a good cause, Susie's mother taught her, and she often wondered what Ivy Bannon would think if she knew the half of what was in Susie's heart.

Husband and wife stared at one another, their breath stirring into one current. Almost at once Greg's anger blew away, as it always did, easily as the wind, and he rolled over her. All Susie could think was, *When did I stop loving him? Why?* He stayed the same gentle, caring human being she had started out with, and his feelings for her not only endured but solidified into granite. Yet at some point in their marriage Susie knew she'd passed Greg by, on a different track altogether, and grief and guilt scratched on her like a hair shirt.

Somehow Greg's hand strayed to her breast. She wanted even less now to make love than before, but as he teased her nipple with a steady rhythmic motion of his index finger, her body, uncurling from a cool nothingness, roused with old familiar sensations. A butterfly slowly fluttered its wings between her legs. Her mind screamed *Leave me alone!* but her hips arched as Greg pulled up the nightgown.

For a second Susie, blinded by the memory of the shelter closet and that other man so forceful and unwanted, thrusting her legs apart, stabbing at her with his rigid battering penis, struggled to disengage her husband, to restrain him. Her efforts, however, only served to excite him.

"Not tonight, please," Susie muttered between clenched teeth as Greg plunged between her legs, spreading the buried softness with his fingers and lowering his head to lick greedily. "No!" Susie whinnied, buckling.

"Let me, I want to so much!" he breathed, his breath hot against her wetness. "Just lie there, don't do a thing. A rag doll, limp. I'll do it all."

He ran his tongue in long, slinky motions, then in quick darting laps, before she could protest further. A tide of fire slowly rolled through her insides as he circled her clitoris, and involuntarily she raised herself higher. He stroked the small hardness until she moaned in a breathy panic, then he lifted up and moved into her just as the long steady roll escalated to a rushing current and she exploded.

"Oh yes, like that, oh yes, Susie love, you're so good to me!" he cried, stiffening, and she felt the pulsing of his orgasm. He froze, then dropped down on her. She lay still, her thoughts in rapid, frantic flight, her body, cooling, distant. When Greg withdrew and fell immediately into sleep, she touched the damp, sticky curls of pubic hair, covering her secret place with both hands. For a long while Susie stayed awake, but then she too finally, in exhaustion, slept.

8

"Lisbeth, I'm sorry," Charlie Morgan said for the third or fourth time, "but when the chairman of the department asks you to dinner, to discuss, as he puts it, something important, you just don't suggest making it another night."

Lisbeth, who could say no to anyone, hadn't understood this at all. Why didn't Charlie just say they were going to the theater? That's what Lisbeth kept asking and Charlie patiently continued to explain. "Because I can't. You don't make waves, Lisbeth, if you can help it. At least I don't. I like calm seas and easy sailing." But Lisbeth would have blown up a hurricane, especially if she were Charlie, who supposedly cared so much, for her, that was.

They ended up in a fight of harsh words like short, jabbing punches and heavy silences, but no screaming. Charlie never screamed; in fact, he seldom raised his voice. The higher Lisbeth turned the volume of the arguments, the quieter he became.

"You know, Charlie, this Saint Francis act can get to be aggravating," she had told him accusingly the previous day. "Grown people, *men,* don't go all silent in a fight like Helen Keller."

Charlie wouldn't be baited. He'd explained and apologized. His smile turned down on his mouth when he said, "I know how you feel, Lisbeth, disappointed I mean. I am too. But it's useless to harp on it, to keep saying I'm sorry again and again." He was a sane, sensible man and he tried to use reason with her when she needed instead a wild, frantic passion, a refusal to put her anywhere but at the top of his list of priorities.

Her anger with Charlie should have abated, for she knew he hadn't abandoned her. But it didn't. A small voice chided her that she was being unreasonable, that Charlie's breaking a date was no big thing, but the anger continued to rise like a fever through the next day and a half.

Now, taxiing up to Forty-fifth Street to meet Quinn, who was going to the theater with her in Charlie's place, the anger knotted between her breasts in a clenched fist. Her vision blurred from the rage as she stared beyond the cab window at the West Side of Manhattan. The dirt-stained buildings, the sidewalks dappled with trash, the double-parked cars and swerving taxis, the people—lopsided figures in a child's sketch, skeletons with clothes draped on hanging bones—swam together in abrupt, quirky motions, then stilled, held unmoving, a television configuration of dots and lines becoming startlingly vivid, then rushed suddenly into confusion before Lisbeth could process what she saw. Which was nothing, just the city, dark but not dark except in patches, mostly brilliant, garish, so striking it was hard to look at. That was why so much of it smeared, she reasoned, ran like liquid, for when the shapes and colors merged the explosiveness of things diminished.

Watching the city, separated from her by glass and motion, she suddenly saw the anger as a thing apart, though *inside* her, not *of* her, engendered by Charlie but having nothing really to do with him. She felt *inhabited* as the taxi rocketed across Forty-second Street and she dry-swallowed Valium. The tranquilizer would take a few minutes to work, but even the expectation calmed her jitters, the dancing bears she called them. The taut muscles along her neck and shoulders eased, tension draining off like rain water.

In the pretheater traffic snarl Lisbeth's cab crawled bumper to bumper to the front of the Lyceum, where she assumed Quinn would be standing off on the side, carving out a small, invisible zone in which to be inviolable. To her surprise, however, Quinn was waiting in the thick of the crowd, unaware of or not caring about the touch of strange bodies brushing against her.

"Here I am!" she called as the taxi disgorged Lisbeth and they struggled toward each other, swimming in a sea of flesh. And right away, though the Valium's smooth, velvet easing hadn't begun to flow yet so that the noise, cacophonous here on the street, drilled into her skull, Lisbeth sensed something different about Quinn. They were in their orchestra seats before she realized Quinn was less wan. Bright spots of color hung like pennants high on her cheeks and she agitated the air about her, set it humming with her suppressed excitement.

Lisbeth asked, "What's happened?"

"Later. I have the most interesting thing to tell you." Her smile, always so frugal, was effusive.

Lisbeth, lulled, the interior bears caged rather than out in the main ring, settled back and watched the musical. It was more ardent than tuneful, though the actors, with sweaty expressions stiffened into rigor

103

mortis, worked hard as miners. Lisbeth's thoughts shifted to Quinn beside her. In the semidark Quinn glowed faintly, more the girl she'd once been in Cabot. But her shine, or young hopefulness, had lasted only the shortest time, changing while they were still in school, Quinn grew quieter, more somber, took on a grayish coloration as she retreated further into a self-possession that now so defined her. She had gotten older before the others gave up being young.

"Not another soft-shoe or a song that sounds like 'Yankee Doodle Dandy,' " Lisbeth protested, tossing her cashmere shawl carelessly about her shoulders as she urged Quinn to leave after the second act.

They walked over to Joe Allen's, the city's clamor overwhelming them, without trying to talk. Once seated midway down the long, half-empty dining room, however, Lisbeth leaned against the brick wall and said, "So tell me before curiosity kills the cat."

Quinn, sipping a gin and tonic, arched her brows. "I've found Will."

"Will?"

"My brother."

"Your brother! I don't believe it," she said, watching Quinn in whom a locked door had been cracked open.

"It happened the other night. Just by accident. I was walking the dogs; he was crossing the street. Another minute either way. . . . Fate, Lis."

"Fate? From Quinn the scientist? Next we'll have gypsies reading tea leaves, palmists, the future cast by the stars."

Quinn's face reddened. "Don't make fun of me. It just was so unexpected, after all these years!"

"The sailor home from the high seas. Well, Quinnie, where's big brother been all this time?"

Quinn repeated the story Will had told her, and then she described going over to Brooklyn and having dinner with Will's family. The word "family" emerged from between her lips like a pearl.

Most of the time, even with the three women, Quinn kept words to a minimum. More miserly with language than she ever was with money, Quinn, banking in some hidden vault both thoughts and sentiments, surprised Lisbeth by running on at length, if not quite flinging out sentences with Dinah's abandon. This change in Quinn, so sudden, worried Lisbeth as much as it pleased her. A stone monolith on Lisbeth's only certain landscape came loose and moved from the center of the plain to nearer the horizon.

She shivered with an inexplicable nervousness. Nothing should change right now; nothing should be different. The friends especially must remain as they'd always been, for they represented a certain stability. The women joined together and formed a raft in a river furious with chaotic currents.

Why was this? Lisbeth wondered. *Because* I'm *different, changing? . . .* No!

The lapses of memory, the forgotten hours, meant nothing, only the moments when she concentrated on something else, when her thoughts were filled with *Silver Street,* mattered. What could happen during that darkness that she had to wipe it away as effectively as an eraser across a blackboard? Nothing of importance, Lisbeth promised herself.

Quinn talked on. "I still can't take it in, Will with a family too, those three enchanting children and a wife and living in Brooklyn. He's a carpenter, my brother, blue collar. Oh, really, I don't know whether to laugh or cry. Will with his Harvard education."

"And," Lisbeth said, "a father rich as Croesus."

Quinn pursed her lips disapprovingly. Websters didn't say such things. Lisbeth laughed. Rosenthals never mentioned money either, but then there were so many subjects they veered away from. Death for one. Anne, Lisbeth's mother, refused, always, to discuss Ferris Rosenthal.

Even when Anne Rosenthal took Lisbeth to Campbell's in a black limousine and they stood before the closed coffin in which—impossibly— her father lay, her mother said nothing. At the cemetery as the casket was lowered into the earth, Lisbeth gritted her teeth, half convinced she was an involuntary player in some monstrous game.

Lisbeth kept her suspicions. Family meetings between her mother and her father's brothers would cease abruptly whenever she entered the room. She'd hear *what if, what if,* beat like a metronome during the silences. Then, the telephone would ring and there'd be no one on the other end, only static or a deep, galactic quiet.

Your father, your father, her uncles would shake their heads, occasionally smile, more often look sad, hiding things they couldn't or wouldn't tell her about. Anne Rosenthal said the past is the past and I don't like to talk about it. Then she'd kiss Lisbeth's cheek or lightly brush her shoulder.

Quinn kept on about Will, and Lisbeth's response was the start of a headache, a rippling pain that sent slow, spiny tentacles stretching across her temples.

Lisbeth tried to conjure up the feel of Charlie Morgan's strong hands when they kneaded her spine and worked at the vertebrae of her neck like a skilled pianist. This practiced technique of his, half erotic and half therapeutic, often calmed her dancing bears and other beasts without completely subduing them. But leaning her head back against

105

the brick wall listening to Quinn, Lisbeth couldn't recall Charlie Morgan enough to make him real. He was drowning in a sea of torn images, of old memories. For an instant he was superimposed on her father's image—Ferris Rosenthal in his double-breasted pin-striped suit.

They had both ordered hamburgers, rare, but when the waitress placed the food before them, Lisbeth's stomach revolted. She poked at the meat, sliding it away from the bun, stabbed the browned outside, digging into the center. Juice and blood ran in a reddish stream.

Quinn had the hamburger up to her mouth, eating, chewing, pink lips claret, a sanguine smear on her chin. It looked like blood on Quinn's mouth, as though she ate raw flesh. Lisbeth could almost smell it, sweetish and sickening. She broke out in a cold sweat.

"Lis, are you all right?" Quinn returned the hamburger to the plate and dabbed at her mouth with a napkin. "Lis, what is it?"

The spell snapped for some reason. Quinn's unremarkable face swam up in Lisbeth's vision without a stain.

"Fine. Okay," she said, and sat back in the chair.

"The accident . . . ," Quinn started to say, unbloodied lips moving. Lisbeth shut out her voice, while allowing the other sounds in the restaurant to rise in a symphony, all the clattery noises of plates and silverware, glasses being used. Lisbeth heard the distinct ping of wineglasses clinked in a toast at the next table.

"I'm tired of the accident," Lisbeth blurted out, surprising herself. "And my spectacular recovery. A real miracle, or God's gift, or your favorite, Quinnie, fate. Or Susie's explanation is the best. For why I came back from the dead, I mean." Lisbeth rushed on, "Not the right time, remember? As if somebody throws a dart the day you're born and arbitrarily picks a number. April seventeenth, nineteen-ninety. Okay, Buster, that's your departure date."

"I don't know what you're raving about, but I think you're working too hard, worrying too much about the play," Quinn said, annoyed.

Lisbeth laughed. "Gilly Aronberg's turning *Silver Street* into a peep show, didn't I tell you?"

"Susie mentioned there was something which upset you. But I'm sure you're overreacting, Lisbeth. You often make too much out of too little." Quinn's tone was lecturing. She sounded so certain, she might have been instructing a group of graduate students, and Lisbeth turned the sound down again.

Smoke curled in from another table, wreathing Quinn. The core of the human brain, Lisbeth remembered, was a snake's, and she shivered with a fear she couldn't name.

"It's late, we should go," Lisbeth said, pushing away the plate. "I think I'll wander up to Charlie's.'' She had almost forgotten their argument.

Quinn sniffed. "Oh, Charlie Morgan.'' To her he was only another man, another lover, just an alternate version of Billy Reynolds, the one Lisbeth actually married. So Lisbeth would know what she thought of Charlie, Quinn asked, "Do you ever hear from Billy?''

"Well, not *from,* but before I left L.A. someone mentioned he was living in Mexico these days, down at the end of Baja in Cabo San Lucas on a cabin cruiser. He fishes whenever, Billy does, and he still drinks cuba libres, but supposedly he's grown fat as Sidney Greenstreet and finally lost the last of his hair.''

Quinn had once met Billy and they'd hissed at each other like rattlers. But Quinn never took to any of Lisbeth's men she'd known. Each and every specimen d' Lisbeth some harm, or so Quinn thought.

"You're well rid of that one,'' Quinn said as they paid the bill and waited for their change.

"Oh, Billy wasn't so bad. He actually made a good picture once, but then drink got him and coke. The screaming meemies after that for Billy-goat,'' she said sadly. She had cared for Billy Reynolds once upon a time. He was funny; he made her laugh. And he had talent, if not the iron in his soul to withstand the battering of the movie business. Hollywood drove Billy crazy because he wanted to trust people.

Lisbeth sighed. "It was never true, Quinn, that he stole money from Metro. Billy never cared about money enough, and he wasn't that kind of clever. But in the last waning days of our less than spectacular marriage, I did see him shoplift a pigskin wallet at Bullocks.''

"How terrible!''

"He was stoned. Winding up there in gaga land or he'd never have tried a stunt like that.'' Lisbeth's headache ebbed, now stroking the back of her skull in a weighty caress. She imagined a man's hand riding along her neck, down in the valley between her shoulder blades.

Talking of Billy made Lisbeth even sadder than just thinking of him usually did. She forced herself to concentrate on the present.

The restaurant had filled up while they ate, the theaters out at last, and the maitre d' eyed their table covetously. At the front of the bar, just inside the door, several people waited.

The waitress finally returned and Quinn stood. Lisbeth sat a moment longer. She wanted to stay at the table now, sit and have more coffee, to talk, to be the old Cabot Lisbeth. *Oh, for some laughter!* she thought.

Quinn gathered her things impatiently. Lisbeth suspected she was irritated with her for not being terribly nice about this prodigal brother.

But her mother might be right after all. The past is the past, the long gone and the dead are better left in the mists. Hadn't that last frame just before the crash been of lilies-of-the-valley?

He was waiting for her, the black car double-parked, blended into the shadows. She instinctively knew it was going to be Neff when she stepped from the cab and he called, "Lisbeth!" She knew before she even saw him. She had expected him, she realized, since the night she met him with Charlie.

Until next time.

There won't be a next time.

What a lie! She'd dreamed of his large hand with the blunt nails, and not of Charlie's, stroking her neck in a cobweb touch.

Neff came through a wedge of darkness and in the thin sliver of light she caught the scar; it shone, a ridge of silver.

How had he found her? she asked.

Neff laughed. "You're in the phone book."

They started up the front steps. Lisbeth stopped. In Joe Allen's she had decided to go to Charlie's, so how had she gotten here, in the Village, home? She turned to Neff suspiciously. Had he done that too? Drawn her downtown where he wanted her?

Neff took the key from her hand and unlocked the doors. He never asked a thing, not whether he could come in or not, and he said not a word about Charlie. With one shoulder slightly raised, he moved as if he had to part not air but heavy water.

Inside he carefully looked around, casing the room in his cop's squinty-eyed way. He pulled off a leather jacket and tossed it on the couch.

"Where's the bar?" he asked.

Lisbeth pointed to a tall French armoire.

He crossed the room to pour himself a scotch and she saw the gun stuck in his belt. Against the pale blue of his shirt, the butt lay dark and heavy.

An uncertain visitor in a strange land, Lisbeth stayed near the door until Neff came over. He slipped off her coat, letting it drop to the floor. They stared at each other and his eyes had the black emptiness of bullet holes.

She touched his scar, running soft fingertips along it. "What happened to him, the man who gave you this?" she whispered, her mouth dry, filling up with sand.

"I shot him through the heart."

He kissed her and his mouth was softer than she would have thought. He tasted unexpectedly of vanilla. Just as she foretold, he caressed her neck and shoulders. She arched closer and he slipped his hands beneath the silky sweater to the warm, even smoother feel of skin. He found her breasts unfettered and cupped them.

"Golden apples," he whispered surprisingly.

The room tilted, the house and East Tenth Street. The planet faltered on its axis, keeled into limitless space as Neff lifted Lisbeth—boneless, loose as feathers—and carried her into the bedroom, then laid her on the bed and undressed her like a doll, raising arms and legs, then shed his own clothes. He was hairy as a bear, hairy all over, a thick pelt covering back and chest, in leggings on thighs and calves. Warmth blazed from him when he embraced her. She expected him to be rough, abrupt in his lovemaking, but he took her slowly, easily, his touch feathery, his tongue like velvet.

He flicked her nipples until they hardened, licked soft liquid circles around them, then sucked, gently nipping. Lisbeth's breath came in balls of pain as her body quivered and desire rushed her toward a mounting joy.

Neff swung around and she opened her mouth for his thickness. Slowly she drew him in, down to her throat. He filled her up. She felt she would take him into the earth itself, for she was the earth, sucking at Neff. But at last she loosened her hold on him, as with darting butterfly caresses, she rode him up to the cap. His shudders and whistles of pleasure sent her spinning, sent her further as he leaned over and parted her, his lips licking the wetness between her legs.

"Oh, oh," Lisbeth shrilled, rising. Quickly Neff, sensing how near she was, turned her around and entered in a long, slow thrust. Her whole body, united for once with all the selves of Lisbeth, rose as if gravity no longer exerted a pull. And Neff drove, jolting thrusts that penetrated to the very center of her, again and again, until she soared through time and space, a sea creature, a ghost creature, screaming.

Minutes passed, hours, Lisbeth couldn't tell. Neff sprawled on top of her, his hand covering her mouth, her breath and the last little cries seeping between his fingers. Slicked with sweat, he pressed his face into the pillow as tiny minnows of pleasure continued to shoot along his limbs. She couldn't see his eyes, and only the edge of the scar. Neff shriveled, pulling away from her, severing their flesh, and as he did he became a stranger, someone she knew not at all. Neff could be anybody. Lisbeth thought of Charlie Morgan, so much bigger and smoother, not, despite his size, bearish in the least, and she forgot why, if she ever knew, she was in bed with this cop, this foreign Neff who had slid his gun under the pillow.

Neff's sweat mixed with her own, turning to an icy glaze. Cold, Lisbeth struggled to wrap the loose quilt over her nakedness. The motion was enough to open up a further distance between her and Neff who, moments later, left the bed. When he returned he carried a drink. A cigarette dangled from the corner of his mouth. He swaggered, looked street tough, surly as a gangster.

He didn't lie down again but sat, naked in the chair, one leg over an arm. At ease, at home, he smoked and drank and stared unblinkingly at Lisbeth.

What was he doing here? All of a sudden Lisbeth didn't want him. With startling clarity she saw how she had simply accepted this cop who arrived on her doorstep. He entered her apartment, entered her, as if he possessed a legal warrant for such invasion. *I let him,* she thought, *wanted him.* . . . But were there reasons besides desire and seizing the moment?

"Go home," she said.

"I thought I'd spend the night," he replied.

"No."

"Come on, Lisbeth Ross, don't play hard to get." He smiled.

Lisbeth yelled, "Get the hell out of here, cop!" She threw a book from the night table, which sailed over his head. Before he could move she followed it with a hairbrush that hit him in the chest.

"Hey, stop it!"

Leaping off the bed, she threw everything she could grasp. Neff dodged the barrage, cursing, as he worked a path across the bedroom. But just before he could secure a hold on her, Lisbeth sprinted for the bathroom. Inside she bolted the door and screamed, pounding her fists against the wood. "Go away, go, go, go . . ." until she wore herself out. Sliding down the door, she made a burrow of towels and huddled on the tile, so sleepy all at once that she slept.

At six in the morning when Lisbeth awoke she couldn't recall at first what she was doing there, but slowly pictures of Neff, quick cuts—Neff pelted as though in an animal's fur by his own skin, Neff moving in indolent motion, sliding into and out of her flesh, Neff rising, jerking in spasms, crying *ohohohohoh* as he came—slipped into her memory. She grew excited again, remembering, even as a voice cried *Lisbeth, how could you? What about Charlie?* But she didn't listen as she turned on the shower and stood under the hot cascade of water touching herself until a quick spiral of relief flamed.

9

New neighbors arrived beyond the still-disheveled hedges, in the Bergers' old house, which now sported a wintry coat of white paint.

Almost immediately, from the rectangular brick chimney perched in the center of the roof, a plume of smoke revolved one afternoon, curling in a child's long ringlet, a gauzy spiral that dissipated in the brisk wind. It might have been a temporary visitor, however, for Dinah, who watched as much as she could see of the neighborhood since she had little else to do, hadn't noticed a moving van. But the next day when she glanced over the hedges in their jungly spread, the smoke sailed up once again through a drizzly rain until the woolly clouds overhead swallowed it entirely.

In the afternoon when the rain stopped, Dinah went out to the side yard and peered through a narrow channel in the privets. She was rewarded with a glimpse of the new owner's face crosshatched by the intersecting twigs. A burning eye, black and smoldering as a charcoal briquette, sunk into swarthy skin, a few scraps of oily brown hair flattened to and somehow held in place on a pinkish scalp visible in odd-sized patches. He was of medium height and somewhat burly, built along the lines of a sumo wrestler. He also had pointy ears like Mr. Spock's.

"Mom, you're being weird, acting like a peeping Tom," Mikey criticized when he caught her watching the stranger.

But Dinah's world these days was a place where little happened and none of that very pleasant. Besides trying to get her sea legs, she was lonely. She imagined herself a leaf fallen from a tree, and all crinkly, blown away. Divorce had separated her from the rest of the suburban society as effectively as a hatchet chop.

The bridge group that gathered twice monthly, rotating houses, dropped her. As Moira Mason explained, "It's nothing personal, Di-

111

nah, but we need couples. Now, if you can find another man by next Friday . . .'' She sounded dubious.

"And if I get wings, Moira," Dinah replied tartly. But Moira complained she didn't understand what wings had to do with it, and Dinah slammed down the receiver.

A dinner party to which Dinah had been invited got canceled at the last minute, and for another one she forced a reluctant body into party clothes and out to the car. But she couldn't turn the key in the ignition. She sat in the driveway for almost an hour. The idea of entering a room full of people she'd known for years, of strolling in *alone,* just sandbagged her.

Walking Rebecca to the end of Delphinium Lane one afternoon, she saw Jan Archer come out on the front porch of her antebellum and waved at her. As Dinah pulled the Airedale down the center patch, she suddenly remembered that Jan lost a husband about five years before, literally lost him on a trip to Hawaii. J. J., overweight and in his late forties, had gone off with a stewardess, a redhead he met on the plane from Los Angeles. Jan had had to fly back east alone. The whole lonely trip apparently so unnerved her that the first thing she did on returning to Westport was to build a big bonfire in the back yard and burn J. J.'s clothes. The blaze grew so large two fire trucks came out and Jan had to be restrained when they doused the flames. After that she had a short stay in a nearby rest home.

"The only relevant fact," she called when Dinah got near enough to hear, "is who left whom." Dinah could tell by her expression that Jan knew exactly. In some mysterious fashion all of Westport, or at least those factions of it with whom Dinah was familiar, possessed the details of her collapsed marriage.

"What difference does it make?" Dinah stood at the bottom of the porch steps while Becky pulled urgently for a nearby rosebush.

Jan's arms were crossed over her breasts. She didn't seem about to ask Dinah in. "It's the whole can of ravioli, that's all."

"Really?"

"Don't kid yourself, Dinah. If you walked you're going somewhere, but if Hatch did then you are standing still like a piece of old furniture."

Jan Archer smiled smugly, welcoming another loser to a select group. Dinah, thinking of slugging her, of leaping up on the porch and throwing a full punch, growled under her breath. Dinah was a peacenik, anti any armed encounter, and had never hit a living soul before; but Jan Archer's tacit assumption that she had become a member of the living dead maddened her and excited a prickle of guilt besides. Well, you have been feeling sorry for yourself, *poor baby Dinah,* the voice of conscience issued a reminder. And why not, she started to argue, but the why not was blatantly evident. Because then she'd grow into Jan Archer with a pattern of discontent stitched across her face.

"I'm doing fine, Jan, and thank you for your kind words of encouragement," Dinah said, tilting her chin way up in the air.

Just then Becky squatted, and whatever Jan might have retorted with a rapier thrust of malice got lost in a shriek of panic. "What is that damn dog doing on *my* lawn!"

"Shitting," Dinah told her, and when Becky finished they both pranced off.

So the lacks in her life, and the fact that it was rather easy, given the geography, got Dinah concentrating on the new man next door. As long as she still lived in the colonial—from which she expected Hatch to yank her at any moment—she might as well act neighborly.

His name was Mario Ellis and he owned a cheese importing firm in Manhattan, according to Mae, the cleaning woman. Mae got her information from Ruthie Rudolph, four houses up on the north flank of the lane, and the neighborhood gossip. Mario Ellis was single, a dark man in the thicket of middle age somewhere. "Not black like me," Mae, a honey-brown shade, offered, "but maybe Eyetalian, Mrs. Rudolph says." Dinah tried for a closer look to decide for herself. But this Mario Ellis was elusive.

Three days after Dinah had joined her friends for dinner at Lisbeth's, she awoke with the world's championship headache. There existed some correlation between the jackhammer behind her temples and the empty bottle of gin she found when she descended, carefully as though on eggshells, to the living room. Adding the gin to the lengthening list of what she banished from conscious thought, she carried the bottle into the kitchen hoping the thunderous pain might ease with a gallon of coffee since today was her first meeting in the city with her lawyer.

Mikey was standing by the window. "Mom," he said, "you're not going to believe this." Dinah didn't either, not even after she stumbled out the back door and across the dewy lawn, to weave a wobbly path along the privets as trimly sheared as a Marine recruit. Here and there were scattered broken scraps of brush that whoever had clipped the hedges to their current geometric neatness failed to pick up. All in all, she had to admit the phantom privet clipper had done a better job than poor, expensive Mr. Alonzo. Perversely, this perfection infuriated her. Standing in the early September chill, she felt put upon. What right had anyone, never mind this stranger, this Mario Ellis whom she knew not at all, to trim her privets, to clip away at something that didn't belong to him? As if she had no voice in the matter, a thing, a small child, a cast-off an about-to-go-mad-like-Jan Archer abandoned wife.

"I am still a person!" she shouted into the wind, shaking her fist. She glared at the cottony sky as if confronting the Almighty who had decided otherwise.

"Hey, Mom, come on in. You'll catch a cold!" Mikey called from the back door.

Her son forced Dinah into motion and she staggered up and down the yard, patrolling the shorn privets, crying, "How dare he!" She even ventured out onto Delphinium to see if she might catch Mr. Ellis on open ground, but the house looked closed up this morning, shuttered and uninhabited.

Back in the kitchen finally, Dinah muttered into the cup of instant coffee Mikey fixed for her, inhaling the steam. "Sneaky!"

"Look at it as a present from a secret admirer, Mom," Mikey teased. Dinah glared at her smiling son. He certainly had come out of his blue funk over the divorce, and a short funk it had been too. She wondered if he would have missed her if she'd been the one to go off, but she was smart enough not to ask.

Mikey shoved his arms through the holes of his knapsack and went off to get his bike from the porch. By the time school and swim practice ended and he wound his way home through the kitchens of his various friends, the privets would be yesterday's news. But Dinah, stuck to the kitchen chair, the house humming conspiratorially around her, the ice maker in the refrigerator dropping its cubes like distant grenades, wouldn't be able to tolerate hedges so elegant, so Hatchlike. She wanted the privets shaggy again, just as she yearned for her husband back in his rightful place, home and with her.

In Serendipity Dinah sat on an uncomfortable ice cream chair at a small round table, waiting for Susie and trying to erase the recent meeting with Harold Isaacs from her memory. Hi, as he liked to be called, had been the first lawyer Dinah thought of when Hatch's attorney—and best friend—phoned to say she'd need legal representation. Since Ned liked Dinah enough to make a ritual pass every New Year's Eve when his wife wasn't looking, Dinah thought she could believe him when he said, "Di, find yourself a lawyer."

As for Hi, he had once whispered in her ear as they did a rather ragged fox-trot at a Legal Aid gala, "Your husband's a horse's ass." She'd gotten mad at the time, but now that remark sounded sensible. So she called Hi's office, gave him the bald facts, over which he tut-tutted sympathetically, and signed him up to represent her. Great. Now she had a lawyer who said, "He's going to try not giving you a cent besides Mikey's support, and he'll probably get away with it." Dinah hadn't needed to hear that. She had a notion she would punish Hatch for his betrayal by stripping him to the bone. Unrealistic. She was going to be the one out in the cold, bare-ass naked, at least according to Hi Isaacs.

"As far as I can tell, Hatch has everything in his name, what little there is." He shook his head sadly. "Lawyers are notorious for obscuring the facts. We can hide almost anything." He preened a bit as he said this.

"There's the house," Dinah asserted, not ready to give up and play dead.

"In Hatch's name."

"Hatch's name!" She fell back shocked.

Hi stared at her foolishly through little round glasses not much bigger than bottle caps and just as thick, which made him seem Dickensian. "And mortgaged to the hilt."

"Oh no!"

"You're lucky he's not charging you rent."

Dinah hung her face over the glass of Perrier and imagined a bound and gagged Hatch down among the ice cubes. "What about stocks, bonds, things like that?"

"What about them? From what Ned Wilkins told me over the phone there's basically diddly-squat, a savings account in Manufacturer's with about two thousand in it. Plus a couple of checking accounts, one up in Westport. The cars and Hatch's salary of course, but other than that . . ." His voice trickled off into silence and he folded pudgy hands on the desk.

"The boat!" Dinah cried, springing forward again.

Hi lunged away. "What boat?"

"We have a boat, nothing elaborate, that's in dry dock now for the winter."

"Kind? Size?" he asked, pen poised above a long legal pad with depressingly little written on it.

"Oh, I don't know. I never went out in it. Seasickness," she explained.

"I'll look into it." He scribbled a note. "But if he's been planning this for a while, he probably sold it."

"And what about the money he got?"

"Gone, I suppose, buried, like everything else. Hatch is pretty smart."

It was on the tip of Dinah's tongue to remind Hi of his previous comment, but she was too disgusted with herself. How had she trusted Hatch with financial matters all these years? Though Dinah wondered why she should have expected Hatch to be faithful with their joint account when he hadn't been with his penis, never mind his heart. Feeling sick again, she turned away from Hi's face, which shone with a slick sweat. Maybe the attorney was sick too, but Dinah didn't ask. For all she cared Hi Isaacs could be terminal, just don't let him tell her about it. Her life these days brimmed with things she hated to think about and she didn't need Hi's melanoma—if he had one—to send it spilling over the top. Dinah glanced nervously around his office instead, questioning as she took in the cramped space, with only one desk and two chairs—no couch or coffee table—and a single grimy window staring onto Fifty-eighth Street, whether she made the right choice in legal assistance. His diploma from Hofstra and his New York University law degree both hung framed behind his head, while on the wall to her right a swan sat smugly in a pond of lily pads. Dinah closed her eyes and heard Hi's sing-song, "Now, now," thinking, obviously, that Hatch's abandonment sent her back to infancy. Dinah ruffled indignantly, though it was true. She felt like a child lost in the woods, alone in the night. All that darkness and the strange threatening sounds. . . . Dinah's heart almost stopped from the fear and the pain.

In the din of the lunchtime restaurant, voices flinging themselves against Serendipity's mirrored walls, Dinah shut her eyes again, closing out the women in their Bloomingdale's best as she tried to find some glimmer of light in the blackness. Instead she heard Susie's voice. "Meditating?" Suz asked.

Susie sank onto the opposite chair, not lapping over the sides like Dinah, and patted her friend's clenched fist. "It can't be that bad, Di. Divorce, for all its heartaches, is very commonplace. You'll find another husband just like that!" She snapped her fingers and smiled, meaning well, but Dinah scowled. Susie wouldn't remember how hard it had been to unearth Hatch.

"How do you know I'm thinking of Hatch? Maybe it's the national debt." Dinah scowled, feeling more out of sorts with Susie's presence than relaxed.

"Oh, Di!" Susie laughed. "That's it, hold on to your sense of humor!"

But Dinah felt about as funny as two dead men, and glaring at Susie's sunny face—her almost-Cabot face—with the white, white teeth glittering in what used to be called in the radio days of Dinah's childhood an Ipana smile, there was the forbidden, snaky thrust of that awful memory. Beyond the darkness there was a dead space, more frightening, much more, than being overweight and alone, even unloved. That was the ultimate, and Dinah, shaken, gripped the glass of Perrier, and when she raised it to her lips she saw Susie again. Their glances snagged. Susie knew and quickly she turned away, looking about Serendipity, saying how crowded it was, and on a weekday, a glum one too. . . . Susie talked too much.

Lunch accelerated Dinah's depression. She rode a plummeting elevator downward, particularly since trim Susie nibbled a spinach salad, murmuring about her diet, while Dinah consumed a quiche and a slab of chocolate mousse cake. How would she ever lose weight when she was so unhappy? And, like a final bucket of ice water thrown over her, Susie asked while they sipped espresso if she'd informed her mother yet. Of course she hadn't, principally because it slipped her mind. But she'd have to be insane to want to call Hanover, Nebraska, and say, "I'm getting a divorce." Her mother, a spike for a nose, a chin never, never lowered, and eyes that hadn't cried once in Dinah's lifetime, would pluck the truth that Hatch left her with malevolent expertise no matter how Dinah strove to conceal it. Her mother wouldn't smirk but she'd certainly think Dinah delinquent, assume whatever marital mistakes had been made were hers.

Her mother was an area, roped off, that Dinah seldom allowed her thoughts to nudge up against. But, though she certainly could do without yet another emotional quagmire, she had to remember to make that call.

As Dinah walked west to the train, elbowing a passage through the crowds, she recalled not her mother but her father. If he hadn't died and were alive right now, he'd hear her out and say, "Reap what you sow." And then probably add, because he hadn't any meanness in him, "Well, there's always tomorrow."

Like Lisbeth, Dinah grew up an only child. She was born just after her mother turned thirty-five and when she had given up the idea of having children at all. Her father, Dinah supposed, must have been bewildered about her arrival in his well-ordered, humdrum life, for all through her childhood, in fact until he died, a year almost to the day after her Cabot graduation, he'd stare at her with a glaze of wonder on his face as if to say, *Who are you?* He made Dinah feel like a tool out of place in the hardware store he owned. She always expected him to pick her up and put her high on a shelf.

Her father had one passion in his life, a car, a Model T, one of the

117

first off Henry Ford's assembly line. It had belonged to his father, who bought the contraption when there were no paved roads in Hanover and everyone drove wagons or buggies. He kept it spic-and-span in the garage, dusted and polished under a blanket winter or summer, except for when he drove it wearing a white jacket and a boater in the July Fourth parade.

Once, when Dinah was ten or so and Harry Esterman had taken the T's engine apart, spreading the parts carefully on a plastic cloth, tinkering and cleaning, replacing what he decided had gotten worn, Dinah came out of the house and, squatting down beside him, asked, "Can I help?"

Harry, humming an uncertain tune that existed nowhere but in his head, replied, "I don't think so."

He smelled sweet, of Yardley's after-shave lotion, and even though his hands were black with oil, crescents of grime beneath his squared-off nails, he seemed so neat. Not a strand of his faded blond hair considered sticking up and his wire-framed eyeglasses sparkled. His old plaid shirt and green work pants hung on his spare frame crisp and wrinkleless.

"Why not?" Dinah pressed, having to bend and crane her neck to look up into her father's Gobi Desert of a face as he hovered over some part of the engine that he revolved slowly in his hands like a priceless jewel.

"Hmmm?" he replied, not paying attention.

Dinah bumped his arm and insisted, "I want to learn about cars and stuff, what makes them run. You know, Daddy!"

"Girls aren't interested in auto mechanics," he mumbled as he took a wrench from his tool chest and made a slight adjustment to a nut and bolt. "Girls learn how to cook and sew," he said, "like your mother. Girls," he went on, giving her the same lopsided smile he offered a customer in the hardware store when a purchase was rung up and bagged, "play with dolls."

When her father died, Dinah's mother sold the T before they even buried Harry Esterman, when he lay on view smooth and polished as a piece of waxed fruit in the town's only funeral parlor. Dinah, who had returned home for the somber though tearless ritual, threw a fit, for she thought she'd get her hands on the T at last, and her mother thwarted her. Neither of her parents liked the other, but both, for separate reasons, Dinah always supposed, considered it a duty to love her, and she took her father's dying and her mother's selling the T as two different forms of rejection.

Her mother surprised Dinah at the coffee-and-cake gathering in the living room after the services by suggesting Dinah remain in Hanover, for whatever strange reason she didn't say, but there lurked no hint in the bald statement that the older woman either wanted or needed her. Of course Dinah couldn't, for even if she and her mother got along better, the flat, open spaces of the plains where she'd grown up before escaping to New England made her feel anxious and vulnerable. The land, level as a sheet of glass, possessed neither beginning nor end, rolling on into infinity, and the only sound she seemed to hear was the low, eerie moaning of the wind.

The afternoon of the funeral, Dinah found herself saying she'd stay a week, but a day later she drove out of town into the open country-side, trying to imagine herself in all that emptiness which should have been familiar but wasn't. She braked at the side of the two-lane and got out. Though she'd spent four years in the East, coming back to Hanover for the briefest visits she could get away with, the loneliness of so much space, of that eternal openness, gripped her once more. It was as if she'd suffered with a virulent disease, which had gone into remission for a short while but now returned deadlier than ever.

Poised on the white line that ribboned forever down a watery road, shimmering all the way to nowhere, fear settled beneath her breastbone. She wanted to hide, in a cluster of trees, against a mountain's stony flank, in a city's caverns, anywhere rather than stick out naked on that Nebraska plain, her soul as well as her flesh exposed.

In the anonymous throng of commuters with whom she now marched, only one of the pack, Dinah remembered far down that straight high-way a spin of lazy smoke, much like Mario Ellis's spiral, and she saw again the broad, metallic face of the diesel rig with its lip-split ugly grin as it approached. Again she heard in the city's atonal symphony the growl of the rig. It shook the earth and the macadam rumbled under her feet, shooting seismic quivers up her calves, and she waited until it drew so near that the sun vanished behind it before she ran back to the car. When the truck thundered past, the driver, perched far above on his traveling throne like some distant monarch, waved at her.

Dinah left for New York the next day without a word of explanation to her mother, for how could she say that if she stayed longer she might stand on the road outside Hanover, beyond the point where the town was visible and even its mirage had faded into the horizon, and might not step aside for the next diesel, that she might be trapped on the white line. From that day to this her mother was even frostier toward Dinah.

———

On the train back to Westport, Dinah realized she'd made yet another mistake. She should have stayed in the city, gone down to see Lisbeth in the Village or arranged for an early dinner with Quinn. Instead, going home as she was meant to, she took seriously what Hi Isaacs said and what Susie unknowingly echoed over her salad: that Dinah must get a job. She didn't want to go to some office, or worse a shop, where she would have to start at the bottom of the employment ladder at her age, for who'd take her past advertising experience into account? If only she painted better! But now wasn't the moment to hoodwink herself into believing she enjoyed an artistic talent so striking she might earn money by it. Maybe she could wangle a job painting daisies on china plates, but not much more.

Home, sitting at her kitchen table, Becky's wet nose pressed against her anklebone, Dinah grimly circled the slightest possibilities in the local want ads and then made a list of the town's few employment agencies. When she finished, she glanced up at the clock above the refrigerator and saw, with a sigh of relief—her first all day—that it was edging toward five. She had to make dinner and feed the dog, and since it was Monday the hamper of dirty clothes needed to be washed. Legitimately she could put off until tomorrow finding employment, or as Susie said with a smile, as though it would be delightful, "making a new life" for her deserted, soon-to-be-divorced self.

Two days later Dinah, finally admitting to herself that she needed advice on job hunting, called Lisbeth at ten o'clock in the morning. She woke her up. "Oh God, sorry, Lis," she said. "I'll call back later."

"No, it's okay." Lisbeth sounded further away than Manhattan, and her voice had a smoker's foggy texture to it though she seldom touched a cigarette these days. Except grass, Dinah supposed.

"I have to get a job," Dinah confessed from her Westport kitchen, "if I want to eat and keep out the rain."

"What about Hatch? And alimony? He'll have to cough up child support, you know."

Dinah imagined Lisbeth propped against the headboard with pillows, four of them, all down filled, at least sixty dollars each in Bloomingdale's. Satin sheets and a feathery quilt too, and she probably wore a lacy negligee in some made-up color like crème de cacao. Lisbeth spent more money to sleep elegantly than Dinah did for a whole winter's wardrobe. With the money that had come to her from dead Ferris Rosenthal and what she earned as the queen of the Hollywood scriptwriters, why not. She could clothe her slim, beautifully proportioned body, taut as a twenty-year-old's, in hundred-dollar bills if she wanted to.

Dinah explained. "According to my hotshot divorce lawyer, between us Hatch and I own *nada,* and what he admits to owning himself is even less. If I'm lucky I'll get a pittance for Mikey and a buck and a half a month for me." She tried not to whine, remembering that people well provided for think people without money are always exaggerating. She forced a laugh that echoed down the phone lines like the last hack of a tubercular.

"Are you all right?" Lisbeth asked.

Now Dinah imagined Lisbeth pulling her knees up and leaning forward on them. She had, after all, four years' experience seeing Lisbeth in bed. "Sure. Just struggling to get my feet on the ground." *Getting your feet on the ground* was an expression Susie had used over lunch. Susie's feet, of course, were always shod in Ferragamos or Charles Jourdans, and she rode more often than she walked. Dinah responded like the poor country mouse with her wealthy city friends, though Westport wasn't Appalachia and she couldn't say even now that she lived on the poverty line. But for how long would this last?

"A job!" she suddenly shouted into the phone. "God, Lis, I have to find a job, by yesterday." The specter of welfare pressed between her shoulder blades.

"Okay, you'll get a job, Di. Don't panic!"

Panic? She wasn't panicking, not exactly. "*Absolutely* not!" she said, suppressing a nervous giggle.

"First you sit down and make up a resume," Lisbeth said, being practical.

Dinah grabbed a pencil from a mug beside the phone and wrote on the edge of the *Times,* which was delivered every morning and which she had canceled as of the end of the month: "resume." "But what do I write? I haven't done a lick of paying labor since we moved to Westport." She stared out the window at the hedges, a steady cause of heartburn, along with the invisible neighbor—who was never home as far as Dinah could tell—and wondered if Mr. Alonzo might hire her. After all these years of keeping him on over Hatch's disapproval, didn't he owe her something? Not that hedge clipping was exactly what she had in mind for a career.

Lisbeth was saying something about "plumping up your advertising and putting in the volunteer work you've done."

What volunteer work? Lisbeth either thought all housewives in-
dulged in charities or she mistook her for Susie. The only helping hand
Dinah gave was addressing envelopes occasionally for the PTA and
serving coffee to the adults at the yearly Halloween party in Mikey's
school. "That's fairly skimpy," she reluctantly confessed.

"Then make it up."

"Make it up?"

"Sure. Why not? Nobody will check up on you."

Dinah opened her mouth to say, *But that's lying,* then wondered
if Lisbeth would consider her naive. Well, maybe she was, stuck
in her colonial in Connecticut in comparison to tough, realistic Lis
who'd paddled the shark-infested waters of Hollywood. Dinah perked
up. If anyone could teach her how to survive in the strange climate
of singlehood, it was Lisbeth. "Lie!" she scribbled alongside
"resume."

"Okay. Now what?"

"Well, what do you want to do? What kind of job do you have in
mind, Di?"

No job actually, or nothing that would propel her out of the house,
which she had a sinking feeling she'd be forced to vacate eventually.
What were the chances Hi Isaacs would be able to snatch the house
from Hatch and Ned Wilkins? She considered again finding a bigger
lawyer, a real shyster, though Hi's tiny office made her hope his
fee would be payable if she were compelled to cough it up herself.
On the top of the business section she penned: "Who pays legal
fees?"

"What kind of job? I'm not exactly sure." Such equivocation must
rankle, especially with Lis, who'd had motivation and firm plans for as
long as Dinah had known her. "Maybe something artistic?" she ventured.

"Hmmm, well, let's see." There was a pause in which Dinah
pressed the receiver tightly against her ear hoping to hear Lisbeth's
breathing. She worried the other woman would lose patience with her
neediness and her, yes, Dinah faced up to it, her *stupidity*. And why
had she awakened Lisbeth so early? Why hadn't she waited until after
lunch? Because she gripped the bit between her teeth and wanted to
launch herself on the cold world *now*. The sooner she consolidated her
position the better she'd feel about Hatch and that strumpet Stacy
Delmonico, or at least Dinah hoped so.

Lisbeth announced, "Museums are out. You need all sorts of
degrees for that kind of work. There are art galleries, of course, but I
don't think they pay much. Probably just the minimum wage."

"That's something like four and a quarter per hour—less than I give Mae, the cleaning lady!" Dinah yelped.

"All right, Di, you don't have to yell."

Dinah didn't think she was, but apologized anyway. "Sorry."

Lisbeth continued. Magazines were out because usually they hired younger women, all bushy tailed and bright-eyed, girls straight from college, ready to slave for the glamor and a pittance of a salary. Besides, the magazines were all in the city. Because of Mikey, Dinah thought it better if she worked in or around Westport. There were art supply stores, but clerking was clerking and there was nothing artistic in selling oil paints and brushes.

"You could give lessons on how to paint," Lisbeth suggested.

Dinah didn't judge herself competent enough. "I need more lessons myself," she confessed. Whatever Lisbeth came up with Dinah rejected, swearing, "I'm not being difficult." She raised her right hand though Lisbeth couldn't see it.

"You are, Di. Difficult and negative, which is not the way to go about this." Lisbeth's temper was fraying, Dinah just knew it. "There seems to be nothing you can or want to do except lie down and play dead." Her tone was ominous.

Dinah, smarting, cried, "That's not true! I want . . ." What she wanted was to stay home and paint in the attic studio, be grungy in sloppy jeans and Hatch's old shirt, and maybe make some effort to improve her culinary skills. Since Hatch left, about all she'd been up to was watching game shows on TV. It made her feel good to witness people winning refrigerators and tape decks, cars and money too. If it could happen to all those screaming, clapping women, maybe it would happen to her. Some such unexpected luck. God knows she needed it. But this wasn't something she'd confess to Lis, who would probably slam the phone down in disgust. "I want to work in another agency!" she burst out, then pressed her cheek to the cool windowpane.

"Fine. But are there any advertising agencies in Westport?" Lisbeth asked.

"I don't know."

"Damn it, Di, go check the yellow pages! I'll hang on."

It occurred to Dinah as she ran to the phone table in the hall that Lisbeth wouldn't have had her coffee yet or brushed her teeth. No wonder she was testy.

"Yes, here, four, no, three of them," Dinah panted on her return.

"Great! Now you've got a target, something to shoot for."

Lisbeth took her through the rest of the steps, from writing the letters to telephoning, to forcing the agencies into giving her an interview and how to bring it off when they did. Dinah felt herself shriveling and shrinking in her kitchen, like Lily Tomlin in that silly movie she and Hatch had seen once, until she became a diminutive person, one incapable of getting a job. There was so much to do! Such manipulation. She thought of going back to bed. What would happen if she just refused to move? Mikey'd call Hatch and he'd commit her to some snake pit, that's what, she thought, so don't even consider it.

"Do you have all that?" Lisbeth asked at the end of the hour call.

Dinah nodded her head, then collapsed. "Every word of it!"

"Good, now, before I perish from caffeine deprivation, have you spoken with Quinn?"

"No, why?"

So Lisbeth related the story of the lost brother, which acquired, as she told it, the coloration of something she'd create for the screen.

"I'll have to call her," Dinah said as Lisbeth finished. When she could better tolerate somebody else's good fortune, when Quinn's joy didn't exacerbate Dinah's misery. These days she'd rather hear of disasters, of people worse off than she was. Other people's happiness, excluding that of the winners on television, who didn't exist in the real world, rubbed away at her like a rash.

But I will get a job, I will be out in the world, a wage earner again, a contributor, somebody like Lisbeth. Sure I will! she sneered inwardly, trying not to sink in a miasma of depression. Even as she crouched at the kitchen table with her old Smith-Corona from college, laboriously picked out the letters one by one because age caused the keys to stick, she thought, *Lis will get a Tony and Quinn will win the Nobel and Susie, oh, Susie would be handed the keys to the city on the steps of Gracie Mansion for being the best volunteer in fifty years, or something like that, while I'll be a stoop-shouldered receptionist.*

Depression and negativism notwithstanding, Dinah forced herself to type up a passable resume and a letter to each of the agencies, then drove down to the post office to copy everything. When she finally put the three envelopes in the mail slot she sagged, a wet dishrag, her hair straggly, arms and back throbbing from the strain. She wanted a hot bath and a vodka and tonic; she yearned to luxuriate, so she stopped off at Crabtree and Evelyn for a bottle of bubble bath and one of bath oil before she drove home. One bright light flickered on the horizon, she realized as she fought the traffic, she hadn't a blessed thing to do, for a week anyway, not until she telephoned the three agencies and put step two of Lisbeth's job plan into action.

124

Dinah's "vacation" lasted less than a week, for she received her first morsel of luck four days later when one of the agencies called her. A woman from Connors and Connors phoned to ask if she might come in the next day at three-thirty.

"To discuss *my situation*! That's what she said!" Dinah screamed all the way from Westport to Greenwich Village. She barely needed a phone, she was so exuberant.

Lisbeth stayed calm. "Remember, a dark suit, heels, only gold, no flashy jewels."

"I don't have any jewels, period, just my engagement ring." Hatch couldn't demand that back, she worried all of a sudden.

"Every hair in place. And makeup. A dab on the eyes, but *no shadow*. A little rouge, and a pale lipstick, nothing garish."

"Yes, yes."

"Check your stockings. No runs!"

"Of course not."

"And, Di, be forceful. Tell these people what you can do for them, why they should hire you," Lisbeth instructed, a general sending the troops into battle.

They should hire me because I need a job, Dinah thought, but restrained herself from saying so, not to Lisbeth or to the nice man who wasn't at all the formidable dragon she expected at Connors. It was Joe Connors himself, president and the only Connors. "Two sounded better than one," he explained. A balding, barrel-chested, laid-back kind of a guy was his personal description. "I'm easy"—he laughed— "and that's the way I run this shop. Nothing high pressure. Not that we don't have deadlines; it's the nature of the business. Got them all the time, but I see we start each job early enough so nobody's hassled. One reason the clients like us and stay here is because we're reliable, we deliver what and when we say we will. Got the picture?"

"Yes, Mr. Connors."

"Call me Joe."

He had a pleasant smile, though a small one that never revealed his teeth completely, and his eyes were large and round and thickly lashed. If it weren't for the hump on his nose, evidence of a long-ago bad break, and his ears, which stuck out like open taxi doors, he'd be a good-looking man. The nicest thing about him, however, was his voice, slow as a southerner's. It fell on Dinah like warm rain. In a shorter time than she would have imagined, Joe Connors had her relaxed and pouring out her life story—or Lisbeth's rewrite of it.

125

"I like," he said when she paused, "that you stayed busy while raising your son. So many women just sit on their duffs and watch television. Soap operas and game shows." Joe Connors gave a disparaging snort. "But you've got an impressive list of charities you raised the sweat for. Congratulations, Dinah."

"Ah, thank you." Heat flushed up her face and she tried batting her eyes demurely as Cybill Shepherd did on *Moonlighting*. She just wished she could remember better the mythical list of organizations she'd supposedly labored for, and what she'd described as her duties. *Please don't let him call anybody!* she prayed. But he never asked for a name, and Dinah sighed as though she'd just swum the Bosphorus when Joe Connors stood up.

"I'll get back to you, or Minnie, my secretary, will. And Dinah, I'm sure you've got a score of irons in the fire. But don't do anything, make a commitment I mean, before checking over here. Okay?"

"Certainly, Joe, whatever you say." She smiled, chirpy as a blue jay, and allowed her hand to be sandwiched between his two large ones.

Dinah rode home on a cushion of air, fantasizing so much she ran a red light and just escaped being broadsided by a bus. After that she banished Connors and Connors, Joe and the agency, from her thoughts, waiting.

She wasn't even put off when the other two agencies said, "Nothing now, maybe later. Check with us three, four months or so."

"I've got a live one," she told her friends, and painted two large canvasses as she kept herself occupied, poised, tense in expectation. She'd already decided what she'd wear her first day on the job. Only neither Joe Connors nor his secretary Minnie called.

Finally Lisbeth bullied her into phoning. "So sorry," that Minnie person lied, "we've hired another assistant in the art department. Maybe next time."

Dinah asked to talk to Joe himself, but he was out of town. "That son of a bitch!" Dinah stormed when she slammed down the receiver. She kicked out at Becky who was nuzzling her knee. Even though she failed to connect, the dog shrieked. "Oh Beck, poor thing! I didn't mean it!" she apologized, and sat on the floor hugging her Airedale as both of them cried.

10

Will and his family again drove in to Manhattan for dinner at Quinn's, and this time Maria and the children seemed less frightened, less guarded in the apartment with, as Maria said, "So many beautiful things like a *museo*." As for Will, he might have been retreating in time, inching closer to the brother Quinn loved once, then lost. *His doing,* Quinn reminded the middle-aged woman she now was when those moments of pleasure, at again sharing Will's life, overwhelmed her.

Quinn also returned to Brooklyn. In fact, she came to expect to be invited. One Sunday, after the big midday dinner, she took the children to the movies. It was the first science fiction film Quinn had ever seen and she was as enchanted as Carlos, Isobel, and Sarah with the space vehicles and robots.

"Why, it's a whole different world," Quinn, awed, said to Will when they got back.

"Hell, Quinn, there are thousands of different worlds besides your little one, and not just in the movies."

Quinn, stung, supposed he meant his for one; family, children, a house in such alien territory as Brooklyn were all still strange as the distant galaxies.

Quinn watched carefully, learning the customs, the rules. The children were strictly disciplined and Maria deferred always to Will. Also, Quinn couldn't help noticing that money was scarce. Will worked, but often the jobs were small and sporadic. She considered offering help, but held off for the moment and bought the children presents instead, sneaked them pocket change.

Having always had an abundance, Quinn struggled to imagine need and doing without. Will, too, once knew a life in which desires were easily satisfied, and a scrimping, parsimonious existence must, Quinn suspected, anger her brother. But though he had moved a considerable distance from Boston, he still was a Webster and kept his own counsel. He hadn't lost his pride.

One Saturday Quinn taxied the children over to Bloomingdale's and outfitted them in jackets, sweaters, boots, hats, gloves, scarves, warm corduroy pants, and designer jeans. It wouldn't have surprised Quinn if, on their arrival back in Brooklyn, Will reacted angrily, but he didn't. He merely lifted a shoulder and reminded the children to thank their Aunt Quinn.

Quinn felt no guilt about being able to buy out a department store any more than she did about her mother's estate, half of which had originally been left to Will. But Will disappeared. Their mother waited, hoping, believing the errant son would reappear as magically as he'd vanished. Only a week before she died did the lawyers prevail and she changed her will, leaving everything to Quinn as the only child whom it was known with certainty survived.

The money could have been his, Quinn thought.

Will seldom mentioned the past, and then only in recalling pleasant incidents or certain friends, less often dead George, Junior, and their parents. That long-ago, that jettisoned life and world, impinged on the present, however, for at times when talking of summers at the Vineyard, the sloop he'd gotten on graduating from Harvard, holidays in Boston, Red Sox games he and George would sneak off to, dancing school they all suffered on Tuesdays and Fridays, parties and that precious first legal drink at the Ritz bar, a light inside Will would spark, blaze, then quickly fade, snuffed out by time and the choice he had made.

Rarely did Will bring up the subject of their father, and so stiffly, as if, like Quinn—despite the fact that he left while she stayed—he had still to hold that towering figure at bay, keep the dying man at the other side of the barricade.

"And he is dying," Quinn promised. "It's not imagination, or one of his ploys. Besides, he hates the sympathy, and the few times I've talked to him on the phone, he won't even tell me how he feels."

"True New England to the end," Will said. "All granite and no complaints; weathering the elements."

Quinn was swinging on the porch glider, Will half sitting on the railing. Despite the chilly night air, it was pleasant in the shadows, with the comforting light seeping through the curtained window.

Quinn asked suddenly, "Do you want to see him one last time?"

"What for? I still despise the son of a bitch and he probably feels the same about me. Dying's not about to change him. Besides, if I had the temerity to appear at his door, he'd slam it in my face."

"I don't know," Quinn said, "he is old and sick and has such a short time." She hesitated, not sure why, before telling Will how ardently Edmund Terhune pursued her on the old man's behalf as well as his own.

Will might never run off now, but still Quinn didn't entirely trust him. It had only been weeks since they were miraculously reunited, but already the relationship was frighteningly important to her. As a child, then a young girl, she looked up to her brothers. First George, Junior, disappointed her by choosing death. As for Will, of the two Quinn's favorite, she remembered sometimes while going back and forth to Brooklyn, when she had nothing to do but sit and think, how angry she'd become when she realized he'd gone for good. After a while her temper had quieted, but the ache in her heart was harder to assuage. On the long rides Quinn recalled both the anger and the aching, but the moment the cab pulled up in front of the small white house all her unhappy memories flew away like a flock of swallows.

She came bearing gifts, and she left leaving more. One night before Will drove her back to Manhattan—the ride had grown into established custom—Quinn opened one of her brother's dresser drawers and put a thousand dollars inside. She thought of this small sum as testing the waters. When Will said nothing, she hid five thousand the next time. The secret game became quite exciting. Though the opposite of stealing, it affected Quinn in what she supposed was a similar fashion. That rush of adrenaline, the shallow breathing and rapid pulse, all indicated she was getting away with something. Then, emboldened even further, Quinn called and suggested that she come out that evening for dinner. Maria couldn't say no. This time, however, Quinn had nothing for her brother. She wondered how Will felt when he pulled out the drawer and found only the usual stacks of socks and underwear.

The next morning when Quinn came in with the dogs from their walk the phone was ringing. It was Will. "I've been thinking," he said, "that you need new butcher block counters in your kitchen."

"What for?"

"It's the style, Quinn."

"What do I care about style? And I don't cook either."

"Too bad. I'm coming over in a while to take measurements." Before Quinn could react he'd hung up the phone.

She had to stay home and wait, fifteen floors up, watching the gray day from the window. Below, the trees were blackly stroked; the dying leaves had only the most tentative hold on the branches.

What was Will up to? He couldn't just take over like this, but then she saw him coming around the corner, crouched into the wind gusting

129

off the East River. He held Sarah by the hand until the wind almost knocked her over. When they crossed the street he had her secured under his arm.

She wouldn't be able to argue this out with Will since he'd brought Sarah along.

"Why isn't Sarah in school?" Quinn asked as she watched Will measure the counters. She liked the Spanish tile he would be replacing with wood, but she had no idea how to stop him.

"Teacher conference day. School's closed," he replied. He scribbled a series of numbers in a small notebook before he moved to the opposite wall.

The corgis' yips of pleasure drifted in from the living room, along with Sarah's laughter, crisp as a waterfall. "The dogs so enjoy playing with a child."

Will snorted. "They're animals, not human you know, or if you don't you should." He ran his steel tape measure the width of the counter and let it snap back with a sharp crack.

Quinn jumped. She felt forced to defend herself and the corgis. "They're wonderful company. And very clean, very *good* dogs."

"You'd be better off if you got married and had *real* children," Will said, facing her squarely for the first time since he and Sarah arrived.

Was he mad about the money? When she left it or when she didn't? Quinn protested, "I realize quite well, thank you, that Yin and Yang aren't people." Then she went out to the hall closet and stuffed five hundred dollars, all she had in the apartment, into Will's windbreaker pocket.

Sarah followed her back into the kitchen, tugging at her sleeve. Quinn, startled, asked, "What is it, Sarah?" She longed to smooth the child's silky hair but she lacked the skill of touching. Now that she wanted to make such intimate contact, she had no idea what to do. Could it be only as simple as reaching out a hand?

"Yin lost her ball under the bed."

Quinn shook a finger at the ball of fluff in Sarah's arms. "Naughty girl," she crooned in mock anger. Yang, running a course between the child and Quinn, yapped excitedly.

"Does she have another one?"

"Oh my, yes. In the pantry are all sorts of toys."

As Quinn started to cross the kitchen Yang, in his frenzy, darted between Will's feet. Will grabbed onto the edge of the counter to keep from tripping. The measuring tape flew out of his grasp. So swiftly Quinn wasn't sure she actually saw the blurred motion, Will swung a foot at the dog. Yang, screeching, rose up in the air, sailing off Will's boot.

"Will!"

"Daddy!"

"God damn dog!"

Quinn gave Will a key so he could come and go while building the counters. She meant for him to keep it, however, and told the doormen that her brother was allowed to use the apartment as his own home. But Will's dislike of the corgis worried her. Furry rats, he called them. Not that he would really hurt them. . . . *Yang doing his somersault on the kitchen floor.* Quinn couldn't settle on whom to defend, the dog or her brother. She wanted Will to like the corgis even if he disapproved of them. Maybe he was right, that they were children substitutes. *Will,* she asked herself, *whom does that hurt?* Surely Will didn't really think that at forty she should start having children.

Sometimes when Will intently stared at her with a dark, haunted look, she wondered if he was seeing her now, Quinn grown, tallish for a woman and broad, carrying too much weight, her square face, flat as a plane, with the stubby nose and wide mouth, so uninteresting, or a younger Quinn for whom some hope remained.

"What happened to you?" he asked Quinn just once. "You've changed."

"Of course I have. Nobody stays the same."

"No, I don't mean that, I mean in some basic way."

What could she say, I have rooms with closed doors, corners I never look into. I won my share of secrets, twenty years in the making, and they require that interest be paid. If there were things she never told the Cabot friends, how could she tell Will? Will had run; he wasn't a fighter. Neither of her brothers had stood his ground. *And me,* she asked herself, *am I any different?*

She'd gone to the apartment at noon to see how Will was coming along with the counters. Quinn was glad now that he was changing her kitchen and sorry that the job was nearing completion. The counters provided an excuse to spend more time with Will and she couldn't get enough of him. Irrationally, she was afraid. Of course he'd stay, and with him the children—but would he? Would the money keep him? Quinn thought she should mention it, but held back. She waited for Will to say something and he didn't.

Quinn had something else to worry about—the dogs. They stayed away from Will. This lunchtime she found them curled on the pillows of her bed. They refused to follow her into the kitchen.

"I hate little dogs," Will said. "They have no reason for being. Rich people's luxuries, like fur muffs."

Quinn saw there was nothing to say. Will had a closed-up look on his face. It seemed such a minor issue to become angry about, except to her. Quinn loved the corgis.

Returning to the university Quinn had the cab drop her around the back of the building. Ever since Derek Sonderson killed himself so publicly, she used the service elevator, which clanged and groaned and smelled sour. Today the heavy doors were about to close when Verensky stomped up to her with a demonic glint in his pitchy eyes that reminded Quinn of a Rasputin she'd seen once in a movie. Despite being a genius in his field, Verensky was a perpetual shambles, none too clean and always in costume. Being in America seemed to mean to Verensky a constant movie in which he starred dressed like Gary Cooper.

Puffy cheeked, his hairy face damp with pearls of sweat, Verensky babbled something in Russian.

Quinn raised her voice. "What did you say?" she shouted. She presumed that when he jettisoned English he could be retrieved more rapidly if one spoke louder, as to a deaf person or one mentally deranged.

Verensky lurched into the elevator, which groaned under him. The doors closed and they started up.

"Lost keys, damn it. You got a set maybe? To inside lab, not out?" He stared at her.

"Now why would I have keys to your lab, Verensky? Do you have keys to mine?"

"*Nyet!*" He tossed his leonine head and moved closer to Quinn. The sweetish scent he gave off caused her to back up against the rear wall of the elevator.

Verensky hunched his shoulders, lowered his chin, and peered at Quinn in an alarming fashion. "What is all this stuff about?" he waved, flapping his hand.

"I don't know what you're raving about," Quinn replied.

"This . . ." He curled his arms about his barrel chest and hid his face. "This crinking violet business."

"Shrinking," Quinn corrected automatically. "And I still don't have the slightest idea what you mean."

"What you think, some other stupid idiot will blow his head inside out when we get upstairs?"

"No, I don't think any such thing!" she yelled.

Verensky hung so close to Quinn she could barely breathe, and the elevator, always sluggish, now rose so slowly that it seemed they'd been traveling upward forever.

"Too afraid, Quinn. Of everything. You Americans . . . bah!" He made a spitting motion. "Weak, foolish people. No iron, here!" He thumped his breastbone. "And, you, I no understand it, such a smart woman."

Hours passed as the elevator continued its endless journey. Around them the building lay in a silence as mysterious as still water. It might have been uninhabited. Just when Quinn was starting to think that like a nightmare this imprisonment with Verensky would never end, the elevator settled.

"What rubbish!" Quinn snapped, sliding around to the front of the car, but Verensky danced with her, blocking her way when the elevator doors parted.

"What you do to this idiot that he acted so crazy?"

"Verensky, you are neither a policeman nor a psychiatrist. Now leave me alone!" With that, Quinn, though disliking the feel of the hard, thick flesh, disliking it before she reached out and pushed, nevertheless shoved Verensky out of her path.

"Ah, Quinn," he cried, following her from the elevator, "you are different. A hard, hard person. No one should fight with you, like that son of a nobody you killed."

"I never—!" Quinn screamed, whipping around, but the Russian was too fast for her. He had already gotten through his door and disappeared.

Verensky stubbornly clung to Quinn's thoughts all afternoon, and trailing in his wake, the floating tail of a kite, came ghostly Derek Sonderson, a nickel-sized red caste mark dead center in his forehead. *Afraid . . . weak . . . foolish . . . kills . . .* Verensky's booming Slavic voice kept intruding though Quinn struggled to obliterate him completely. His presence, the very weight of the man as he tried to overwhelm her—just as her father had once done, and dying, shrinking to half the man he was, still did, would do even in death—pressed her down, held Quinn in place. She, tall as Verensky, felt smaller, insignificant, one who falters and is capable of bursting into tears though she hadn't done that, not at all, for years. Not since she was a child, when Will—

Quinn pushed back in her chair, the pencil she held poised above a row of numbers dropped. Stevie came to the doorway, about to say something and hand her a folder of results from twenty-five, but she retreated from the stormy look on Quinn's face as Quinn, remembering, saw herself at ten, under the trees, reading in the hammock.

Will came along, taking the shortcut from the courts, swinging his racket, whistling. He snatched the book out of her grasp, and Quinn, shrieking, chased after him, but plump and awkward, she stumbled while Will, laughing, easily outran her. Even now, in her office, thirty years later, Quinn experienced that rage, which rushed up inside her chest. Wanting something and not being able to get it, knowing she'd never better her brother or run faster. And even if by a miracle graceful Will tripped, fell, sprawled for a second on the ground, he'd still fend her off. Not strong enough, or quick or good enough. . . .

Never before or since would a stone be thrown by Quinn with any accuracy, but this rock arced through the air and struck Will, still laughing, on the brow.

Blood, a red blooming. The two images, Will's tanned skin and Derek's milky whiteness, merged together, both disfigured. Quinn felt sick while still remembering how good the feeling when the old man said it was the first interesting thing he thought she'd done, or that he knew of, taking her revenge. Her mother wanted to punish Quinn, but her father laughed and said *Not at all,* and for the longest moment she stood beside his chair as he stroked her hair.

The day disappeared, going more quickly than Quinn liked. The window behind Quinn darkened, and Stevie, sitting opposite, was bathed in the cruel light from the overhead fixture.

"That should be it for twenty-five," Quinn said, closing the file folder and handing it back to Stevie.

Stevie stretched and said, "Then I guess I'll quit for today. What about you, Dr. Webster? Going to leave soon?"

Quinn lifted another folder out of the in-basket and opened it. "No, I'm staying on for a while. One of the grants is coming up for renewal, so I have to start on the reports they want." In her peripheral vision she saw Stevie tug a strand of pale fine hair behind an ear and poke a stubby finger at the bridge of her glasses. Stevie manifested a peculiar neuterness and appeared to be of indeterminate sex. She had the bland look of a blancmange, all pale and pudding.

"Well, don't stay too late." Stevie hesitated before offering a rare personal remark: "You look tired." She dawdled, and Quinn who repelled the slightest familiarity, grabbed a handful of papers and swung around to the window. After a pause Quinn heard the door click softly, and when she glanced over her shoulder and saw Stevie had gone, a sigh escaped her and she slumped wearily.

Not too long afterwards Quinn left the lab, hurrying through the empty building and out into the night. The temperature had dropped and the air was chilly, leaden with the threat of rain. She shivered as she walked rapidly along the path spun yellow by the sodium lights. Few people lingered about the campus, for there were no evening classes. Here and there she saw the shadowy figures of the security guards in their gray uniforms drifting along the walks.

Silence settled like mist. Quinn listened to the beat of her steps on the ground, to the creaks and groaning of the dark, as if the earth itself stretched and settled. Out beyond the wall and the heavy iron gates the city rumbled, traffic sparse. A bus came up the avenue and its brakes hissed when it stopped. A car horn shrilled in indignation; an ambulance siren blew peevishly a few blocks south.

Quinn ached, a steel bar bending against her shoulders, her arms dragging her down with their weight. Dreariness burdened her soul and she had an uneasy premonition that the night promised to exacerbate her black mood even further, that sleep lurked as far in the future as the dawn, and that bad dreams would take wing, swirling like primordial creatures out of their secret caves.

Quinn passed through the gates and stood on the curb until a taxi screeched up to her and braked. She rode home trying to think of a hot bath and a light meal, perhaps a glass of wine, and the dogs, but none of these promises gave her pleasure. Unbidden, a grinning Verensky entered her thoughts. No memories, no terrors stalking the past, could keep the Russian from enjoying himself, from living life to the fullest. And for the moment she so hated him for his exuberance, his passion, and the steel will to survive, that she wished him dead as Lenin in his glass tomb. But quickly Quinn stopped herself, thinking instead of Will and how seldom her brother laughed anymore.

The doorman saluted Quinn as she passed through the ornate marble lobby to the elevator. She rode up to the fifteenth floor in gold leaf splendor, but at the apartment door, the key in the lock, she faltered. Some intuition stayed her hand.

If only Will still worked in the kitchen. They could eat together, share a bottle of Beaujolais and talk about nothing that mattered. Or maybe they'd remember the good times. Surely there were some of those, but standing uneasily in the hall Quinn was unable to recall when she hadn't plodded, when she hadn't put one determined, sensibly shod foot before the other.

Opening the door she crossed the threshold calling out, "Yin! Yang!" Usually the dogs with their sensitive hearing knew the instant she reached the floor. Even if they were asleep on the bed some instinct alerted them that she'd arrived, and they'd come, barking joyfully, clicking up music on the parquet.

Why weren't the corgis scampering about her feet begging to be picked up?

On a small William and Mary table a lamp spilled a vivid aurora of light. Quinn moved and a splash of yellow hit her feet. Beyond, to the living room on the left and down the long hall, there was only darkness. On the right were the sliding doors to the dining room, closed, a soft glow tatting out from under them.

Quinn hung back, calling the dogs again, then once more. An eerie quiet filled the apartment and she couldn't decide what direction to advance in. She hesitated, frozen, hanging back like a guest, afraid to move on. *In my own apartment!* she chastised herself, taking two steps into the murky living room. Her hand pushed through the gloom as though underwater until she found the switch on a standing lamp. When she sent the darkness scuttling, everything appeared untouched, the furniture in place, the books still anchored on their shelves.

"Yin? Yang?"

She retreated to the foyer again, staring down the black hallway, and turned toward the doors on her right. Silently they slipped in their grooves and Quinn stepped through the opening.

The crystal chandelier glowed, the diamond tears sparkling brilliantly. The glare stung her eyes and Quinn flung up a hand. Before her the long Empire table was elaborately set for four with the Rosenthal and best silver. A Waterford goblet and wineglass stood by each place. Upon the plates were lace-edged Irish linen napkins cinched by engraved rings. To the left of where Quinn normally sat a sterling ice bucket held a bottle of Dom Pérignon. And for the centerpiece, on a large piece, on a large antique china plate, were the dogs. Yin faced the kitchen while Yang peered sightlessly the opposite way. Even with the small wax apples stuffed in their little mouths Quinn could tell the corgis apart. Their black button eyes were glazed and wide and their pert ears stood up stiffly. Later Quinn discovered that one-inch nails hammered into their skulls acted as cruel armatures for those ears. The reddish fur blazed and blood still dripped slowly about them. The lush, foxy tails curled, each hugging the other. The dogs looked alive except for the carving knives—bone handles and stainless steel blades protruding from their backs. The final touch was the pink ribbons tied about the knives into bows.

Quinn slipped into a half crouch, a throaty keening primitive in tone, mournful as a dirge, bursting from her throat. She huddled on the floor moaning for what might have been hours until she crawled, hugging the wall, to the foyer where, after three tries, her badly shaking hand managed to dial the phone.

11

"Let Mrs. Sloan answer it," Greg said.

Susie saw the slim elegant figure in the mirror, hair upswept and pinned in tiny ringlets, the long sequined dress, shoulders draped with mink, turn and stare at the phone.

Greg's voice rose imploringly. "We're late!"

The phone rang again as her tuxedoed husband rolled his eyes and ran nervous fingers through his carefully arranged hair. "Jesus, Susie, we'll never get there!"

Oh, if she could only please him as she once did when his happiness meant everything. But now, without knowing how it happened, they pulled in different directions, or at least Susie did. What year or month or day had that begun? Before she started going to the shelter? she wondered as her smooth hand lit by a large pear-shaped diamond reached for the receiver.

"Hello?" Susie said, asking endless questions of the violet eyes reflected in the mirror.

"Quinn knows other people. Didn't you tell me she found that long-lost brother of hers? Why doesn't she call him? Or Lisbeth?" Greg, standing beside her under the awning while the doorman whistled down a cab, was unhappy. He stroked his upper lip in memory of a mustache he'd had for a brief while years before and which he'd disliked except for touching it. He'd shaved it off, but that stroking had become a habit. Susie thought it must have a soothing effect, but tonight the reflex failed to ease his distress.

"You don't have to come with me. Go ahead. I'll meet you there later, after I find out what's wrong with Quinn." But whatever had sent Quinn, strong and usually so calm, into hysterics, Susie knew it wouldn't be something easily dealt with. For Quinn, weeping unrestrainedly, to be so out of control that she cried into the phone, "Please come over! Help me!" the cause had to be truly awful. Quinn wasn't likely to cry wolf.

"These tickets cost two hundred dollars, you know. And we're sitting at a very good table. McGrath will have the whole shebang to himself if we don't show up."

I don't care, Susie thought blasphemously, fervently praying under her breath that Quinn wasn't physically hurt.

Greg's career had always been their first priority, that and getting ahead. Money, success, and dancing about in a cotillion with the right people once meant everything, until one day Susie awoke and found none of it mattered. But she'd yet to tell Greg how she felt.

"What's so wrong with Quinn anyway?"

"She didn't tell me, but she was crying."

Greg sighed. "Well, I can't see her calling you out on some wild goose chase. Quinn's not one for a case of the vapors." Despite his resentment of the women and the time Susie gave to them, he tried to be accepting, was certainly kind. "But it still might be nothing so terrible," he said, struggling to create a reality that pleased. As with Betts—whom Greg had yet to confront or allow Susie to—he wanted the truth not to distress him.

The burden of Greg's complaint against the friends was that they represented a choice he hadn't made. They were, or Susie's relation to them was, outside his control. She understood that and how it saddened and disappointed rather than angered Greg. This area of her life that he couldn't share, except peripherally, symbolized an ongoing revolt. In all fairness to her husband, however, Susie had to admit that he'd warned her before they married how old-fashioned he was. "I want," he'd said—in his shiny youth already ponderous and middle-aged—"a traditional home, family, a wife who will take care of me and our children. I don't want a lady lawyer or doctor or even an interior decorator, Susie. I'm sorry!" Even then he'd sounded grieved and slightly ashamed of himself, but his eyes were warm, brimming with enthusiasm, and he loved her so much.

He'll be a good father and husband, and given his drive, quite successful. You'll have a good life, Ivy Bannon had pronounced to her daughter.

Susie, between her mother and Greg, and yearning as she always did to duplicate that comforting Baltimore life, felt years later that she'd been trawled in effortlessly. Surely she knew then as she knew now that Greg, for all his positive attributes, for all those admirable characteristics, was tissue-paper thin.

139

The doorman had finally caught a cab on Eighty-sixth Street and rode it down to the building. He hopped out and held the door. Greg started to join Susie inside. "No," she said, "I'll go by myself. Make my regrets and as soon . . . or when I can, I'll be there."

"Well, I don't know. I mean what if something's really wrong . . ." Greg said, but Susie motioned the driver to be off and slammed the door. Greg might have called *Wait!* but the cab surged forward, quickly spinning into a U-turn and heading for the transverse.

The Quinn who flung back the door was a woman Susie had never seen before, with a face blotchy with tears and eyes inflamed. "Oh, thank God you're here!" she cried, and, another surprise, let Susie's arms enfold her.

Susie reached up and smoothed Quinn's wheat-colored hair back from her moist brow. "What happened?" she asked softly.

Quinn jerked her head toward the dining room doors, closed once more.

"Something in the dining room?"

Channels of pain flowed over Quinn's face as she stared past Susie's shoulder. It seemed possible that she saw through the wood.

"Quinn?"

But Quinn never said another word as Susie, graceful in the long dress swaying about her legs, went up to the doors. Though when she pushed them apart, Quinn expelled a whinny of panic.

Susie crossed the threshold unthinkingly, the air humming with mystery, while Quinn hung back in the foyer; and when she actually understood what she saw, the dogs like suckling pigs, her hands flew to her mouth. She cried out, words and sounds of no meaning. Horror cinched her throat. It was moments before she could breathe and whisper, "They look real. Their eyes—"

From behind her Quinn cried, "Yes, like rubies!"

"Oh, how could anyone! So sick!" Susie shook, shivering under her fur and dress. She backed away, and out of the dining room shut the doors. Eyes closed, she tried to block out the dinner table, but the elegant china and silver and crystal and the dogs were etched on the inside of her lids.

Susie looked for Quinn, but Quinn wasn't there. She had curled herself into a corner of the sofa on the far wall of the living room. Susie sat next to her and took Quinn's hand, cold and feeling as dead as the corgis.

"We should call the police," Susie said.

140

Quinn's eyelids fluttered in surprise. "No police!" she groaned.

"Oh, Quinnie, we just can't—"

Quinn dug fingernails into Susie's arm. "The door was locked. Whoever did this had a key, and . . . oh, please, Susie! I just want it all to go away, to never have happened!"

The phone rang, startling them both. Quinn screamed and Susie stared at the instrument as though it were lethal, letting it shrill twice, three times, before she snatched up the receiver and breathed, "Hello!"

"Susie? Are you okay? What's going on there?"

"Greg."

"Honey, I should have come with you. This is only one more business dinner. Listen, I'll grab a cab and get over there if you need me."

"No," she said hastily. "Things are under control." Greg was concerned, but faced with the dead corgis Susie could see her husband, for all his good intentions, stiffening, insisting, *This doesn't concern either one of us.* He'd try and force her to hand over the "problem" to the authorities.

"Well, what is it?"

Susie lowered her voice. "A family affair, something I can't discuss, but Quinn's terribly upset, so I doubt if I'll make it to the dinner."

Silence at the end, and then Greg said, "You do what you think best, Susannah." The use of her full name signaled Greg's disappointment. She rejected his help, which meant rejecting him. Wasn't he supposed to take care of her? More and more often now, Greg's love afflicted Susie and became a burden.

"I'll see you at home," she said, and quickly hung up the phone.

Quinn said, "A few weeks ago somebody sent me a dead mouse, a penknife stuck in its little belly. All wrapped up in a shoe box."

"God!"

"It was the day Derek Sonderson shot himself. I supposed he'd left the package downstairs before he died. A parting gift!" She laughed in a screech of rusty gears.

"Derek Sonderson didn't do this," Susie said.

"Who could be so cruel!" Quinn's scream tore through the room.

Susie supposed her courage had limits to it. She often thought of herself as a hider, yet she had survived being raped, her body being invaded and used, she'd withstood that degradation. She'd neither fainted nor died when Miss Allen made her suggestion about Betts; in fact, Susie was going on, watching and worrying but staying in control of herself. So why now, outside the closed dining room doors, her palms wet with sweat, fear stitched to her insides and the grisly arrangement on the table imprinted in memory in all its vivid, Technicolor detail, was she immobile? The dead dogs stuffed like suckling pigs ready to be carved and eaten were appalling but distant from her, neither her body nor her child. *I will not be afraid!* She swore and tugged the doors aside, three quarters back on their tracks so that she had a long view through the gap of the entire table, the chairs ready to be sat upon and the glittering chandelier with its tiers of glass drops like icicles.

For the first time Susie noticed the peculiar smell, much stronger now as she stepped into the room, long and angular—like a coffin, she thought. She was sure the odor was of blood, though she couldn't remember ever smelling blood, but then, only once before had she seen so very much of it. Up close, holding on to the back of a chair, she saw that the large plate on which the dogs were so artfully arranged was filled with a soupy pool of red. Tiny bright spots sprinkled along the white cloth, but it wasn't the blood or the sight or the sweetish aroma that captured Susie's attention now and caused the tight feeling in her chest. It was the little white card before the dinner plate in front of her. *Quinn Webster*, it read. Susie moved to the left and saw Lisbeth's name inked on a similar card. She sat opposite Quinn, Dinah to the right. There was no mistake. Susie, once more shutting the doors on the dinner table, walked with heavy feet into the living room and called Quinn's name. Quinn lifted a despairing face from one of the cushions. Susie said, lips stiff, "There's a place set for each one of the four of us at that table."

"No!" Quinn cried in a desperate whisper louder than any scream.

Quinn got the shakes and Susie had her lie down on the bed under the covers.

"I'll make you some tea," Susie said. "Have you eaten anything?"

Quinn's teeth chattered, but she managed to shift her head back and forth on the pillow. Susie's heart almost broke looking at the pitiful Quinn, all that bigness crumpled.

"I'll get you some toast, too."

The only way to the kitchen was through the dining room where the scent of blood hung heavier now, almost making Susie gag. She breathed through her mouth, hurrying by the table, the corgis watching her, their jeweled eyes flashing malevolently. She couldn't touch them, just couldn't, but she had to remove them from the table and dispose of them somehow.

While the water boiled she called Lisbeth and got her machine. Susie left a message to call her here or at home.

Inching the kitchen door open, Susie gazed through the narrow crack and sweat broke out at the nape of her neck. Both dogs stared at her over the china and crystal. *They'd moved! No, that's not possible,* she thought in a rush of panic, the door slipping away from her hand.

A fever burned under her skin and a red flush of dizziness swam in her head, threatening to topple her as with unsteady hands she poured the boiling water into a cup.

I won't be able to do it, she thought, *not alone.*

Dinah was home when Susie phoned, Mikey said. "But she's asleep. Well, sort of half asleep and half passed out." His young voice, cracking on the high notes, dripped with disapproval. "Mom drank too much. Half a bottle of gin, anyway," he said.

Susie supposed men like Hatch Johnson had once been boys like Mikey. *Be kind,* she wanted to say to Dinah's son, but couldn't take the liberty. She and Dinah had an unspoken agreement never to interfere with one another's children.

"Just leave her a note to call me in the morning, okay?"

"Sure."

"And when you go to bed, Mikey, don't forget to lock all the doors," Susie quickly added, then wondered what there was to fear in sleepy Westport, though Mikey accepted the suggestion without comment.

Susie put the tea and toast on a tray and shouldered her way back through the dining room, not glancing at the dogs at all, but she felt their dead presence pressing at her. In her flight along the hall to Quinn's bedroom she imagined she heard them growling.

Some color seeped into Quinn's floury cheeks as she sipped the hot, sweet tea. "Are they . . . ?" she asked.

Susie quickly promised, "Don't worry. I'll take care of things." *But how?* she wondered.

"Did you call Lis?"

"Yes, but she's not home. I left a message on the machine."

Quinn's eyes focused sharply. "She's probably with that Charlie person. The professor." Even in her anguish Quinn remembered to disparage the new man in Lisbeth's life. Susie ran her hands along the sparkling sequins of her dress, like shiny fish scales. "I called Dinah too. She's drunk, dead to the world." No sooner had the words come out than she shuddered. "Passed out I mean."

"Why?" Quinn cried suddenly. The cup rattled on the saucer; tea sloshed over the fluted edge. Taking it out of her hands, Susie for a moment thought Quinn meant Dinah and her drinking. "They never harmed anyone!" Of course; she meant the corgis.

"I don't know, Quinn, but those place cards . . ."

"Why?"

Susie made no answer, but she crossed her arms over her breasts and stared at Quinn until Quinn turned her head.

A chilliness seeped into the bedroom from somewhere, maybe just from their imaginations. But it was cold enough to pucker her nipples, as if she were undressed and naked sitting in the silk-covered slipper chair so near to Quinn. Quinn must have felt the cold too because she slid further down under the covers. The tray teetered on her lap, the cup and saucer tinkling. Susie rescued the tray and put it on the floor.

"You shouldn't stay here tonight," Susie said. She expected Quinn to give her an argument, since she hated sleeping in any bed but her own. But Quinn surprised her by saying nothing, only closing her swollen red eyes. "I thought Lisbeth's, but she's probably gone until morning. Or Dinah could have driven in to get you if she was sober." Susie didn't add that if Quinn went home with her she'd have to lie to Greg more than she already planned to, and so much of her life with her husband was a web of dishonesty and half truths.

"What about your brother?"

Quinn pushed herself up. "Not Will."

"Not Will what?" Susie wanted to know. "Surely he'll put you up for a night, or come sleep here?"

"I . . ." Quinn started to say, stopped, and rubbed at her eyes with clenched fists like a child. "Will . . . Will hates my dogs."

Susie didn't point out the mistake in tenses. It would take Quinn time to deal with the loss. *They had been her children,* Susie thought, as Quinn's eyes leaked tears again. The tears slid down her cheeks as if she didn't know they were there.

"He won't refuse you a bed, Quinn, because he hated the dogs," Susie said softly, waiting for Quinn to stop the useless tears. Quinn always hated crying. It never does any good, she'd say, pursing her lips. But now, thick fat tears continued in an unending wash.

"Not Will. . . ."

It took Susie a full minute to catch what Quinn meant. "Oh no," she cried, "you can't think Will did—did *that*!" Her denial rang loudly in the quiet. "No, Quinn. Think! The place cards with our names on them. Why, none of us ever even met Will!"

"He thought the dogs were an indulgence."

"Maybe they were. But it's a big jump from there to killing them.

You never said Will was crazy, and Quinn, think. You're the doctor. Doesn't it take a crazy mind to have done that?''

"I gave him a key. And today, earlier, he was here."

"I think that makes him even less likely," Susie said. Yet how easy it would be if Will's feelings about Quinn had spun insanely out of control. But those place cards . . . and their names in fine scripted black lettering. . . .

"I suppose you're right." Quinn wiped her eyes. "Will's not mad."

"And I don't think it's just you, Quinnie. Somebody's got it in for us." She remembered suddenly: "The flowers! Somebody sent me flowers with a razor blade buried in them. And Quinnie"—she grabbed her arm—"they were lilies of the valley!"

"Oh no, Susie, that's impossible!"

"Well, it isn't, obviously," she said, tossing her head. "But what about Di and Lisbeth?"

Tears swam in Quinn's eyes again, but she blinked them away. "My babies might not be the only ones."

Now Susie backed away from what she couldn't tolerate thinking of. There were too many whom she held dear. Superstitiously she kept from naming them even to herself.

"I'll call Will," Quinn said.

Susie handed her the phone from the bedside table. "Don't tell him too much. Not how the dogs died."

"No. I couldn't anyway."

Susie waited for Father Simon on a gilded chair in the lobby. She'd seen Quinn into a cab, then went back upstairs to call the priest. "I need help," she whispered urgently into the phone, shaking and near tears too now that Quinn had gone and she didn't need to hold herself together.

She couldn't stay in the empty apartment. An undercurrent of ominous sounds, creaks and groans, a reedy hissing like escaping gas, was everywhere. The evil emanated from the dining room like something palpable; Susie felt the icy-cold heft of it against her back. The smell of blood, more rancid than before, seeped through the rooms, clung to the draperies, insinuated itself between the sofa cushions, burrowed into the fibers of the carpet. Even when the dogs were gone, Susie couldn't believe Quinn's apartment would ever be free of that odor.

Rushing to the lobby, Susie waited bundled in her fur coat, drove her hands into the pockets. Her breathing was labored as if, in her silver sandals, she'd been running through the night.

"Mother of God!" He crossed himself, and for a moment Susie saw the priest again instead of the man. "Who did this? And *why?*" he asked, turning to Susie, who, now that Simon was with her, sensed nothing in the apartment, just waves of silence. Whatever force had been there, or which she imagined, had fled, leaving the pitiful sight of the little dogs, so tortured it seemed the memory of all their pain was reflected in their dead eyes. Not evil, suffering. Susie stifled a sob and put her hand on Simon's arm. She needed the reassurance of another human being.

"A terribly cruel joke," Susie said, telling a lie, her first to this man. Would that one falsehood take root and flower as all her other deceits had done? She thought fleetingly of Greg and what a creation of deception their marriage had become.

"A joke?" His eyebrows rose inquisitively, but that was the only movement on his impassive face. His *priest's* face. Simon, in Quinn's dining room, was more the cleric than he'd been at Claire McGrath's talking about The Good Shepherd and man's obligation to his brethren. Susie might have invented their walk in Central Park, hands linked together, and especially the longing in him that so surely mirrored her own.

"It's so senseless, what else could it be?" She assumed an air of innocence as he journeyed slowly around the table. The four place cards burnt a hole in Susie's evening bag.

"Who lives here?" he asked, staring at her above the china and the crystal. If she kept her eyes up she'd avoid seeing the dogs.

"A friend of mine," she said. "A woman. They're her corgis."

"And where's this friend now, Susie?" He stood once again beside her looking down. A wave of longing broke within her. In the few days since they'd seen each other she'd almost managed to forget this effect on her.

She bristled. "Why are you interrogating me?"

"Because it's pretty peculiar, don't you think? Dead dogs in a very fancy East Side apartment. In the middle of the night. Like a movie, Susie, or a thriller. You can't really expect me not to be curious, can you?"

He sounded so rational. He always did. The even tenor of his voice calmed her. *Nothing to fear from him,* she thought, *nothing,* and yet a faint, inner whisper said: *Everything.*

"She went to stay at her brother's. I promised I'd . . . I'd take care of all this. She certainly couldn't. But then, you see, Simon, neither could I. The idea of touching them made me physically ill. So I called you, for help. I wasn't able to think of anybody else, anybody I trusted more." Lie two.

"Does your friend have any idea why someone would want to kill her dogs? Not just kill them, but make a spectacle of them too?"

The apartment, so icy before, had warmed up. In fact, it had gotten hot. Steam poured out of the radiator by the window. Susie, shaking her head from side to side, telling the third lie, wondered if Simon could see the plume of steam or if she conjured it up somehow.

Susie pushed the mink coat back off her shoulders. "No."

For the first time Father Simon appeared to notice how she was dressed. "Were you at a party?"

"On the way to one when she called."

"Where's your husband?"

"He wanted to come but I sent him on without me."

"I see."

He was behaving so priestlike, though in the circumstances Susie couldn't decide how she wanted him to act. Still, he probably did understand, since it was so commonplace even among Catholics, wives and husbands unhappy with one another. *But I'm not unhappy with Greg!* she thought. Only not happy, either, and that was the truth Simon undoubtedly sensed.

He stared at her a second longer and Susie glimpsed her stricken reflection in his eyes. She thought between the dogs and the priest she would faint and tried to distance herself from this room in which they seemed stranded, disengage from the macabre table and the smell, sickly sweet like cheap perfume.

Simon must have caught her fear as strong as the stench of blood. "Why don't we go into the kitchen. You find a plastic garbage bag and I'll take care of the rest. Then I suppose you want to put all the dishes and things away so there's nothing at all."

"Yes."

"Okay, then, Let's get started." He nudged her arm, directing her toward the kitchen, and kept Susie from getting a last look at the table, for which she was thankful.

When they finished Simon carried the dead corgis wrapped in shiny green plastic out of the building in a Bloomingdale's shopping bag. The doorman regarded them strangely, almost as if he knew what they had.

On East End Avenue they walked to the north corner, crossed, and headed west.

"Now the trick is to find a trash can where we can bury them under some garbage. And where some poor soul in search of treasure won't disinter them." On Second Avenue they discovered just such a wire container next to a phone booth. They deposited the shopping bag under piles of old newspapers and assorted trash. "There. Nobody will notice it," Father Simon said, slapping his hands together.

They wandered up the entire block to Third Avenue before either of them said another word. "You could have caught a cab downtown on Second," Susie pointed out.

"It doesn't matter." He dug his hands into his pockets, and with his long hair curling untidily about his ears, he might have been any ordinary man standing on a late-night corner. He asked, "Are you going on to your party?" Like Susie, Simon seemed to want to delay their good-byes a moment longer.

"It's too late, and I'm not exactly in the mood." But she had no desire to go home either. If Greg was already there and if he'd had a few drinks too many, they'd lurch into one of their rare fights. Greg would be angry thinking he'd disappointed Susie, let her down by not going to Quinn's, by choosing business rather than her. He'd get angrier still at Susie's allowing him to make the wrong choice. *Poor Greg,* she thought, *how he liked to do the right thing, and how sorry he felt afterwards when he knew he hadn't.*

Susie, looking at the priest's face with the dark hollows under the shadowy ridges of bone, and the full lips she ached to stroke with her fingertips, let Greg slip out of mind as easily as if he had no leverage, and she suffered guilt pangs about this too, as she did about so many other things.

"Buy me a drink, Simon," Susie said, walking south on Third Avenue before fears and regrets could overcome her. She drifted on a dangerous course, sailing into the wind. *Don't think about this, just feel,* whispered in her head.

Halfway down the next block Susie—Simon at her side—turned into a bar with misted windows. *The Green Man,* it said above the door. The cluster of men, along the bar, only five or six this late, were full of wonder at the sight of Susie in her mink and sequined dress. She moved like the night sky glittering with stars amid the rickety tables and mismatched chairs. The floor was sawdust-covered and a Schlitz clock and a color TV hung above a pyramid of glasses and a wall of liquor bottles, a mirrored expanse in which Susie and the priest appeared. The hand of time locked at ten to twelve, and Johnny Carson, turbaned, in fancy dress, made silent jokes as the drinkers came to life on their stools, shifted stiffened arms and leaden shoulders, swung their heads as Susie first, then Simon, disappeared into the gloomy recesses in the back.

They were a suspicious pair, Simon coatless, in his jeans and corduroy jacket, Susie furred and elegant, and it was partly this which captured the drinkers' interest, but even more was her luminous face shimmering in the darkness like the moon.

Seated across from one another in a booth, Simon's gaze fastened onto Susie and held. She shivered and willed his touch, his hand to travel across the table and curl with hers.

A silent cry knotted in her throat as the priest talked of the dogs. There were so many secrets she longed to tell that priest part of him. Urgency brought a sinner to the confessional, and she wondered if, in this dark hidden place, this bar that could be at the end of nowhere, he might offer her forgiveness. Yet no matter what he said to her or she to him, Simon's absolution wouldn't bring Quinn's dogs back to life, nor would it halt what Susie intuited lay ahead, waiting in blackness, for the rest of them.

The waiter brought them draft beer, and Simon clinked his glass with hers, but Susie didn't drink. "Are you all right?" he asked.

She smiled, expecting any moment to scream. She thought of the corgis and how she'd been raped, and of Betts, troubled perhaps by youth or, God forbid, something worse, and of Greg who loved her still, passionately and kindly too, and of this man, this priest who caused her very blood to burn.

Up front, someone put money in the jukebox. Old songs, the ones that last forever, those her mother slowly danced to with her father out in San Diego where they met, and the ones that touched Susie also, poured softly out the ceiling speakers.

"Dance with me," Susie said, rising, holding out her hand, not waiting for his reply. It was a command as she used to issue when younger to the men in her life, and that forgotten audacity almost made her cry. How sure she'd once been of everything, of life, and how little she knew now.

"Susie . . ." It was a plea, almost, but he went anyway and took her in his arms. Only for a moment, as they found the rhythm of the music, did space separate them. As they moved, longing drew them closer together until Simon pressed lightly against the length of her. Pleasure rose in a wave from Susie's sex to the pulse of her throat and she would have fallen if Simon failed to brace her.

"I want to make love with you," Susie heard the words, hers. She

149

was breathless, but she couldn't gaze into Simon's eyes. Their looks bypassed one another, but she lacked the will to stop from bringing her mouth up to his. They brushed tentatively, like the wind, the tip of Susie's tongue licking Simon's full, throbbing lips. *I must be mad,* she thought, drowning in desire as she slid her face to the side and tucked it in against his jacket.

Simon brought his head down. "You know," he said, warm breath stirring her hair, "I'm in love with you." His sigh as he tightened his embrace held centuries of regret.

12

Charlie Morgan lived uptown near Columbia, on a side street off Broadway in a narrow limestone house, its bolted half-glass, half-steel door flush to the sidewalk, the glass itself reinforced with wire mesh. Separating this uninspired structure of ten floors from its neighbor to the west—a dilapidated single-room-occupancy hotel, once the ornate residence of a railroad magnate, with windows now latticed by metal guards—was an alley only a few feet wide that ran from front to back. Another, larger alley, whose space above the ground was filled by a fire escape attached to the side of Charlie's building, paralleled the eastern flank. The apartment house bordering this, on a typical New York street in transition, was a more elaborate building, viney scroll-work sculpted up the front. Two gargoyles were in residence at the corners of the roof.

Lisbeth thought Charlie should move next door, into one of the recently renovated co-ops where the rooms, spacious and with high ceilings, had more character than the boxy squares in which he now resided, rent controlled, and had since his divorce six years before. But Charlie, easygoing, slow moving, and ponderous, liked the cave he had constructed with almost wall-to-wall bookshelves, wood-varnished shutters, comfortable old furniture, and a perpetual dusk, for the apartment faced the rear. The apartment fit his cumbersome self. He humored Lisbeth, however, by saying, "I'll think about it."

Charlie almost never said no, to Lisbeth or anyone in his professorial life, for he hated to displease, and could not tolerate arguments or unhappiness. A raised voice, the first intimation of dissension, and Charlie's big pleasant face tightened like a screw. He heard on the spinning rise of anger his father's roar, his mother's whine of complaints and counteraccusations, and his younger siblings' cries behind closed doors. He heard too the terrible sound of flesh striking flesh, his father's hand to the curve of his mother's cheek. There were other

151

sounds, worse, which Charlie deliberately buried, such as the grinding of bones when twisted, or the snapping twiglike papery sound when they broke. Yet these too could fly like an old familiar song back into memory if an argument got too heated. So Charlie Morgan, strong as a Kodiak bear, aware that he could wreak havoc, that like both his parents he could blow a tempest of pain and destruction (indeed, that anyone really could if he had the desire), became gentle as the wind. Some people called the large, shambling man with the loping gait and the soft easy voice a patsy, and he acknowledged that too. He knew, for example, that if his ex-wife hadn't run off, though he'd long ceased to love the woman, he would have remained with her until death put them into separate graves.

A small thing, breaking a date for the theater, particularly for something as professionally mandatory as the chairman's invitation to dinner, yet Charlie suffered agonies over the anger Lisbeth hurled at him. He felt attacked, bruised, struck by rocks; his defenses were weakened, he himself so vulnerable. Size was deceptive. He tried to tell Lisbeth as much. "It's not a matter of strength," he said. "I'm not afraid of other men, of muggers, fires, speeding cars, you know. Things like wars and battles, Lisbeth. Only anger. People getting mad. Friends. Those I care for. Even strangers. New York is the wrong place for me, don't say it. I know, but here I am." Charlie smiled, but the confession had been wrung from him. His earnestness was real enough to touch.

Lisbeth wasn't like those poor women, pulpy and with no steel to their hearts, who believe whatever men tell them. Lisbeth never believed a word of Charlie Morgan's, though she wanted to and knew he never lied. Charlie was the best man who ever came down the pike, as she told Susie, and still she weighed his words as carefully as a thrifty housewife the produce in the supermarket.

Lisbeth seldom believed anyone about anything. People lied outright when they didn't fantasize, and reality, never mind truth, existed only in some dreamlike, pretend state. Hollywood was in part responsible for Lisbeth's attitude, for in the movie business people only took as gospel what they said at the time. The moment in the celluloid capital was complete in itself. Truth and the lie were therefore interchangeable.

Make believe and let's pretend. Lisbeth always thought that like an alchemist, she could turn what isn't into what is. She refused for those few early years to accept that Ferris Rosenthal lay in his grave, but he remained just as dead. Until she was sixteen, she told people who didn't know that her father traveled.

Lisbeth had more success with her other deception, changing Elizabeth Rosenthal into Lisbeth Ross when she went up to Cabot. She let her hair down and threw out all the pretty outfits she owned. Gone were the pleated skirts and cotton blouses, the cashmere sweater sets and cultured pearls. She wore jeans and overalls, tee shirts and sweats, striped stockings and no bras from then on, even when vacations came around and she returned from New England.

"I hate how you look, so common, so like everyone. Girls on the street, on television, carrying signs and storming the barricades in protest of God knows what. Girls whose pictures turn up in the newspapers," Lisbeth's mother said. She meant girls who never look like *me* or *my daughter*.

"I can't take you anywhere," Anne Rosenthal complained, "not even to a decent restaurant. Not when you wear those ragged pants and a denim jacket. Of course that doesn't bother you since you've given up meat and barely subsist on grains plus a few lettuce leaves."

Her mother, after several skirmishes with Lisbeth—whom she continued forever to call Elizabeth—didn't so much as give up on her daughter as pretend that Lisbeth was the way she wanted her, though most times that was hard to do.

"What do you mean you're going to Cuba? You can't. Americans aren't allowed. The State Department takes a dim view of any communications with the Castro regime. It's out of the question."

"No, it's not. I've already got the tickets. I fly from here to Mexico City and out of there to Havana."

"You won't."

"I will. I'm twenty-one." Not only legally an adult she meant, but in possession of her own money, the estate bequeathed by Ferris Rosenthal. Whatever his financial misdemeanors—which she'd later decide were what her uncles' silences and long sighs had to do with—what he left to Lisbeth multiplied over time. Money makes money, and by Cabot graduation she was better than well off; Lisbeth was rich.

Charlie Morgan couldn't care less if Lisbeth was rich or impoverished, but then Charlie proved different from most men, most people, Lisbeth had known. Charlie, so big, with so much hard-packed flesh on his bones and that lazy voice, allowed Lisbeth to hammer at him, allowed her to be vague, then maniacally alive, incomprehensible and clear as glass. Charlie, so far and despite his fears, had withstood all of Lisbeth's assaults, hadn't allowed her to repulse him as she had Billy and so many others. A promissory forgiveness was what he offered before her misdeeds, whatever they might be.

In his own way Charlie was sly. He realized the value of time, how most problems were ultimately resolved by waiting. He'd go into hell like Orpheus and stay if it would win him Lisbeth, though he would never put it that way. He'd just simply say, *I love you, Lisbeth.* As if that explained everything.

Several times Charlie asked her to marry him. Lisbeth would laugh. "I've already *been* married, Charlie."

"That's a fact. And so have I. That's another fact. But marry me anyway."

Charlie had never considered marrying after his divorce, supposed he'd be a crusty old sociologist, writing dusty tomes and having the occasional affair. Love seemed impossible, a romantic literary notion more appropriate to the English department. But then he met Lisbeth.

Lisbeth didn't want to get married yet, if at all. Charlie had another suggestion, that they live together. He longed to bed down with her every night and wake up with that long, lean naked body beside him in the morning.

"I'll even buy an apartment in the building next door. Or I'll move down to the Village and take the subway up to a Hundred and Sixteenth Street every day. How's that for devotion?" he'd ask. And when Lisbeth shook her red mane of hair, Charlie offered to live anyplace she wanted.

There was no getting a definite answer out of Lisbeth, so Charlie teased and waited. "I won't pressure you," he promised, and he didn't, not even about meeting the Cabot women or her mother and stepfather.

Lisbeth's decision to introduce Charlie to her friends wasn't, she assured herself, an assuagement of guilt. What could she possibly feel guilty about? Neff? Certainly not, for the homicide detective meant no more to her than an episode of masturbation. She didn't think of him as a real person, more like a character in a screenplay she wrote. He wasn't even Charlie's friend, only a visiting expert. Charlie always took those out for drinks or a meal as a way of saying thank you. Neff offered Charlie's criminology class educational sustenance, and Charlie reciprocated with alcohol. He would have fed Neff too, if Lisbeth hadn't sent him off.

She didn't mean to see the cop again. *Once,* Lisbeth assured herself, *doesn't count.* Still, she cared for Charlie (a small voice whispered she should care for him more). He'd be hurt if he found out.

Lisbeth intended to have Charlie and the women for dinner, for Susie to bring Greg, but then Quinn's dogs died—not died, Susie said, were *slaughtered,* elaborately put to death, and Quinn was grieving. *Just as though the dogs were human,* Lisbeth thought, angry with

Quinn though she wasn't sure why. She should sympathize despite her indifference to animals. But she had no intention of thinking about the dogs. Yet she dreamt about them the night of the day Susie called. Awake, Lisbeth wouldn't have been able to describe them except that they were small and yappy. Asleep, however, she saw them sitting on a shelf with their jeweled eyes and hair like silk. She thought they were toys, stuffed animals, and she reached out to pick one up. The little corgi bit Lisbeth when she touched him, and she awoke. For a moment in the dark she actually felt the impression of those tiny teeth on her skin.

No, she didn't want Charlie to meet Quinn then, not when Quinn would be so full of the dogs. Instead the two couples, Lisbeth and Charlie, Susie and Greg, met for dinner at the Café des Artistes.

"We should have asked Dinah," Susie said when they were seated at a table. "But if we did and excluded Quinn . . ."

"Oh, the dogs. Let's not discuss the dogs," Lisbeth said.

"Those dogs ruined my evening," Greg said, "and I still don't know what happened to the damn things except they're dead."

"What dogs?" Charlie Morgan asked.

"A vodka tonic," Lisbeth ordered.

Charlie looked around the artfully decorated restaurant and said that such elaborate and expensive places always made him think of the revolution.

"Are we having a revolution?" Greg asked.

"We will be," Charlie said.

Susie apologized, "I always think of this as in the neighborhood. Not like Le Cirque or Lutèce."

Lisbeth laughed. "Once upon a time I was a vegetarian. Now I eat steak, Charlie. And I haven't signed a petition since I was twenty-five."

Greg said, "Lisbeth, you should never sign your name to anything without a lawyer."

"Never! But in my youth . . . in our youth"—she nodded at Susie— "I marched, handed out leaflets, went to rallies, *protested,* and signed every piece of paper shoved under my nose."

"Well, don't. The past can come back to haunt." He smiled at Charlie. "Women, don't you know!"

"I want something light," Susie said. "Veal, I think."

Charlie didn't smile back at Greg. He knew, by his own admission, little of women other than as people, sociological entities who were part of the main. Charlie still, though judiciously, involved himself in liberal if not radical causes.

Susie liked Charlie Morgan quite a lot, though the men found very little common ground on which to meet. Politics were out, as was business. They settled, tentatively, on baseball.

Dinner proceeded in fits and starts. Lisbeth felt Susie watching her when she should have been watching Charlie. That was what she brought him for, for Susie to see (she didn't care what Greg thought) and to please Charlie. Yet the dinner seemed to be a success, if success meant, as she said later to Charlie, that no one got into an argument. And the pain in her head stayed faint, far off. But she didn't say that to Charlie, who knew nothing at all about the headaches.

Later she went uptown with Charlie, who, lying beside her in his bear sleep, sighed as he dreamed. His breath stirred across the pillow and caressed Lisbeth's bare shoulder. Charlie, before he fell asleep, said, as he always did, that he loved her, and that something within her, the brilliance and what he called quirkiness, the mystical feeling, her intuition, all of Lisbeth that he knew or thought he did. He loved, too, "Your hair, your skin smooth as a polished apple, your eyes, sometimes a sea green, then in a certain light deep emerald, the line of your chin, those high cheekbones. Your neck," he whispered, "the slope of your shoulders, your breasts like fresh peaches." Charlie thought she resembled a Modigliani, and her beauty, heightened by the years rather than diminished, awed him. "I don't know why me," he said when he embraced her, "but I'm grateful."

Lying awake while Charlie slept, Lisbeth thought he lived in a strange imaginary country with her, whether or not she dwelled there with him. No matter how he suffered from her bouts of anger, how much of him was worn raw, he rode up and out of the numbing silence into which he had to descend in order to save himself when Lisbeth's voice began its spiraling.

Despite her efforts Lisbeth thought Charlie a fool when he'd say he wasn't angry after one of her tirades. How could he reassure her time and again, always returning that fragile inner part of himself, handing it over courageously once more? She'd never felt that safe.

Lisbeth had gone back to Charlie's bed from the Café des Artistes, and he undressed her, stroking her skin, whispering along the soft hairs down her arms. He licked the ridges of her backbone, stopping only to tug off his clothes.

His large hands with the thick, strong fingers traveled over her naked body as Lisbeth lay splayed upon the pillows. "Bring me something to drink," she ordered him.

Quickly she turned on her stomach and hid, trying not to think, and heard a pop, like the Porsche's tire blowing. Lisbeth veered and jerked up as a cold cascade trickled onto her buttocks.

"Here," he said, "taste," and he gave her his wet hand. Lisbeth sucked his fingers as he bent and licked the champagne from the cleft of her buttocks. The pleasure surged and he poured more of the bubbling liquid to lap it from her fleshy softness until Lisbeth hummed.

He had her face up, washing her in Dom Pérignon. Her nipples puckered from the chill, rising like plump firm cherries. Her sex swelled as his tongue rode down the slope of her belly. She reached for him, and he was huge, so big he barely fit in her hand. When Lisbeth brought him into that wet, pulsing center, he seemed to expand, grow larger, as she screamed.

Lisbeth rushed in a wave, in a great burst of speed, riding the highway, the finely tuned car flying, tires leaving the pavement, sailing into the emptiness of space. Suspended for an endless second, all breathing ceased, a roaring of the engine thundering through her bloodstream as the brakes screeched. All the parts of Lisbeth's body loosened as with a stupendous, deafening eruption she passed from there to somewhere further on her planetary freeway orbit.

Eventually, in the ashy dark, she arrived, knowing from the absence of that white, burning light that she was no longer in the ICU, that she had, miraculously, yet again, arrived. It took several minutes more before she realized that she was stretched out not in Charlie Morgan's bed but in her own.

When had she left and come downtown? Why?

An arm heavy as dead meat over her waist. Lisbeth cried out, afraid, and pushed the man away. He started to rise, but even before she saw his face she knew it was Neff.

Neff disappeared at dawn. Lisbeth slept, awoke to find her bed empty, and would have imagined that Neff was made up except for the empty champagne bottle on the rug.

She went back to sleep and Charlie called. "Why did you leave?" he asked.

Lisbeth couldn't even remember going, nor how she got down to the Village and Neff. "I'll call you later, Charlie," she said, putting him off. She recalled not Charlie's gentle lovemaking but Neff licking champagne from her breasts, biting the nipples until the hurt became pleasure.

About noon she left the apartment and walked to Sixth Avenue for the *Times*. When she came back she found Gilly Aronberg standing on the front stoop of her brownstone. No one could mistake the producer in his voluminous, dramatic cape that made him look neither like Barrymore nor like Count Dracula, but simply foolish.

"Well, there you are!" he bellowed when Lisbeth was three buildings away. "I was afraid you'd gone back to L.A."

"No, Gilly, I'm right here." Lisbeth climbed the stoop, moving right past him, unlocking the door while he waited.

"You've never given Corbet the rewrites, Lisbeth." Gilly flung off the cape, sent it billowing over a chair, and dropped himself on the sofa. "Any coffee in the pot, sweetie?" he asked.

"No," Lisbeth said.

"No what?" Gilly grappled his way up from the too soft cushion to stand so that he wasn't at a disadvantage with Lisbeth, on her feet, staring down. Lisbeth, knowing so much of Gilly's behavior was calculated playacting, smiled, amused. And yet she recalled all of a sudden, on a plane once, flying into Athens, how her seatmate, a handsome Iranian businessman, advised that in a hijacking you should never get on the ground or the floor, never allow yourself to be humbled, made a victim of. "Look them always straight in the eye," he had confided. "It's much harder to kill you that way."

Gilly was saying, "No coffee or rewrites?"

"No to both."

"Lizzy-bet!" Gilly rolled his eyes.

"We haven't settled our dispute, Gilly, so why should I work my fingers to the bone doing rewrites." Lisbeth went into the kitchen and Gilly pranced behind her. She poured a glass of orange juice from the pitcher in the refrigerator and didn't offer him any. She wanted Gilly gone, far, far away.

"Stalemate, is that what you're saying?" Gilly kept his aging baby face impassive as a mask.

Lisbeth shrugged. "I suppose so, Gilly."

"I'll take *Silver Street* off the boards," he purred softly, as if he weren't uttering a threat.

Lisbeth thought Gilly would lose too much money if he jettisoned *Silver Street,* thought he was shooting his mouth off, trying to fake her. "Go on and do it then," she drawled, eyebrows arched, calling his bluff. But anger speeded up inside her and she felt the promise of the darkness.

"Why, why, oh God why are you acting this way!" Gilly shrieked with theatrical fervor, tugging at his skimpy threads of hair. "What have I ever done to deserve such base treatment! All I want," he howled, trotting on his dainty little feet close up to Lisbeth, tilting his face near to hers so he dissolved into coarse pores, "is to make you famous!"

"Give me a break, Gilly! I'm famous enough already," Lisbeth said calmly, leaning against the sink and sipping her juice. The image she presented was deceptive, however, for she fought to keep her muscles from tensing, to hold her body at ease and thwart that stiffening that seized her before she lost control. Before, Lisbeth thought, the holes in remembering came—nothing burnt out of something—as if the glowing end of a cigarette had been fixed, momentarily, to time.

Gilly found her unbelievable; he told her so.

"I won't have *Silver Street* cheapened," she said. "It's not a movie. There's no reason to pander to every creature in the universe. My one time, Gilly, that's what this play is, to see what I've written, to have *my* vision up there whole."

"How self-indulgent," Gilly said, curling his lip. He glanced around the kitchen. "A whole kitchen, where you can sit down." He nodded toward the tiny butcher block table and went to perch on one of the two little caned chairs. "This apartment must be costing you a mint. How many bedrooms?" He smiled at her avariciously.

"Why, are you thinking of subletting from me?" she asked, trying to sound amused and at the same time douse the anger Gilly was igniting like an autumn bonfire.

Gilly laughed. "No, darling, I have digs over in Murray Hill, have had them for years and years. Just being a nosy bird." He held her gaze, silence ticking away on a Mickey Mouse clock on the counter, until Lisbeth turned about. She put the empty glass in the sink and let the weight of Gilly's presence commandeer the kitchen, accumulate at her back until he pressed in on her like a northern wind.

Clouds gathered in her mind, gray puffs of sky sails. Lisbeth held her breath, down in a deep well.

He said, "You don't need a good box office to live from day to day. It doesn't matter to you or your banker, sweet, if we drag our little ship out to sea or if we sink. Back to Hollywood and more movies. Ah, Lizzy-bet, have you ever known what it is to have bills to pay, or a sick brother eating up the insurance like Corbet's is, or all those actors and actresses waiting on tables between gigs, getting unemployment? No, no, art for art's sake."

"I've paid my dues," Lisbeth said, bent over the sink, unable to look at Gilly just then. She gazed into the shiny steel bottom instead, into the distorted reflection of her own face. She appeared minted, like a coin, and when she pressed a finger against the lips, she felt only the damp cold.

159

"That's nice, Lisbeth. My congratulations. They'll give you a plaque at the Writer's Guild. But I want to make a decent return on my investors' money. I want to be sure of that." Gilly sighed and scraped the chair's legs along the quarry tile.

"What's sure in the universe?" she asked, coming full circle. He was closer to her than she knew, and her hand brushed his sleeve. She thought the wool clawed over her skin like wire shavings.

"That we'll close in a week, maybe two if luck's on our side, unless we add a little punch, something to drag them into the theater without kicking and screaming."

"Stop trying to make me into a thief, Gilly!" she screamed. "I'm not taking food from your mouth or Fleis's, never mind that sick brother's."

"There are no guarantees."

"I never asked for any, Gilly," she breathed painfully.

He shouted, "Well, la de da to you, Lady Astor! But I need a hit."

"Then put on *My Fair Lady* or something by Neil Simon!" Lisbeth heard herself yell from the distance.

Gilly swept the clock from the counter and at full tilt sent it flying on a wide trajectory across the kitchen. It slammed against the wall, crashed to the table, skidded onto the floor.

Without a pause Lisbeth swung at Gilly, catching the side of his skull with her palm. He staggered in a little two-step, and Lisbeth's hands found his throat. They grabbed hold of Gilly Aronberg's neck as though it were the stalk of a plant. And they squeezed. Surprisingly, for all his marshmallow softness, Gilly's neck was tough cartilage, and Lisbeth couldn't snap it like a twig. Which she might have meant to do, or perhaps she intended nothing more than to shake him for his insolence, for being such an annoyance and rousing a beastly pain, a storm of oncoming forgetfulness. But she couldn't know, or not for sure, because there was only the sensation of Gilly's talcumed skin beneath her fingertips, nothing else. Lisbeth had no consciousness of choking Gilly Aronberg, perhaps to death, nor was she aware of how or when he exerted surprising strength and broke free of her grip. But suddenly curtains like those hanging across a proscenium whipped apart, and she saw Gilly staggering on his tiny feet in their shiny penny loafers through the living room and out of the apartment.

Lisbeth rushed out of the front door and half down the steps as Gilly whipped along Tenth Street. "God damn you!" she shrieked, stiffness gripping her face as if she'd been shot full of novocaine. Her whole skull was encased in an iron mask.

Gilly stopped and whirled around. "You're crazy! Mad as the

March Hare! No, worse! Elizabeth Rosenthal!'' For all his hysteria and insults, it was Lisbeth's old name that he flung vituperatively along the shady street like a curse.

He clenched his fists, stamped at the sidewalk as if to gouge a hole in the concrete, his cheeks fiery red and his eyes brimming with terror. Even from the distance, midway along the steps, Lisbeth, painfully aware of each object now—the cars and the people on foot, lampposts, the stoops and iron fences fronting the brownstones, the sidewalks, the trees and their outstretched limbs—even with so many things, human and otherwise, impinging on her, Lisbeth saw Gilly's eyes. They had the black, bottomless depths to them of terror.

Later, Lisbeth's mother phoned and reminded her she'd been invited to dinner. "You promised to come."

"Did I?" Lisbeth asked, having forgotten. She was at the dining table in the alcove, the play separated into scenes spread out before her. Gilly's acquiescence, given by Corbert in a whispering, reluctant voice over the phone, set her to making the last of the changes for the end of *Silver Street* and she'd been moving from the Selectric on the desk to the table. Tighten, shorten a scene, add a longish speech of exposition, give the male lead a snappier line of dialogue just before the end. Corbert's suggestions, and Lisbeth agreed. The director had an eye; he saw what she missed.

"We see no more of you since you live in the Village than we did when you were in Los Angeles," her mother complained.

Lisbeth's eyelids twitched. Anne Rosenthal's voice, neither strident nor obtrusive but rather upper-class indifferent, spun a spiral of pain through Lisbeth's skull.

We, Lisbeth heard again. *We* meant that stepfather, so timid a man half dead in a wheelchair, gasping away what little life remained, leaning toward oblivion, poised at the doorway where he'd hesitated for years now. What did Paul Morell care if he ever saw her or not? He possessed enough children of his own in Argentina, three sons, a daughter living, another incinerated. Lisbeth thought she had to be a blight on this unwanted refugee from France to South America in thirty-nine, on his marriage to wealthy Anne Rosenthal, no matter how he smiled and complimented her talent. "How proud to have a picture maker!" Paul Morell would say. "Now a play! We look forward, Lisbeth." He always slurred her name, the "i" to "e," the "s" hissed to a "z." Unlike her mother, Paul Morell never called her Elizabeth.

Yet for all the years of that resented marriage, Lisbeth said silently, *You're no relation to me*.

Her mother, who swore she'd never marry again, married Paul Morell only a month before Lisbeth went to Tijuana one moon-washed night with Billy Reynolds. They traveled fast, seventy, eighty miles an hour all the way, the top back on the Mercedes, the wind stinging her eyes. Twice they got tickets, the first just past the Los Angeles county line, the second entering San Diego. Billy laughed and sang cowboy songs, an aria from Verdi, the entire *Yellow Submarine*. Lisbeth kept thinking of her mother in Buenos Aires marrying some unknown man with a crooked left leg, short and looking undernourished in the snapshot Anne sent. Paul Morell's features in his swarthy, bony face were faint, undescribable, not at all like Ferris Rosenthal's. He had the haunted look of someone who had barely escaped. Long distance, Anne whispered that his stories were horrible.

In that picture they stood, her mother and Paul Morell, before a high, narrow window cast with thin, vertical stripes of shadow like the bars of a cage.

"Only twenty minutes late," her mother said when Lisbeth got off the elevator. She waited, the door held open, a bemused smile on her still-attractive face. For all her troubles, past and present—a husband only a bundle of sticks, wheezing and chronically short of breath, drowning in his own fluids—Anne Rosenthal made it a point to look her best. The years had faded but not burnt away her beauty.

"Sorry. I'm in the middle of rewrites."

"It doesn't matter," she said, eyebrows raised, meaning it did. Still, Anne lifted up her face and Lisbeth laid cold lips against the silky cheek. Her mother smelled of lilacs.

How small she was, Lisbeth thought, and how much smaller she was becoming, dwindling, folding up like a lady's fan.

Anne asked, "How's the play?" She closed the door behind Lisbeth and nudged her toward the living room. That would be where Paul Morell waited. When she thought of her stepfather Lisbeth used his whole name, as if otherwise she might forget him entirely. Yet there were moments when he trailed through her memory like a ghost, a living wraith among the dead.

"Ah, here at last! Such a stranger!" Even Paul Morell's voice sounded watery. It's a curse, this disease, Anne repeatedly lamented, meaning the emphysema. It was destroying his lungs, turning them into pulp, and would eventually kill the meager man in the wheelchair. His skin was stretched in tawny leather over the plains and crevices, creped in an underhang below the sharply jutting chin. He existed like a bare, leafless winter tree, seeming more dead than alive, but underneath, in some hidden recess, life pulsed urgently. Paul Morell hung on tenaciously past his time.

Behind the wheelchair, on a shelf like a luggage rack attached to the frame, rode an oxygen tank. A tube with a black mask resembling a largish suction cup lay draped over the dying man's shoulder. Often he'd crouch with the mask to his mouth, almond eyes peering above the top, sad and surprised as he sucked in another moment of life. Lisbeth imagined his thoughts at those moments, gray and hideous, of the gas chamber in which his older brother and parents died, his grandparents too, and innumerable distant cousins.

He is even now, Anne wrote in that letter, more dead than alive.

Was that why she married him? Was she guilty for surviving, living out the Holocaust time high in the clouds, so above everything? Lisbeth wondered. Luxurious, that had been Anne's life when other Jews were being paraded naked under ashen skies to a crowded death in the gas chambers. It could have been otherwise. Only luck gave her mother Fifth Avenue and Paul Morell's relatives Auschwitz.

Lisbeth maintained a judicious distance between herself and this man her mother married. She kept an emptiness in her heart that she would not let him fill no matter what he did or how hard he tried. *For no reason,* she thought. *I don't dislike him any more than I like him. He is just not there.* But he was and she did her best to ignore him.

Perhaps Anne waited too long to remarry and Lisbeth simply accepted her mother as she was, like a cold, unchanging star. Whatever the reason, when Anne wrote I love Paul, Lisbeth replied, I don't believe you. There was no answer to such bluntness, or not for a long, long while. Eventually Anne Rosenthal shattered the silence, but by the time she did Lisbeth had built a high wall of resentment. She believed the chilliness between them was her mother's fault or was because of Paul.

Lisbeth strolled around the vast living room that her father in his laughing way had called the parlor. "My little fly," he'd say, and hug her on the couch. The Chinese rug had faded, the vividness worn away in spots. Lisbeth saw her young self tumble about it with Ferris Rosenthal. She heard their laughter, and it teased a pain in her temples.

"Now, tell us news of the play," Paul said, rolling slowly after her, a tight grimace manacling his mouth in what passed for a smile. He cornered her into sitting on an art nouveau upholstered armchair, the velvet brushing the back of her legs. "Rehearsals going good, yes?"

He was childishly wide-eyed about the theater and bragged, Anne told Lisbeth, to his family in Buenos Aires about "our celebrity." He was certain *Silver Street* was going to be a huge success.

163

"Need any help with dinner?" Lisbeth asked Anne foolishly, for her mother seldom set foot in the kitchen.

Anne laughed. "Of course not! Cook will serve in a few minutes now that you're here. Roast chicken. New potatoes. Broccoli. Salad. I hope that suits you, Elizabeth."

"Fine. Whatever."

In the antiseptic atmosphere of the room, draperies clutched tightly over nighttime windows, shadows weaving in the moldings around the ceiling, the women found little to say to one another, less even than traveling strangers. If they'd ever been close, time and death and their disparate life-styles pushed them to opposite shores of an unbridgeable ocean. Anne Rosenthal, in tones of pink and ivory, curly silver hair shaped close to her scalp, vivid green eyes twin to Lisbeth's own, no longer tried. Her thoughts and life were devoted to pleasing the man in the wheelchair, the pitiful wreck whose only connection to the world was a plastic tube to a tank of air.

Lisbeth's jaw ached from clenching her teeth.

"You look thinnish," Anne complained. "Tired, too."

A pillowy woman in white, colorless hair scraped back and pinned in a knot, appeared just inside the living room. "Can I see you for a minute, Mrs. Morell?"

Lisbeth crossed to the fire blazing in the fireplace, hands outstretched as Anne followed the cook out of the room. Nearer the hearth the heat billowed and the room suddenly felt like a tropical jungle. Lisbeth swayed, light-headed from the fire flaming orange and yellow, and to the side Paul sat dwarfed in his chair like an ancient version of a Cabbage Patch doll. Without a word she rushed to the outer wing of the apartment and her old room.

Here it was chilly as she passed through the darkness to the long rectangle of window hung against the black walls like a movie screen. Looking out she saw a long-ago film of the fairy-tale kingdom.

Oh Daddy, how beautiful it all is! The diamond lights.

Some day it will all be yours, Ferris Rosenthal whispered behind her. And Elizabeth sighed, placing her palms on the glass, blowing cloudy circles over the park, the streets in ribbons, the starry buildings, like sugar castles.

Time passed, then Lisbeth inched back, feeling for the rocker, for her father, ready to climb in his lap. But she banged her hip against something solid that shouldn't have been there and cried out.

In the shadowy room monsters seemed to hulk everywhere. They clung bundled in the bed, danced on the tops of the dresser, scampered along the carpeting. All those dream monsters who'd wake the little

Elizabeth screaming from sleep suddenly crowded the room. But there was no Ferris Rosenthal to soothe her. Loss rushed over her along with the remembered fears. Lisbeth backed against the wall, fumbling for the light switch.

Where am I? She forgot that the room had been changed, done over long before, and expected in that first moment when the light exploded to find the lovely trundle bed, the rocking chair, the shelves with her books and lacy-gowned dolls. Gone was the old room, buried now in time and memory, along with Ferris Rosenthal.

I want my father! The child's voice rang in Lisbeth's head, and she remembered night after night going to bed believing it could have been a lie, that Ferris could be alive and well somewhere.

She waited until she was sixteen and then, though she had only a learner's permit, Lisbeth secretly took Anne's Cadillac and drove out to the Long Island cemetery. Her mother had put her father in the ground and left him there. Or had she? Lisbeth wondered, sitting on the soft grass.

The stone was wide, a smooth brown marble speckled with flecks of gold that reflected the sunlight. Ferris Rosenthal born, died. The grave itself mounded only slightly, and when Lisbeth stirred the grass on top, it felt no different from that to the side. Earth, rocks, lay underneath.

She heard her mother crying, *Forget it, him. Get on with life!*

Lies, Lisbeth knew, were told all the time. Lies were a kind of currency that her friends used with one another, in school, at home. Truth, on the other hand, was sparse, and there were degrees of it. Often, too, people did their best, for whatever obscure reasons, to hide the truth. No one was ever sure of anything, which didn't surprise Lisbeth six months after John Kennedy died. One man with a rifle? Never! The KGB, the CIA, the FBI, the Mafia, the Cubans, several, or at least one other on the grassy knoll back in November. Conspiracy was rife in Lisbeth's world, so why wasn't it possible that Ferris Rosenthal hadn't died, that his death and burial were deceptions?

This corner of the big cemetery was deserted on the warm, spring afternoon. Lisbeth stretched out upon the grave and concentrated, willing a narrow tunnel through the layers of dirt. An inner eye traveled in the dark earth and all at once she saw the coffin. Stones or maybe a scarecrow in Daddy's best suit, the eleven-year-old in Lisbeth's memory howled. But she pierced through wood and tufted satin to her father, shrunken and yellow, waxy, inhuman.

Lisbeth would always believe that by some magic trick or a psychic talent she had actually seen Ferris Rosenthal, as dead as dead could be, lying under a ton of dirt in his coffin, saw him as surely as she did the blue sky when she rolled on her back and the blossoming clouds sailed overhead in schooners.

Lisbeth remembered the clouds, the swoosh of traffic beyond the cemetery, the feel of the breeze stirring her hair, then the trip back on the Long Island Expressway. But once home, she forgot her father, the grave, the earth. She had a fever; she was sick. She slept and slept, and surfaced only when her mother forced her awake long enough to drink water, fruit juices, whatever medicine the doctor ordered. In a week or two she returned to school and never again thought of her father alive.

"Lisbeth, are you all right? You ran off when I thought we could have a little talk," Paul said. Moving by instinct she must have fled out into the hall and back into the living room.

"And just what do you think we have to talk about? The stock market? The state of the country? International affairs? Or the theater maybe? Yes, you'd like me to sit and tell you lots of theater gossip, Hollywood gossip, little tidbits you and my mother could pass on!" Her anger, her disappointment that once again it was *now* rather than *then,* and she was grown, that more of life trailed behind than beckoned with promise ahead, made her strike out. The pain crawled up her cheeks and dug with grappling hooks into her temples. Pain and anger mixed and Lisbeth wanted to tear at the past as if it were a sand castle, as if she could destroy and rebuild.

"What do you mean?" Paul asked, the tendons in his neck tightening. He pulled upward, then fell limp and started to whistle. Only it wasn't a tune, but a thin spindrift of air and spittle seeping through his lips. When he inhaled the sound grated and dragged. His skin paled, tinted an icy blue. His eyeballs started to protrude and his hands flew about his chest in frantic gull motions.

"Tank . . . oxygen," he wheezed, twisting, a loose arm flopping for the back of the wheelchair, straining to grasp the mask. He struggled for the air that would come flowing down the long plastic tube. Sweat beaded on his brow in shiny droplets.

He was a flailing, gasping thing, a fishlike being flung ashore, beached in the metal chair, wanting Lisbeth to do something, but she couldn't think what. A mist separated her from it, white trailing streamers crossing a black pit of emptiness into which she was being sucked as she watched the thing, halfway to the carpet now, slung over the shiny arm, tiny little feet in patent leather dancing slippers tap-tapping against the footrest, the music atonal as it fell and lay not on the Chinese pattern of tangled vines and miniature fire-breathing dragons but on snow.

Oh yes, she screamed, staggering backward, *kicking up flurries, it's so cold! All that snow. And the monster in the middle of it with the handle sticking out of its chest.*

"Ooooooooo!" The scream tore a wound through Lisbeth's head, a pathway into the bone and gray swirls. A steel rod might have been stuck into her skull, as, weakening, she descended not into the soft white cottony drifts, but on the sofa as Anne came running.

"Paul! Oh my God! Elizabeth, help me! Elizabeth, why didn't you do something? Why didn't you give him his mask?" Anne wept, throwing herself beside the crumpled heap of clothes and snatching the tube with the mask, jamming it over Paul's mouth. These images played before Lisbeth in a montage, one collapsing into another, blurring until tiny dots of color peppered her vision.

"Paul, please, breathe! Yes . . . that's it. Again!" Anne's tears clung to her cheeks in icicles.

Paul's skin tone lightened from mauve to pink, and his limbs relaxed, his chest stopped its frantic heaving.

Carefully Anne stretched him out, his head elevated in the well of her lap as the withered heart beneath the starched white shirt ceased to struggle and staggered once more into its normal, ailing beat.

When Paul could get enough air into his ravaged lungs without the mask, Anne sagged and turned a face of fury on her daughter. "You almost killed him!" she swore.

"No, *ma chérie,* please, it is all right," Paul whispered.

Lisbeth clawed out of the sofa, trying to catch her own breath. The mists swirled slowly and spun along the oriental rug, out of the room. "It happened so quickly," she said, not even sure what had. Paul was sprawled on the floor, Anne at his side. "I'd better go." And she ran, in the hall calling out to the kitchen, "Cook, come right away, they need you!" Then she was gone, entering a blackness, going nowhere she remembered afterwards.

13

Having exhausted all the job possibilities she could think of in West-port without landing a future source of income, much to Lisbeth's disbelief—"You should have turned up *something,* Di!"—Dinah jour-neyed into the city. So be it, I'll have to commute, she groaned as the train lurched in a shuffling stop-and-start motion through the suburbs.

Dinah had almost convinced herself that working in New York wasn't as awful as cancer. All she needed was the right attitude to make it a positive experience. *Chin up,* her father always said, and *Rain before the rainbow.* Even out in the dizzying maelstrom of mid-Manhattan where in her previous working life she thrived like a weed, she forced herself to feel purposeful, to stride through the crowds like a woman on her way someplace exciting, in her Alexan-der's Chanel copy that hid the worst bulges and was so out of date it had come full circle back into fashion.

The first of the employment agencies on the lengthy list she had copied from the Yellow Pages insisted on Dinah's taking a typing test, which she huffily refused to do; and the second was so mobbed with females, most of whom were dewy and pink cheeked, she'd have had to wait at least an hour and a half. The next agency and the one after that found her "old" experience too far in the past: one interviewer, with red hair in Rastafarian braids, had been born the year Dinah graduated from Cabot. Jobs Galore, a more upbeat group of sunshiny women in glass modern offices, cheerfully added Dinah's name and particulars to their roster, but they weren't too optimistic. A young woman with glittery braces on her teeth suggested Dinah not get her hopes up. "You're so unfocused it will be difficult to slot you."

At one-fifteen Dinah, feet burning from their unaccustomed pound-ing on concrete, her skirt wrinkled, and an ink smear on the cuff of her blouse, bought a hot dog with everything and a Diet Pepsi from a wagon in front of the public library. Though it was a chilly gray day with the raw feel of rain in the air, Dinah sat on a bench in Bryant Park chewing slowly, not for her digestion, but to drag out these few minutes before she hit Executive Placement on Forty-fourth Street.

Dinah had now tried five employment agencies since disembarking from the train and not one suggested sending her out to interview for a job. Surely a company existed that could utilize her talents. *What talents?* she thought despairingly. Rejection did nothing to motivate her into trying harder; rejection had her fantasizing about crawling into the empty kingsize bed and yanking the covers over her head.

Initially, the afternoon promised to be an improvement over the morning. "EP," as the search team assistant familiarly referred to the agency, had nothing for Dinah, who wasn't "in their track," but Twelve Star Careers hurried her over to a market research company to discuss an opening for an executive liaison officer, whatever that was. Dinah lasted ten minutes before the personnel manager, a prissy little bantam of a man in a double-breasted suit, got her to admit she had no idea what market researchers did.

The rest of the day collapsed in a mudslide. Though Dinah left her resume with another half dozen agencies, no one was optimistic. Her lack of experience in the last fifteen years and her age militated against her, though the latter was hinted at rather than baldly stated because of recent suits brought for age discrimination. Dinah's volunteer work, bogus or not, failed to impress the hard-boiled New Yorkers. Money earned mattered in the Big Apple, and giving away one's time and talents was considered bizarre except for women in the social register. "A big salary and an important title are what counts," one agent told her, not unkindly. By five o'clock, Dinah was beginning to face facts; the only career opportunity she had looming before her was suicide.

She planned to have dinner with Quinn on the upper East Side, but she called from the only working pay phone within ten blocks of Grand Central and begged off. "I'm worn to a frazzle and too depressed to eat," Dinah told Quinn, not bothering to add that Quinn's having a firm, useful place in society depressed her even further. Dinah had to cover her exposed ear to hear what Quinn was saying, and then she barely caught a dangling phrase about something next week. Damn the cost, she'd call Quinn later from Westport.

Once again on the train, this time standing because the 6:09 was packed with commuters, Dinah shuddered at the idea that she'd have to do this tomorrow and the day after that, every weekday, in fact, until she captured that elusive creature, a job. Then she'd be sentenced to this trek, as bone rattling as a Conestoga across the prairies, for the rest of her natural life, unless, of course, she won the lottery. Dinah, crammed

169

into the aisle of the 6:09, vowed there and then to play the lottery religiously.

By the time her car eased along the Westport platform, her mind was blank and her legs might have been amputated because she no longer felt them. She walked on faith off the train, down the steps, and across the parking lot to her station wagon.

"I could eat a live cow, tail and all," Mikey barked as he burst through the door thirty seconds after his mother. Dinah hadn't even had the time to pour herself a stiff vodka for medicinal purposes, though she'd advanced as far as the liquor cabinet and was holding a bottle of Stoly aloft. "What's for dinner?" he asked, kissing the air somewhere in Dinah's vicinity.

"Your hair's still wet," Dinah said.

" 'Cause I've been swimming."

"You're supposed to dry it before you go outside so you don't catch a cold or something worse," she huffed, thinking, despite her strong maternal instinct, of doctor bills.

"Mom"—Mikey raised his voice as though she'd gone deaf—"what's for dinner?"

"Nothing yet. I just got home from the city."

"Great! Let's go out to eat!" Mikey had a successful career ahead of him as a restaurant critic. About the only trait that he inherited from his father, as far as Dinah could thankfully tell, was this business about eating away from home.

"Money . . ." Dinah hissed.

"Ah, c'mon, Mom, I'll settle for Burger King." He grinned at her winningly, as if he could charm her into agreeing, which he could and did. Dinah found herself, drinkless, directed up the stairs with orders to be quick in changing clothes because Mikey was going to die in the front hall from starvation.

Burger King had a line out the front door and around the sidewalk. "Either the food's improved or everybody's dead broke," Dinah said, idling the wagon in the parking lot. There wasn't one free slot into which she could pull the car. "Let's go home. I don't want to wait. We'll be here until Christmas."

"What about the mall? That way we can have our choice of junk food," Mikey pleaded.

"Mikey . . ."

"Ah, Mom, you know you're goofy about that Sicilian pizza they sell."

It was true, the thick crust gave her more of a sense of biting into something substantial, and it was less greasy, which probably equalized the calories with the regular stuff. "Well . . ." She hesitated, thinking how much she'd enjoy anything comforting. Food was dangerous when she felt depressed, but just one more time couldn't hurt. Besides, she'd taken off four pounds, hopefully straight from the hips. The pizza, at most, would only put back two, and she'd been about to eat a burger anyway. "I must be crazy. I'm too fat and dead broke, so we shouldn't be spending money. We should be growing our own food in the back yard," Dinah said, but she swung the car around and headed out for the highway.

"It's October," Mikey reminded her. "You can't plant a garden just before winter."

From the backseat Becky nuzzled Dinah's neck with a moist nose. "Get down," Mikey said, not even having to swivel his head to know what the Airedale was up to. The dog was a creature of habit, and every time the car started rolling she'd slurp whoever was driving in gratitude. It sent Hatch wacky, but no matter how he yelled and threatened, the next light brought Becky up beside his ear.

"Rebecca will have to stay in the car," Dinah said.

"So? She'd have to at Burger King."

"It will take us longer at the mall, all that walking and those escalators. Then we'll probably stop to look in some stores, but no buying anything. Promise?"

"Promise," Mikey replied solemnly. Dinah still wasn't sure her fourteen-year-old got the message that money was at an all-time low. Hatch continued to pay the bills, but was decidedly reluctant to fork over any ready cash.

A full moon hung in the sky like a decal and a skeletal parade of birches stood lateral to a stubbled field and waved their bony limbs. "Halloween's around the corner," Dinah said as she speeded up, the highway unfolding ahead of the station wagon in a frosted ribbon that had no end to it. How far could they travel in the dark before they reached the dawn? Some urge inside Dinah encouraged her to try it, to just keep doing a steady fifty-five, but there had been few impulses in her lifetime that she'd followed up. Back at Cabot it had been different. The East, when she came out of endless flat Nebraska, loosened some interior bindings, and for a little while Dinah Esterman was regarded as impetuous. During her marriage to Hatch, however, she went from running at full throttle to idling. Being a suburban wife and mother had drained her. Her energy and high spirits leaked away until she became what she most often felt like, a statistic.

"I'm too old for Halloween, all that silly stuff about ghosts and goblins,'' Mikey was saying as they entered the parking area and found a place up near the sprawling building.

"Well, there goes one of my two honest-to-God volunteer commitments,'' Dinah said, locking the car. She left the driver's window open a notch so Becky would have air. The Airedale, already whining, pressed a furry face up against the glass, marble eyes wide and staring with unhappiness. *Always left behind, just like me,* Dinah thought.

Few people were wandering around the mall, though the stores were open until nine, and Dinah heard her footsteps and Mikey's echoing as they trotted along the west wing of the first level to the escalators bunched in the center. The restaurants and food stands were on the third floor. As they rode up from the second level, the pools and fountains splashing below them, Dinah saw Joe Connors, a shopping bag looped off one wrist, descending on the moving stairs. At the moment they passed one another, two '68 Cadillac lengths apart, their glances crossed and snagged like a hook and eye.

"Joe Connors!'' Dinah cried as he slipped by her, as he raised his shopping bag in an awkward salute. He turned to watch her rise up and away.

"What?'' Mikey asked, but Dinah didn't answer.

At the top of the escalator, Dinah said, "Go see what you want. I'll be back in a minute.''

"Mom!''

Dinah was already hustling over to the down escalator. She searched the next level for Joe Connors as it glided down. *Damn! I've lost him,* she thought, wanting to find him because he'd been her one "almost" job. He'd also been kind. Maybe—Dinah crossed her fingers—if luck shines, something else opened up in his agency.

Dinah discovered him finally in the opening of a large bookstore, idly leafing through a paperback, shifting from one leg to the other as if his pants were too tight. Surreptitiously he threw quick glances over his shoulder toward the escalators. Dinah, who couldn't imagine he might be waiting for her, was afraid to blink. In an instant he could be swallowed up in the huge cavern, sucked into one of the cavelike stores.

When the stairs flattened at last and Dinah was deposited at the second level, she lost sight of her quarry momentarily, now hidden behind a vast tangle of indoor vegetation. But when she hurried around the greenery, she saw Joe Connors still in the same place, though he'd put the book back in the cardboard dump and was reaching for another.

"Mr. Connors!'' Dinah cried. He didn't look quite as she remembered him. For one thing he dressed more casually out of the office, in jeans and a turtleneck and an expensive suede jacket. He seemed furrier, too, his hair scant at the forehead and curling about his ears in wings. His jaw was shadowed with sooty bristles. *He has to shave twice a day,* Dinah thought, ridiculously pleased by this meaningless fact.

Dinah offered up a smile, the first after a day with personnel ladies that was entirely sincere.

Joe Connors, all interest in books put aside, smiled too, a bit sheepishly. He was taller than she had thought, hovering several inches above her, and slightly stooped, as if his height burdened him.

"Hello. Nice to see you again."

"It's nice to see you too, Mr. Connors."

The amenities over with, the two middle-aged strangers shuffled about in embarrassment. No reasonable idea drifted into Dinah's mind except the hope that the floor would open up and give her an escape. Why had she ever come chasing down here after this man?

Joe Connors wasn't any better at creating instant, trivial conversation. He opened his mouth once or twice, but only air emerged.

"Shopping?" Dinah finally asked, an unnatural froggy croak in her voice.

"Only a few things." He held up the shopping bag dangling from one wrist. "You?"

"No, no. My son and I just stopped in for a quick meal. A night out, ha ha, from the kitchen."

"Oh, well, don't let me keep you."

"It's all right, really."

The little spurt of conversation made them heady, at the same time wearing them out, and they once more lapsed into a tricky silence. How long they might have stood there without saying another word they'd never know, for Mikey trundled up on his mother's flank, his Reebok laces trailing, swinging his long teenager's orangutan arms, peeved to be kept from his food. "Mom, are we going to eat or not?" he asked, his eyebrows settling into a vee of annoyance.

Quickly Dinah introduced the two males. "Mr. Connors, this is my son, Mikey."

Mikey allowed his hand to be squeezed by this interloper who'd captured his mother's attention, dragging her away from her duty, which was to feed him. Like a young animal in the brush, Mikey sensed danger on the wind. He peered suspiciously at this adult. A noise far down in his throat, like a warning growl, was Mikey's only reply when Joe Connors said, "Pleased to meet you."

"Mom, let's eat, okay?"

"Hey, you two go on. I don't want to hold you up," Joe Connors said, backing off.

Dinah breathlessly found herself asking, "Would you like to join us for a hamburger or some pizza?" Such forwardness quite excited her.

Joe Connors's face lit up. Mikey snorted behind his mother's left shoulder, but Dinah paid him no attention. Neither did Joe Connors when he said, "If you don't mind the company, that would be great. I honestly hate to eat alone."

Somehow they all got into motion, heading for the escalator. "Why don't you eat with your wife?" Dinah asked, thinking herself foxy sly. Memories of being single flickered on and off in her head.

"Because I'm divorced, that's why I don't eat with my wife," Joe Connors said, chivalrously standing aside to let Dinah get on the escalator ahead of him. Three steps down from Joe's back Mikey sulked in icy aloofness, his arms crossed over his chest.

Up on the third level Dinah and Joe, after some consideration, decided on Chinese food. Much more slimming, Dinah reminded herself, and she needn't worry about shoving a slab of greasy, dripping pizza into her mouth in front of a strange man.

Mikey got two hamburgers, a large order of fries, and a milk shake, all of which he downed in record time, eager to put space between this couple, one part of it being his mother, and himself. "I'm going to wander around," he said, scooping up his trash. "Meet you here in twenty minutes." He seemed for all his gawkiness more the parent than the child, and sent his mother a harsh, disapproving look that she airily deflected with a wave of her hand.

"Okay," Dinah replied, and continued saying to Joe Connors, ". . . and of course I do have options so I'm taking my time."

He had asked her about the job search and Dinah was presenting him with an imaginary, upbeat version as they ate. Nimbly, Joe Connors lifted awkward strands of noodles from his plate with chopsticks while Dinah used a fork for her fried rice. She wouldn't dare run the risk of dropping half the dinner in her lap.

"It's better not to rush a commitment," he said.

Dinah, though eager to fly into any situation that paid her a decent wage, nodded her head in agreement. "Oh, you are so right. Taking one's time is . . . is *grown-up!*"

"Hmmmm," he said, bush brows rising. A lump of chicken disappeared between his lips. Joe Connors chewed with his mouth slightly agape, in a way Dinah's mother would disapprove of. Still, Dinah found the man at the other side of the rickety little Formica-topped table quite good-looking. He had the dark sexiness of a terrorist.

Dinah wished he had hired her because she ached to settle down with a salary, to remove herself from treadmill days like today, but, and she couldn't deny it, also because Joe Connors was an attractive single man. Maybe there lingered some chance. . . .

"I'm sorry I didn't get the job with you," she said. "I'd have loved working at your agency. It seemed such a, oh, I don't know, such a dynamic place."

The compliment pleased him and he started to speak at the same moment a mound of noodles passed into his mouth. He coughed and choked; his eyes ran. Hastily Dinah pushed his root beer into his hand. "Are you okay?"

A few seconds passed before he could hoarsely say, "Just something going down the wrong way."

Don't talk with your mouth full, Dinah could have told him. "Do you want me to get you some water?"

"I'm fine, really."

Dinah leaned forward. "Do you think something else might open up? My square edges accommodate to any round hole, honestly."

Joe Connors broke into another fit of coughing. When this new spasm subsided, he angled the chopsticks across his plate, obviously deciding it was no longer safe to eat. He said, "Ah, well, I'm not sure."

"Is something wrong?" All of a sudden Dinah had a premonition that she hadn't lost the job to someone with more experience. "I mean, you would have hired me, wouldn't you, if a woman, or maybe it was a man, didn't come along with better qualifications? Mr. Connors?"

"Call me Joe."

"You were interested in giving me a job, Joe, or was I mistaken?"

"Dinah . . ." He looked stricken.

"What?"

"I wish you hadn't brought that up. That was business, this is pleasure."

"Why didn't you hire me?" Dinah practically shouted.

Joe Connors swallowed. "Your resume, with the list of all those charities. Minnie, my secretary, said that at least three of them don't exist."

"Oh shit!"

They stared at one another in dismay. Joe Connors was as upset about Dinah's lies as if the fabrications were his own. "I honestly was going to offer that job to you, but Minnie became so indignant. I mean it's not like you had your hand in the till on your last job." He apparently forgot that the last time Dinah received a paycheck was a millennium or two ago. "I mean, everybody puffs themselves up a bit on paper. It's human nature."

Dinah was so still, her body obviously continuing to occupy the chair, though her mind had flown. Joe Connors hesitated in the hope she'd say something but no words emerged. Gently he reached over and patted her hand. "Look, Dinah, I thought, I mean think, that you have just the right qualities for our agency, but Minnie is such a damn gossip that if I had hired you she would spread it all over the shop about your resume. Then all the wagging tongues would say I hired you for some other reason."

"What other reason?" Dinah asked, staring at a spot in the middle of his forehead so that while her eyes aimed in his direction, he saw nothing but a glazed, outer covering.

The deep silence that fell lengthened until it threatened to shatter like glass under an imponderable weight. "What reason?" she hissed, shifting her anger from Lisbeth and her own foolishness to him. She bared her teeth as if she meant to snap like Becky at a cat.

He gulped. Dinah hadn't heard any male gulp since high school. "Minnie thought I'd been taken with you personally, more than the other women I interviewed. Of course, one must have weighed two hundred pounds, and another, just out of junior college with the worst case of acne I've ever seen. A few were just ordinary. And then, you."

Dinah's gaze traveled down the bridge of Joe Connors's nose until they were eyeballing one another. "Are you a pervert?" Dinah asked seriously.

Joe Connors roared. He laughed so hard that, tipping back on the frail chair, he almost bowled himself over. "God no! Or at least I don't think so. Actually I'm probably conservative, in that area anyway."

"It certainly seems perverted to me, making fun of a poor female with no money, no job, left out in the cold by a crazed midlife husband, and with a dependent child to support!" As always, when Dinah found herself in the wrong, she attacked. She yelled so loudly, waving her arms in the process, that everybody eating at this end of the open floor turned to stare. Bright spots of anger burnt on her cheeks, and her eyes shot off electrical sparks. With her dark hair wildly disheveled because she had tugged at it, and in a vividly printed blouse and a wide black skirt, she looked like a mad gypsy.

As Dinah rose from her chair without leaving it completely, Joe Connors leaned forward, reaching out, trying to hold her in place as he cried, "Dinah! I'm sorry. I didn't mean . . ."

Dinah knew her mouth was working faster than her brain, and that she should draw herself up smartly, making a dignified, ladylike exit, but she tumbled, helter-skelter on a downward slide, unable, to her increasing horror, to stop herself.

Somehow Joe Connors had captured her hands, but she yanked free. "What's funny to you is a life-and-death matter to me. Food in the fridge and a roof over our heads!" she seethed. She started to push the table back, the mists of fury having cleared enough for her to make her escape, but somehow, as she always seemed to do in life, she miscalculated. The large plate still partially filled with a Chinese combination got mysteriously dislodged from the table and Dinah saw it sitting in her lap.

I will die, she thought, rice and noodles, plus the vegetables and bits of pork all over the front of her moving with her agitated breath like a nest of insects. Utter humiliation silenced Dinah at last and made her head droop.

"Here, let me help you clean that up," Joe Connors offered, thrusting out a wad of napkins.

"Go away," she snapped, "just go away."

"Listen, I'll get some water, so—"

"Disappear this minute before I start screaming rape!" Dinah choked, tears in her eyes, wanting nothing more than the source of her humiliation, Joe Connors, gone.

"Well . . . if you really don't need . . . ah, I guess then . . . yeah, okay." "I'm sorry," she thought she heard him whisper again before he fled, but she didn't care.

Dinah's fits of bad temper were only occasional storms that blew up to dissolve almost at once. But Mikey, who found his mother in the station wagon with Becky half in her lap, knew enough to wait until the fit passed before he asked her what was wrong. They drove home in silence, but the silence had a leaden feel to it, like the thick air before a tornado.

Dinah's anger would have cooled by the time they arrived at the colonial if she hadn't entered the house and suddenly, sniffing, strode into the living room, looked around and cried, "Your father's been here!"

At the foot of the stairs Mikey stopped. "How do you know?"

How did she? Dinah's eyes closed down into narrow slits and she sniffed the air again like a bird dog, as if she actually caught Hatch's scent. Becky who smelled nothing, lacking for some reason this canine trait, slunk under the coffee table expecting to be hidden by the glass top.

177

Slowly turning in a circle, her arms extended as if she found it hard to maintain equilibrium, Dinah stopped before she completed the whole one hundred and eighty degrees, pointing dramatically at the bookcase. "There!" she shrilled.

Mikey came to stand beside her. "There what?" he asked.

"It's gone!"

Mikey peered closer, following his mother's finger. "What is? Oh," he said, advancing toward the far wall. "The barometer's not hanging where it always does."

Hatch once found an old ship's barometer at an outdoor flea market. "For when I set off to sea," he'd joke. *Well, he certainly had gone to sea now,* Dinah thought, running through the rooms to see what else her about-to-be-ex-husband had wandered off with. As she searched, definite holes appeared in the fabric of the house. A lithograph from their bedroom and a watercolor from the downstairs bath were both missing, leaving anemic rectangles on the walls. The shelves displayed gaps like an eight-year-old's teeth, where books had been and were no more. It took Dinah a full shocked minute to realize that both bedside lamps were gone as well as the old patchwork quilt draped over a rocking chair. All of Hatch's drawers were empty. Only dust balls floated around them and one mateless sock, which brought a rush of tears to Dinah's eyes. She clutched the crumpled scrap of black wool to her breasts and bowed her head.

In the kitchen Dinah couldn't believe her eyes. The Cuisinart no longer stood on the long butcher block counter next to the Braun coffee maker. But then the coffee maker was also among the missing.

The wine! Dinah remembered all at once and flew to the basement steps where, Scotch-taped to the door, she discovered Hatch's first note.

"I see you finally got around to having the hedges cut. In the dark they look pretty good. Hopefully in the light they still look trim which will mean you hired somebody other than Mr. Alonzo. Congrats."

Dinah clenched her teeth and growled, her heart pulsing rapidly. She was light-headed with rage. She ran down the steps to find note number two.

"Can't take most of the wine this trip. Will come back for it later."

"Oh no you won't!" Dinah screamed, and, grabbing a bottle of pouilly-fuissé from the rack, flung it against the cement wall. It smashed with a wonderful sound, glass and wine spraying in all directions. Breaking the bottle made Dinah feel so good a warm, comforting hand might have been patting her back. She threw another bottle and another and another.

Mikey appeared silhouetted in the light at the top of the stairs, watched the bottles being tossed like hand grenades, and hastily withdrew.

A tart, winey smell permeated the basement as riverlets of white and red wine, of pinkish rosé, flowed in all directions. Shards of glass crackled underfoot as Dinah, with a maniacal laugh bubbling through the froth on her lips, happily destroyed the wine, happily damaged Hatch too. It was Hatch she sent flying across the cellar, cracking his head on the damp, bloodied spot where a bottle of burgundy had hit. The next loud, smacking detonation was Hatch's spine being snapped. His skull burst open like a watermelon as a California rosé crashed on the bannister and pinky brains leaked out.

The spray sailed back onto Dinah from a very good chardonnay, and she licked her lips. A clear thought seeped through her rage, and for a moment she wondered if she should drink the remaining wine rather than painting the basement with it, but she was having so much fun she hated to stop. Every bit of anger was being purged, with Hatch, with herself for being such a wimp all these years, with Joe Connors too because he hadn't hired her, and Lisbeth who made a mistake, something Lis never did, with Perfecto and their perfect trimming of the hedges, and her fury involved the new next-door neighbor also because he lived in the Berger house. Dinah wanted the old couple back, up from death, because they always had chicken soup. "Come sit, eat, we'll listen to you," they would say. Right now, more than anything, Dinah needed the Berger brand of comforting. Blood had nothing to do with it, for calling Nebraska would evoke a colder reaction than caressing a tray of ice cubes. Dinah, thinking of this, seethed hotter, and grabbed a particularly fine French Chablis by its skinny neck. She aimed at the wall, but the bottle detoured to a shelf heavy with gardening tools, and as the hand rake, a small shovel, and a metal watering can all became airborne, Dinah screamed, "Mother!"

When the last bottle, a Marquez '75, met its end against the steel door to the furnace room, Dinah wiped her moist face with sticky fingers and heaved a long sigh, a moan of regret, that her bacchanalia of anger had come to an end. But immediately she laughed, clomped up the steps, passed a worried Mikey in the kitchen, went along to the liquor cabinet from which she snatched a bottle of gin, and climbed higher, to the master, now mistress, bedroom.

In the shower, slugging down the gin as the hot water sluiced over her, she wished there were a skylight cut in the ceiling, for it would have been nice, it would have been perfect right then, to see the stars hanging in the sky like diamonds.

Later Dinah woke from a dream whose particulars she couldn't remember, and thought of Joe Connors. His face, spotlit and shimmering, hung in a medallion on the black bedroom ceiling. Personally interested in her? *Personally?* What did that mean?

Dinah's head fell back against the pillow. *He sees me as a woman, a female.* And before she had the opportunity to think such a startling idea over, she was once again asleep.

"I don't believe you did that, Dinah. It was such a juvenile, such an immature thing to do. Never mind that you destroyed hundreds, maybe thousands of dollars worth of property. *My* property!" Grief as much as anger was in Hatch's voice.

"Well . . ." She couldn't think what to say now that Hatch had gotten her on the defensive. Dinah didn't understand how that happened. She called him because the last check to the Grand Union bounced, costing ten dollars and making it impossible for eternity to pay at the supermarket except with cash. You were supposed to have put money in the account, she'd accused Hatch, firmly she hoped. He'd countered by bringing up the wine. Not that Dinah forgot how in a drunken fervor, drunk with rage not alcohol, she'd wiped out Hatch's cache of wine as effectively as an avenging angel. How could she forget? The house reeked of fermented grapes, since she still hadn't cleaned up the wreckage in the basement.

"How did you find out about the wine, anyway?" Dinah asked suspiciously.

A sudden hum of silence came on the line before Hatch cleared his throat. Lost in time for a moment, Dinah hoped he wasn't coming down with a cold. Then he said, "Mikey told me yesterday when I phoned."

"Nobody let me know you called yesterday. Where was I?"

"Now why are you asking me where you were, Dinah? Surely you can keep track of yourself." Hatch, at his most exasperated, snarled, and Dinah wished not a head cold but pneumonia on this stranger who'd once been—still was, by law—her husband.

Dinah was thinking fleetingly of love, misplaced somewhere by Hatch, not her, and still wanting him home, when he said, "Mikey was very distressed by your craziness."

Craziness? That stuck in Dinah's craw along with the idea of her son the turncoat, the Benedict Arnold! Hatch had left Mikey too after all, so how come he wasn't angrier? Storms ahead, Susie had pointed out, and Dinah, feeling betrayed, wondered if divided loyalties might be one of those squalls.

A book on children and divorce, maybe some sessions with a psychologist, Dinah thought, determined not to allow her son to flounder, but the immediate problem was, "My check, Hatch, remember?"

Actually Hatch was already saying something about ". . . and there you are in the lap of luxury." She hadn't been listening closely enough. He added, "So stop complaining for once in your life, Dinah."

"Who's complaining? Just because I think food's essential to life, and I don't see starving myself to death, nor *our* son either so you can play house with some Barbie Doll, doesn't mean I'm complaining," she shouted down to Manhattan. "Hatch? *Hatch?*" But he had hung up, just like that, no good-bye, no promises that the check was on its way by Federal Express. He simply cut her off like an old dead dog.

"Aiiiiii!" Dinah screamed, slamming the receiver with a loud crack, and tugging her hair in both hands as she slid off the front hall cobbler's bench to the floor. She buried her head in her arms and rocked like a roly-poly doll, moaning. *What's happening to me?* Life was sliding out from under her like an old banana peel. Oh God! She wished all of a sudden she remembered how to pray—effectively, that was. It would do no good to mumble a bunch of meaningless words. She wanted to impress her neediness upon some higher power, as she hadn't with Hatch the urgency of getting cash into the bank account. *I certainly was a big flop with that,* she thought, *so why should He listen to me?*

All the rolling around on the hardwood floor wasn't making Dinah feel any better, though it probably did some good for her behind. So when a cold, wet nose pressed up against her hand she stopped. Rebecca crouched hesitantly before her, regarding Dinah with soft, velvet eyes.

"Becky!" She reached for the Airedale, who, the minute she had Dinah's attention, bounded toward the front door. She pawed the wood and cocked her head like a curious bird.

"Oh, all right." Dinah wiped her eyes on the sleeve of her sweatshirt and grabbing the edge of the bench pulled herself wearily up. Of course she'd rather sit on the floor and hug the furry dog, as comforting as a large teddy bear, and weep. But nature beckoned. She thought Becky might as well have her way, since everybody else seemed to. *Except me,* Dinah reminded herself in another flurry of self-pity.

The Airedale in an explosion of energy and pure joy at being loose in the wide-open spaces of a Westport residential street made a running swan dive to the sidewalk, hanging for the blink of an eye in space, then soaring to the lawn. She squatted, and Dinah, envisioning a burnt yellow circle in the dead grass, yelled, "No, Becky! Stop! Not there!"

Dinah was too late. By the time she nudged the dog with her foot, Rebecca had finished watering the lawn and leaped up from her squat. She rushed frantically in one direction, then the other, along the walk to tumble in a pile of leaves, scattering the brightly colored patches. Then, up and out, she bounded in sheer abandon across the road to the lawns opposite. Ears back, tail floating behind her, the Airedale cantered until she almost disappeared in the distance and Dinah, yelling her name, summoned her back.

Panting, breath in puffs fluttering her whiskers, Rebecca trotted more sedately now at Dinah's side. When Dinah put a hand down, Becky nuzzled the palm, forcing the fingers in the direction of her ruff. Next to running loose as a wild animal like one of her fiercer ancestors on the scent of a hare, Becky loved most a good hard scratch about the neck and ears. She groaned with pleasure as Dinah's nails dug into her fur, and then flung away from such happiness by sprinting forward as they approached their own walk. Galloping in the opposite direction now, Becky hurtled in front of Mario Ellis's house.

The terrible screech of brakes tore through the morning quiet and stabbed Dinah's heart. "Becky!" she shrieked, fear thick as cotton batting gumming up her mouth.

A black Jaguar, its long snout poking out of the driveway, had stopped with a suddenness that spun the car to the side. Its back wheels dug two troughs at the edge of the lawn.

"Rebecca!" Dinah screamed again, panic billowing through her. *I'll kill myself, she swore, if anything happens to her.* I'll kill that man, that Mario Ellis it must be, framed in the driver's window of the expensive car. He had a face before noon like a Dürer etching or, worse, a Grosz, all quick, jagged lines and cumbersome features.

Dinah's fists balled as she leaped toward the Jaguar, but before she could assault the car Mario Ellis drove off. "You son of a bitch!" Dinah screamed down Delphinium Lane into the Jaguar's exhaust fumes. She would have rushed, but then she saw Becky. The Airedale sat on her haunches, head at that particular Rebecca angle, grinning a furry smile before she scrambled into Dinah's arms, or tried to, all four feet leaving the ground at once. At the garage where Dinah got her station wagon serviced, the bunch of unemployed hangers-around who used the Esso station as a social hall called the Airedale "Becky Dancer" for her sure-footed grace. It was "Becky Dancer" that Dinah, suddenly weeping, murmured into a silky ear, stumbling back, tottering on the verge of losing her balance as she hugged as much as she could grasp of this creature whom she loved almost more than life itself, almost more than Mikey, though not quite.

The phone was ringing as Dinah and the dog entered the house. It was Lisbeth to relay the news about Quinn. The recent fright with Becky froze her heart. She knew how Quinn must feel.

"Oh, poor Quinn! Those corgis meant everything!" Dinah sat on the bench and pulled Rebecca close to her as if there were something in the house, something nearby ready to leap, from which she had to protect the dog.

"We're all having dinner later in the week. Here. Chinese food probably. Maybe pizza."

As Lisbeth talked on Dinah wondered, surprised that she never knew, if Lisbeth had ever owned a dog. Or any pet, a cat, maybe a canary, or at least a goldfish. There was such detachment in her recitation of Quinn's tragedy, even the macabre, horror-movie details.

"God, I think I'm going to be sick."

Lisbeth chastised her, "Pull yourself together. You should be out looking for a job, remember. No one is about to wander into your house, Di, and offer up some lucrative employment."

"Yes, yes, you're right. I know," Dinah said, but her stomach sank at the thought of more job hunting. Why couldn't she simply win the lottery and be done with the annoying problem of how to survive?

With her black suit, the skirt hooked closed by a safety pin, she wore a red blouse for color. But the perky little bow under her chin, seen in the pallid reflection of the train window, looked like a bloody garotte choking her. Her powdery cheeks had the texture of worn velvet. *Oh—* she shut her eyes—*I'm getting old.* Fat, forty, and aging badly. *Could life be worse?* she wondered, then remembered Quinn's corgis and wanted to kick herself.

Settling back in the seat, Dinah folded her hands, took a deep breath, and whispered silently, *I will pull myself together, later if not sooner, as long, God, as you do nothing to Rebecca and Mikey. Deal?* No Almighty voice answered, but Dinah felt satisfied and proceeded to try and hypnotize herself into a calm serene state so as to minimize stress, something she'd read about in *Ladies' Home Journal.*

Once in the city, however, instead of being relaxed and confident

183

enough to beard the employment agents who hung on to their cache of jobs like Caribbean pirates, she was even more agitated. The bows on her sling-back pumps hung crooked, and bending to straighten them, she inadvertently snapped the right one loose. There was no way to reattach it. Which left her with mismatched shoes, or having to remove the other bow. Unfortunately the metal hook that held the bows to the pumps now showed plainly. *Oh shit!* she thought, and tossed the bows into a trash basket, *I can't go job hunting.* The way she felt about herself, no one would hire her to wash dishes.

God damn Hatch! Dinah fumed, angrier with her husband, ex to be, than she'd been yet, not only for the embarrassment of being dumped but for making her needy. Why couldn't he continue to support the two of them, her and Mikey, while he sported with his popsie? Not that Dinah didn't want to work, rather the opposite. She'd slave like a coolie if the tooth fairy would only slip the job beneath her pillow while she slept.

Wandering along the East Side of Manhattan, growing more furious with Hatch at every step, she circled closer to his black glass office sky-scraper until she found herself only three blocks away. Well, why not get him right now and pry a good-sized check out of him? Dinah moved purposefully ahead until her image, captured in a window display, flung the smudged and limpid impossibility back at her. Her roots were abysmally gray in hair too long and frizzy. *I can't see Hatch looking like this!* she despaired, stranded, lost, lonely, and a mess on the sidewalk.

One last spark glowed in Dinah somewhere, and before she thought once, never mind twice, she marched into the next beauty salon clutching her Visa card like a magic wand. She'd worry about paying for an overhaul a month from now, but damn it, what was it Lisbeth said? *Be good to yourself.*

Three hours later the colorist, hairdresser, makeup lady, and mani-curist all sighed in unison, "You look like a new woman." It was true. The soft waves of dark brown hair framed a face made up in an attractive pinkish shade of beige, with feathery brows arched neatly above the palest violet shadow, giving Dinah a gauzy, slightly unfocused appearance. Not one hard edge remained to her.

"Perfect, Sweetie, except for that suit," Eric, the spare young hairdresser, complained.

After Dinah signed away more than Mae's monthly salary, she steered herself into Bloomingdale's, up the escalator to the better dress department and into a navy and gray silk that draped in becoming folds and hid her shape. Next it was a new London Fog trench coat, high-heeled pumps, and last, a spritz of perfume as she passed the Chanel counter on the main floor, on her way to Hatch's. Dinah's mood was light-years away from the gray funk she came in with on the train. She felt not good but simply miraculous. *From now on,* she promised—as if God Himself were listening—*I won't be good to myself, I'll be better.*

Dinah arrived at Hatch's building a little past five. Walking tall, her shoulders thrust back, her spine poker-straight, she saw no reason why she and Hatch couldn't go for a drink before she went to Lisbeth's, maybe somewhere like Peacock Alley, and talk sensibly about their marriage. Swimming through the crowds of departing office workers, she rode up thirty-two floors in an empty elevator, practicing her response to Hatch's "My God, you look terrific, Di! What have you done to yourself?"

"Nothing, really. It's just the same old me." Shrug.

"Why didn't I ever realize how beautiful you are?" A sigh of regret.

"You know how it is, Hatch, people who live together for years think of one another as old shoes." That didn't sound right, and Dinah was pondering another response when the doors parted and she stepped smartly out into the ample reception room of Myers, Sandberg, Morgan and Leibowitz.

The cool-as-a-popsicle female behind the semicircular desk, a lean lanky creation of chocolate brown, not a hair out of place in an intricate construction piled high on her head, pursed mauve lips at Dinah and said, "Can I help you?"

The last time Dinah stopped at Hatch's office, months ago, the receptionist was an older, smiling woman, comfortable in polyester, who reminded Dinah of an Eastern Star friend of her mother's in Hanover. That receptionist, Hester, always remembered her name and Mikey's too. "How's that young swimmer of yours, Mrs. J.? Ready for the Olympics yet?"

This praying mantis gazed past Dinah's ear with bored eyes even when she replied, "I'm Mrs. Johnson. I'd like to see my husband, please."

Purple nails longer and sharper than a cheetah's tapped out Hatch's extension and the message was relayed to Lureen, his secretary. A longish pause followed during which the receptionist turned glossy pages of *Harper's Bazaar*. Then the receptionist's eyebrows arched and she mumbled, "Sure." Hanging up the phone she said, "Sorry, Mrs.

Johnson, but your husband's tied up in a meeting. He'll call you at home.''

The rebuff, stinging like a slap, raised a flush of embarrassment on Dinah's cheeks. She glared at the woman, as if she had physically assaulted her. But the receptionist, having delivered the message, once again gave full attention to her magazine. She never even noticed Dinah sidling off through the door to the inner sanctum beyond.

It might be quitting time at other firms, but at Myers, Sandberg, Morgan and Leibowitz, people bustled about as if it were the middle of the day. In the offices Dinah passed, men and the occasional tailored female were crouched over desks writing, reading, or on the phone. Dinah hesitated at an open doorway through which she saw Bill Charles, an old law school buddy of Hatch's, dictating to a fat, gray-haired woman.

"And as the party of the second part, we hereby . . .'' He paused, mouth open, as Dinah waved. Staring at her puzzled, with a look of "I know who that is, but I just can't come up with the name right now,'' he fluttered his fingers in reply. Since they had known one another for years, either Bill Charles needed glasses or her transformation was more startling than Dinah realized.

Winding her way into the center of the rabbit warren, a sudden cold chill seized her. One of these offices held the home wrecker Stacy Delmonico. Dinah carefully inspected the females she saw, but not one of them struck her as important enough to disrupt a marriage of fifteen years.

"Hi, Lureen!'' Dinah smiled. She shrugged out of her coat and tossed it, along with the Bloomingdale's bag that contained her old suit and blouse, on a chair by the secretary's desk.

Lureen, a plain, scrawny bird of a woman who'd been with Hatch for seven or eight years now, gasped, "Dinah!'' Behind her the door to Hatch's private office was shut. Dinah, patting her coiffeur, waltzed around Lureen before the surprised secretary could vault from her chair, scattering a mound of file folders she held on her lap, and try to bar the way. "He's in a meeting!'' she exclaimed.

"Oh, that's okay. I'll just tell him I'm here.'' Dinah smiled so broadly her teeth ached.

Lureen gave a squeal and lunged at Dinah as Dinah threw open the office door. Hatch's head bobbed up with the snap of a startled turtle's. "What the hell?'' he yelled.

"Hatch, I told her,'' Lureen apologized over Dinah's shoulder.

A skinny young man, shirt sleeves rolled up, sat in the center of

Hatch's couch, the marble slab coffee table before him strewn with papers.

"I just wanted to tell you I'll wait," Dinah sputtered, treading on Lureen's foot as she tried gracelessly to retreat.

The young man unfolded to a standing position. "Listen, Hatch, I've taken enough of your time. I think I can unscramble the rest of this miasma myself." He shuffled the papers together and hastily slithered out of Hatch's office, closing the door and leaving Dinah and Hatch alone.

Hatch yelled, "What the hell do you think you're doing, busting in here like the Gestapo? Lureen told you I was in a meeting, didn't she? Didn't she, Dinah?"

"Hatch, I'm sorry, honestly, but I thought, well . . . I thought . . ." What had she been thinking, and why was there a whipped-puppy tone to her voice? Dinah nibbled her pink passion lips as perspiration began to make inroads in her deodorant. "That we might go have a drink," she said quickly.

"A drink! You thought we—you and I—could go have a drink?" Hatch was off his desk chair, bouncing on the balls of his feet as if preparing to pole-vault. "Just like that, you barge into my *private* office, interrupt an important meeting, and say, 'Hey, Hatch, what about us having a drink together?' You're crazy, Dinah, you know that?"

Hatch never noticed the new hairdo and the softer, more feminine look of the artfully applied makeup. He had eyes only for the old Dinah. She might as well have worn the usual jeans and sloppy sweatshirt as the expensive silk dress from Bloomingdale's.

Look at me! she wanted to scream in high C. I look terrific! But the four hundred dollars spent to transform Dinah's usual self into a female quite different was wasted. Feeling guilty and ashamed, Dinah reverted to her original complaint, the reason she'd come to Hatch's office in the first place: "There's no money in the bank! My Grand Union check bounced. I'll never be able to show my face in there again!"

Hatch turned to stone. "So that's what you're after. I should have known. Greed!"

"No . . . !" She hadn't meant to say it, or not right out, so baldly. After a couple of drinks, when Hatch was beginning to feel he'd made a serious blunder with his life. "Hatch!" Dinah reached out imploring. An ocean of tan berber carpet stretched between them.

"The check," he seethed, "is in the mail. And don't think I'm not considering deducting the amount of all the wine you destroyed from our final settlement, Dinah, because I certainly am."

Dinah's temper climbed. She could almost see the red line of the thermometer rising to the little bubble at the top. The boiling point neared, and then, why then, she'd give him what for, she'd tell Hatch Johnson exactly what she thought of him. Until then, she simply shouted, "You louse! You no good miserly rat!"

"Hatch, darling!"

The door opened so soundlessly neither of the combatants heard it. A willowy blonde, the kind of woman Dinah wanted to kill on sight, stood, one hip jutting out, just inside the office. An enigmatic smile, kin to the one Leonardo painted on the Mona Lisa, creased her full mouth. Her eyes were thickly fringed, her skin a silky peaches and cream. Her nose must have been sculpted by a plastic surgeon; it was too perfect for nature.

"Will you be ready to leave soon? We have to meet Daddy for dinner, don't forget," she said, baring a fortune in orthodontic work. Her gaze slipped across Dinah as if she were lying next to a garbage can on Broadway.

"I'll be through in a few minutes," Hatch was saying.

Dinah, crossing her fingers, hoping against hope she was making a terrible mistake, pushed out the words, "You must be Stacy."

The blonde cocked her head, a spill of gossamer hair floating along her cheek. "Yes," she drawled. "But I don't think we've met."

"Not likely, you bitch!" Seizing the first thing her hand alighted on from Hatch's desk, which was a loose-leaf calendar, she flung it overhand at Stacy Delmonico. The calendar slammed into the door, breaking its plastic spine, and the days of the year flew in a shower. Stacy Delmonico was so surprised she never moved, not until the Rolodex came sailing at her. Then, galvanized into motion, she fled, screaming.

Hatch scrambled around his desk and yanked Dinah's arm. "What the hell do you think you're doing?" he shouted.

"So that's your whore!" Dinah yelled in Hatch's face, flecks of spittle striking his chin and shirt collar. "Young enough to be your daughter! You pervert!"

"Dinah, get out of here before I lose control! And Stacy's twenty-eight, not that it's any of your business!"

Dinah slapped Hatch's face. He gasped, dropping the arm he'd gotten, and Dinah leaped to the other side of the desk. She grabbed a glass paperweight, threatening to fling it. But Hatch dove at her, both arms outstretched as if he intended to wrap his maddened wife in a bear hug. He got the other arm and they battled, struggling about the office in a new kind of dance.

Hatch yanked at Dinah's elbow so violently, she thought for a second he'd dislocated some bone, but it was just the silk dress, the sleeve parting from the shoulder. "Oh!" she cried, tears springing to her eyes, as she dropped the paperweight. It fell in a blizzard of spinning snow onto Hatch's foot.

"Ouch!" he yelled.

"You tore my new dress!" she shrieked accusingly. Dinah held out her arm. "Look what you did!"

"What *I* did? This is all your fault. Out!" Hatch thrust a hand in her direction and Dinah kicked for his knee. "God damn it! That's it!" He jumped, getting a grip on one shoulder, and with surprising ease, frog-marched her to the door as he shouted for Lureen.

The door opened so quickly she must have been leaning against it. "Yes, Hatch?"

"Hatch, I'll kill you for this! I swear," Dinah sobbed. "I'll get even!"

"Get a rope and hang yourself, Dinah. I don't give a fuck!"

"You bastard!"

He tried to force her out the door, but she sagged on him, becoming deadweight, and he had to turn and drag her, her new pumps digging gullies in the carpet. "No more Mr. Nice Guy!" Hatch hissed in Dinah's ear.

"Drop dead," she said, but she said it automatically.

Hatch wrestled her the rest of the way to the door, and before Dinah could do anything else, he tossed her, panting and heaving, out of his office. A large crowd of secretaries and lawyers, drawn by the commotion, stood about watching curiously as Dinah stumbled into a heavy-set black man, almost knocking him off balance.

"Excuse me," she mumbled, rushing back for the door, which was already shut and locked, she discovered, when she jiggled the knob. "Hatch!" she yelled. "You bastard! Let me in! I came here for a friendly meeting, for a civilized drink maybe, and you attacked me. Hatch! Hatch?"

At the other side of the heavy door a silence pooled thick as syrup. Dinah pressed her ear to the wood and listened, but there was nothing to hear. "Hatch!" she yelled again.

"Dinah, don't you think you should go now?" Lureen whispered by her ear.

Dinah swung wildly about and the secretary warily moved the desk chair between them. "What did you say?" Dinah asked.

"That it might be best if you left." Lureen dripped sympathy, looking mournfully at Dinah in the same way friends and neighbors in

Hanover did when Harry Esterman passed on. The rest of the office curious had shifted along both wings of the hall, and now they stared at Dinah as if she clung to the bars inside the monkey cage. Humiliation covered her like a layer of dust, obliterating the impact of her expensive remodeling job.

"Please, Dinah, leave. Hatch is probably calling the building security this minute. You don't want them to put you out on the street, do you?" Lureen implored.

Lureen inched closer. She had a huge pimple like a snowcapped mountain in the center of her chin. It oozed, just ready to pop. Dinah stared at it, fascinated. "Acnomel, the stuff teenagers use. It smells awful, but put some on that pimple and it will dry right up," Dinah advised. Lureen's mouth gaped open in surprise. Dinah picked up her trench coat from the chair and put it on. She buttoned each button and belted it neatly.

Lureen's hand approached tentatively and touched Dinah's sleeve. They stared at one another. Dinah thought Lureen's eyes looked like melting balls of ice cream. "My father walked out on my mother for some divorcee who lived down the block. So I know how you feel," Lureen offered sadly.

Dinah shook her head. "No, you don't. I'm not even sure how I feel, except dead, like a stone."

The crowd parted as she moved off down the hall, only a small tug inching out into the channel. Her mind had shut down the way it did when she caught a cold, her head and nose logjammed.

Out in the reception area two overweight security guards in gray uniforms, clutching their walkie-talkies, leaped from the elevator as Dinah sailed between them and got into the car. The doors closed, but Dinah didn't bother to turn, and she rode down to the ground facing backwards.

14

Icy rain fell all during the day and night, turning the city wet and slick, with guttering rivers along the curbs and ponds pooling by the drains. Far to the north an early winter storm swept across the plains in white drifts and churned up a cold front that rolled over New York heading for the Atlantic. By morning the drizzle could freeze; there might even be an unseasonable snow. Just past midnight, however, the chilly showers whipped through the streets, tapered off for a little while, exploded without warning in a drenching downpour, and finally found a slow continuous rhythm.

Charlie Morgan went to bed early, after a scotch and a joint following another argument with Lisbeth on the telephone. He wanted her to come up and have dinner. She wouldn't. Later he called and asked if he could go down and spend the night. She said the weather was too disgusting for him to bother. He said he didn't mind, that the rain wasn't so bad. He said it would be nice to curl up together on such a cold, wet night. But Lisbeth hadn't wanted him down in the Village.

Charlie had spent the kind of afternoon he hated, correcting exam papers, endless essays that seemed to have been written by illiterates; indecipherable handwriting, bad grammar, and answers that convinced him his students dreamed through his lectures like the dead.

He needed Lisbeth, and the need set him to cursing when he hung up the phone after a bland supper of canned soup and a cheese sandwich.

When he was lying in bed sipping the scotch and taking short little hits of the harsh, soothing smoke, he kept telling himself that of course Lisbeth was working, that she had to have her "space." The old-fashioned word bellying up in his thought irritated Charlie, made him feel foolish. Love reduced him to the level of his students, turned him again into a young man. A bungling colt, he thought of himself then, with two left feet and a stuttering heart. Older, he was happier, and all he wished was to settle down with Lisbeth even if only for moments, or in sleep.

Thinking of Lisbeth, his anger at least numbed by the scotch and the grass, Charlie eventually drifted off.

He never heard the intruder or felt the knife as it penetrated through sheet and blanket into his flesh. It was an ordinary carving knife with a six-inch serrated blade, and smoothly it sliced a narrow passageway between Charlie's ribs. Charlie, dreaming of standing on a high cliff, dreaming that he was about to take off and fly over some dark sea, was penetrated as easily as a stick of softened butter.

Dawn lightened the eastern edge of the sky when Neff, trench coat collar turned up against the rain, climbed Lisbeth's stoop and punched the bell. He wore a gray face, a long-night-with-no-sleep face, and seemed a stranger.

"I was at the Twenty-fourth when the report came in. They were pleased as pigs in shit when I said I'd take it." He took off his wet coat and threw it over the Eames chair, the trickles of rain falling on the leather. He poured himself a drink and said, "You've got the luck of a lottery winner, you know that."

"Why?"

"Because I know the professor. Because I told Petrelli that I'd come see the broad whose photograph is by the bed. The fucker said, fine, he was wet enough for one night."

He swallowed a long drink of scotch and put the glass on the mantel, where he leaned his arms, his back to Lisbeth. Kicking at the charred logs in the fireplace, he waited for Lisbeth to ask him what happened to Charlie. At last she did.

"Somebody shoved a knife in him," Neff said.

The last viny tendrils of sleep left Lisbeth and she watched herself coming awake, an evolving figure passing in a mist. She saw herself on a screen, black and white, in slower than normal motion. She didn't think she wanted to hear this. Nothing bad should happen to Charlie Morgan. The best man who'd ever come into her life, that was Charlie, she repeated silently, and went into the bedroom.

"Aren't you even curious if he's alive or dead?" Neff called after her.

"That's not funny," she said, hoping Neff would disappear.

Neff didn't go away; he followed her. "You better believe it's not funny. It's a frigging miracle. A hair left or right and the professor would be dead meat."

Lisbeth put a tape of the *Brandenburg Concerti* into the cassette player on the night table and lay down on the bed. Neff was a bad dream, Neff with his sly smile and his news of Charlie Morgan. Charlie was safe in his own bed, asleep, loving her even while dreaming. That was what Lisbeth wanted.

Neff leaned against the doorjamb. "Morgan's tough. He was sleeping, but being stabbed wakes you up fast enough. The assailant must have thought the professor bought it, because he left and Morgan crawled to the phone."

Lisbeth pushed up against the pillows, fighting dizziness. The Bach played on relentlessly, but the music came muffled, taking forever on its journey to her ears. The notes hung, one by one, deliberately in the bedroom's sepia light, and Lisbeth inhabited her own skin like an intruder. She sensed some stranger lurking in a crevice she couldn't quite find. Before Neff arrived Lisbeth thought she'd been dreaming, but no memory remained of being in bed, asleep and waking. Only emptiness lingered until the first recollecting, standing by the door letting Neff in out of the rain. Rhinestone drops shone on his gigolo's face and slicked-back hair.

"I want to go see Charlie," Lisbeth said.

"No rush. He'll live. He needed a lot of stitching, but there was no real internal damage apparently. I called in on my way downtown. He's still in never-never land. Wait until noon."

"Be serious." Suddenly frantic, Lisbeth was up off the bed, standing.

"Who'd want to hurt the professor?" Neff asked, not moving.

Lisbeth dropped the velour robe on the floor and stark naked, not caring about Neff, started to get dressed. "Hurt Charlie?" She laughed bitterly. "No one would hurt Charlie. He's everybody's friend. People love Charlie!"

"Do you?" The question was pro forma. No hint of curiosity touched Neff's voice.

Lisbeth zipped up her jeans and turned, her breasts bare, to face him. "Yes, I love Charlie. He's the best thing that's ever happened to me." She repeated the line like a child reciting.

"It wasn't a junkie, which is what you'd think in that neighborhood. Not the usual breaking and entering. The door was unlocked; the window on the fire escape cracked an inch. The whole fucking Russian army could have gotten in."

"So? So what do you want from me?" Suddenly the urgency to see Charlie, to be sure he was all right, burned in Lisbeth like a fever.

Neff's glance was lethal as moving toward her he said, "Nothing was taken." Anticipation prickled the back of Lisbeth's neck. "Tell me about Charlie,'' Neff continued. "Give me a couple of names. Next of kin. That sort of thing. Have to call people with a situation like this. Let them know, because they'll be interested that one of their loved ones almost ended up in a body bag.''

"Go away,'' Lisbeth whispered. "Call the chairman of his department if you have to call somebody. Charlie's family lives down in North Carolina. He hasn't seen them in years. His ex-wife is over in England. He hasn't been in contact with her either.''

Neff was close enough to touch now. "And where were you?''

Where was I? She screamed, "Sleeping! I was sleeping, you son of a bitch!''

Lisbeth thought of the darkness, those dead black periods of time, and she remembered the Porsche. Was that what the darkness meant? A return to that moment, that pool of ebony into which she must have descended as she'd once before when racing on the San Diego Freeway? *I was a conquistador,* she thought, *rushing south to north, the mountains sprawled at the skyline, the snow—*

No snow in California, only so cold. . . .

There was a stinging blow as the Porsche hit a wall of metal and Lisbeth's head smacked the windshield like a melon. No pain then, not like this. Lisbeth fingered her cheek. Shocked, she glared at Neff slowly coming into focus. "You slapped me!''

He half apologized. "You were leaping around like a tuna out of water.''

Lisbeth spat, "Stop trying to make it sound as though I had a fit!''

Neff sighed. "Christ Almighty.'' He went into the living room for another drink. When he returned he said, "Scotch before breakfast, scotch *for* breakfast.'' He put the glass down. "Christ, I don't want this. You got any coffee?''

"Get out of my house, Neff. I'm going up to see Charlie.'' But Neff ignored her and went into the kitchen.

He ground beans for French coffee. "There was fifty bucks on the dresser and a handful of change. His watch. The TV's still there, the VCR.''

Lisbeth's head started to ache. As Neff, watching her, talked on she listened to the rattle of the garbage cans in the alley, the hoot of a horn in the distance. The day had begun. She imagined Charlie in the hospital where time existed only in the routines, where the fluorescent tubes were lit forever. Lisbeth heard the hushed fluttering of the nurses gliding along the corridors, disappearing, whispering without words. Their voices rose up not in Lisbeth's memory but in actual sound, like the stealthy slither of spiders crawling.

"Coffee?" Neff held up a mug.

She felt Charlie's near death, the pain of the stabbing, the luck of his survival. Dragging nervous fingers through her hair, she shook her head violently as if she could dislodge her own hurting.

"I have to see Charlie," she whispered finally.

"God, you're beautiful," he said softly. He ran a finger down her neck to the cleft between her breasts.

Lisbeth's heart pounded with a terrible feeling. She shouldn't be here with Neff, but at the hospital waiting for Charlie to surface into consciousness. She owed Charlie her concern and her presence. She licked her lips and tried to speak to Neff but couldn't.

Neff said, "You're like a constant high. I think of you and can't stop. You make me crazy. See how much I want you." He took her hand and put it on his crotch.

Lisbeth jerked away and ran; Neff's voice faint, fading. Escaping through the swinging door, she crossed the near corner of the living room and rushed down the hall, one foot deliberately before the other. Still she stumbled into the walls, careening like a drunkard.

She heard Neff behind her and tried not to listen. Just at the doorway, Neff, so much faster, grabbed her by the hair. She fell back and his arms came around her, his hands finding her breasts.

Lisbeth struggled but Neff was too strong. Perhaps she didn't fight him enough. *I don't want to,* she thought; *I do.* The desires mixed inside her, ran as confused as a river. It was impossible all at once to separate the currents of longing.

At the bed they stumbled and Neff shoved her down.

"I don't want you," she cried, clawing at his back with her nails as Neff fell on top of her.

He didn't answer and he didn't stop. His breath roared in her ear. She felt the sharp pain of his teeth as he pushed down and bit her on the neck. The hurting was everywhere now, not just in her head, and for the first time the pain was exciting. There was pleasure in it, such pleasure that she heard herself screaming.

Neff ripped off her jeans, his own clothes, and tumbled her about on the cold sheets. Her teeth chattered; she was suddenly freezing. Her own bed felt like a field of snow under her skin until Neff thrust himself inside her.

15

Dinah was in the bathroom crying. Not that she couldn't weep in Lisbeth's living room with Lis and Quinn, or with Susie, who arrived after she did, but standing at the sink, trying to restructure her hair into the expensive hairdo, brought back that awful afternoon at Hatch's office, and tears began a slow winding course from her eyes. She hadn't willed them and they wouldn't dry them up. The tears possessed a life of their own, and Dinah watched them trickle down her cheeks like lines in an old map.

Lisbeth appeared in the doorway. "Come on, Di, stop it. Have a glass of Chablis. It'll cure whatever it is."

"Misery," Dinah said, staring at the heavy, elongated face with the ruffle of excess skin beneath the chin and recognizing that ridiculous woman as herself. It was such an unlovely face, unloved, and imprinted with faint genetic memories of her mother.

Quinn poked her head over Lisbeth's shoulder. "What's wrong?"

"I'm feeling sorry for myself and hating the experience," Dinah wept. "Especially when I think of your corgis."

Susie arrived at the bathroom. "Darling, honestly." She wrapped an arm around the slumping shoulders. The two faces, framed together, hung in space, Susie's in perfect smoothness, Dinah's an old cat caught out in the rain.

"We're forty, all of us, and we'll die some day, soon, sooner, soonest," Dinah whispered.

Quinn groaned and Lisbeth pushed out of the bathroom. "Not for ages and ages," Susie's mouth formed the words, but Dinah neither saw nor heard them.

"What am I going to do with my life?" Dinah screamed at the two women.

"Sssh!" Susie hugged her tighter. "You're going to have a glass of wine and one of Lis's tranks if you want, and we'll order in Chinese.

And talk, Di, the four of us, just like the old days, the way we always have. And really, Di''—she squeezed the soft shoulder—''life won't seem so grim. We won't let you down, not ever. Friends to the end of time, right? Isn't that what we always said?'' Tugging gently, Susie detached Dinah from her umbilical connection with the mirror.

''You were always the butterfly,'' Quinn remarked to Susie as she stepped aside. Susie smiled with sad eyes.

''Fly . . . let's fly away! Tonight!'' Dinah cried, drying her tears.

''Oh, what for? No place is any different,'' Quinn said, shadows sweeping over her.

''Is anybody going to make sense tonight?'' Lisbeth sat in the Eames chair, stockinged feet tucked up under her. She drank, not wine but something amber over ice cubes.

Outside the rain, on and off for days, began again. A harsh wind blew and splattering drops struck the windows in a hail of bullets. A siren moaned somewhere south of Tenth Street.

Lisbeth had lit a fire and the warming blaze drew Quinn to it. She huddled on a throw pillow, long, heavy legs in tartan pants pulled up, arms about them, a cheek resting on her knees.

Susie poured herself a glass of wine and lit a cigarette. Lisbeth pointed a finger, cocked an imaginary gun, and pulled the trigger. ''You are going to hell in a hand basket.''

Susie smiled. ''That's what my father says when he reads the newspapers.''

''How is Dr. Bannon?'' Dinah asked, curled up in the opposite corner of the sofa from Susie. They held hands, however, like two schoolgirls.

''The same, but older. Last week when I talked to my mother she said Daddy's building a harpsichord from a kit in the rec room. When he finishes he plans to take lessons. He's tone-deaf as far as any of us know, but he says it's time in his life for music.''

Quinn asked Lisbeth, ''Did you order?''

''The usual. If I don't know what the rest of you like I never will. Cashew chicken and steamed dumplings, pork fried rice and Hunan chicken. Let's see.'' She tapped her front teeth with an unpolished nail. ''Oh yes, Di's sweet and sour shrimp. Buddha's delight and pork lo mein.''

''Some things never change,'' Quinn said.

Dinah's eyes had closed. With hands clasped in an attitude of prayer against her breasts, she seemed to be either dead or sleeping, but she started, crying out, ''Some things do, like your poor dogs.''

None of the women said anything, and Susie hoped that was the last

197

mention of the corgis. Though she couldn't, she wanted to forget the poor creatures, killed and dressed like piglets.

The morning after, with a quivering voice, she had described vividly to Lisbeth how macabre Quinn's dining room table looked. A dinner party elaborately set, for four, for *us*. Lisbeth at the other end kept so still Susie was certain she'd gone away, just put the phone down and wandered off. But finally she said that Quinn had loved the dogs too much, and Susie retorted that was no reason to kill them. Much less so fancifully. *And why?* she cried, afraid. Hating herself all the while, she waited for Lisbeth to answer. The words were cold in Susie's mouth—*Did you do it?* But she couldn't say them. Such a question would have been too great a betrayal. Yet she had come right up to it before backing off.

She didn't tell Lisbeth about Simon either, how he helped her to clean things up in Quinn's apartment.

Since that night Susie hadn't seen or talked to the priest, but it required little imagination to feel again his arms around her when they danced in The Green Man, and afterwards when the bar latched its paint-scarred steel door and he put her into a taxi.

Susie, these last days, ached from guilt, because of Greg, because, too, of the boisterous Irish wing of her family. All righteous Catholics, they'd be condemning if they had seen her slowly circling the dance floor with the priest, if they knew what she felt or, worse, the words Simon whispered.

All non-Catholic women have this "thing" about priests, the aunts often joked. Susie supposed they'd blame Baptist Ivy Bannon for the blasphemy.

Quinn was saying, "And Will accused me of substituting Yin and Yang for children."

"Half-baked psychology," Lisbeth snorted. "Not all women are brood mares or devotees of baby talk and pabulum—excuse me, Dinah, Susie. I've never had the slightest interest in children. Even when I was a child myself I disliked them." She wrinkled her nose. "Give me grown-ups any time. Never a life of diapers and three A.M. feedings, dirty fingerprints on everything, or teenagers with their pimples and hormones. Not that I'm wild about dogs either, Quinn."

Susie, who loved Lisbeth, who loved her from that very first day at Cabot when she met the skinny girl in overalls and bare feet, legs long as stilts, that fiery flood of hair swinging free to her waist, thought about asking this present Lisbeth what she did love, or whom. But without posing the question she suspected Lisbeth would say: I love you, Quinn and Dinah, too, in an old shoe sort of way, but you especially, Suz. I love Ferris Rosenthal, she would add, as if her father hadn't been dead so many years. And the men I sleep with, but only for a little while. Susie thought, oh Lord, the damage love can do! The damage love had already done to all of them so many years ago. What it still might bring.

How could she suspect that Lisbeth had harmed Quinn's dogs? Because Lisbeth was different since she moved to New York, vague and silent, less intense (and yet at times more so), given to dark fits of brooding? *I'm mad. . . .* Yet she watched Lis, searching for some sign.

"Will has three children," Quinn said. "I think I told you. The youngest, Sarah, just ten, is so like my mother. Some nights I wake up—I suppose I've been dreaming—and I see the two faces come together as one. And I want Sarah," Quinn confessed. "I yearn after that child as I don't after the others." Speaking of Will's daughter, her heart speeded up alarmingly. The loss of Yin and Yang had somehow gotten entangled with the impossibility of ever having a daughter like Sarah or Sarah herself.

"I can see how those distraught women you're always reading about in the paper snatch babies from the supermarket. I understand that, especially now after the dogs," Quinn said, sorrow gouging lines along her mouth.

"Oh, Quinnie!" Susie cried, stretching out a hand, but Quinn never moved to receive Susie's comfort. Touch wasn't healing, not for her.

In the fireplace a log sputtered, its underbelly burnt away, and crashed with a shower of sparks. The sudden noise silenced them. For a few seconds they gazed at the fire. Quinn stabbed the wood with a poker, rearranging the remaining logs.

Lisbeth rattled the ice cubes in her glass. Her voice had a catch in it. "Charlie Morgan was stabbed the night before last, in his bed. Somebody meant to kill him. He'll be okay, but it's a fluke."

"Your Charlie? Someone tried to kill your Charlie?" Susie cried, astonished. "But why?"

"I guess you'd say, Suz, the wheel just turned his way."

"A thief," Quinn suggested.

"No, seems not. Mur-dah," she slurred. Susie realized that Lisbeth was quite drunk. "Murder, my dears, that was what some person had in mind for Charlie."

"Like Yin and Yang," Quinn said, shuddering.

"It's too silly. I don't believe it," Dinah protested, throwing a cushion off the couch angrily.

"We're being persecuted," Quinn said.

Dinah cried, "For Christ's sake, Quinn, don't be so dramatic!"

Lisbeth laughed shrilly. "Oh, Di, now that *is* the pot calling the kettle dirty names."

Impossible, that big friendly man being stabbed. It couldn't have happened, yet it had and the attack brought a sudden rush of relief to Susie. She felt light-headed. Lis would never have hurt Charlie. Something else, a reason they couldn't comprehend. Quinn had called them persecuted, and Susie remembered the flowers with the razor blade. The lilies-of-the-valley.

"It's Lily," Susie said.

"Lily *Vaughan*?" Quinn asked as if she'd never heard the name before, but she drove her hands through her short cropped hair until it stood up in tufts.

It was hard to tell if Dinah was going to laugh or cry. She said, "That was twenty years ago, damn it. And Lily's dead besides. What do you think, she's up and walking around? A zombie, straight out of *Night of the Living Dead*?"

"We forgot, closed off the past as if it didn't matter, and now it's come rolling over us in an avalanche," Susie said, certain.

"Oh, stop it!" Quinn pleaded.

"No, you all have to listen! Quinn, please, the dogs and that beautifully set table . . . there were place cards with our names." She looked from one to the other. "Yes, cards with our names, one at each of the four places. Why? *Why?*"

"Well, I don't know!" Dinah shouted, but a thin current of memory stirred through her mind. Quickly she poured herself an ample brandy, drinking most of it down.

"And Charlie Morgan, a man *you* care about, Lis, hurt. Then, earlier, the beginning of September, somebody sent me flowers. Lilies-of-the-valley with a razor blade buried in them."

"That's sick!"

"I bet I wasn't the only one who received a reminder of Lily."

Lisbeth ran a finger around the rim of her wineglass, making it sing. "I think of Lily Vaughan quite a lot. Not that ferrety person alive and annoying, but dead Lily, Lily in the snow. *Back then*, I think, as if Lily were a place or a time instead of a girl. And there's that kitchen knife sticking out of Lily's chest."

"Enough!" Dinah cried, leaping up and pacing the room. She paused at the window and held the curtain back, staring out into the dark street. "Where's the food? I'm starving. I want to eat, not remember Lily."

"Lily's remembered by someone!" Susie shouted. The others stared at her in surprise, for Susie seldom raised her voice. Tendrils of hair floated about her face; there was a smudge of color at the corner of her mouth. She looked mussed, her beige silk shirt pulling free from her jeans.

Quinn stood up. "Wait, the white mouse. After Derek Sonderson shot himself, I received a package. A shoe box with a mouse in it. And the poor thing had been stabbed. I assumed it was more of Derek's . . . well, a parting gift."

"Some gift!" Lisbeth laughed harshly.

"What about you, Lis?" Lis raised her shoulders in a shrug. Susie turned to Dinah. "Di?"

Dinah left the window, arms windmilling, yelling, "Susie, let it alone! Real life's bad enough without ghosts, a dead girl we knew once walking around killing dogs and sending flowers!"

"Lily wasn't just a nobody to us, Lily was—"

"Damn it, I know who Lily was!" Dinah flung herself into the other end of the sofa.

"Suz, you really think that the piper's come with the bill, that after all this time we're going to have to pay up?" Lisbeth asked.

"That's ridiculous!" Quinn said.

"No, Suz is right. I feel it, Quinnie. We've got to face Lily at last."

Dinah clamped her hands over her ears. "I won't listen to one more word about Lily and how she died!"

Quinn echoed that. "It's finished, and so is Lily!"

Susie, who had started the squabble, withdrew, clutching a pillow to her breasts. The others fell silent too.

The doorbell rang.

"The food!" Quinn said with a sigh of relief. "We need to eat." She hurried to the door.

Lisbeth went for the dishes. Dinah, setting out the placemats and napkins, said to Susie, "I don't know why you started this. If I felt rotten before I feel horrible now. Lily Vaughan! Honestly, why'd you have to bring her up? We said we'd never talk about her. Why, Susie, why?"

"Because we had something to do with her dying and we know it." The other three women stared at her in silence and she met their gazes defiantly, having at long last said the unforgivable.

16

He noticed her the moment she came through the doorway at noon, the collar of her camel's hair coat turned up against her cheeks. Jose had cooked up a hearty soup from scraps of meat and bones, potatoes, carrots, lentils, a few turnips. Garbage soup, Father Simon, who loved it, called the concoction. Steam wafted from an enormous pot placed in the middle of the long serving table against the far wall, and a tantalizing aroma filled the room. The warmth and the smell of food made already bleary eyes water.

Simon handed Jose the ladle and came around the table. He paused to say a word here, another there, as his hand touched a rounded back, a torn sleeve, but his eyes never left Susie. She moved toward him slowly, recognizing a few of the homeless, smiling. One of the women, her face rough as a riverbed, said, "How are you, Missus?" But most ignored her. On a blustery day when the wind unsettled any poor soul who crouched in a doorway and the promise was only for worse to come, snow and icy rain, the killing cold of winter, no one cared about violet eyes and silky hair. Beauty wouldn't save them, beauty was irrelevant. Susie sensed the indifference.

"Susie," he said, finally meeting her. He closed the door to his office after her. "Here, let me hang up your coat." He helped her slip out of it and his hand brushed her shoulder, setting off sparks of static electricity. "I'm very glad you've come back."

"I had to sooner or later," she said. Why had she? Staying away, rape would be only one more memory, and possibly even its vivid details would fade.

If only she could pretend that it had happened to someone else. Oh surely, she thought on the taxi ride downtown, pretense would be better than reality. Only now that she was here, pretending became impossible. Standing in the priest's cluttered office, she knew that two floors above, almost directly over her head, was the linen closet.

"You don't think he'll show up again?"

Simon shook his head. "It doesn't seem likely."

"No, I suppose not," she said, knowing at last that no exorcism Simon might perform would vanquish the ghosts.

When she and Simon reentered the main room of the mission, Jose shyly met her with a smile. "Hello, Susie. Long time no see." He didn't ask where she'd been. The volunteers were as transient as the homeless. At the shelter no one posed questions; as Father Simon said, we're just grateful for whatever, whomever, we get.

In the kitchen where Susie went for another tray, Sven was standing at the big double sink filled with soapsuds, his massive hands moving among the glasses and plates. "Been away," Sven said.

"Yes, but I'm here now."

"Good." He nodded. "More Tang made up in pitchers on top shelf of the 'frigerator. You need?"

"No, we're okay for a while yet. Just more sandwiches."

They worked quickly together, two old men who were regulars at the shelter helping them, and a plump, chickeny woman in a stiffly pressed housedress and a sweater, a Mrs. Ryan from a church in Hell's Kitchen. Father Simon came in and explained, "The ladies of the sodality take turns, bless them." He introduced the women, and Mrs. Ryan's pinched features took on an expression of humility.

"Penances, helping the poor, ain't that the truth, dear," she said, staring unabashedly at Susie. Susie agreed, beginning again to feel at home here, as impossible as it seemed.

The patient lines, the cracks in the walls, the smell of soup, the scuffed floors, the long metal tables and wood benches, the iron cots and thin wool blankets upstairs, the rust-stained showers and tubs, the creaky stairs and loose panes of window glass, the naked light bulbs, all comforted her. She needed this home as much as the indigents, though again she wondered why.

Claire McGrath will probably bring in a team of painters, cover the floors with carpeting, get the poor matching china and stainless steel, Susie thought. She could even see Claire hanging Utrillo prints in the dormitories and Picasso posters in the large downstairs main rooms. *I'll hate it then,* she thought, and felt a stir of guilt, for she always left here and went uptown. For the poor there was nothing better than The Good Shepherd, only worse.

Lunch ended at two and Sven began carving up whatever had been collected from the markets and restaurants for dinner. Jose swabbed the floors with a wet sponge mop. The two old men wiped down the tables and collected the trash in big green plastic bags that brought back an instant memory of the corgis. Mrs. Ryan buttoned her sensible black coat to her wattled chin, donned a knitted red cap with a pom-pom, and got ready to leave. "Have to be home for the kids," she said, nodding good-bye to the rest. "I believe in it," she stated firmly. "No latch-keys for mine."

Do they do well in school? Are you worried they're on dope, running wild, doing things you never dreamed about and are scared of? Will they be priests and nuns, doctors or lawyers, happy wives and mothers supporting their husbands, or lost souls, wastrels, floating about in the world? Susie wanted to ask Mrs. Ryan these things, but Mrs. Ryan was too much like the Irish aunts, if poorer, and she would only have snorted in embarrassment.

There was a lull in the shelter's routine, a half an hour or so when nobody moved too quickly. Time to sit and think, or dream, or even nod off in a light doze. Simon read or prayed then. Today he said, "Come with me, Susie. We'll walk each floor, look in every room." Lay the ghosts he meant, return the building to its familiar state.

She didn't take his hand, or he hers, until they were halfway up the first flight of stairs, their footsteps echoing, their hearts pounding. "How's your friend?" he asked, steering Susie along the second floor.

"So so. Sad," she said. "Another friend, her"—what should she call Charlie Morgan?—"fiancé . . ." Susie said, though she knew Lisbeth would never marry Charlie. Her one marriage to Billy Reynolds had been enough. "Her fiancé was stabbed in his bed. He'd been sleeping."

"Is he—?"

"No, he's alive, but hurt."

Simon showed little surprise, but then the world in which he lived was populated with people who got stabbed and people who wielded knives, with policemen and squad cars and howling sirens.

"Did they catch the guy?"

"No." Susie didn't ask why. It was someone who remembered Lily, no matter what the others said. Getting even. As Lisbeth put it, time to pay the piper. Penances due. Susie knew about guilt. It had been guilt that had driven her here to The Good Shepherd, to Simon.

"Coincidence, things happening to two of your friends," Simon said as they walked down the hall, the floorboards creaking.

"It's evil, that's what it is."

They stopped at the doorway to the dormitory, all the narrow beds stripped, skinny mattresses exposed. He gripped her upper arms and urged Susie around so they faced one another. "What's evil?" he asked.

"You should know about evil, Simon. It's part of what you do. The way my father knows about suffering."

"Your father?"

"He's a doctor. And every day he has to deal with suffering and pain. That's his business." She stepped out of his grasp into the long barrackslike room. The light entering the dormitory through the high, smudged windows was dirty. Though she wanted him to touch her, she kept just far enough away so that he'd have to reach an impossible distance for her.

"I didn't know your father was a doctor," he said, "but then I really know little about you."

She smiled back at him apologtically and almost said, *I'm sorry.* "Yes, he's a doctor, in Baltimore. An obstetrician-gynecologist. What he really likes best is delivering babies, but somehow the women with other things, the bad things like cancer, always find him." She walked to the end of the even rows of beds and circled back. "The way evil seems to be finding my friends," she added, thinking, *What more will it be for me?*

"Susie, it's nothing like that, just New York. Random violence." He held out an arm as though he expected her to slip under it. With his boyish grin and all that tousled hair, in jeans and a work shirt, he looked like somebody's brother. As she came up to him, Susie wondered if he'd give her a rough, affectionate, a brotherly hug, but at the last moment he veered off and they slipped out like strangers.

In the hall, she asked, "Did you think Quinn's dogs were random? That a cat burglar broke in and killed them so elaborately by chance?"

They reached the stairway to the third floor, and she hung back. Simon clasped her elbow and began guiding her up the steps. "What else is there to think?" Her feet were dragging and gently he persuaded her on. "There's so much you don't tell me."

"No, don't be silly." The sound she made was half laugh, half cry. Simon brushed her shoulder, but it was enough to turn Susie around. There he was again, not the priest but the man she danced with, the man who kissed her as they danced. Longing stripped his face of every emotion but hunger as his arms circled Susie and his mouth descended like a falling moon.

An uncontrollable shaking seized her. No line existed where she ended and Simon began, and his heartbeat resounded as her own. *Flesh of my flesh . . .*

Somehow they had gotten back into the second-floor dormitory. Simon must have half carried her because her legs were useless like sticks. They leaned against the closed door and she felt enveloped by him as she had when they danced. He took her in to him, surrounded her entirely.

"Oh, Simon!" she gasped.

He lifted her up in his arms as though she weighed nothing. Susie's eyelids fluttered shut and she hid in the curve of his neck until he gently put her down on one of the cots. When he lay beside her, his breath bathing her face in a warm tide, she looked at him. His back was to the light and darkness layered him. Susie sought his mouth again as if she could push such blackness away.

"I can't stop thinking about you, Susie, day and night," he murmured. "You haunt me."

"No, I don't mean . . ." she started to apologize, but the breath caught in her throat as his hand whispered across her breast. *I will die,* she thought, *from such longing,* and she squeezed her legs together, frightened as a girl.

Simon lifted up her sweater. The wisp of lacy bra hooked in front and with trembling fingers, she flicked the catch open.

"Susie, oh Susie, I never imagined . . ." She lay on her back as he caressed the small breasts, fondling the erect nipples, rubbing them against his palms. His fear passed from him to Susie in the tips of his fingers.

"Kiss them, please!" she whispered urgently, a pulse between her legs beating in her groin.

He bent his head and soft lips found her, sucked a nipple into his mouth and lapped at it greedily with his tongue. Susie cried out, arching up, wanting Simon inside her as she never wanted Greg, as she never knew she could want any man before. On fire she whimpered, "Simon, oh Simon," over and over, his name a prayer.

Then, suddenly, he was gone, leaving a hole in space. He clung to the far wall by the windows and his shoulders shook. He was weeping.

Susie straightened herself and left the cot. She felt light-headed when she stood, and the long rows of beds undulated like the tide.

"Simon . . ." she pleaded, but he couldn't hear her. He was praying. The Latin sounded strange in the dreary, airless dormitory. "Simon," she repeated, pulled in two directions, to rush to him and fling her aching arms about that bent shape, and to escape.

He must have sensed her approach, for he threw out a hand and cried, "Susie, don't! I'm so sorry. I must have lost my mind. Dear Jesus, forgive me!"

Susie flew away, light as the wind, heaviness in her heart, thoughts of darkness, Simon's words echoing. Rushing down the stairs, she never stopped until she retrieved her coat from the office and pulled it on outside in the windy street.

———

All the long ride uptown in the cab, Susie shivered as though coming down with the flu. The taxi lurched in a stop-and-start pattern, but she saw nothing of the city pressing against the window, nor heard the driver's curses. Finally arriving, he told her that she was home, and still she remained motionless until the doorman offered a hand to help her from the cab.

Mrs. Sloan heard her fumbling with the key at the apartment door and let her in. Tia was home already. She came into the bedroom where Susie was stretched out on the chaise lounge and recited the events of her day, her small face eager. "Laura took the Yodel right out of my lunchbox," she said. "She promised me a Twinkie but then she said her mother must've forgotten to put one in. Which is a lie. Laura's mother never gives her anything good 'cause Laura's too fat." Susie made no reply and Tia noticed her silence at last. "Are you okay, Mommy?" She sat on the edge of the chaise and nudged Susie's leg.

"What?" Her head swam as though she stood up too fast.

"Do you feel sick or something? You're so quiet, Mommy." She watched Susie with a mixture of curiosity and fear. Mothers weren't supposed to behave peculiarly, or not hers, and Susie seldom did. She had always been the most reliable of parents.

Susie opened her arms and let Tia, all disjointed parts, bony angles of elbows and knees, climb over her. Her breath smelled milky when she pressed a cheek to Susie's. Like a deep-sea diver pulling her up from the ocean's floor, Tia's presence urged Susie out of the void into which she had descended from those moments in the dormitory.

"I'm fine, Sweetness," Susie whispered into her daughter's hair, and hugged her. "Just tired, that's all."

Greg's secretary, Denise, called around five to say he wouldn't be home for dinner.

"Should I keep something warm?"

Denise put Susie on hold; then Greg came on the line sounding harried, sounding like a man rushing off somewhere. "Don't bother," he said. "I'll grab a sandwich."

"You need a proper meal," Susie said, "and nothing processed or high in cholesterol, remember." Guilt made her worry even more than usual about her husband's health. "Try to have a salad," she suggested, "and no coffee!"

"Susie, you're the best"—Greg laughed—"and I promise to behave myself."

When Susie hung up the phone she wandered into the living room and poured herself a brandy. The chill she couldn't shake iced her bones. Sitting by the window, she gazed out into the night. The park's lights sent up a silver glow and she could see the tops of the naked trees, their gaunt, twisted arms stabbing up to the overcast sky. Beyond, the buildings opposite were pricked with sparkles of gold. Once the city thrilled her, enticed her with its magic. Now it was only one more place in a world full of dirt and noise, threatening people, acts of madness and brutality, horrors that were never supposed to touch Susie Bannon Lamton. She struggled not to hear her heart's whisper: *Filled with love, too.* For what kind of love could it be, this love for a priest, she wondered, sick to her stomach.

As Susie dreamed, her face pressed against the cool window, Mrs. Sloan came in and said, "Betts isn't home yet, you know."

"What?" She looked up dazed and found she sat in darkness. Mrs. Sloan, an anonymous shape in her gray uniform, moved purposefully about the living room switching on the lamps. She left pools of light behind her as she came toward Susie.

"Betts hasn't come in from school."

"What time is it?"

"Nearly six. She's never been this late before." The women looked at one another, and Susie saw disapproval in her housekeeper's eyes.

"Did she call?" Mrs. Sloan shook her head. "Maybe Tia knows where she is."

"No, I asked her."

Had she put off confronting Betts for too long? The city down below had monsters in it. She should know. But it was one thing for her to meet the demons, another for her child.

"Maybe I had better phone around to some of her friends," Susie said, fear fueling worry. How much more dangerous life had suddenly become. "She probably stopped off somewhere, though she certainly should call. Children!" Susie cried, talking too fast as she went to the phone on the hall table. But she no sooner picked up the receiver than Betts came in. A rush of relief swept the fear from Susie's shoulders. Mrs. Sloan disappeared into the kitchen on silent feet as Susie said, "Where have you been? I was getting worried."

"Out," Betts mumbled, walking right by Susie as if she weren't there. Her hair was a mask tumbled about her face.

"Out where?" Susie meant to be calm but somehow the question turned into a complaint. Betts never glanced back and Susie had to follow her into the bedroom. "Betts," she said, "I'm talking to you!"

"You're talking *at* me!" Betts flung her down jacket in the direction of the closet and collapsed across the bed.

"Betts . . ."

"You never talk *to* me. You always raise your voice and let me have it, like I'm a wall or something." She flopped over on her stomach, burying her face in the pillow. A bedraggled stuffed bear, minus one black button eye and with a chewed ear, more bald patches than fuzz, got snuggled up under her arm. Susie half expected Betts to jam a thumb in her mouth, and the panic that only a few seconds ago gripped her heart gave way to the more familiar, almost equally painful tugging of motherhood. No one ever churned up deeper emotions, and no one ever would, not even Simon, she thought, than her daughters.

"If you're saying I treat you like a thing instead of a person, that's just not true." Betts left no room for her on the bed, and she perched awkwardly at the edge of the desk. "Betts?"

"Lemme alone. I have a headache," Betts said, her words muffled by the pillow.

"From what? Where have you been?" Susie took off down a long hill, picking up speed, unable to halt now that she'd started. "You're only fifteen, Betts, and I'm concerned."

"Mother!" she wailed.

Susie shouted back, "Don't 'Mother' me!"

Betts rolled over and stared up at her. "I want to be alone!"

"I have no intention of leaving you alone until we get some things straight." She waited one beat, two, then continued, telling herself she was under control. "You're not doing as well in school this semester as last. As well as you can do and should."

"How do you know? Marks aren't out yet."

"I had a meeting with Miss Allen."

Betts laughed sourly. "Oh, great! What did Allie have to say? Something awful probably. She hates me!"

"Hates you? Why should she? Don't be silly," Susie said.

"You don't understand."

Susie heard herself saying the same thing to Ivy Bannon: *You don't understand!* How bad, then, could this be with Betts? Not so terrible. An ordinary rite of passage, Susie thought. "Try telling me and see if I do."

"Mother . . ."

"No, Betts!"

"No, what?" the girl shouted, abruptly sitting up. She hurled the tattered bear across the room.

Susie drew in a deep breath and tried to stare Betts down as she said, "Miss Allen thinks you're doing things you shouldn't, that maybe you're taking dope."

Betts froze; the color drained from her face, leaving a blank slate that looked nothing like Susie's child. "You want to look for track marks?" She thrust out an arm and yanked up the shirt sleeve.

Susie stayed firm, though the cold wind of indecision blew through her. *Am I going about this wrong?* she worried. "Are you smoking grass, Betts?" Susie resolved not to imagine worse than that.

Betts jumped off the bed, whirling her arms like windmills, leaping about the room wildly. She forced Susie against the wall as she cried, "Sure, I'm on grass and coke and crack and horse and bennies and acid and speed and . . ."

"Stop it!" Susie yelled. For a second Tia appeared in the doorway, her round, childish face a pale moon of fright; then she ran off.

"You think I'm an addict, Mommy!" Betts outyelled her. "I hate you! I hate you worse than anything!" In her rage she swept the dresser clean, bottles, books, a picture of the four of them in a gold frame, the leather jewelry box, papers, pens, magazines, and pencils, all flying off, airborne. The room was a missile range as Betts danced about destroying whatever her fury touched. Susie screamed at her, but Betts wasn't listening, her litany—*I hate you!*—a record she seemed unable to stop. As she spun around the bed, Susie reached forward and slapped Betts's face. The crack of hand to cheek exploded like a rifle shot. A dreadful silence inundated the bedroom. That terrible action, Susie thought in horror, would remain with both of them forever, a fixed ghostly imprint on film. And even when she drew back, when her hand dropped, she could feel the pain. She almost cried to Betts, whose eyes were unfocused, *That hurt me more than it did you, it will hurt me always.*

Betts never moved. She said nothing, as if she could no longer speak. Susie forced down a scream and fled. In her own room, slamming the door, throwing the bolt, she hid herself away, pulling the darkness around her like a shroud. And yet, her eyes closed tight, she couldn't escape the thought: *I've always run off and tried to hide.*

17

Quinn hated the apartment now. She hated the quiet, too, so thick at times that it felt as though she'd lost her hearing. She wished she could avoid the dining room, but there was no other way into the kitchen except through the service door. She would have removed the room altogether if that were possible; and she considered replacing the chairs and table. But new furniture, she knew, wouldn't really make any difference.

With no dogs to walk in the morning, she should have left earlier for the lab, but she slept the extra time away and in fact began going in later. Some mornings she wanted to stay in bed, logy and light limbed, lying flat on her back and floating. She dreamed every night now, but even on first awakening, when wisps of whatever came to her during the night should linger in memory, nothing remained.

The days, once Quinn got up, were bleak, endless hours of creeping time. The friends couldn't give enough consolation; no one could. Besides, they had other worries. Quinn tried to dismiss the attack on Charlie Morgan as coincidence, a vicious urban event, but it didn't work. And despite her resolve she kept remembering Lily. *Little Lily!* A stick when she stood next to Quinn, skinny, just five feet, and with birdlike bones. We weren't going to speak of Lily, not ever again; that's what we said, Quinn told the others, told whichever woman was on the phone. But somehow Lily entered every conversation now, an unwanted guest, and they couldn't let her go. Susie's flowers. Quinn's corgis. Charlie Morgan. Dinah was the most ardent of the women, vociferous in her denials. Mistakes, all of it, she'd cry. Quinn longed to believe her. Often she'd call Dinah rather than Susie or Lisbeth just to hear Di yell down the wires, It's a lie that anything has to do with Lily! This is real life, she maintained, not one of my horror movies. No ghost, no dead friend seeking revenge after all this time, or . . .

Neither Lis nor Susie had any suggestions as to who it might be, or *what*.
Susie simply said we have to feel guilty, and Lisbeth said, it's time.

Quinn thought they were collectively losing their minds, yet it was
too painfully true that somebody had slaughtered Yin and Yang. By
design. The carefully laid table, the place cards. All of Quinn's training
screamed, *Pay attention to the evidence!* Still she struggled hard to
choose forgetfulness.

Other things came more easily, like the lie. When Will asked,
"What the hell happened to your dogs?" she swore that pneumonia
carried them off.

Will and his family offered Quinn the only relief from weariness,
from depression and grief. Brooklyn was a place to go. Maria cooked
large, elaborate meals, Mexican food now that she knew Quinn better
and could express not who she was, which was a private matter, but
where she came from. And there were the children. Especially Sarah.
Sitting in Will's little Brooklyn house, she read Sarah Sherlock Holmes
stories, which Carlos liked to hear also, or *Eloise at the Plaza,* a story
the older children had outgrown. She'd read under a lamp that threw
too weak a light, conscious of the cheap furniture, the skimpy carpeting, and almost hated her brother for all he'd gained. By running away,
Quinn meant. She stayed and what had she gotten? Not a thing now
that Yin and Yang were dead. It wasn't fair, that was all Quinn could
think, childishly, sitting on Will's old couch, with Sarah by her side, a
draft caressing her neck.

There were shadows and more shadows in Quinn's life these days,
and bending into the wind this morning on the way to the lab, she
hoped to banish them for a short while by walking. Though Stevie
expected her half an hour ago, she didn't hurry. For the first time in all
these years her research bored Quinn more often than it engrossed her.
Gene splicing, once the cutting edge of medical research, the impossible tinkering, as critics once called it, was commonplace. Now it was
simply a matter of endless labors, of countless trials and experiments,
to discover the right combinations that would ignite a shutdown im-
mune system. For the high flyers in Quinn's small world, the scientists
who played Godlike games, nothing was ultimately beyond reach.

Once research, uncovering the elusive element, making the connection, the leap from the unknown to the certain before anyone else,
being the first and not only walking off with the prizes but the
acknowledgment that *she* had achieved, set her humming with pleasure. Discovery promised to redeem her. But now depression under-
mined joy, told her that whatever successes she might attain in the lab
were, in the most profound and personal sense, meaningless. They'd

never transform her, not even for the moment, and when the accolades faded to whispers, she'd still be the same woman she'd always been.

The snappy cold and the wind nudging against her shoulders finally hurried her along.

Quinn waited for the light to change and headed west on one of the narrow side streets. The block was a grimy pocket of poverty lined with dilapidated tenements. A fat black woman, muffled in a knitted ski helmet and layers of sweaters that strained over her pillowy breasts, swept debris off the sidewalk into the gutter. Her lips were working but no sound emerged. When she first came to the city, to medical school, Quinn had been fascinated by such people, those who talked to themselves, and the others, the ones who talked to her. Once, a skinny young man, neat and clean if in old clothes, begging with an open hand outside a coffee shop, told her he came from Mars and was trying to return. She asked how he'd do such a thing at the same moment she handed him a quarter, and he stared at her as if she were the stupidest female he'd ever seen. Why, just take the bus from the Port Authority! the man exclaimed disdainfully.

She remembered a day with Lisbeth, before she moved out to California, walking together in St. Mark's Place one Sunday afternoon. Lisbeth watched her watch the crazies. "They fascinate me," Quinn observed, "like the inmates of a mental ward, or a primitive tribe in some hidden jungle. Those who are different, who live by their own rules, rules for the simplest things, for time and space. They refute physics and dictionary definitions. It's amazing."

"Well, what are we, the four of us I mean?" Lisbeth said. "Our exclusiveness, the secret pacts we have, the signals. Not that I'm complaining, just the opposite. I like being inside a circle, a closed world, where nobody else can get in."

Supposing any similarity to *them,* the lost, the mad ones, frightened Quinn, and she began backing off, until she came to ignore the derelicts as everyone else in the city did, stepping around the gesturing figures, the mutterers and ranters, as if they were things rather than people.

Quinn had no affinity for the city; she wandered through it unmoved. The noisy ferment, except for that intense curiosity of long ago, left her indifferent. At Cabot she had thought, *Now life's begun,* but it hadn't been true. Even Will's reappearance, the discovery of his children, had the feel of theater to it. Only the corgis and the women ever crossed from the audience to the stage. With the dogs gone now, she was abandoned, some part of her amputated. But she still had the friends, and in this darkening last quarter of the year she was more wedded to them than to herself.

Quinn entered the university grounds through the back gate, a narrow pedestrian passageway that brought her around on a macadam path to the front of the building.

The limousine startled her. It waited, its engine quiet, and she didn't need to see the Massachusetts license plate to identify the car as her father's. Terhune had returned. She would have slipped off if she could, but it was too late. Earl had seen her and was already getting out of the car.

"Miss Quinn!" he called over the shiny black hood.

Quinn came forward. "Hello, Earl," she said. "I didn't expect to see you so soon again."

"We've been waiting near an hour, since a quarter to nine. Thinking you came in to work early." The old man couldn't hide his disapproval. *Too bad Terhune had to sit here,* she thought, and realized Earl's annoyance wasn't for himself or Terhune when he said, "*He* shouldn't have made a long trip like this at all. Not in his condition."

Her *father* was in the limousine? Quinn took two steps backward even as Earl went around her side of the car and opened the door.

The interior of the limousine was dark as a cave. She could just make out the pale blur of a face. Her heart pounded wildly as Earl urged her nearer. How long had it been since she'd seen her father? Years now. Only a few disjointed phone calls, more pauses than speech, and what words were spoken seemed tossed in the air like balloons.

"Quinn." The raspy voice called her name. It sounded like the wind through the last of the leaves, so insubstantial she barely recognized it.

Earl, with some vigor, motioned her closer. "I—" Quinn started to say. *I can't get in that car.* Why did she have to see what the old man had turned into? She knew the disease that was about to kill him. She had seen its ravages often enough during her residency and with her mother, and the relics who refused to die quickly as the cancer ate them alive. She thought, *I can live without firsthand knowledge of his disintegration.*

"Quinn." Again her name floated from the car, and she remembered her father when he was big as Will, upright, strong, standing on the great lawn calling them through the gathering dusk. She saw her younger self running over the grass. Did he really put his arm around her, or touch her hair as she wanted to touch Sarah's, as they entered the bright house?

"Hello, Father," Quinn said, slipping into the car. Earl shut the door quietly, plunging Quinn into the watery twilight.

The old man hunched over like a crab in the opposite corner, his shoulders blades of bone under the suit jacket, his head, fringed with faded wisps of hair, hanging down as if his neck were no longer strong enough to support it. He reminded her of a rotting iris or a tulip in the Vineyard garden whose stem had softened; he was a dying growth.

"You're well, I trust," he said.

"Yes, Father. I'm fine. And you?"

Small black-currant eyes under white wings glared at her angrily. "Almost dead. Soon. Not much time left for me." He wheezed through the pursed, bloodless lips, and seeing the sallow skin, the shrunken chest, she was startled by a sudden pang of regret. Quinn thought, *He's right.*

"You shouldn't have driven all this way. The trip's worn you out." She spoke harshly, for her father, as always, confused her. She hadn't wanted to see him and now she had. Pity mixed with the tumult of all the other feelings.

"No choice," he said complainingly. The expiration of breath whistling from his mouth took forever. It sounded like escaping gas.

Quinn lowered her head. "You sent Terhune. He must have reported what I said."

"Not good enough. The name. Webster. There's only you. Think if one of your brothers were alive I'd come crawling like this?" Quinn kept her face impassive, refusing to reveal how much his rebuke hurt her.

"But you don't have my brothers, do you? All that's left is me." She choked up and had to hold her breath for a moment before she could go on. "What you really want is that I should die too, that the whole world be erased because of you." Now Quinn couldn't stop what she was saying. "Well, I'm not going to die right now, Father, no matter how angry you are. Nor am I going to chair those meetings in the boardroom with an obsequious nod to your portrait. No, not at all, none of it. How dare you even ask me!" She was screaming.

Earl slid open the panel between the front and back seats. The old man scowled at him and waved his hand, but Earl had been too long with the Websters to be chastised. "Is everything all right?" he asked Quinn.

"Shut up. Mind your own affairs," the old man wheezed.

Earl, used to insults, glanced from father to daughter, his servant's face impassive. "The doctor said he wasn't to have too much excitement," he stated.

"He should be home in bed," Quinn said, feeling her racing heart slow. It had produced a childish thrill to yell at her father; now she experienced another, talking about him as if he were powerless, a thing even.

"He's so stubborn. Has to do what he does, Miss Quinn, you know that."

"I do indeed, Earl. Only now he's dying." She swung back on her father. "Dying people should mind their manners. They can't make mistakes."

The old man's hand slapped a steady, angry beat against the seat.

"How he must hate being imprisoned in a disintegrating body," Quinn said to Earl as though George Webster were not there. "Losing control, his energy, his life slipping away, between his fingers just like sand. Wouldn't you agree, Earl?"

"Miss Quinn—"

Quinn opened the door. "I'm expected in the lab."

"Stubborn," she heard her father say.

"Miss Quinn, we're going over to the Harvard Club if you want us," Earl said. "Told him when we left Boston in the dark that even if he's up to coming and going in one day, I'm not. Last time wore me out for a week."

"Old fool," her father snapped at Earl, and Earl quieted down.

Quinn climbed from the car feeling for solid ground with her foot, almost expecting to find a void beneath her. The morning light splashed warmly, reassuringly against her face. Taking a deep breath, she turned and walked away.

Will called soon after Quinn got home, and she described the meeting with their father.

"He looks terrible, shriveled, fifty pounds lighter; only, inside he's the same. Nothing's changed." Quinn meant, *He still doesn't love me, but she didn't say it.*

"Shouldn't he be in the hospital?"

"When he gets chemo he goes in and stays a few days. It's easier for him that way. Soon, of course . . ." She left unfinished the obvious statement.

Will asked, "What was he doing down here, anyway? He hates New York."

"He's still here. At the Harvard Club, but only because Earl refused to drive back without a good night's sleep."

"How is old Earl?"

"Old, otherwise the same." Quinn hesitated before telling Will what their father wanted of her, but at last she explained.

The silence seeped through the phone. Finally he asked, "Are you going to do it?"

"Don't be ridiculous! Of course not. I have my own life here. Besides, I hate the company just as Mama did."

Will's laugh was bitter. "Mama was a Monroe, she could afford to hate the company."

"What does that mean? I haven't heard you talking about how wonderful it was working for *him*."

"He didn't ask you that, Quinn. After he's dead he wants you to take over as chairman," Will said. "Different. No Joe Stalin reminding you day and night who runs things, who does it better, more successfully than you ever could."

The tension in her neck fluted up her scalp and set off a pounding in Quinn's temples. She said, louder than she meant to, "Who cares! It's still Boston and Webster Incorporated." *And it all makes me feel like a child again, impotent,* she thought.

"You'll be the head," Will repeated.

"I don't want to talk about it anymore," Quinn cried. "How are Maria and the children?"

"You're an ostrich, Quinn," he said, but then he told her how Carlos had done on his math test and that Maria had a cold before they hung up.

Later Dinah would say there was no reason for Quinn to be surprised, that she set it up, if unconsciously, and Lis would laugh, Oh how nefarious, our Quinnie! Only Susie would understand Quinn's pain, whatever the reason.

Still Quinn insisted, I never for a moment imagined. . . .

"—the best thing to call you first. Not only because you're family, Miss Quinn, but a doctor too." Earl was breathless at the other end of the phone, though no less so than Quinn, whose heart pounded as though she'd been running miles and miles. "In case the shock does something bad to his heart. It's not only his lungs, you see, but the ticker too. The disease makes it tricky, Miss Quinn. Miss Quinn?"

"Yes, Earl, I'm here."

"What should I do? Let Master Will up to his room? Or maybe

bring him downstairs?'' Master Will. They both in a way remained children to Earl. He was only calling Quinn because he had to call somebody; the possibility of the old man's dying was too real. Quinn supposed he could have phoned Edmund Terhune, who was as close to her father as she'd ever been, probably closer. After all, the two men shared one mistress, the company. But Terhune, of course, was in Boston.

Earl nervously chattered on. ''I couldn't believe my eyes. Master Will looking like he always did except for that bit of snow in his hair. A real man, and oh how your mother would have loved to see him, Miss Quinn. Wept she did, day and night, simply worrying, right up to the minute she passed on. But you remember that. Oh, it's a miracle, that it is, Master Will's popping up like he has.'' Will might actually have died and risen from the dead.

Even as Earl talked, Quinn was pulling on her coat, checking her purse for money, keys. ''I'll grab a taxi right now,'' she said. ''Keep them apart until I get there, and Earl, don't tell either my father or my brother that I'm coming.''

Earl waited in the small lobby, shifting from one foot to the other, jumping each time a new arrival pushed through the door. There was nothing strange about a chauffeur at the entrance of the Harvard Club, though Earl neither wore nor carried his cap, but the look of panic on his face made Quinn think immediately—*Accident. He's died.* That was why Earl rushed forward with such relief when he saw her. Now she could handle the details. Already she was considering ways of transporting her father's body back to Boston, and trying not to think whether she bore responsibility for this. Had she let Will know where the old man would be so that he'd go running? Why? For the money, all that money he'd given up—access to it, anyway—and now wanted back? How she had hoped, she realized entering the Harvard Club, that Will would have acknowledged the money she gave him so surreptitiously, like a children's game or a foreign agent passing secrets. But he hadn't, and the more money she hid for him to find, the more the transactions, the simple giving, became perverse.

Will had always liked money so much.

Then the memory came back to Quinn crisp and clear. *Money missing, close to twenty thousand,* she'd heard through a door mistakenly left ajar the Thanksgiving after Will had vanished. *No!* her mother had cried.

Will was gone and the money too. Her mother wept, and still, Quinn remembered, listening, she'd stood up to her husband and insisted Will had never done *that*. Later, when Quinn asked her, she swore no such thing ever happened. Will ran off, for whatever reasons. He didn't have to go, she said. He could have stayed, should have. Will belonged at home in Boston. The money, Quinn said then, and her mother squeezed Quinn's hand, stared close into her eyes, and said, He's an unhappy man and I don't know why. Hard and unhappy. Made of flint. She meant Quinn's father.

But money and Will's leaving had nothing to do with each other. She must forget such an idea, Quinn's mother had cried. She was near hysteria, yet forceful, so Quinn, obedient, had. She forgot it, that was, until now, standing in the quiet lobby of the Harvard Club. Will had taken money, Father's money, and run off, like a guilty dog with his tail between his legs. She blushed with shame, as if the transgression were somehow her fault.

"Oh, Miss Quinn, thank God you're here! I tried, I really did, but you know he has some sixth sense, and he just jumped all over me. What are you hiding now? he kept asking, and so then I had to tell him. Of course he went white as a bag of flour, and my own ticker did some fancy two-step, let me tell you, because I thought that was it, he was going right then. But he's steel, I swear your father is, Miss Quinn, and nothing would do but for me to get him into some clothes again and bring him downstairs. Five minutes or ten, that's all it's been. He and Master Will are in one of those private little rooms at the back."

Quinn followed Earl through the somber club, quiet except for the distant rumble of voices. At the door Earl raised a hand to knock, but Quinn stopped him.

The room was small and dark, like a well-appointed cell. Heavy blinds screened the windows, and the two chairs before the hearth, where a fire was laid but not lit, were high-backed brown leather. Paneling covered the walls, and the only decoration was a series of hunting prints. *It was such a* man's *room*, Quinn thought, and neither her father nor Will seemed uncomfortable in it. As the door opened, she saw the old man's lips draw back over yellowing teeth. He resembled a gargoyle. No one who hadn't known him before disease struck—bringing as baggage the devastation of age—would have believed he had once been the handsomest of men. But Will still was. Standing by the furthest of the chairs, he resembled his father twenty years before.

Even without the fire the room was stifling, and Quinn broke out in a sweat. She wanted to throw open one of the hidden windows and bathe her skin with the cold air. She felt a tightness in her lungs, and like her father knew the horror of struggling for breath.

The door closed, leaving Earl outside in the hall, and still no one said a word.

Will froze, not a muscle moving, and with his hands jammed into the pockets of his jeans he reminded her of Edmund Terhune. Poised by the fireplace, he became what he'd been groomed and educated to be, what he'd been under the skin from birth—a Brahmin.

The old man spat at Quinn as if she were to blame for all his pain, "Twenty years!" His ragged voice set off waves of motion. Quinn removed her coat, and Will came around to take the other chair. The sound of that dying relic, their father, wheezing, dragging horny nails across his trouser legs, scratched at Quinn. She felt, not the unremitting power, the despotic authority, but a sharp, exacerbating regret. Soon he'd be in the grave, laid between their mother and George, Junior, on a slope of green hill, with a bowed chestnut dripping its branches behind the marble stones. No wind would bother him further, no daughter or son either, not even a rudderless company. There were no dreams in that eternal sleep their father was being dragged toward so reluctantly.

Now, however, a flush reddened the old man's cheeks and a shine of fractured light glinted in his sunken eyes.

The dark mouth, as if stained with old blood, spasmed as he fought for speech. The rattle of tortured breath rolled through the room. "You knew about this," the old man accused Quinn.

"For a while. Not so long." Then she looked at Will. "Why didn't you let me know you were coming over here?"

"Why, Quinnie?" This time she heard him use the childhood form of her name not affectionately but to shrink her. Quinn, standing like a servant while the two men sat, thought, *I'll always be a female.* The lesser part of her brother and father, never their equal despite her accomplishments. She shook with anger at how these men made her feel diminished.

"Earl is worried you'll overextend yourself, Father," Quinn said, turning to the old man and voicing concern for something to say.

Father and son appeared so at ease with each other, more comfortable under the circumstances than seemed possible. At the least, Quinn expected some initial awkwardness, hesitations, those shufflings strangers make as they're adjusting. Of course the old man had so little time. The clock was ticking his last minutes, and he'd known Will for as many, or more years, as he hadn't.

Allowances must be made for the dying, Quinn always remembered a professor saying in medical school. The dying were different; they saw not the light at the end of the tunnel but the black pitch of nothingness and were being rushed toward it most often against their will. So when her father snapped, "Whatever it is you want, Quinn, I'm busy now," she kept her temper and never screamed back though the rebuke stung, identical as it was to those of childhood.

"It's marvelous, isn't it, Father, finding Will after all these years," she countered, chattering foolishly, anxious to be gone from the little room, yet knowing she couldn't leave the two men who sat so companionably together.

Quinn continued, "And I'm pleased you're not angry with him."

Will laughed, but the old man scowled. "No time for anger. Too much to do, arrangements to be made."

How, in hours, things had changed. Earlier the old man held his tongue, striving for patience with Quinn. He needed something badly enough to behave. Now she no longer mattered, the tall, broad woman whose wide shoulders were slumping. He averted his gaze and almost smiled at his son. Quinn's stomach lurched and a sour taste filled her mouth.

Will crossed his legs and picked up a glass from the end table by his chair. He looked not only Bostonian, but perilously close to duplicating their father. "We'll be moving as soon as possible. Father and I decided there's no sense even in waiting for the Christmas vacation. What for? The children will all go into private schools anyway. And as for a house, why, there's ours. Home, I mean." His voice, which had possessed a flat, unidentifiable quality, an intonation that could have placed him anywhere geographically, rolled in the long drawn-out vowels, caught on the sharp ragged consonants of Boston. Chameleonlike Will shed one persona for another or, rather, reverted to who he once had been, at least in manner and demeanor.

"What about your career?" Quinn asked, roused to anger at last. "Are you planning to fix doors and windows, build cabinets, and put in kitchen counters? I understand there's quite a lot of new construction in Boston. Whole areas of the city are undergoing renovation, so you shouldn't have trouble finding jobs."

"What garbage are you babbling about!" the old man said, coughing. "Will's going to run Webster, Inc."

"You asked *me!*"

"Didn't want it. Told me so. Besides, who else was there? Just you. George dead and he was gone." He looked at Will. "No right to do that. We knew nothing."

"Never cared, either," Quinn cried, and rushed the old man, put her hand heavily on his arm, "and doesn't now. It's a trick to get me to change my mind. I'm the one. You said so."

Quinn bent over their shrunken father and caught the tainted stench of his breath rising from the rotting lungs. She stared into the muddy eyes in which the darkness almost obliterated the white. A flicker of light lit up the tiny figure reflected there and Quinn saw herself, diminutive, not large at all.

"No, not you, Quinn, Will. If I can choose. True now. The two of you. A man's what the company needs." He taunted her. "Too soft, women, like your mother."

"Leave Mama out of this. And I wouldn't brag so if I were you, Father. There are laws these days against discrimination. Ask Edmund Terhune." How silly she sounded, and tried to straighten up, but the old man clamped down on her wrist, pinning her against the arm of the chair. She could have broken loose if she struggled, but the power in George Webster was of another sort, a high-voltage intensity not so easily thwarted.

"Quinn, be reasonable. You never considered for a second moving back to Boston or giving up your research. The money doesn't matter and you hate the company," Will said quietly, but with firmness and a trace of arrogance.

Her father let her go and she was on Will, though not quite touching him. The hem of her raincoat whispered against his knee. "So do you, damn it. You hate the company, and Boston, the rich and all our privileges, Will. Remember how you raged about those months when you worked for Father? A tyrant, a monster, that's what he was. You said so! You left because it was indentured servitude, a job at Webster. You told me all those things, Will. Have you forgotten? On and on!" Her rising voice must have penetrated even the thick walls of the Harvard Club, for Earl suddenly opened the door and just as suddenly closed it again.

"You're dramatizing, making my complaints sound worse than they were. I was young, adventurous, with little desire to be serious and settle down." He shrugged and a shy half smile curled on his mouth. When he had looked this way, so endearing, boyish, their mother gave way and Will took whatever he wanted.

"I know my priorities were all wrong," he went on to confess with a slow nod to his father. His sincerity was thick as treacle, and Quinn in an abrupt, blinding fury swatted the air before his face. But he was, as he'd always been, much too quick for her. In a graceful, sleek feint he escaped her hand. Quinn stumbled and Will had to steady her.

"Be careful!" He was harsh rather than solicitous.

Quinn screamed, "What about the money, the twenty thousand dollars you walked off with?"

"I don't know what the hell you're talking about," he protested. A nerve ticked at the corner of his eye.

"Oh yes you do!" She saw at once that it was true, the whisper she'd heard winding through the house that Thanksgiving. It had been her father, then, who was in the right and her mother who lied. She needed Quinn's silence, and Quinn's forgetfulness too, so she could put Will's theft out of mind, make it into something that never had happened.

"Forgive and forget?" she asked her father, turning from Will. "What's twenty thousand dollars, anyway! Just that!" She snapped her fingers.

"Why the devil are you carrying on? Those dead dogs must have unhinged your mind," Will accused her, the Boston twang more pronounced.

"Shut up!"

"Something did." Will stood and drank the rest of his whiskey. He slammed the empty glass back down on the table. "I thought you'd be pleased, the prodigal son accepted into the bosom of the family. No more out in the cold, in Brooklyn! But, Christ, you're screaming like a banshee."

"Why shouldn't I be?"

"Why should you?"

The old man watched them avidly. There was no escaping his scrutiny even when Quinn turned aside. The glancing blow of his eternal disapproval struck midway between her shoulders.

"I suppose you suspect me of taking some unfair advantage, and what can I say? You're wrong, Quinn."

Her brother, having outflanked her, didn't really want explanations. He wanted her gone. And what could she say, that for these weeks and months she'd been the *bigger* one, that he'd been dependent, searching in his underwear drawer, the pockets of his jackets, for *her* money. A hand outstretched, Will, who'd always outrun Quinn, been the handsome, oh so loved one, had become a beggar. She gave or not as the feeling moved her.

Quinn's cheeks burned.

The old man started a tottering rise from his chair. "Enough of this. Going to bed." Standing, shoulders stooped, George Webster had shriveled to her level. Yet, shrunken and ill though he was, she realized he still kept himself immaculate, not a hair out of place, manicured fingernails, white cuffs, a gray pin-striped suit. His silk tie was held in place by a handsome gold clip, a snake surrounded a small Roman coin, Augustus in profile.

Quinn remained in the old man's path. "I'm not finished, Father. You owe me the truth about the past, about that money."

"I don't owe you anything. My money, my business."

Why, oh why, couldn't she stop herself, just turn and leave! What difference did it make if Will went to Boston? *Sarah.* Even so, Boston wasn't running away, disappearing. There were holidays, vacations. The shuttle took less time than a taxi to Brooklyn. Let him go make his compromises, bury his lies. Will was family; he had children.

Her father glared with a direct fiery gaze not dimmed by either age or illness. "Childish. Get out of my way, Quinn. I'm tired."

Quinn shrank from his disdain. How miserable, how pitiful this man thought her! Her throat tightened as her father waited patiently for her to move, while Will hovered. It struck her with some satisfaction that he was still not wholly confident.

She had to make him realize she was someone in her own right, but it took effort for her to protest, "I am a physician, Father. I'm involved in important research."

"That's nice, Quinn. Now, to bed," he said. A shaky hand wavered, as if wiping aside what she'd done, who she was, and pushed at her arm in an attempt to get by.

Quinn shoved, and her father fell backwards, a hip striking the high side of the chair.

"For Christ's sake, Quinn, are you crazy!" Will yelled.

She ran for the door. "I don't give a damn. About you or him. No one since Mama died." A lie, she knew, even as the words left her lips. The women, she cared about them. They were everything, and now, so unexpectedly, there was a child of Will's—Sarah. Pushing past Earl, who had faithfully stationed himself out in the corridor, Quinn slammed from the club. *Fool, fool, fool!* She was suddenly afraid that Will in revenge for her tantrum and bad behavior would keep his children secreted away. Will, she remembered with a chill at the nape of her neck, always got even.

18

Charlie Morgan recuperated from the knife wound faster than the doctors expected. Within a week he was discharged from the hospital and home in his apartment. It would be another week or two, however, before he'd resume teaching. Meanwhile, as he told Lisbeth, he had an unexpected vacation, time during which he could work on his book. Publish or perish was Charlie Morgan's professional nightmare. His occasional articles in the small journals were no longer enough to assure him of tenure and he was writing a full-scale analysis of the rehabilitated criminal and his long-term adjustment to society. He'd have at least two chapters to show for his time at home and sounded almost pleased about the assault for providing this.

He did, however, want Lisbeth with him all the time. Charlie saw no reason why they couldn't work in the same apartment, though in different rooms, of course. Then she wouldn't have to travel from the Village to the Upper West Side, which she did often now that Charlie was home. She found it difficult to resist his requests after the stabbing, and because she gave in in ways she never would have before, she resented him. *I love Charlie; I almost lost him.* But telling herself this made no difference. Most nights she couldn't wait to leave his apartment, where she refused to sleep, and hurried downtown. Often Neff would be waiting, though there were too many times she couldn't remember and she only knew she'd been with him by the evidence. Her body was sore and there were bite marks on her thighs. One morning she found a painful welt across her back, as if she'd been hit with a strap or a belt. She didn't ask Neff how she'd gotten that, though. The blackness and the lost hours were her secret; she wouldn't even tell Susie. Secret, like the headaches that often blinded her no matter how much Percodan she swallowed, so that she moved tentatively with other people, watching what she said. The women said that Lis was calmer, more subdued. Charlie thought she was being quieter because of him. Only Neff didn't notice or didn't care. But mostly she only recalled Neff talking about Charlie and who might have entered his apartment to stab him.

Charlie possessed no curiosity about his assailant's identity. An ordinary breaking and entering. A daily occurrence in New York City, he said without animosity to the police and to Lisbeth. A personal vendetta? Never, he protested, and Lisbeth wouldn't tell him of the corgis or Susie's flowers any more than she had of her own apartment being trashed. He hadn't heard of Lily Vaughan, and the friends agreed there was no reason he should now.

Let the poor man think whatever he wants, Susie had said earlier over the phone to Lisbeth. We have no proof, except in our hearts. But we must, we absolutely *must,* be wrong, Susie thought, even as the familiar tightness invaded her chest.

She stood before the bathroom mirror screwing in her diamond earrings. In the background she saw Greg passing back and forth putting on his tuxedo.

Guilt sticks like mucilage, leaving white patches even though you try to scrub it off, one Susie whispered silently to the other.

Greg called, "Where are my gold studs?"

"Top drawer of your dresser. Under the handkerchiefs."

"You sure? I can't find them." Susie turned the tiny screw as she heard the rumble of the drawer being pulled out. "Oh yeah, here they are."

In a moment Greg appeared in the doorway. He handed Susie the studs, then stuck out his arms. "Do you really want to go?" he asked.

"Miss *Silver Street*? Never. And why should I?" She looked up at him curiously.

"Susie, I hate to upset you, but the word is that Lisbeth's play has no underpinnings. All surface, and worse, nothing snappy to draw in the crowds." His eyes were pained. Greg disliked telling Susie something that might make her unhappy.

"Now where did you hear that?"

"Oh, around." He shrugged. "It's just the word."

"The word? From whom?" Susie laughed. "Honestly, you and your secret information! Sometimes I suspect you of being a spy. A regular James Bond," she teased her husband.

"Laugh, but what happens if the play proves to be a dead bird? Are you going to lie to Lisbeth and say it was up there with *Macbeth*?"

"I'll love it," Susie swore. "I always love what Lis writes."

"You'll just never learn to make informed judgments," he said, shaking his head and wandering off. Susie watched his retreating back in the mirror. He meant so well. Face facts, Greg always instructed her. He'd set himself stiffly as a soldier and insist, There's no escaping what is. Yet with Betts so far his attitude was, let's not jump the gun. Some mistake here, he insisted adamantly. We could make it worse, he complained to Susie. But he did take Betts for a long walk in the park and both girls out to see the latest Eddie Murphy movie. And, almost politely, he'd say to Betts, I love you.

"You're going to have to face the truth, Susie," Greg called from the other room as if on cue.

She sighed and wondered if Ivy Bannon knew her husband as well as Susie did Greg, and how much did that familiarity sadden her?

Taking a brush to her glossy hair one last time, Susie tucked an unruly curl in place, then stepped back to view the overall effect. The long white knit dress clung from shoulders to ankles. It suddenly seemed too revealing, though only the merest sliver of skin showed below her neck. She considered changing, wearing something loose, a dress that draped in ample folds of fabric beneath which she could hide. Hiding was what she longed to do with herself, secrete away the physical being as Arab women did under their galabias, only eyes watchfully peering out above the mask.

Greg returned, pointing to his watch: "Time to go. We have to allow a good ten minutes for the doorman to whistle down a cab at this hour." Susie waited for Greg to comment on her appearance. "You look beautiful," he said.

But you always do, he'd add.

"But you always do," he echoed.

"Thank you, darling." She smiled, following Greg out of the bedroom. In the mirrors, the various shining surfaces, she charted her passage through the apartment, the facade recognized, known, but behind the makeup, the jewels, the expensive dress. . . . *You can't feel a void, nothing, what doesn't exist,* Susie thought, trying to catch a glimmer of light in her eyes when she saw them reflected. Emptiness, that was all. The memory of Lily's special flowers, blood on her finger, and those dead dogs, rose up to haunt her.

I won't think of this now. . . .

They stopped to say good night to the girls and called out to Mrs. Sloan; then Greg helped her on with the fur coat. "I think we're overdressed for off-Broadway," he grumbled.

"No. We all agreed to make a splash for Lisbeth. Diamonds and furs. The works. And there's a party afterwards at Vanessa on Bleecker Street. We were there once with the Hurleys. You liked the food."

"Oh right, right." Suddenly he grinned impishly.

227

"What's so funny?"

"Just imagining Quinn Webster in a mink coat. I bet she'd look like something you'd point a gun at in the woods."

"That's cruel!"

"I'm sorry." He quickly kissed her cheek as they waited for the elevator. "But you've got to admit—"

"Greg!"

"Okay. No more jokes about the Cabot girls!" The cab arrived. As they stepped inside, Greg, confronting himself in the glass, straightened the bow tie just a hair. "Oh, by the way, you never told me, what did happen to her dogs? You just said they died."

"Just died, that's all," Susie said. "And don't mention it. Quinn gets very upset." *And so do I.*

The truth was that Quinn didn't want her to stay overnight, and nothing would convince Dinah otherwise as she drove around the crowded Village streets searching for a place to park. Cars hugged the curbs from the start of a block to the end, bumper to bumper as though welded to one another.

She wanted to sleep at Quinn's after the party rather than drive back home to Westport, but Quinn worried about Mikey. Don't leave him alone! she cautioned with the dreadful sonority of an oracle. Really, as if something could happen to him, as if this ridiculous Lily business, which had nothing to do with Lily Vaughan in the least, Dinah had firmly decided—the flowers and the dogs only sick jokes and Charlie Morgan's assault a coincidence—might reach out and touch him. Oh, Quinn, despite her scientific brilliance, was silly, Dinah thought, turning the corner onto Twelfth Street, because no reason in the world existed to worry about Mikey.

There, was that a space? She pressed the gas and speeded up to the center of the block, but found only another fire hydrant. Damn! Dinah drove east, bisecting Fifth Avenue, glancing at the clock in the dash. Still time. She hated to make Lis wait, especially tonight.

There was not so much as an available inch of legal parking space all the way to University Place. Some spite in Dinah half goaded her just to stop at a traffic light and get out. Let a tow truck drag the old horse off to the pound. Why not? Free, free, she whispered, driving on.

Hope fired up in Dinah like a hot flame at the sight of a promising indentation just ahead on the left. She speeded up only to find a tiny Triumph snuggled in the hole. She clenched her teeth. Nobody should own a convertible in Manhattan.

Working her way up to Fourteenth Street, Dinah sensed that the two-piece silk dress she wore under her good black coat with the fox collar was wrinkling. Little creases crept beneath her legs each time she stirred. *I'll look like a washerwoman,* she despaired, taking a deep breath to feel the tight waistband dig into the soft fold of flesh about her midsection. Why had she eaten that frozen pizza just before she got dressed? Well, who knew when they'd get fed, and maybe nothing more than a few little hors d'oeuvres. And the play was hours long. Oh, how she hoped, whenever she thought about it, that Lisbeth's *Silver Street* was a big success. Not that she needed any more accomplishments in her life, money either. Richer than a ship-owning Greek, that was Lisbeth, from all that Ferris Rosenthal wealth.

Please, Dinah started to pray, *give me somewhere to park!* Traveling east once more, she would have put the wagon in a garage, but the few she passed were either full or closed by ten o'clock. *Damn Quinn!* she thought again. *Double damn!* Because the other thing was, with the car she wouldn't be able to drink, not more than a glass, possibly two, of wine since she had to maneuver the parkway to Westport without killing herself. The night was fraught with disappointments.

There, at last, miles from Lisbeth's apartment, a slip of curb free of any impediment, unmarked, into which she backed the station wagon, sent it forward, kissed the Ford in front, shifted to reverse and bumped the Renault behind. After a sweaty struggle that dampened the curls on her neck, Dinah breathed a sigh of satisfaction. She had parked the car.

Now, hurrying along, her highest heels pinching her toes and giving her an awkward gait, Dinah checked her watch. Five minutes late. Not too bad. She paused for the light to change, rushed west to Fifth, then down, too warm, out of breath, but setting her shoulders back despite the strain. *Another few blocks,* she thought, wondering if they'd have time for her to take an iron to the skirt, maybe wash again under her arms, touch up her face, and. . . .

Out of nowhere, attached with the suddenness of a mugger leaping from a dark brownstone well, the afternoon she'd gone to Hatch's office sprang into Dinah's mind. She stalled, blundering against the barrage of memory. What a fool she'd made of herself that awful afternoon!

Afterwards, back in Westport, Dinah blocked out the trip, held all her carnivorous memories at bay. But one after another, they crept in on her when she slept. She'd awaken at four A.M. in a cold sweat. The dying hour. Body at low ebb. Most sick people went then, she remembered, listening to the pounding of her heart and seeing Hatch's snarl.

He had been ready to kill her. In defense Dinah banished the afternoon, but it kept resurfacing at unguarded moments like now.

Dinah shook herself and walked rapidly on, right into remembering that time at Cabot when Lily caught her shoplifting a gold bracelet from the boutique in town and threatened to tell. Nasty Lily with her pointy teeth, a vampire smiling and promising to bite, had bobbed up out of nowhere just as the gold links slipped into Dinah's pocket. She'd had to give Lily the bracelet to keep her quiet and then suffer for months through her sly innuendos.

Well, Lily Vaughan, you're dead now, aren't you? And good rid-dance! I hope you're burning in hell. Lily gone gave her immense satisfaction, but as Dinah approached the steps of Lisbeth's building, she thought involuntarily of the blood and the flowers, Quinn's mur-dered corgis and the wounded Charlie Morgan, and ice settled about her heart.

As she climbed up to ring the bell, Dinah heard the roar of a car. She turned around and there, just a few feet down the block, something long and dark pulled out, leaving a space at the curb large enough to park the station wagon. Dinah took this missed opportunity as an omen, a bad one.

If the scheduled event had been anything other than the opening of *Silver Street,* Quinn would have begged off. A cold was coming on, beginning to fill up her head with that faint, waspy buzzing, and a leadenness was settling in her limbs. Oh, for a day or two lying in bed and being sick, feverish, eyelids forever closing. Floating down into a cottony sleep, that was what she now longed for. As it was, she had spent three days not going to the lab, though she couldn't beg off tomorrow. Stevie's latest calls were frantic. I'm too inexperienced to track this experiment by myself. That was the unspoken cry whistling down the phone lines whenever Stevie managed to catch Quinn on the other end. Tell me what to do now, and after this. And if this happens, what?

What Quinn did with this time had no consequences. Without plan-ning it, she returned again and again to the Metropolitan, wandering, without purpose, and most often coming to ground in the medieval section, peering narrowly at the carved ivories or running dry fingers surreptitiously over the madonnas. Sometimes she sat in the tiny chapel or out in the new American wing. The museum rested her.

Only once had she started over to Brooklyn, but just before the bridge she had the taxi let her off. She called Will from a pay phone on a windy corner, drops of cold rain sliding down her collar. Maria answered, and after all these years of living in the United States, she seemed to have forgotten her English. Quinn, who spoke no Spanish, kept crying, *I don't understand!* Finally Maria managed to say, Don't come now. Not now. Maybe after. He goes off to Boston three, four days.

And the children? Quinn screamed against the city's clamor. But Maria had already hung up the phone.

Yes, anything but the opening of Lisbeth's long-awaited play, and Quinn would have said, *I can't*. What energy she possessed these days was necessary for ordinary motion.

Will's betrayal and the old man's cruelty, coming together as they had, were doubly hard to endure. Their indifference, the little thought they'd given her, and the abrupt dismissal dragged Quinn reluctantly once more back to childhood. She suffered again the taunts at her awkwardness and the lumpy body, the plain, uninteresting face.

I should hate Mama if I were you, Will once said, pulling her straight drab hair as they watched from the front window their parents in formal dress leaving the house one evening. Quinn was six or seven then, but already she understood what her older brother meant as the tall, floating woman in the long velvet gown crossed the sidewalk to the car. How disappointed their mother should have been in having a homely, gawky bird of a daughter, yet it was their father who'd been angered. Her mother always said, You have lovely eyes, Quinn, and soft skin, and what's most important, you're smart. Her mother had sustained her; then she was gone. Quinn hated the Webster men, even dead pusillanimous Georgie, who'd been handsome despite his weak chin and whose suicide she'd always considered a desertion. Quinn loved the only person who had pronounced her wonderful.

Quinn hadn't told the friends about Will and how he was moving to Boston to do what she had rejected. It was her father's asking, almost begging, as well as Edmund Terhune down on his pin-striped knees and her refusal that had felt good. But then they snatched all that out of her grasp, the old man and Will. I only asked, not because it was you, but because there was *only* you. The awfulness of that scene in the Harvard Club still made Quinn physically sick.

She should tell the women, for who else was in her life who could or cared to listen, to sympathize? And really, these twenty years since Cabot they'd shared so much. (How could they not, a tiny voice whispered.) They clung closer than sisters, than parents and children.

231

Always the four of us, only us, Quinn thought with some comfort, taxiïng through the night to the theater.

She leaned against the cracked seat and stared not out at the disappearing streets but inward at the Cabot memories, whitened, blanketed with snow. *The past, the past.* She sighed, and her eyes filled up with tears for all of them and especially for the corgis.

19

Lisbeth tried to watch *Silver Street* from the back of the theater, but she couldn't stand still for long. Nervousness would seize her and she'd have to grip both elbows to control the shaking. Several times she walked out to the lobby for a drink of water. At the sight of her, Gilly muttered, "So now we'll see who was right." Having withdrawn the nude scene or, being both spiteful and angry, as he tattled to the cast, "Forced to do so, my dears, by the original Queen of Sheba," Gilly was unforgiving. Though his own fortunes were tied to the success or failure of *Silver Street,* it seemed as if a part of him wished for a flop so he'd be proved right about the need for a naked body. He'd been heard to snip, "I hope the bitchy Ms. Rosenthal falls on her skinny derriere," and reportedly bragged, "I've produced so many plays the outcome of this one really means very little to me."

After the dress rehearsal, which went as badly as those things usually did, Lisbeth met up with Gilly backstage near the light board and shoved him into the wall. She grabbed his shirt and bending low, whispered in his purpling face, "You're just a nasty aging faggot, Gilly, without an ounce of talent or much of a brain."

When Corbert protested to Lisbeth later about this display and her public treatment of Gilly, who "does have credentials and calling him tasteless names won't change that," Lisbeth couldn't remember the incident. Her memory of the dress rehearsal ceased somewhere in the last act. The rest of the evening was obliterated, time wiped clean, but Lisbeth had no intention of telling Corbert Fleis or Gilly that. So the animosity deepened from a pool to a lake. They were truly enemies now, and Gilly would have happily killed her if he'd been able. Not that such hostility dented Lisbeth's indifference. She cared about *Silver Street,* a story of a *hate* affair in Hollywood and ability both aborted and spent, not about the play's producer.

233

She leaned against the glass doors. A rising wind blustered down the empty street, stirring up bits of debris, sending kites of newspaper into spins.

"I'll never do another thing of yours, Lizzy-bet," Gilly spat at her.

Lisbeth, knowing that if the reviews came in raves Gilly would be on his knees begging to stage her address book, said, "Take a walk. I wouldn't let you." That much wasn't fake. If she made a hit with *Silver Street*, everyone in New York would come to call. Nothing makes more friends than success, Lisbeth had quickly learned in movie-land. Failure, on the other hand, produced the same result as bad breath.

Gilly continued to glare at her, but she was not about to retreat into the theater and take her seat between Charlie Morgan and her mother. Paul Morell had come after all, his wheelchair on Anne's right in the aisle. He wouldn't have stayed home for anything, Anne informed Lisbeth coldly, as if to say, Not that you deserve such loyalty. Her mother was as unforgiving as Lisbeth, and Anne's allegiance was to her crippled husband.

This is your night, savor it, Charlie Morgan had urged her. But the distance kept widening between Lisbeth and *Silver Street*. One Lisbeth spied another reflected in the glass door, chewing her bottom lip and playing with the long red tangle of hair.

The inevitable headache clawed up her temples. She swallowed a Percodan with a mouthful of warm water, and as the evening wore on, the second act of *Silver Street* moving into the third, the pain shriveled, drew in its nails. Just to be safe, however, she had taken another capsule with a glass of acidy red wine during the last intermission.

Silver Street rushed to its curtain, five minutes shorter than in rehearsals, and time suddenly collapsed like a house of cards as the audience rose with a burst of applause. The cast, smiling, took their bows in sweaty exhaustion. Then it was Corbert's and Gilly's turn, with Lisbeth in the middle, all three like lost children holding hands. The glare of the lights, the thunder of palms slapping against each other, all rose up and rolled over Lisbeth. She staggered during the few steps she took on the stage and would have fallen if the two men hadn't been holding on to her. Gilly shot her a furious glance as the curtain fell. Corbert, stunned that everything was over, his future in the slippery hands of the gods, looked more and more like the sole survivor of a plane disaster.

Lisbeth sleepwalked around to the front of the theater. The others had already gone over to the restaurant in the limos Anne hired for the evening, but Charlie was waiting patiently with the shaggy good humor of a Saint Bernard. "A terrific play, just great!" he said, encircling Lisbeth in a careful embrace. "A hit, no two ways about it."

"How do you know?" Lisbeth asked, breaking loose from Charlie's arms. She sounded belligerent though she hadn't meant to be. But there was no loving at all in her tonight. She needed *Silver Street* to be a success too much to be the least bit giving, and the need made her gag.

"Trust me, Lisbeth, the critics will love it. That Roger Clark was perfect, wonderfully smarmy in the part. I also liked Tilda what's-her-name, and the one who played the agent. Sensational casting, and you know, I was surprised after what I've been hearing from you, but Fleis's direction was good—better, first-rate." Charlie's words should have thrown a safety net under her despair, but as they taxied west to the party she only grew more depressed.

The crowd was collected about the bar and scattered among the tables, talking animatedly as she and Charlie entered the restaurant.

"Another mountain climbed," Susie, kissing her cheek, whispered in Lisbeth's ear.

Eyes closed, Lisbeth clutched her. "All those bears going over all those mountains," she murmured as Susie giggled.

"What bears? What mountains?" Greg asked.

"Our junior year, when Lis got her jeep," Susie explained, "the four of us spent most of our time driving around the countryside singing kid songs."

Susie reached out and hugged Lisbeth again. Lis sighed and said, "Ivoire by Balmain."

"A lucky guess," Susie said. Lisbeth had an infallible nose for perfume.

"Here, Lisbeth, have a drink. You probably need one." Greg insinuated an arm between the women, pushing a glass of champagne at Lisbeth. The amount of physical affection his wife displayed with her friends unsettled him. Greg had a streak of old-fashioned prudery in him, though he pretended to the sophistication appropriate for a successful financial expert living all these years in New York City. In his heart of hearts, though, he found something unseemly in women always touching each other. *Pawing.* As for the women, they sensed how desperately Greg longed to tuck Susie away on a high shelf, unreachable by anybody else.

Quinn broke through the crowd to join them. She too kissed Lisbeth's cheek, but with the mere brush of lips. "Wonderful, Lis," she said about the play. "I thoroughly enjoyed it, though they were quite awful people. Are there actually that many liars and cheats in Hollywood? I thought such deceit was the province of Bostonians."

Before either Lisbeth or Susie could say anything, Dinah was on them. She had a glass of champagne in one hand, an hors d'oeuvre in the other. "Loved *Silver Street,* Lis. Cuckoo about it. God, it's the best thing you've done, even better than *The High Valley,* and you know how much I adored that." Dinah's smile was already glazed.

"You better put more food into your stomach before the champagne drops a depth charge," Susie suggested.

"Oh, not to worry!" Dinah said, smiling and licking her lips. "I never get besotted on bubbly, not me."

"I seem to remember one Winter Carnival," Quinn was saying.

Dinah, however, had already swung around to Charlie Morgan. "Lisbeth never mentioned you were built like a bulldozer."

Greg hurriedly whispered to Susie, "There's someone from Morgan Stanley over in the corner we really should talk to." He slipped a firm hand under his wife's arm, but Susie removed him.

"You go on," Susie said.

"Still a pretty weak machine, actually." Charlie was laughing.

Lisbeth, knowing Dinah in her cups only too well, realized she was going doggedly on, ready to ask Charlie where he'd been stabbed and maybe, if he wouldn't mind, unbuttoning his shirt and showing the wound to her. Lisbeth never cared what any of them did, made no judgments on these friends, but as Dinah cried, "I hope you don't mind my asking, Charlie, but where exactly did that mugger stab you?" She suddenly saw Dinah with a different eye, unmasked by affection. *She drinks too much . . . she's too sorry for herself. . . .*

Lisbeth's hands curled into fists, the nails digging into the palms. A rush of dislike, even hatred, swept through her. *I care about Dinah, love her even, though not as much as Susie,* Lisbeth promised herself, but she couldn't dislodge the hostility that had her shivering.

Charlie pointed just right of the center of his chest. Dinah blew at a strand of hair across her face and said, "Could we see it? The scar, I mean."

She's foolish. A drunk, too.

Dinah stared at Charlie. She looked silly, almost goofy. There was a smear of lipstick at the corner of her mouth.

Lisbeth found herself wanting to slap her, almost felt Di's cheek under hand. Then, suddenly overwhelmed by loss, she bent forward and kissed Dinah exactly where the stinging blow might have landed.

"Oh, Di!" Susie laughed, and Quinn snatched Dinah away from Charlie Morgan and walked her over to the buffet.

In the distance Anne Rosenthal motioned to Lisbeth. Lis had no choice but to move in that direction, sliding slowly through the crowd, stopped every few feet by people wanting to talk to her. Not until she reached the table by the wall of windows did she realize that Charlie had stayed with her. She was forced to introduce him as he sank into a chair across from Paul. Even in the dim lighting she could see that Charlie was pale, and when he raised his glass, champagne spilled.

Anne, who seldom missed a thing, asked, "Are you feeling ill?"

"No, no. Not at all. Just had an accident a few weeks ago, and I guess I overdid it a bit. Plus all these people!" He smiled apologetically, as if he was responsible for the milling crowd.

An accident! Lisbeth thought. *Doesn't he take anything seriously? Some accident, Charlie. A knife got shoved into you while you slept.* His complacency annoyed her and his big, happy face, just as Dinah's had a moment before. It was as if familiar landmarks were changing as she watched.

Charlie and Paul launched into conversation, smiling at one another, momentary acquaintances transformed into friends. This made her angry too.

Her head hurt. She was lifting a hand to rub her temples when Anne said, "And what about you, Elizabeth?"

"What?" She dropped her hand quickly, afraid of acknowledging the pain to her mother or Charlie.

"How do you feel?"

"Fine. Why?" Lisbeth sensed sympathy passing from Anne to her, but she shrugged it off.

Anne sighed. Even amid the clamor Lisbeth heard that sigh. It had been Anne's response to the difficulties, even the tragedies, of life as long as Lisbeth could remember. "I just thought that, finally, you might be content."

Whatever her mother meant, she heard the comment as a complaint. Hadn't it always been like that? What are you wearing? Where did you find that friend? I suppose you did as well as you could. Why not try it over again, Elizabeth? Anne not only understood nothing of magical kingdoms, she never found that the real world matched her expectations either. Lisbeth wondered again why Anne had chosen Paul Morell, a man so crippled within by terrible memories and outside by a maimed leg.

"Elizabeth?"

The old name, the one other people had given her that made a prison in which she was forced to be whom it was *they* said, came at Lisbeth like an arrow. We bring things into existence by naming them, people too, she started to tell her mother sitting at the other side of the table.

"Mother—" she began just as Paul Morell said very loudly how well acted *Silver Street* had been. His normally soft voice turned her around; in that single blink of a second she imagined it was Ferris Rosenthal sitting in the chair.

The headache crawled to the back of her skull and barbed wire dug into her scalp. Sometimes the darkness surged like that, rising up as if from the earth itself, black and loamy.

Lisbeth touched her brow with light, tentative fingertips.

"What is the matter with you?" Anne cried.

Lisbeth, not taking care, drowning in the anger that threatened to swamp her, cried, "I'm not the perfect girl, Mother. I'm about to disappoint you again." As she spoke, some intuition told Lisbeth *Silver Street* was going to fail.

"Of course, you're not perfect," Anne answered, her tone modulated as always. "No one is. And I never asked that of you, anyway. As for disappointment, well, Elizabeth, I don't know what any of us has done this time to so annoy you, but please, let's not discuss it *here*. This is neither the time nor the place."

Charlie came halfway up from his chair and asked if Lisbeth wanted something to eat.

"I'm not hungry."

"The food's supposed to be great. You should try some of it. Just tell me what you want, okay?" Charlie was trying to soothe her.

"I don't know which is worse, the kind of men so self-centered and arrogant that they see everyone else in miniature, or men like you, Charlie, so damn *accommodating*. You'd crawl across the Sahara to get me a cracker and cheese! So sweet you make my teeth ache!" Lisbeth cried, angry at Charlie Morgan's kindness, at how *nice* he was. In spite of herself, she wanted to hurt him even more than the knife thrust had.

People at the nearby tables turned to stare at her curiously.

"Stop it, Elizabeth!" Anne ordered, in distress.

"Sit, sit," Paul said, patting the arm of the chair next to him and not looking at Charlie, whose face had the stony lifelessness to it of marble.

All three would trap her if she sat down, so innocent and loving, sheep, all of them. So at home with one another. She saw them as linking together, standing in a solid wall against her.

Retreating, Lisbeth bumped into Corbert, his reedlike physique clothed in an antique tuxedo, the lapels of worn velvet. "It went well, didn't it? I mean it played great?" He begged for some assurance. Lisbeth passed him by as she would a cowering dog, and catching Susie's eye nodded toward the ladies' room.

There were three women Lisbeth didn't recognize posturing before the mirror. She moistened a paper towel and dabbed at her burning eyes. Two of the women left together, and as the third pulled open the door to go, Susie slipped inside. "God, there's a mob out there!" she said, squeezing Lisbeth's hand. "You should be pleased as a maharani."

Lisbeth lowered her head and the world came apart beneath her. The white porcelain of the basin oozed and spread, filling her vision. Snow covered the ground in an unbroken sheet and she shivered.

"Lis, what is it?" Susie's arm gripped her tightly and kept her from sinking. The cold of the frozen earth moved up her legs. Her breath puffed in white clouds.

"Cold." Lisbeth's teeth chattered.

"Here, let me get you into a stall. You can sit down on the john."

Once inside a cubicle Lisbeth moaned as Susie started to leave. "No, stay, Suz."

Susie latched the door behind her. "Too much champagne or too much everything?"

Lisbeth couldn't answer as Susie stroked her hair. The gesture was comforting, familiar, though when Lisbeth tried to remember her mother's hand in such a motion nothing came to her.

She moved back and forth under Susie's touch, stretching like a cat, wanting more. Susie's fingers trailed down one cheek. "Oh, that feels good!" Lisbeth murmured.

The outer door creaked and they heard two women come in chattering.

". . . Would you believe?"

"Well, I never thought he was that sort."

"He is. Take my word for it."

There was the splash of running water.

"Do you have any mascara?"

Susie moved closer. Lisbeth's arms came and circled around her. She laid her cheek against the smooth flatness of Susie's stomach.

"No, just eyeliner."

"Hmmm. Makes me look like a raccoon."

"Okay, back to the fray. Ready?"

Susie's tremors passed into Lisbeth, whose hands still held her tightly. Lis rubbed her face against the weave of the dress, humming softly, too low for the women outside to hear.

239

"Yeah, as much as I'll ever be."

The door hushed shut again and the tiny cubicle filled with the harshness of their breathing.

"No, Lis, no," Susie whispered urgently.

Girls' love, that's what they called it, Susie's mind recoiling even as she felt those same sensations again, after so many years. Desire and excitement, need and love. "Lis, don't." Her hands gripped Lisbeth's shoulders and inched her back.

"Do you remember?"

"Yes, but that was so long ago; that was then. This is now. We were young and—" And what? And we loved one another? We still do. "But not like this," Susie added as if Lisbeth could read her thoughts. Gently she raised Lis up.

They held one another and Lisbeth said, "I'm scared."

"Of course you are," Susie said, comforting, "we all are." *But,* she thought, *of different things.*

A large Sony had been hooked up at the bar. Gilly flipped the dial from channel to channel. The three reviews they managed to catch were remarkably alike. The cast displayed a slick professionalism, the director had wrung them for every ounce. The sets had elegance. But the play itself was badly flawed. After the first review people catcalled, but by the third, silence settled over the restaurant. Surreptitious glances were darted at Lisbeth; then people turned away embarrassed, avoiding the erect figure standing with the implacability of a totem pole. Charlie held on to her arm, but Lisbeth never looked at him. Down toward the other end of the bar, drinking champagne, Greg whispered to Susie, "No underpinnings."

Susie's cheeks stung. Whatever her feelings, she had no intention of crossing the crowded room to stand at Lis's other side. To do that would make Lisbeth seem in need of support, point up how much she must be hurting. Yet Susie had to force herself to stay where she was, for Lisbeth had said what she never had before: *I'm afraid.*

Gilly sent one of the stagehands over to the nearest newsstand to wait for the early editions. He returned just as Corbert switched off the TV with shaking hands.

"Great! The *Times!*" Gilly shouted, waving the paper. He smiled, his teeth exposed as though he were preparing to take a bite out of somebody. The stagehand offered Lisbeth the *News.* She ignored it. Charlie took it instead.

Frank Rich was less enthusiastic than the television critics, but he approved of Roger Clark. The star bowed his head modestly and shrugged. *Silver Street,* the critic wrote, had more of the feel of a movie than a play. It never stopped long enough for relationships to be plumbed, and what revelations there were seemed deliberately timed, so many an act. The man in the *News* was even more succinct. He admired the labor that went into *Silver Street,* though he wasn't sure why anyone had bothered. Surely the stage didn't need its version of *Dallas* or *Dynasty.* Surely there had to be writers lurking about who could create genuinely interesting plays.

In the funereal hush of the room, Dinah cried, "Well, I loved it!" Angrily Quinn quieted her.

"Come on, let's get out of here," Greg urged Susie, pinching her elbow. But Susie shut her eyes and thought, *I'd be a fool to push my way over there now, to put my arms around Lis and just let her hold on. Lis has never needed succoring.* And she thought, *Lis never learns.* But then, she said to herself, *I suppose I don't either.*

People began wandering off into the night. A failure was shameful; they ran away.

Gilly stalked in front of Lisbeth on his march to the front door, a phalanx of slim young men in a half circle about him. He shoved the *Times* in her face. "I told you so, Lizzy-bet, now didn't I? But you knew better than Gilly. You're the big Hollywood literary expert." One of the boys giggled.

The periphery of Lisbeth's vision darkened, and she saw Gilly at the end of a long tube, a fat, jumpy little man dancing about in jerky puppet gyrations. Her hand shot out on a trajectory for Gilly's baby face, but another of the young men, faster than Lisbeth, grabbed her narrow wrist and bent it back.

"You tacky little bastard!" Lisbeth spit.

"Nudity would only have agitated the critics more. It certainly wouldn't have mollified them," Charlie Morgan said, freeing her wrist.

In a whirl, as people scattered, Lisbeth's faction surrounded her, but Charlie urged everyone to leave.

"There will be other plays, Elizabeth. You must let this one go and move on," Anne Rosenthal said to her daughter, her manner gentler than it had been in weeks.

Paul Morell, a captive in his chair, had such pity for her that Lisbeth's rage rose in a bloody tide. She would have wreaked worse damage on him than on Gilly Aronberg if Anne, totally unaware, hadn't pushed him off.

"Come on, we'll go up to your place, light a fire, and drink ourselves silly,'' Charlie whispered in Lisbeth's ear. He grabbed an unopened bottle of champagne off the bar and with his hand against her spine directed her toward the coatroom. The attendant returned the blue fox coat and Charlie pulled it around her.

It was raining and the drops struck Lisbeth's hair like thin needles of glass.

Out on the corner a taxi squealed to a stop. Lisbeth climbed in but held Charlie off, pushing at his chest. The way he winced told her she pressed against the still healing wound. ''I want to be by myself for a while,'' she said tonelessly.

''Not tonight. You need somebody, Lisbeth,'' he replied.

''I don't need anybody!'' she yelled, shoving him backwards and slamming the door. ''Drive!'' she ordered the cabby, who responded to her urgency by stomping on the gas. The taxi shot up Sixth Avenue.

''Where to, lady?'' he asked when they hit the next light.

''I don't care.'' She curled into the corner, wrapping herself in the warm fur.

The driver, suspicious, watched her in the rearview mirror. ''Come on, give me a hint. Uptown? Downtown?'' Lisbeth offered no answer. ''Grant's Tomb? The Top of the Sixes? Saint Pat's? Or what about the Staten Island Ferry?''

''All right.''

''All right what?''

''The Staten Island Ferry,'' she said indifferently.

The cab swung west, took the next left, and rocketed south. Lisbeth never noticed the bumpy ride or the dark city outside. Time, the present, Charlie Morgan and the love he nurtured for her, ceased to exist. The headache was fierce, worsened by the humiliation that claimed her. Never in a long career had Lisbeth suffered a true failure. She had scripts optioned that weren't bought, or were bought to lie on some dusty shelf, or even produced never to appear in the theaters, or once up on the screen distorted beyond whatever vision she created. But whatever she had done, her talent, that gift for characters and dramatic scenes, the cadences of her dialogue, had always brought her a certain acclaim. She believed in her ability, and now she'd been flung from that one place where she never had had to put up her guard. Oh, God damn the Gillys of the world!

The speeding cab flung itself around another corner, and Lisbeth was back remembering racing the Porsche through the winding, slippery streets of the Hollywood Hills and that last shadowy ride on the San Diego Freeway.

It was impossible that she'd never seen those flowers even once in all those years, but if so she had no memory of them until she found the lilies-of-the-valley covering an entire table in the nursery. The sight of the tiny white heads nodding like a gathering of obsequious schoolchildren brought back Lily Vaughan. They were *her* flowers, patterned on her blouse, across her bed sheets, in a large poster above her desk. Lisbeth bought them all. Wrapped in brown paper and filling the passenger seat, they urged her to drive even faster. She remembered Lily taunting, sly Lily with a tongue as forked as a snake's.

Lisbeth pushed the gas to the floor, and the Porsche shrieked down the 405 into blackness.

The present had splintered in the careening taxi, and a riotous garden of vivid memories bloomed in Lisbeth's head.

She remembered the windshield ruffling in waves of white as the van appeared out of nowhere, and then she raced not along the freeway but through time, into a cold Vermont winter, across snowy fields, roads, hummocks rising in the distance like secret burial mounds. In the junction of then and now the Porsche exploded, and Lisbeth, the pain rushing in a wall of moving fire, flew against the taxi window. The blackness billowed and her eyes closed, her breathing slowed, and her heart quieted in an adagio.

Unknowing, Lisbeth traveled through the night, winding down the narrow island along the silent Hudson until the land ran out and the cab slammed to a stop.

The back end shimmied on the damp pavement.

"Okay, lady, we're here. Lady? Hey, lady, you awake or what?"

How cold it was. In this place. Still and cold and with a white, icy light. The moon's giant face hanging on the ridge. It spoke, but what did it—who?—say?

The snow all around. The light drained down a tunnel in the ground. Somebody moving. Reaching out. A hand.

"Ouch! That hurts! Get away!"

The driver was at the back door, pulling her arm, dragging Lisbeth from the cab. "You can't spend the night in my cab, lady. It ain't the Waldorf."

She stumbled out onto the asphalt, falling to her knees. The driver yanked her up. She swayed in the slashing rain and the wind that cartwheeled off the river. The blackness, which had been ebbing, closed in again. The night water rushed to the ocean behind her.

The cabby stuck his ruddy, pocked face into hers, shouting, "Now dig into that itty-bitty pocketbook of yours, lady, and find my fare.'' White eyes, round beams of light, suckered onto Lisbeth like barnacles.

"I'll take care of it," a voice yelled against the wind. A curling shadow slipped around a parked car.

"All right, Lisbeth, unless you're planning to go to Staten Island, I'll drive you home." As he led her to the car a small window rose in Lisbeth's mind.

"Neff," she said, staring at his wet face.

"Yeah. What?"

She said nothing as he dropped her on the front seat. He slammed the door, and the marauding wind was shut out. Neff slid behind the wheel. He started the car and switched the heater on. Hot air blew on Lisbeth's legs and into her face.

"It's cold out," she whispered, reaching numbed fingers to the vent.

They drove off. Neff said, "You don't say."

The heat, the ride north, and the city lights spilling through the windows, spinning kaleidoscopes of color, loosened the ice floe inside Lisbeth. She came back to herself slowly, as if emerging from a heavy sleep. When she awoke, when she recognized Neff better than she did her own uncertain self, Lisbeth wondered what she was doing in the small car. How had she gotten there? The darkness again, always the blackouts, deep and never remembered.

"Where are we going?" she asked at last.

"I told you. I'm driving you home."

"No."

"No?" Stopped at a light, Neff turned to look at her. He had, Lisbeth saw, half a face. He smelled of dampness, of stale smoke, old cigarettes. All of a sudden she remembered his tongue, felt it drawing circles in her mouth, about her erect nipples, between her legs.

Desire awakened Lisbeth further, but with it came sections of the night, scenes in the theater, bits of *Silver Street*, the party at Vanessa, and Anne Rosenthal's hard eyes—You would have let Paul die! rang like a clarion—and Paul himself, gentle as an injured rabbit.

"Where, then?"

A splash of water splattered on the windshield. The wipers pushed against the pool and spread Gilly Aronberg's sweaty face across the glass.

"Leave me alone!" Lisbeth cried to Gilly and to Neff also. But when Neff's hand came down on her knee, fingers scrambling at the material, she didn't push him away. He turned a corner. The rain pummelled the car, racketing on the metal. Gilly slipped away as easily as a greased pig.

"Didn't like the reviews?" Neff asked. He drove into a narrow alley cramped between two old buildings. The alley was dark as Neff pulled to the back beside a jumble of overflowing garbage cans, and the stone walls pressed in like the sides of a mine shaft. In the yellow cones of the headlights she saw pinched brown rats flee up into the shadows.

"What do you know about the reviews?"

"Heard them on the tube, read the early editions." He switched off the lights. Neff's face disappeared into nothingness. The man behind the wheel could have become anyone. When he pulled her across the seat, she searched for his scar and finding it kept her palm against the ridge. Now she knew it was Neff whose mouth was on hers, Neff sliding up the long dress.

He pushed Lisbeth down, the silk rucked about her waist. She grew limp, weightless under his hand, not fighting at all, not caring even when he ripped her panty hose.

"Failure's not your style," Neff said. "Must be driving you crazy." His voice was raspy, a file working on metal.

He moved back to unzip his fly. Lisbeth lost the scar. Above her, he was only a large shadow of a man, any man.

"Ever not gotten what you wanted?" he asked, shoving forward.

What did Neff know about it? She turned a cheek against the cool vinyl and his lips wandered down the slope of her neck. He nipped the soft skin and a warm flush rustled through to her groin.

Neff took her hand and put it around his hardness. "Put me inside," he ordered, groaning.

Lisbeth obliged him, cool, not quite at home in her own flesh. She lifted up and guided Neff to her. In the darkness she thought she saw his eyes, fires glowing.

Remembering Susie in the toilet stall, Lisbeth moistened, opened up for Neff. He slid into that tight, warm center of her and she shrilled a flutter of pleasure. Her heart sped and she was on fire. She pulled Neff's head down and kissed him, her tongue running frantically around the inside of his mouth. Rising, rising, her tongue rushed; she sucked Neff's lips and pushed his hand down so he'd touch her there, just at the swollen nub of her desire. When he did she reached the edge and hurtled, blinded, maddened, a pent-up creature suddenly let loose. And Lisbeth screamed into Neff, screamed as he plunged while she clasped him. She screamed *Susie!* but the cry, flowing, was silent and Neff couldn't hear her.

Even so late there was traffic, and Neff swung agilely from one lane to another, the siren shrieking. Lisbeth swept the long hair around her hand in a twist and curled it on her head. She checked her wan face in the rearview mirror as Neff raced, fifty, sixty, through the streets. The radio had squawked just when he'd finished with her. There had been a shooting, one of somebody's birds bought it in a tenement, the staticky voice said. Neff had sworn and backed with screeching tires out of the alley, hurrying north.

"Scared?" he asked, licking his swollen lips.

He seemed pleased with himself. Just because he screwed her, she told him, as if that meant anything. Gilly Aronberg had sex, too, with any number of ambitious lovers. Right now he was probably in someone's bed laughing at her. Lisbeth didn't say that to Neff. Instead she shrugged. "It wasn't such a big deal."

"I didn't hear you complaining."

"Liking it or not is the same," she said. Yet she ran her hand along Neff's leg to the inside of his thigh. She hadn't had enough of him, no matter how she pretended otherwise. She wanted Neff naked, wanted him to love her again. Except it wasn't love, or not love as Charlie made love. It was like the blackness, terrifying and compelling. That joining with Neff shriveled her insides. She lost herself then. She swam out of control. No one, a voice whispered, can hold you responsible. Like a child.

"I drive you crazy," Neff said, laughing.

"Let me out. I'll get a taxi," Lisbeth said when they crossed Fourteenth Street.

"Maybe I'm not finished with you yet. Did you ever think of that?"

"Don't push your luck, Neff." Lisbeth smoothed down her dress. One of her pearl earrings had fallen off. She ran a hand along the seat but couldn't find it.

Neff entered the park at Fifty-ninth Street and raced along the eastern edge. The red light he'd clamped on the roof of the car spun flashing watery streamers through the night.

"You know I have a wife, two kids. And I don't screw around, or not much. Not for a long while. Until you. Lisbeth the witch," Neff said.

Sometimes Lisbeth thought he was a dream, not real at all, not alive like Charlie Morgan. Charlie almost died. She remembered that and wished he hadn't been hurt, that he wasn't made to suffer. She clenched her fists in anger at the knife wielder.

"Tell me what I'm doing with you," Neff said.

Lisbeth, thinking of Charlie, had momentarily forgotten Neff. "I don't know," she said, "but probably nothing good." She had a sudden suspicion that things wouldn't turn out well for Neff, or not with her.

At Ninety-sixth Street they left the park, ignoring the signal on Fifth and turning north up Madison. In a dozen blocks the city melted into burnt-out tenements collapsing on their narrow plots of ground. Derelict cars lined the curbs. Shadows wavered about the overflowing garbage cans and fled from the beams of the car. Every few blocks a burst of neon or the lights of a bodega splashed into the darkness.

Neff turned so many times through the tortuous streets Lisbeth lost all sense of direction. Then, suddenly, the night disappeared in a white blaze. Police cars, an ambulance, milling groups of people kept back on the sidewalks by ropes. To Lisbeth the scene had the intensity of a movie being shot. Cameras, action. She didn't feel as if she were far uptown or out of her element. Reality possessed no definitive substance for Lisbeth, had no special boundaries. The real differ from the make-believe only when it was happening.

"Wait here," Neff ordered, pulling toward the center of the action and scattering the curious.

Lisbeth sat in the car while the red flags of the turret lights wound round and round. Watching faces stared in at her, hawks waiting for blood, for some awfulness to feed on.

Up ahead Neff listened to a cop in uniform. Joined by a cowboy in a denim jacket and a plaid shirt, the black grip of a gun sticking out of his belt, Neff started talking himself. After a second the men turned toward the car, to Lisbeth behind the windows, a specimen, she thought. Which was how Neff saw her. In her mind she stood out there with the cops and saw a similar Lisbeth, pale, oddly nonhuman, a corpse except for the lips. The lips were a bright glossy red—*Bravado*.

Two paramedics came through a doorway and down the steps heaving a blanket-covered gurney. Its burden was secured by wide straps. Dead, Lisbeth reasoned. Her camera-eye held and she slowly moved Neff to the gurney. He bent, pulled back the covering, and stared at the unseen face. He motioned to the medics and the dead man was hidden again. The medics moved on with their cargo. Neff came back to the car and waved at the cowboy, who lit a cigarette and gazed out over the crowds as if he stood alone in the street.

"Not one of mine. Just another dead shit, brains blown out his asshole," Neff complained sourly. He turned the key in the ignition. "Let's go home. Somewhere."

Neff smelled of death now. Lisbeth put her hand on his leg. He wasn't surprised. She smiled as she said, "All right."

20

Thanksgiving Day dawned blustery and very cold. The temperature fell into the low twenties and snow was expected. A savage storm entombed the Plains states, hurtled on into the Midwest, and worked its way east.

In Westport, Dinah, unable to sleep after the first watery light of dawn, brewed coffee and took a mug of it up to the studio, though like Hatch and Mikey she called it the attic now. She leaned against the window frame and gazed out at the sullen day, leafless limbs of trees tangoing in the whipping gusts of wind. The plump line of hedges, shapeless as muffins and finally sprouting erratic twigs, seemed more blackish in the colorless day than green. No smoke tunneled up from Mario Ellis's chimney, but it was still not long past eight o'clock. Her new neighbor, a stranger secreted in the Berger house where even the old people's memories had surely been removed with the wallpaper and the threadbare carpeting, probably still slept. Westport on holidays lingered late in bed; Dinah usually did herself. But the colonial was empty. She and Rebecca were alone in the house. Mikey had gone up to Boston yesterday with the swim team for a meet. He wouldn't return home until tomorrow night. Dinah hadn't realized how much his presence stirred the air in the silent rooms, how his thundering sneakers clunking up and down the stairs brought life. Her teenage son, full of mysteries himself, sent shadows scuttling in loud blasts of David Bowie and Led Zeppelin. *This,* she thought, sipping the cooling coffee, *is what I have to look forward to more and more, a throbbing emptiness.*

The furnace didn't kick on until six, so the big house with all its corners hadn't warmed up yet. Dinah wore a heavy woolen sweater buttoned to the neck over a flannel shirt and was still cold. Arthritis already stalked her bones, she just knew it. She saw a whitened, calcified sketch of herself aging and folding up like the fossils in walkers or gripping canes she always dodged in the mall. She sighed so loudly that Becky lifted her ears, then sighed herself and continued drowsing. *What do I have to be thankful for,* Dinah wondered, *with no stuffed turkey ready to shove into the oven, no frozen pumpkin pies to be baked?*

Life with health despite being overweight and some future joint disease . . . Mikey . . . loyal Becky . . . and her friends. Oh yes, especially the women, who had taken her from nobody to a person of some importance. There was much to be thankful for, she chastised her sorrowing self, even if no one was coming for dinner.

Susie had invited her to have Thanksgiving with them, but Dinah was so depressed she said no, though Quinn and Lisbeth would be there. Lisbeth had refused her mother and that little dying man.

As she drank lukewarm coffee, Dinah thought about Paul Morell. She never understood why Lisbeth hated him so when he was unfailingly pleasant and very intelligent. Besides, he had that hideous history and a spidery leg that surely earned him some consideration, a touch of tolerance, if not Lisbeth's love. But Lis was hard. Even with *Silver Street* sinking like a punctured balloon, she hadn't thrown herself into the Hudson River, though she'd certainly not been overjoyed. But no tears. Not Lis. What would she cry about? Whatever drew sobs from her, it wouldn't be a sick stepfather.

A sheet of newspaper blew in from somewhere, an unsecured garbage-can lid most likely, and sailed dizzily across the lawn rising almost as high as the hedges. If it caught on top, became impaled on a spiky twig, she resolved to let Mario Ellis retrieve it.

"Oh, Mikey," Dinah cried suddenly as if her son lurked in the room somewhere and not in the chlorine-blue water of a swimming pool miles from home, "why aren't you here!" Only it was Hatch she truly meant, Hatch she yearned to have downstairs sprawled in front of the TV set. She saw herself sitting next to him while the turkey roasted and the pies baked. Dinah could almost feel Hatch's arm automatically drape about her shoulders.

Oh, to be a happy family again! Yet had they really been happy, the three of them? A family? If so, Tolstoy was wrong, for they resembled no one Dinah knew, no other group of father, mother, child or children. Even when they'd lived together they were out of step with one another. *Who've I been kidding?* Dinah wondered.

Her back ached from holding herself so tightly against the chill, and she went to sit in the big chair with Becky. The dog stood up to let Dinah slide under her, then collapsed in furry happiness, licking as much of her wrist as hung out from the woolen sleeve.

———

The phone rang while only cold dregs remained in the coffee mug, but by the time Dinah blundered down the crimped attic steps and into her bedroom, it stopped. She crawled on the jumbled sheets and blankets. Becky had followed her, so nervy herself these last few weeks she seldom allowed Dinah out of her sight. Dinah patted the cushion of quilt at her side, and the dog leaped up in one graceful motion to settle close to Dinah's thigh. Now that Hatch slept somewhere else, she could take the dog to bed with her, and sleep came easier if an arm hung over Becky. Dinah felt reassured by the rise and fall of the furry rib cage, by those snippy midnight cries and whinnies that signaled the Airedale's dreaming.

The phone rang again. Dinah lifted the receiver and immediately wished she hadn't. Her mother was at the other end.

"I just called, but there was no answer. It must have been crossed wires. It couldn't have been your house. That's what I told myself. Not on Thanksgiving. You'd be getting dinner ready, unless you're all going out, or course."

Such was her mother's style, never to ask a direct question, but to make pronouncements and let Dinah tell her if she was wrong or not. Knowing the dreaded moment had finally arrived, Dinah sank down on the pillows. Still, she tried to avoid the inevitable by hurriedly asking, "What are you doing for dinner?"

"Nothing. It's unreasonable to cook a big turkey for one old woman, and you know you can't buy a bird smaller than ten pounds."

"Why didn't you go to the MacDonalds? They had you last Thanksgiving," Dinah said. How would she phrase it? Simply say, Hatch moved out?

"The year before."

"What?"

Her mother said sharply, "You've forgotten, but last year I had dinner over at the Reverend Watkinses'. He and Trixie had several people in. Actually, those of us in the congregation who are alone, without families."

Dinah fended off her mother's dig by asking, "Who's Trixie?"

"Trixie Watkins, *his* wife."

What sort of Presbyterian was named Trixie? And wouldn't such a name, more appropriate for a dog or a stripper, hurt a minister's career? Dinah tried to imagine what a Trixie Watkins would look like as her mother continued, "They asked me again, the Watkinses, but I declined."

"Why'd you do that?" Dinah asked.

"Because I hate being included with that group, old Tom Henry, and Ivy Issinger and they always ask Esther Stickney, and you know she and I have never been able to stand one another. Plus a few more of the church's incontinent aging fools. I was so depressed after last year I didn't leave the house for a week."

Dinah knew her mother wanted her home for holidays, Hatch and Mikey too. Holidays meant cooking huge meals, a blazing fire in the living room, and the sound of live voices, not those from flickering images on the TV set. For the first time Dinah realized with a pang how her mother must feel. Just to hear a male voice raised in a howl of rage or a roar of pleasure over a football play!

"I hope you're making the yams in a casserole with marshmallows instead of just wrapping them with tinfoil and baking them."

"I'm not cooking today," Dinah plunged, tears starting up in her eyes.

"The three of you are going out then. Well, I suppose once in a while it's a relief to let somebody else fuss," she said, waiting for Dinah to tell her the details.

Dinah stalled. "Not Mikey though. He's up in Boston for a swim meet."

"Then you should be with him, Dinah. He's much too young to be traveling alone."

"Not alone, Mother, with the coach and the team."

"Oh, that's all right then."

Silence settled between them like a break in the connection. Dinah sought for the right words. But any words would do, for nothing could change reality or soften the truth. Taking a deep breath, Dinah shut her eyes, just as if she were a child again at the top of the high playground slide down which she must go to reach solid ground. Phantom children clamored behind her on the steps, crying, *Come on, Dinah. Hurry up, willya. Fraidy cat!*

And Dinah soared off. "Actually, Mother, there's been a, well, a change with things here. . . ." She flew down the slide faster and faster until with a cry, she shouted all the way to Hanover, Nebraska, to her disapproving mother, "Hatch and I are getting a divorce. He moved into Manhattan. It's a woman. I'll be getting a job. Mikey's taking it pretty well. So, there you are, Mother. No turkey here, just me and the dog. We'll probably share a can of Campbell's noodle soup and watch television."

Quinn never thought about holidays. When her mother lived she'd dutifully appear in Boston on the requisite occasions, and celebrations were enacted in the traditional ways of the Webster family through the generations. But Quinn derived no pleasure from any of them. She didn't honestly know why even Christmas left her unmoved, bored. Only as a very young child did she recall any happiness. The huge tree, so beautifully shaped and exquisitely decorated in a corner of the big parlor by one of the front windows, the expensive presents wrapped in shiny paper and large bows, the table groaning with so much food, the wonderful little buttery cookies Norah baked and which melted in your mouth. . . . Yet as she grew older all those pleasures faded. As for Thanksgiving, a month earlier, it became just as inconsequential, though her conscience always pricked her when those gathered about the table knotted their hands together and with bowed heads gave thanks for so much bounty, such Godly gifts. It was true, she'd known only a life of material plenty, and her intelligence was considerable. She should have been grateful, though to whom or what she didn't know. No Eminent Presence lurked either in the heavens or in Quinn's soul. While she understood mystery, as did any scientist who gazed through a high-powered microscope at the unseen world hidden beneath the observable, she believed mystery was simply ignorance.

Once her mother died, Quinn automatically stopped traveling to Boston, and Thanksgiving and Christmas came and went like other, ordinary days. Though Dinah and Susie always asked her to join them—and Lis invited her out to California every year where the weather further obliterated the holiday aura—Quinn usually went to the lab or spent the time lazily with the dogs. This last Thursday in November, however, was different.

Somehow, her terrible mistake with Will must be rectified. Whatever her motive, she had blundered badly during that unforeseen meeting between Will and their father. Hearing nothing, she decided on the Sunday before the holiday to take them all for dinner at Tavern on the Green. Though it was late for making reservations, she went over to the restaurant and bullied them into saving a table in the Crystal Room. Then she hurried out to Central Park West and flagged a taxi. Forget a telephone call—the invitation was a perfect excuse for going to Brooklyn.

Quinn's anger with Will hadn't evaporated, but as the days passed and there was only silence from her brother, no plans and nothing to look forward to, the coldness inside Quinn, the resolve, began to crack like late winter ice. She no longer wanted Boston, and had never desired a place in Webster, Inc. *Let Will have them,* Quinn thought. But it was not easy. The old man in his deterioration and collapse, in his slide toward mortality, had given Quinn an opportunity. For the first time in forty years she had had her father's attention. Then, with the skill of a conjurer, Will yanked it right out from under her.

Fool! Quinn thought as the taxi raced through Brooklyn, to pull up in front of Will's house, finally, after what seemed years to Quinn with her fears and memories, with her losses and still that anger, Will's betrayal, the old man's lofty denial and rejection—I don't need you now. At the curb a sudden premonition seized Quinn, who pressed her face tight up against the window. She clenched her jaws to keep from crying out.

The small white house appeared the same, unchanged since the last time Quinn had been there, but she sensed a difference.

The taxi waiting, she hurried up the path to the front door, her eyes fixed on the blank windows. Only darkness lay inside and when she pressed the bell, it echoed emptily.

Dust would gather over the furniture, drift onto the shelves, the floors, the stairs. The air would grow stale and the silence old. Quinn knew this as she walked around the house, peering through a sliver of space between the curtains, beneath the edge of a pulled shade to glimpse only shadows and more shadows.

"Hey, what do you think you're doing?"

Quinn jumped guiltily. A man, small, compact, with a fuzzy halo of white hair and a gummy mouth in which no teeth were visible, came to the fence and stared out of bottle-thick glasses at Quinn.

"I'm Mr. Webster's sister," she said, standing tall and straight, prim as a dancing-class girl. She could have worn white cotton gloves on the hands she folded at her waist.

"They're not home," he said, squinting suspiciously.

"If they'll be back soon, I'll wait." If they'll come home at all and hadn't just gone north to Boston possessionless. Not as refugees. No Webster could ever be that. But perhaps Will simply left Brooklyn and all it meant behind in his decision to once again be what he supposedly so hated—a Brahmin.

The little man thrust his head forward and asked, "Sister?"

"Yes."

"Don't believe you," he snapped. "And if you don't clear off I'll call the cops one-two-three!"

The fusty old man, prying and for some reason angry, disconcerted Quinn, who cried, "No, Will Webster's really my brother. Here, I'll prove it!" She fumbled through her purse for her wallet and some identification, but as she rushed the fence the man, rapidly working his lips, drew back.

"Just stay away!" he yelled as if attacked. "If you was his sister then you should know they went off and how come. Where to." He stopped at once, as if realizing he told her too much, told her that he knew nothing about the Websters, and he shuffled to his own back steps, shouting, "Get off the property, or, I mean it, I'll dial 911."

Greg was annoyed almost constantly with Susie these days. More than annoying him, however, she puzzled him. It was as though a long-term and reliable secretary upped and quit or, Susie thought sourly, an old dog suddenly turned and bit his hand. She hated to have Greg wander around with a look of confusion, or worse, constantly to explode in small detonations of anger, but it seemed she couldn't help it. Forced to choose between pleasing herself or satisfying him, she didn't quite choose at all, but flew off and did what she had to. Good wives never thought of themselves first, if they thought of themselves at all. Good wives were the foundations that kept civilization from collapsing in chunks of broken cement and clouds of dust. Susie no longer considered herself any kind of wife at all, which added to her burden of guilt. Only poor Greg never realized she had walked out on him and the familiar scaffolding underpinning their marriage had shattered.

The Saturday before Thanksgiving, as they sat on a banquette against the back wall of The Odeon in Tribeca, waiting for the McGraths to join them, Greg asked her seriously if she was going through menopause.

Susie had just told him she'd invited Quinn and Lisbeth and Dinah—though Dinah wouldn't be coming—for Thanksgiving, without their discussing it first. This was so unlike Susie that at first, in the crowded restaurant where the mixed symphony of voices hammered against the high tin ceiling, he thought he'd misheard her. She said it again, and that's when Greg charged, "Susie, most times I don't know who you are anymore. Some days I think I'm living with a stranger. Is this . . . I mean, have you started the change of life?"

"Change of life?" She stared blankly. "You mean menopause?" Greg nodded his head. "Good God, I'm only forty!" She was more amused than upset.

Greg continued ponderously, "Well, I've heard it can happen to women just about anytime. Every female's different." He was obviously trying to find some concrete reason, some physical cause, for this transformation. If she suddenly announced she had terminal cancer, Greg would probably sigh with relief.

Greg's bafflement depressed her, and as the waiter put their drinks in front of them, she wished she'd ordered something stronger than Perrier.

"I don't want Quinn Webster and Lisbeth Ross at our house on

Thanksgiving,'' Greg said when the waiter moved off. She was watching a couple two tables away, the woman who wasn't much older than Betts and a gray-haired man at least three times her age. Susie could tell from the stillness of the woman's face, the way her jaw was set, that she was adamant about something. The man, in a dark business suit, flushed. He leaned forward and attempted to take her hand, but she lifted a wineglass to her lips. *What does he need from her that she's just said she won't give him?* Susie wondered. The woman seemed unconcerned with the man's pleading and stared off into the distance. Susie unaccountably wanted to speak to that woman-girl, though she had no idea what she would say. She knew what she would have told the man, however, if she could. *Just leave her alone. Go back to your office and just let her be.*

It came to Susie as no great revelation that she much preferred women to men. Not sexually, not because of that old girls' love she shared with Lisbeth, but from an almost primitive sense of kinship, from the knowledge that women stood on one edge of a great chasm and men on the other. This realization had nothing to do with political and economic inequities, but was biological. And yet, even as she considered sisterhood, she thought of Simon. . . .

Susie turned to Greg.

"You're not listening to me," he said.

"What did you say?"

He groaned, looking put upon. "Susie, my parents always come from Philly. Thanksgiving for us, remember, is just family."

He was right. The holiday happened to be one of the few occasions Greg never mixed with business, and he never knew that each year she invited Quinn or Lisbeth, if the latter was in New York. "Well, I can't very well uninvite them, can I?" she said, deciding to try to be reasonable.

"But why did you in the first place?"

Susie felt like the woman at the other table. "Because I wanted to," she said. "It's no big deal."

"It is to me." The lines in his face deepened with his earnestness. "Family means everything, Suz."

Part of Susie would have agreed, but that underground spring of her being spun about Quinn and Dinah and Lisbeth. Perhaps she would have tried to explain at least some of her feelings, though certainly not the more important ones, but the McGraths approached their table, Claire in a red fox cape like an ocean liner on fire seeking safe harbor. Her expression was grim; she and Harold had obviously been arguing.

Are all women always at odds with their men? Susie wondered, feeling kinder toward Claire McGrath than she usually did. They brushed cheeks and the McGraths sat, Harold rubbing his long, thin undertaker hands and loudly summoning the waiter.

Susie's good feelings evaporated like teakettle steam as Claire flung the cape over her chair and began imperiously to discuss Simon and the mission.

"He runs the place like a candy store. Oh, really, it's so irritating! Somebody will have to take him in hand, and I suppose that means me because it always means me!" She rolled her heavily mascaraed eyes.

"He's extremely competent," Susie said, then hastily added before Claire could ask, However did she know *that*?, "or at least he seems so." The waiter arrived, slipping quickly in by their table, and before Harold could speak, Susie said, "I'd rather have a scotch instead of this mineral water. A double, I think, with a dash of soda."

"Susie! You never drink so much liquor," Greg said, surprised, once again staring at her as if she had been transformed into an alien space traveller.

"Greg—"

Already he was drawing back the glass and saying to the waiter, "She doesn't mean it, not in the least."

Susie opened her mouth to protest at being treated as an infant, but Claire McGrath, leaning over the table, waited hungrily for a scene. And Greg, hair mussed, eyes so full of love and yet so troubled, took her hand and squeezed. Why was it, Susie asked herself, that Greg's love, deep and tested by time, made her feel like such a prisoner? It took every bit of energy she had to sit and not scream at her husband through a meal that seemed to take as long as Wagner's *Ring*. By the time the Lamtons and the McGraths said good night and got into separate cabs, Susie was exhausted.

"You weren't very talkative," Greg said.

Susie slipped to the far corner of the taxi. "I have a headache."

"What's the matter?"

"How could you tell me what to drink? I'm a grown woman!"

Greg sighed. "Susie, be reasonable. If you have a headache now, think how much worse it would be if you'd drunk that scotch. A double no less; oh, my God!"

"I have a headache because I didn't drink, because I wasn't allowed it, not because I did," she said.

"Now that doesn't make any sense."

"Just forget it," she said. Susie hated to argue. Marriage isn't a race where one contestant has to finish in front of the other, Ivy Bannon always cautioned.

"Not discussing things doesn't seem very adult to me," Greg complained, but Susie wouldn't answer.

They rode in silence, and as each block passed Susie felt the weight of Greg's disapproval grow heavier, along with his confusion. From his corner he beamed out those unspoken messages that drifted through their life like confetti. Susie wondered what would happen if she had the driver stop the cab and simply got out. And went where? The shelter? The Good Shepherd took in whoever came to the doors, offered food and lodging and never demanded the right to ask questions in return for such benevolence. As unrealistic, as stupid, as it was, she wished she could vanish into the anonymity of the city, to wander and to drift. *To freeze and starve on the streets, you fool,* she thought.

By the time they reached their building Susie was as angry with herself as with her husband. Greg, in his sulk, stood up straighter in the elevator, angled his chin, and stared at some unseeable spot in the distance.

Susie read the list of messages Mrs. Sloan had left by the telephone. Her mother, Greg's too, and Quinn. It was too late to call anyone and Susie went to check on the girls.

Tia slept soundly on her back, arms opened wide as angel's wings. She expelled little snorts of breath and Susie smiled, tucking the covers more firmly about her. She kissed her forehead and continued to Betts's room.

She heard faint scurrying sounds from the bedroom when her hand touched the doorknob. Betts wasn't asleep yet, but when Susie entered, the room was dark. Betts lay curled up under the covers.

As she was about to step back in the hall, her thoughts congealing around Greg and the argument they didn't have, a creaking from the closet stopped her.

"Who's there?" she whispered, her heart pounding. Quinn's dogs . . . the flowers . . . Charlie Morgan stabbed in his bed. She remembered the afternoon she'd come home and thought someone lurked in the shower. How Tia had scared her! But Tia was fast asleep, and Betts was there just in front of Susie.

No one's in the closet, no one's hiding.

She forced herself to walk across the room, along the slender strip of light rivering in from the hall, and slide the closet door aside.

Susie screamed.

"Oh shit!" Betts cried behind her.

"What's wrong?" Greg's voice came echoing from the other wing.

A thin bony face was wedged in the space above Betts's clothes. One dark cratered eye gazed out at her unblinking. It might have been innocent as a mask hanging from the bar or someone as treacherous as the rapist of that other closet. What it wasn't was the play of light and shadows skating in her own imagination. A man was standing in the midst of Betts's shirts and jeans.

Susie's screams rang as unremittingly as the siren of a speeding ambulance. Even as the desk lamp snapped on and the overhead light, when Betts sat up in her bed and Greg rushed into the room, Susie couldn't stop screaming.

"What the hell is wrong? Susie, stop it before you wake the dead!"

Greg pushed Susie aside and stared at the strange white face. A swatch of cornsilk yellow hair draped over one eye. As the boy slid the swinging hangers along the closet bar, he jerked his head. The hair swayed to the side; then, as he stepped into the room, it slipped back again.

He was tall as Greg and naked except for his jeans. A skinny boy with chickeny shoulder blades and a pale peachlike fuzz on his upper lip, he blinked in the harsh glare.

"Who are you?" Susie croaked.

Greg yelled, "What the devil is going on here?"

"Don't you hurt Jason, Daddy!" Betts cried, sitting up in bed, winding the sheet around her. It was obvious she wore nothing under it.

"Why's everybody making so much noise? You woke me up." Tia stood in the doorway rubbing her eyes.

"Go back to bed," both her parents ordered.

"How come Jason's here?"

Greg asked, "You know this . . . this person?"

"Sure, it's Jason—"

"Shut up, Tia!"

"—he delivers the groceries. From D'Agostino's. You know, Mommy, when you get a big order."

"Susie . . . ?" Greg turned on her.

"Put your clothes on and leave, right this minute," Susie whispered. The boy quickly gathered his things together. Defiantly, Betts handed him a pair of Jockey shorts trapped beneath the blankets. He inched toward the door.

"Oh, no. Dress! I won't have you going down in the elevator half naked,'' Greg said. "Starting gossip. People talking about you! Oh, my God!" he yelled, and swung at the boy, who jumped aside. "What the hell were you two doing?"

"It's not what you think," Betts said.

"I don't even want to think what I'm thinking!" Greg grabbed Jason, who wore his shirt now and denim jacket. He shoved his bare feet into sneakers and stumbled ahead of Greg into the hall.

Greg's angry voice boomed as he hustled Jason to the front door.

Susie, wringing her hands together, said, "How could you, Betts?"

"Don't get hysterical, *Mother*." She glared dangerously at Susie, as if Susie were at fault.

"Would somebody please tell me why Jason was only wearing his jeans?" Tia said.

Susie waved her hands at Tia, shooing her into flight. "To bed, now!" Tia ran. The front door slammed. Betts winced as Susie said, "You're only fifteen!"

"I'm almost sixteen."

"Not for six months. In my book that means you're still fifteen. Not that it matters. What does is that you were . . . you have . . . this stranger from the supermarket in your room while we were out. At . . . all hours. You were . . ." Susie knew what Betts and Jason were doing, but the idea of her daughter as a sexual creature was appalling.

Greg reappeared, flushed and with his tie yanked to the side. Susie worried that at the last moment he'd done something physical to Jason. "All right, Betts," he stormed, "explain yourself."

"Explain myself! Oh Daddy, honestly, you sound like some father on television."

"I do not."

"You do too, and you always tell me that television isn't real life."

"It's—" Greg stopped. The women watched him. He was counting, his lips moving silently. Finally he said, in a steadier voice, "We come home to find you in bed with a delivery boy. That needs explaining."

"I wasn't in bed. Or I was, but Jason was in the closet."

"That's not funny," Susie said.

"No, Mother, but it's *accurate*," Betts retorted.

Susie saw it was no use. Betts would twist and turn, argue them into the ground, keep the three of them in verbal combat until dawn, or longer, until either she or Greg dropped. And what, ultimately, could they do? Spank Betts, lock her in her room, demand she see a psychiatrist? With a sinking feeling Susie recognized that her daughter wouldn't just think about running off, yearn to move beyond the boundaries, but could actually leave. Unthinking as a bird rising in the sky, Betts, despite her intelligence, could escape. (Escape from what? Us? This sheltered life?)

Among the derelicts Susie saw on the streets of the city were the young ones, weary and badly clothed, in need of a meal and a shower. Hands out, begging for the spare dime, still a light—of what? anger? defiance?—glowed in their eyes.

The outside world suddenly pushed in too closely, seemed nearer than the street twelve floors below, and Susie cried, "Enough! We won't settle this tonight."

Greg ignored her. He shoved his fists in his jacket pockets and asked, "Is this why you're not doing well in school? Because you've gotten involved with the dregs?"

"The dregs? You mean the lower classes, Daddy? Because Jason delivers groceries? Is that what's upsetting you? If it was Bobby Howard from Trinity or Drew Wright from Collegiate, would you still be so mad?"

"That's unfair," Susie protested, but wondered if it were true. Would Greg be so outraged if the boy were the son of someone they knew?

"I'm upset because my fifteen-year-old daughter is . . . is . . ." Greg couldn't say it.

Betts said it for him, "Screwing around. Screwing like in 'fuck,' Daddy?"

Greg lurched for the bed and Susie screamed, "Greg, don't!"

She thought Greg was poised to slap Betts, but he stopped and asked, "Are you taking drugs too?"

Betts leaped to her feet on the bed, trailing the sheet around her. She was taller than both her parents now as she yelled, "Oh great, you too! First Mommy accuses me of being some wiped-out addict—"

"Susie, we decided this was a wait-and-see business!"

"I'm sorry," Susie said hastily. "But I don't think that's the issue now."

Betts sank down to a yoga position. "Can I go to bed? I'm tired."

Greg stared at his daughter in disbelief. "Just like that?"

Betts didn't reply and a silence settled in which parents and child all trod water. Susie, finally, groping for the door, said, "We might as well get some sleep. We're not going to solve anything tonight."

Greg, close on her heels as they approached their own room, said, sorrow and rage mixing in his voice, "I don't understand at all. Betts

261

isn't that type of girl.'' Susie could have told him any female was that type, victimized by her desires and wants, but what would be the use? Greg had rigid, old-fashioned categories for women fixed in his mind. He was a holdover from the fifties, a dinosaur on a forgotten landscape, who believed there were still good girls and bad.

"We have to get her some professional help,'' Susie said, unscrewing her earrings and carefully putting them in the jewelry box along with the pearl ring and gold bracelet. "A good doctor,'' she added, thinking of the child-care books she had read. All those chapters on troubled teenagers. She'd never thought any child of hers would be confused or without a clear vision. But then she'd never supposed she herself would come so undone, a rudderless skiff bobbing in deep waters.

"A shrink, is that the solution?'' Greg asked with fear and not a little loathing. Therapy, like with drugs, was the kind of thing that befell other, mostly unacceptable, people.

"I suppose so,'' Susie replied, "unless you have any other ideas.'' Her own anger washed over onto Greg now.

Greg slumped wearily on the edge of the bed, not even starting to undress. "I don't know.'' He looked older than time. While Susie changed, creamed her face, and brushed her hair, he sat dejected.

"Come on, let's try to get some sleep.''

Greg rose obediently. He got halfway to the bathroom before he said, "I really *don't* understand. This is not the way it's supposed to be. My life. Our life. We should be happy.'' He reached toward her, and reluctantly Susie allowed Greg to enfold her in an embrace. "We are, aren't we, Susie, in spite of these . . . this . . . happy, I mean?''

"The only thing you have to be thankful for is that nobody dropped you out the window the day you were born,'' Betts said to Tia. They were in the laundry room off the kitchen, where Tia's hamster lived in a wire cage. The hamster was a new addition, one Tia bought in the pet store on Amsterdam with allowance money she'd saved. Only when she carried the small brown creature home and established him next to the dryer did she inform Susie.

"I was afraid you wouldn't let me get Herman if I asked you first,'' Tia explained, her bottom lip trembling. The storms in the Lamton family swirled Tia up on their winds too. Then she sensed sea changes in her mother. Susie, reaching for this younger, slighter child, her bones like a bird's, thought, *Oh, why shouldn't she have her own small someone to love*. Greg, who feared animals that he considered dirty— "Disease, Susie!" he'd cry—couldn't object to a little ball of fur caged in the laundry room, where he seldom went. Besides, with their attention so fixed on Betts, and all their energy given to the older girl, Tia needed some gesture.

"No one would have dropped me out the window, Betts," Susie in the kitchen, finishing preparations for Thanksgiving dinner, the one meal she always made by herself, heard Tia say. "I was wanted, a lovely wanted baby," Tia hummed.

"Who said so?" Betts asked.

"Mommy, and don't hold him so tight! Betts, stop it! You'll hurt him! Betts, don't!"

"Betts, give Herman back to Tia. He's her pet," Susie called out.

A second of silence, then Tia ran into the kitchen. "Thank you, Mommy." She held up the hamster, which resembled a very hirsute mouse. "Say thank you to Mommy for saving your life, Herman. Betts was squeezing you to death."

"I wasn't hurting the scuzzy thing," Betts, following her sister, groaned.

"Put Herman away," Susie said. "He shouldn't be around food."

Betts said, "He's probably a bubonic plague carrier."

"He's not!" Tia screamed.

"Stop it, you two!" Susie ordered.

Tia disappeared with Herman, murmuring words of loving reassurance. Betts glanced at her mother from the corners of her eyes. She hadn't confronted either Susie or Greg head-on since Saturday night. On Monday Susie got the name of the best psychiatrist dealing with adolescents in the city, and Tuesday after school she took a sulking Betts over to Dr. Feingood's on Park Avenue.

"This is a big waste of time," Betts said, pushing up the sleeves of her uniform blazer as if she meant actually to do battle.

"You need to talk to someone, a professional, with experience," Susie answered as they sat in the waiting room.

"Well, I won't," Betts threatened.

The next day, feeling like a CIA spy, Susie wandered about Betts's room, not quite searching, just looking. She hated herself with each step she took, with every drawer she opened and lightly fumbled through. Even such casual tactics reminded her unhappily of Lily Vaughan. Lily, they all knew, padded about the suite when no one was there. She drew secrets out of the air if she couldn't find anything more substantial and used what she could for barter.

263

The doorbell rang, bringing Susie abruptly into the present, and Betts's tense presence by the refrigerator watching her. "Girls, that must be your grandparents. Go meet them at the door." Tia ran out of the laundry room still clutching the hamster, but Betts dawdled. In my own good time, she might have been saying as she swiped the long hair behind her ears.

Even with Lisbeth and Quinn coming, Susie dreaded this day for which she lacked all spirit. She needed to feed no one but herself, and the mountains of food about the kitchen put her in a black mood. She thought of the shelter and knew she shouldn't be so disdainful of this plenty, yet she was. Scooping the cranberry sauce into a serving dish, she put it in the refrigerator to keep cool.

"Hello, darling. Here, my homemade bread-and-butter pickles." Greg's mother, Eugenia, small and pixyish, appeared. The two women embraced as the door swung in again and Jack Lamton, shadowed by his son and grandchildren, burst into the kitchen with the zeal of the fullback for Penn he had once been. Only Jack's muscles had metamorphosed into fat, and his hawk's beak of a nose was pinkish, with burst capillaries in fire trails down its slopes. Thin red lines webbed the whites of his eyes. When he hugged Susie, picking her right off the floor to an accompaniment of giggles from Tia, the first slight scent of alcohol perfumed his breath. Susie shuddered to think that Eugenia traveled with Jack when he'd been drinking; worse, when he was dead drunk, on the streets and highways of Pennsylvania. In the death seat yet. But her mother-in-law was an accomplice in maintaining the image of her husband as just another good old boy.

"He's an alcoholic pure and simple," Dr. Bannon said of Greg's father in the early years of Susie's marriage. "He'll kill himself with drinking or, more criminally, kill someone else." But so far Jack had managed to maim only the cars he drove or the furnishings in their suburban house. When in his cups Jack threw whatever he could get his hands upon. Eugenia just laughed, at least to Greg and Susie, that Jack gave her a constant excuse to buy something new.

Susie refused to allow the girls to visit their grandparents alone, and this was one of the few issues she'd been adamant about until what Greg, discarding menopause, now referred to as her "recent stubbornness."

Jack Lamton knew his daughter-in-law disapproved of him—more, actually disliked him—and thus made a show of affection for her. He forever grabbed her for a bear hug, kissed her cheek, or patted the top of her head. Once, Susie had expected Greg to restrain his father, but

Greg feared the older man more than he could ever let on. It was in part to deflect Jack Lamton that Susie invited the others. She hoped that with strangers around, Greg's father would behave.

Dinah arrived unexpectedly. "I know I should have called, but I simply threw some clothes on and jumped into the car. At the last minute I couldn't bear those four walls."

"I'm glad you came," Susie replied, feeling the tremors in Dinah like slight earth movements when they embraced, and set another place.

Lisbeth and Quinn arrived a few minutes later, and Susie reminded her in-laws that they had met the three women years ago, at the wedding down in Baltimore. "Impossible!" Jack Lamton shouted, standing by the fire, legs spread, heavy glass filled with whiskey clutched in his paw. "I never forget beautiful ladies, do I, Ma?" he called to his wife.

Eugenia, on the sofa with Tia, laughed brightly. "You forget everything, Jack. Your mind's a sieve. But it's all right."

Greg's father was the sort of man Quinn especially couldn't tolerate. He resembled the Russian Verensky, so cocky and sure of himself, explosive as a boiling geyser. Blundering through life kicking up dirt, he reminded her of similar men as boys when, because she stood tall, rising to their size, they taunted her to fight. Fearfully, she ran from such encounters, but later, in high school and at Cabot, they stopped approaching Quinn, which frightened her even more. Now, a sour taste in her mouth, she wondered what it would have been like to battle it out with a man like Jack Lamton, to push toe to toe and see who could beat the other into a whining submission. She saw the blood, and a murderous rage welled up in her. Her breath felt hot and heavy in her throat and a fishhook of desire almost choked her. Will, as large and broad shouldered, husky voiced, and with, when he chose, a frosty indifference in his eyes, was a man like those others, like Greg's father. Superior beings, that's what they considered themselves. Arrogant cowboys, they stuck together, and yet when Quinn was younger she remembered her brothers and the old man fighting, tearing at one another like pit bulls.

"Is Quinn all right?" Dinah quietly asked Lisbeth, who was ignoring the elder Lamtons.

Lisbeth accepted a gin and tonic that Greg handed her. Greg always shrank and curved his shoulders from the burden of his father's expansiveness and his mother's brittle good humor, but today he was worse. The trouble with Betts increased his bewilderment and caused him to be even warier.

"You look a hundred and twelve. Weary of corporate life?" Lisbeth asked him, licking her red lips. She wore swirling yards of baby-soft wool that billowed, then clung when she moved. "Or is the market ready to take another nosedive?" Susie hadn't told her about Betts yet, so Lisbeth teased Greg to keep him from saying anything about *Silver Street*. She couldn't have tolerated his bland sympathy.

"Just tired, that's all."

"Your wife should give you some vitamins. Isn't that what wives do with droopy husbands?" She laughed, buzzing the air with a kiss by his left ear before she strolled to the window.

Dinah, trying to accommodate her nose to the same angle as Lis's, wandered after her. "I suppose Quinn's still upset about her dogs. I know I would be if something happened to Rebecca," Dinah said, shivering.

"The city is different if you see it from the West Side," Lisbeth said, gazing out the window.

Dinah's glance ricocheted off Lisbeth's wool-covered arm to the spill of park below. The paths trailed among the denuded trees like streamers of spun sugar. She sniffed, ever resentful of that Nebraska childhood, flat and unexciting as the plains, and envied Lisbeth's, spent here. Lisbeth, no doubt, learned to roller-skate and ride a bicycle down *there* somewhere.

"Though *everything* looks different, depending on who you are and where you stand in time and space," Lisbeth continued.

Dinah sighed. "Oh, to be born again, to have another chance at life!"

"What? You want another ride on the merry-go-round, Di?"

"Don't give me that superior, how-can-you-be-so-dumb look of yours," Dinah snarled.

"You're very testy today," Lisbeth said, smiling, which only stoked Dinah's anger.

She snapped, "What else should I be?"

"You mean instead of sorry for yourself?"

Years had passed since Dinah had fought with one of the women. And she'd never really fought strenuously with any of them. How could she? At Cabot she was simply too grateful to be admitted to the circle, and once in, she worried, biting her nails and keeping silent, afraid of being ejected. Dinah's fear was of being kept outside in the cold, wanting and not getting, just as they'd done to Lily. Of the four,

Dinah understood best why Lily sought inclusion in the group so ardently, why she chased after them, willing, Dinah remembered, to do anything to gain admittance.

The Cabot memories allowed Dinah to inhale and reply slowly, "Of course I'm sorry for myself. What else should I be?" She nudged Lis's shoulder. "But come on, Lisbeth, I'm working at it. Losing weight. Haven't you noticed?"

Lisbeth inspected her judiciously from stem to stern and said, "Another fifteen pounds or so, then some very rigorous exercise."

Dinah bared her teeth. "Sometimes, you know, you're a real bitch, Lis," but then, suddenly, Lisbeth hugged her.

"Of course I am, darling, but promise not to tell a soul!" Her eyes were wicked.

Pressed to Lisbeth's bones, inhaling her perfume, Dinah had the ridiculous feeling that there were two people holding her. Lis slipped in and out of focus, much less substantial than Dinah ever remembered at Cabot and the years after.

"Girls, why so quiet?" Jack Lamton was upon them, scooping the women in, each under a wing, gripping them too tightly. Dinah considered kicking him, and for once sympathized with Quinn's phobia of being touched.

Lisbeth was amused, however, but then she had grown accustomed in California to all those producers pawing her. California had an abundance of kissy fat men, as many as, if not more than, the cliques of anorexic, icy women. *Thank God,* Dinah thought for the first time ever, *I live in Connecticut.*

"C'mon, lighten up! Laugh and be merry!" Jack Lamton roared like Joe College, whom he obviously still presumed he was.

Dinah gritted her teeth and tried to pull away from him, but Lisbeth laughed along with Jack. "Because tomorrow we die!" Her retort so surprised Lamton that he loosened his hold. Dinah spun away, almost tripping. *The only man who's put his arm around me in ages and he's a drunk octogenarian,* she fumed. But she was being unfair. Jack Lamton was somewhere in his late sixties.

"Death? Who's talking about dying? Jesus! This is a holiday!" he cried, annoyed.

Susie stepped smoothly out of nowhere with a plate of cheese and crackers. "Remember that old movie, Lis? We saw it in our Cabot film class." She managed to pry Lisbeth away from her father-in-law, who gulped down the rest of his drink and surged to the bar for another.

"You don't really want anything else before dinner, do you, Dad?" Greg asked, trying to step between his father and the bar.

"Death Takes a Holiday," Dinah said. "I saw it too."

"Sure I do. Lubricates the stomach lining for all that food," Jack Lamton said, pushing his son away from the scotch.

Lisbeth laughed again. "Death never takes a holiday."

"What are you talking about now?" Quinn asked from the deep chair in which she'd buried herself.

Eugenia said, "I think I'll have a sherry. This is a sherry kind of day. Honey"—she nudged Tia—"go get a glass of sherry from Daddy for Grandma."

"Pissy drink," Jack growled.

"A lady's drink," Eugenia informed her husband.

Jack prowled around Lisbeth again, staring into the glass she held. "You're not drinking that pissy stuff, are you?"

"But I'm not a lady," Lisbeth told him with arched brows. Jack Lamton yelped with laughter.

Oh, Lis is off and running, Dinah thought, as Lisbeth flirted with Greg's father, almost, but not quite, insulting the man.

Susie went to the kitchen and Dinah trailed in her wake. "Lis is acting cuckoo and Quinn looks like she's coming down with some dread disease. And why is she here, anyway, and not at her brother's?"

Susie turned off the oven, opened the door, and peered at the turkey. "I'll let it sit for a few minutes," she said.

"Are you peculiar today too?" Dinah asked. "I mean, I was supposed to be the one. Hiding out in Westport from any festivities. A Looney Tune for sure. But, you know, my mother called and I finally told her and then I just had to get out of my house. I saw myself at one end of the phone line to Nebraska, and she was at the other. Two lonely women with no men to make dinner for. Yuck! I felt sticky with self-pity." She dropped onto a high stool by the island counter. "Enough already, right?"

"Enough." Susie gave her a glancing hug on her way to the refrigerator.

"But, oh, I expected so much. Out of life, I mean. We all did," Dinah cried.

"Well, maybe we shouldn't have. Maybe we should learn now, before it's too late, to be satisfied," Susie said, taking the salad from the refrigerator. She shut the door with her hip, and even through the gloom in which she was mired with little hope of rescue, Dinah recognized the movement when Susie performed it as hopelessly graceful.

"In the here and now, you mean." Dinah sighed. "I remember that. We were out of Cabot by the time the world got around to living in the present. Which is what we should have been doing, I suppose. Only now the present's such a depressing place.''

"Life will get better for you, Di, honestly," Susie promised with a false smile.

"Always Pollyanna," Dinah said, though not unkindly. She loved Susie, after all, and only envied her on occasion.

"Not always. I'm the one who thinks—"

Dinah stopped with a hastily raised hand like a traffic cop. "Oh, no, not again, not Lily. It's not funny, Suz, thinking Lily's come back to haunt us. Somehow, some way."

Susie ran water over a colander full of cherry tomatoes. "Quinn's dogs get artfully killed and Charlie Morgan is stabbed in his bed. Not funny. I agree. It's scary. And what if there are other horrors waiting?"

"I thought I was the only one of us who liked horror movies. Eeeck! The creaking door!" Dinah tried to joke.

Susie donned insulated mitts and lifted the browned turkey in its pan to the tile counter. Deftly she transferred the bird to a large carving board. "It has to cool a bit before slicing," she said.

"Do you need help?"

"No."

"You're so organized for somebody who cooks maybe five meals a year. It beats me how you do it, Suz. Maybe you should write a book, something like cooking for the noncook. I'd buy a copy for sure." Dinah rambled on, the threat of Lily suddenly chilling the nape of her neck. Her head stuffed up. She felt logy, out of sorts. Frightened was more what she meant but didn't like to think so. With all her other worries, Dinah hadn't realized just how near the surface the "Lily business" hovered. But all of a sudden her fears of being a disenfranchised, divorced female, of wandering lost, unloved, were swept aside by a shaking terror of dead Lily Vaughan. It was as if a huge, bloody sun had burnt away the fog.

Dinah croaked, "You don't actually believe the dead can climb out of the grave and walk!"

Susie dropped the carving knife. "Damn it, Di!" she cried, tears starting up in her eyes, "the dead are dead forever!"

Dinah drank what was left of her vodka and melted ice cubes. "Sure, Suz. But then who's doing it?"

Susie didn't answer. She picked the knife up from the floor and ran it under the hot water. "Somebody who still cares about Lily, I suppose."

"Nobody cared about Lily twenty years ago, so why now?"

"I don't *know!*" Long dark grooves burnt across Susie's brow.

"Suz, oh please, don't be angry!" Dinah hurried to the sink and put an arm about Susie's shoulders. But Susie jerked to the side.

"And I don't care," she added.

"You do, you know you do or otherwise you wouldn't be worrying over it like Beck with some smelly bone," Dinah accused.

Susie, her back still turned, spun swiftly and punched Dinah's shoulder.

"Ooooh!" Tears rushed to Dinah's eyes and she blinked, bewildered. No one had ever hit her, not once.

"I'm sorry, I'm sorry. Oh, Di, I'm so sorry!" Susie had hold of her, smoothing the disheveled hair, touching, breath winnowing down Dinah's neck, tears too soft and warm and wet. "I don't know what's the matter—oh yes I do, it's Betts!"

"Betts?"

Susie explained.

Dinah, listening, thought *This can't be, not Betts, Susie's daughter.* Susie couldn't have a troubled, impossible child. Not only had she long before been touched by luck, blessed with the kiss of some fairy godmother, but such tragedies didn't occur in Susie's kind of family. The Bannons in Dinah's imagination were perfect people. Dinah once longed for Ivy Bannon to be her own mother. She'd dream that morning would come and she'd awaken in Susie's house in Baltimore, that they'd be sisters sleeping side by side in twin beds. She'd be Susie's sibling rather than the strange, peculiar Jody, who wore love beads before they were fashionable and for as long as Dinah knew her was a vegetarian. She recalled that for a while, until she met her guru, Jody shaved her head, donned a white uniform, and joined the Hare Krishnas. Ivy Bannon reportedly wouldn't speak of such outlandishness, and Susie didn't often. Yet Jody was just eccentric, a marcher to a non-Bannon drum, while Betts meant heartbreak and a quicksand of worrying terror. For the first time Dinah could recall, she didn't envy Susie and wouldn't have traded places with her this moment for a million dollars. *Say what you will, Mikey's no problem,* Dinah thought, feeling much less sorry for herself.

"Of course I forgive you," Dinah gushed, dripping tears on Susie's beige sweater, where they left dark dime-size spots.

"And I'm sorry too for mentioning Lily. You're right, she's the past. We have to forget her. And we did, we have, it's just—" Susie swallowed a sob and gripped Dinah's hand so hard the bones ached.

Despite a silent *no!* shrilling in her head, something broke loose in

Dinah's memory and pictures formed of the A-frame, the fire blazing in the large, rock-hewn fireplace, the dancing tongues cleaving the shadows. The women, girls then, and Lily Vaughan. The never-forgotten night pressed heavily against the uncurtained windows on which their reflections turned and turned again, and Dinah felt the past reach with open arms to claim her in a fashion it never had all these years. She thought, *I forgot . . .* and felt the hot and cold on her bare skin.

Greg pushed in the swinging, padded door and stared at the two women, both wiping their eyes. Black bird tracks walked down Dinah's cheeks. Greg asked nervously, "What's happened now?"

Susie searched for at least half a smile. "Nothing serious."

Greg didn't believe her, but he said, hurt, "If that's how you want to be, Susannah. Only, can we please have dinner before everybody dies of hunger."

"This is what I like, a big, happy family!" Jack Lamton bellowed. He had plopped himself down at the head of the table in Greg's usual chair. Everyone was aware that he'd commandeered his son's place, and Jack must have been, too, since he lurched into it a moment before Greg could sit himself. The little byplay, Greg standing, a hand outstretched for the back of the chair in which his father was now collapsed, indecision winging across his face, was missed by no one. Move the man or sit unprotestingly somewhere else? The women watched him avidly, all but Susie, excluded from the drama as she came out of the kitchen with the turkey. By the time she arrived Greg was already seated next to his mother.

"Good food, libation fit for the gods, and pretty women. What more could a man ask for?" Jack Lamton asked rhetorically, an elbow propped in his plate, the glass never far from his mouth. He was drunk enough now to sag, his lower lip falling away from the top, spittle collecting at the corners of his mouth.

"Here it is," Susie said. She placed the large platter in the space cleared for it, nearer Jack now than Greg. There was a flurry of rearranging the dishes and serving bowls so that Greg, up on his feet again, could carve.

"God damn biggest bird in the world!" Jack yelled, and lurched forward. He seemed about to grab the knife from his son's hand, but his momentum reversed and he bounced back in the chair. Jack Lamton with a knife would be lethal as a psychopath.

"Oh, Jack!" Eugenia giggled, a hand before her mouth in a geisha

271

gesture. Quinn frowned, unplucked brows running together. Dinah kicked Lisbeth under the table. The two girls stared at their grandfather, Tia with a ten-year-old's fascination, though she'd witnessed some version of his drunkenness before, and Betts with barely contained disgust.

Susie pretended her father-in-law wasn't there, but Jack Lamton refused to be invisible. He grabbed her hand and, fast as he was crafty, quickly kissed the palm. "Thank you, darling, for a wonderful dinner."

Wiping her hand on her skirt, Susie said, "We haven't eaten any of it yet. Betts, start passing the potatoes, please."

"Doesn't matter. Still damn good."

Talking too loudly, Greg said, "All right, who wants white and who wants dark?"

"Betts, I asked you to pass the potatoes. *Please!* Then start the vegetables around."

Betts glared ominously at her mother. "Here!" She shoved the bowl of mashed potatoes at Tia.

"Don't be so pushy, Betts!"

"Oh, sit down!" Jack yelled at his daughter-in-law. "You remind me of the drill sergeant I had during the war."

Lisbeth smiled. "Want me to pour the wine, Suz?"

"Damn!" Greg muttered, looking up from the turkey. "You forgot the wine, Susie."

"I didn't. It's right there on the sideboard."

Lisbeth was already out of her chair. A bottle of Chablis in one hand, a rich burgundy in the other, she circled the table. "One of each." Jack winked slyly, sailing a wild hand in the direction of her thigh. Lisbeth brushed him off as she would a pesky fly.

"So you girls have all been friends from college days," Eugenia cooed. "How nice!" She had pointedly turned from her husband, whom even she could see was fast slipping from conviviality into sloppy drunkenness. "And you stayed friends all these years. How nice!" she repeated, her smile wilting.

None of the three women had a thing to say. Quinn toyed with the silverware and Dinah dismantled a poppy-seed roll. Lisbeth, having filled every wineglass on the table and replaced the bottles on the sideboard, took her seat again and, sipping the Chablis, tuned into some inner channel that only she saw and heard.

"I still don't know who wants what," Greg said, an undercurrent audible in his voice. "Mom? White meat?"

"Yes, dear," Eugenia said, offering up her plate, which passed on a row of hands to Greg.

"Dad?" Greg eyed his father.

"What?" Jack's chin came up.

"What kind of turkey do you want?"

"Turkey? Turkey? I don't want turkey, I want a girl, just like the girl who married dear old Dad!" Jack Lamton had burst into song, and though he slurred the words, he displayed a fine baritone and kept the tune. "She was the girl and the only girl that Daddy ever had!"

"Jack! Jack!" Eugenia called as if for the family dog. But her husband brushed off her fingers clutching at his sleeve.

"A good old-fashioned girl . . . !" he bellowed.

"White meat or dark?"

Quinn protested aloud, "He's drunk as a skunk!"

Greg heard her and yelled, "Shut up!"

"With lots of . . . with lots of . . . with lots of *what*?" He forgot the lyrics and glared about the table as if someone in this dubious crowd had stolen the lost words out of his mouth.

Dinah laughed so hard she covered her face with the napkin.

"Burlesque," Lisbeth said, "pure burlesque." She had come down from her cloud.

Susie said to Greg, "Do something!"

"Oh, Jack, please, you're making a spectacle of yourself again, and at Gregory's too!" Eugenia patted his cheeks as if the man had fallen into a dead faint.

It was Betts finally who brought the scene to a sudden dramatic climax. Like any accomplished actress, she flung down her napkin, leaped up, and in a stance reminiscent of Ingrid Bergman playing Joan of Arc, cried, "He is disgustingly drunk. Soused. Plastered. Shit-eyed!"

"Betts!"

"Betts!"

"Oh, honey, be kind! He's an unhappy man!" Eugenia wailed.

Betts's fiery glance flew from her grandfather to her mother. "And you carry on about grass. Accusing me! When there Grandpa is like one of the bums who sleep on the park benches."

"Don't you dare talk like that about your grandfather!" Greg yelled.

"I hate you, Daddy! You're as bad as Mommy!" On as good an exit line as she could muster, Betts fled from the room.

Greg shouted, "I don't care if she is fifteen, I'm going to beat her backside raw." But he didn't leave the table.

Quinn said to Dinah and Lisbeth, "I think we should say our good-byes."

"I always believed everyone in Susie's orbit was a proper Episcopalian," Dinah answered softly. The scene buoyed her up as nothing else had this long, preposterous day.

"I suppose so," Lisbeth agreed with Quinn. The women stood and Lisbeth said, "Suz, we'll go. Call me later, okay?"

Susie stared at Lisbeth, and then, her frozen face easing, she began to laugh. The four women left the dining room together, all bunched up, girlishly bumping into one another, their laughter as full and musical as it had once been at Cabot. "And I thought," Susie's voice drifted back to her marooned husband, "my life was perfectly wonderful. For years I thought that. What a fool I've been!"

21

The three women found themselves out on the sidewalk in the wind rocketing along Central Park West. Lisbeth pushed up the collar of her fox coat. Dinah hunched slumped shoulders and stuffed her gloved hands in her pockets. Only Quinn stood tall and straight, her fine hair uncovered in the cold. Their laughter had finally dissolved and they talked of going to a restaurant, but none of them cared much about trying to salvage the holiday.

"Skipping a meal will be good for me," Dinah said as they decided to part, each going her own way. Lisbeth and Quinn caught separate cabs and Dinah walked around the corner down the long block to Columbus and the station wagon.

On the ride back up the parkway to Westport, the humor of the aborted dinner soured and the squalor bore in on Dinah. It reminded her of a Buñuel movie she'd once seen where the gross manners and gluttony of the participants eventually changed from being screamingly funny to being disgustingly bestial. Jack Lamton was an animal, and as for Greg, she had to admit she'd always considered him ineffectual, a slaughterhouse lamb. Eugenia, on the other hand, frightened her, for she gave Dinah the sensation of staring down a long, narrow tunnel to the future. If Dinah had stayed with Hatch she would come to be through some slow metamorphosis not so different from Susie's mother-in-law. The realization sent shivers through her. Maybe it wasn't such a bad thing that Hatch, her tether to the world of married couples and suburban normality, had left. It was the fact that he'd left *her*, like an old used sneaker, and gone with the moist-lipped glistening Stacy that stuck in Dinah's craw. She saw in a flash of enlightenment that if he'd simply galloped off on the usual masculine adventure, to find himself or get his head together, to backpack on the slopes of Kilimanjaro, she might have sighed and said good riddance. Hatch's bunk would have—did actually—set her free. If only he hadn't used another woman to uproot himself from Westport! Yeah, but what else could it be? Hatch hadn't the imagination for adventuring, and he thought Zen was some macrobiotic cereal.

One of the boatier Buicks passed on Dinah's left, and she observed a profiled family, father, mother, and two children on the backseat, traveling straight ahead, and suffered no pangs of envy.

I'm healing! Me!

But then, in one of the swift reversals so characteristic of her inner territory, gloom jerked Dinah up by the short hairs and she rode into the calm of a darkening Westport, lolling in Thanksgiving peace, wondering, *So what comes next?*

One of the quads in the mall she was passing was showing a new horror movie, and before that strangulating depression, which each time it struck made her think, *This is it! Terminal!* clobbered her, she swung in and parked close to the large main doors. There were very few cars in the parking lot, for most people in this enclave of upper-middle and upper-upper Connecticut were probably lazing in front of their dying fires, filled up to the ears with a surfeit of good food. Oddly, Dinah wasn't the least bit hungry, and locking the wagon, she butted her way against the wind into the mall.

Luck was with her, *The House of Horror* had just started. She had only missed the credits, and as she sank into a seat on the aisle, she saw that the small theater was almost completely empty except for a handful of teenagers. She relaxed as an enormous Victorian pile, eerily lit as though for a Halloween ad, filled up the screen.

Severed limbs, heads hacked from their necks, eyeballs popping out of their sockets like giant marbles, bodies falling from high windows, bodies splattering into Jell-O on the sharp rocks abutting an angry surf, dead cats and strangled chickens, none of this blood and gore bothered Dinah at all. That distance between her and the screen soothed her in some peculiar fashion, eased those personal demons, smoothed over her real-life fears of even the Lily Vaughan-haunted present. She entered the land of never-never, of never-could-be, and enjoyed the murderous evil as much as she had, when a child, the animated Disneys.

When the screen went finally black and a pale glow filled the theater, she uncurled from her seat, eased her stiffened legs, and strolled, completely satisfied, out into the lobby. *A good movie, no doubt about it, was almost as good as sex*, she thought, then scoffed. *What do you know about sex?* That twosome game, at least the sensations, was almost as forgotten as tennis since Hatch left. She failed to remember, except for the haziest details, what lovemaking had been like with her husband.

Getting back into the station wagon, Dinah reviewed the silly plot and the gruesome scenes of the movie, feeling a touch ridiculous. On Thanksgiving night, unfed, alone, to shut herself up with a teenage horror picture hinted at the perverse, or worse, a certain immaturity. Yet, as she sat behind the wheel, the key in the ignition unturned, memories of the movie's blood, the surprise slashing attacks, the heart-pounding thrills and terror, sent no tremors up her spine.

I should know better, she thought, *having* really *seen a knife and blood . . .*

There was much less blood, actually only a few small drops spotting the snow, though a jagged patch darkened Lily's sweater around the handle of the kitchen knife. Not a lot of blood at all, Dinah thought with a shiver that set her teeth chattering, had flowed out of Lily Vaughan with her life. She lay on the snow as though on a white ruffled sheet, legs kinked, arms by her side, in a parody of sleep.

Somebody killed her, somebody found Lily outside the house, midway between the gentle slope to the secondary road and the A-frame, and shoved a serrated knife between Lily's cupcake breasts.

In the nighttime parking lot, the long angular shopping mall spread out before her, Dinah hunched and tried to keep the scattered moments of those hours with Lily Vaughan from flying up and out of the depths of memory.

Why had she gotten up and gone out?

Why had Lily left the house when the temperature hovered around zero and the snow was just slackening off? They'd all been so sleepy, after the spaghetti and chocolate cake and the grass. Dinah watched them from here back through the curves of time to the past—Lis on the couch, Susie by the fire now down to a few glowing embers, and Lily in a cushioned chair, still dressed, sleeping.

And after that . . . too much wine, too many tokes. I can't remember. . . . Dinah clutched her head with gloved hands. I was sleeping until somebody's shouts—Lisbeth's or Susie's or Quinn's—woke me up, she told the troopers and Newbury's police chief. And she clung to those dead, dreamless hours of sleep like a drowning man to a raft.

A chill crept under Dinah's coat and finally shook her loose from the past. Flexing leathery fingers to get the circulation flowing, she started the car.

Her feet were now blocks of ice, and hunger pangs set her stomach rumbling. These ordinary feelings affirmed life. She lived when Lily died, she thought with satisfaction. Her own awful life was all at once wonderful, and she laughed until tears came to her eyes.

The hunger escalated into a craving that needed to be sated right away, and Dinah swung into the Burger King. She left the car and practically running for the well-lit building, pushed her way inside as she thought, *Lily's dead, so what? The miserable twit deserved to die. Nobody deserved to die at twenty,* she answered guiltily before she could stop herself, throw up the protective barriers she'd constructed all this time. She had for so long locked that house in the country, the snow, the knife, the blood, and Lily frozen stiff and gone forever, into a corner of her mind. And ordering two Whoppers, fries, a chocolate milk shake, and apple pie, Dinah realized that just as Lily like a George Romero zombie refused to lie in the grave of her own memory, she'd sprung back to life in someone else's. So what if Lily had been murdered in 1968? What did it matter now?

It matters desperately to someone, Dinah thought, before she could stop herself. Susie was right. . . .

Dinah's order arrived at the counter, and she took the tray to a table by the window. She bit into the burger and thought not about real life, so untidy, a growth with too many errant tendrils to it, but the pretend and satisfying fright of the movie. Dinah nibbled the fries and drank the milk shake and buried the memories under the food.

"I thought that was you."

Dinah leaped up off the chair and banged her knee against the underside of the table. Joe Connors, his hair rumpled, stood just to the side in a green duffle coat.

"I saw you through the window as I was driving by. At first I wasn't sure, but then I turned around and drove along this side." He smiled and, suddenly shy, ducked his head.

"What are you doing here?" Dinah cried, feeling for the chair under her and sitting down again. Joe Connors scared her as nothing in *The House of Horror* had. And she just knew she looked a mess with ketchup smeared on her mouth.

Joe gazed at her puzzled. "I just told you. I was on my way home from my sister's after dinner and I saw you. So . . ." He halted abruptly, then cleared his throat in an embarrassed harumph, harumph. "Do you mind if I sit down?" he asked, already claiming the chair opposite. They stared at one another like two train travelers stranded for a long journey.

What can he want? Dinah wailed to herself. *The last time we met I dumped food in my lap. Oh, why doesn't he go away and let me finish eating in peace.* But she was unable to eat another fry or take one further sip of the gooey shake, and if he abruptly vanished, she'd throw herself on the floor in a fit of hysterics.

"Maybe I should get some coffee. Do you want some?"

"Okay." She'd have agreed to a cyanide cocktail.

Joe went off to the counter. Dinah never took her gaze from his back. He could be, after all, another hallucination, soon to be gone, poof! up in a dervish swirl of dust. But he quickly returned clutching two paper cups of coffee.

"You want anything in it?" he asked.

"No, just black."

"I thought so."

"Why did you think so?" She cocked her head like a curious bird, or like Becky trying to translate human sounds into dog speech. There were so many things in the world that were inexplicable, such as Joe Connors sitting at the other side of a plastic table in Burger King on Thanksgiving night.

"You look like the tough black coffee type." He grinned. Dinah noticed one of his incisors was a bit out of line. "Now, the last time we were together," Joe Connors said, making their previous encounter sound like a date, "we ordered tea because you always do with Chinese. But"—he held up a finger—"we also had sodas."

"If you say so," Dinah replied. *How could he remember?* she wondered, nervously pushing the small paper boat with its cargo of cold fries around the table. Krazy Glue might as well have attached her tongue to her teeth, it was that difficult to speak.

They eyeballed one another for the longest minute, then Joe said, "You must have eaten pretty early."

"What?" Why did she keep saying that one word? *God, I sound like a mynah bird!*

"Turkey dinner. I mean, Thanksgiving's always such a pig-out that if you're already hungry—" He stopped with a jolt as it obviously occurred to him that maybe Dinah never ate turkey today at all.

"I was just at the movies," she explained, sidestepping the question of the usual feast.

"Oh, what did you see?"

"The House of Horror."

Joe blinked. "Was it good?"

"So-so. Not as bad as some." She tried not to sound completely cuckoo as she enthusiastically added, "The special effects were great."

Joe Connors flashed a smile. "My kids really love horror movies."

"You have kids? I didn't know that," she said, trying to steer him off the subject of her bloody hobby.

Some inner glow, perhaps love, infused the dark skin stubbled in a grayish shadow on his cheeks and chin. "Yeah, two. Twins. Girls. Both seventeen." He laughed, embarrassed. "I mean they're seventeen. Of course they both have to be. Twins, well, what else."

"How nice. Twin girls. I always thought I'd like a daughter. Besides Mikey, that is," Dinah said now, more at ease for some reason than Joe Connors, wiggling on his plastic chair like an angleworm.

"Where is your son?"

"Mikey's competing in a swim meet up in Boston. He'll be home on Sunday."

"A swimmer! Hey, that's terrific! My girls play tennis, but their hearts aren't in it. I think they do it just to please their old man."

A pimply-faced adolescent in a brown and orange uniform pushed a mop around the tile floor, leaving a dry semicircle about the table at which Dinah and Joe sat. The swish, swish of the mop entered their silence like music.

There were even fewer people in the restaurant than when Dinah arrived. Only a pair of burly men in drab-green work clothes and hobnail boots, elbows on the table like a set of bookends, and midway down the other wall of windows, a slender black woman, ebony skin glowing beneath gray curls that Dinah suspected were a wig, reading a paperback. The distance made it impossible to see the title, but a huge sunburst flared across the cover. Something inspirational, probably.

Dinah, so awkward, so often stumbling through life like a hunchback dwarf on crutches, cursing herself for the inevitable clumsy encounters, sat speechless with Joe, afraid. All sorts of sentences battered at her secured teeth and lips, but she wasn't sure she could speak straight and not tangle herself into trouble. Look what had happened the last time they'd sat just like this. Not that Joe Connors seemed angry over getting a piece of her mind, and she, after all, had gotten a lapful of Chinese food. In fact, he lolled quite comfortably now, the duffle coat unbuttoned. His long legs jutted over to her side of the table, and he simply stared, a goofy smile tugging at his mouth. What did he look so pleased about? Was the man dim? No, of course not. He was a successful businessman. Well, maybe he got his jollies by picking up overweight, sloppy single women in fast-food restaurants.

"Would you like to do something?"

"What do you mean, something?" she asked suspiciously, giving him a slitty-eyed glare.

"Oh, I don't know. Like go to a movie. No, no"—he waved a hand—"you've just seen a movie." *Is he being a smart-ass?* Dinah wondered. "And, of course, neither of us is hungry. So how about a drink? Maybe find someplace to have a beer, or whatever, and we could dance if they have music."

Dinah opened her mouth but no sound swept out. She closed it again and tried to think. All she came up with was "I have to go home and walk the dog."

"I could go with you."

"I have to feed her, too. She eats her big meal at night. I put some dry kibble in her bowl to fend off starvation, but that's not the real thing. She also likes it mixed with granola and heated up in the microwave."

"What kind of dog?" he asked.

"An Airedale."

"With the real fuzzy face?"

She wasn't sure if that was a compliment or an insult to Becky. "Rebecca's a beautiful dog!"

He pulled back hastily. "Oh, absolutely. I mean, I'm sure she is. I'd like to meet her. So, we can go feed her and walk her, or walk her first, and then go out for a drink." He smiled hopefully, waiting for an answer.

"All—" Dinah started to say when it struck her with the speed of a major league fastball. The man was asking her for a date! Nobody had asked her out since before she'd begun going steady with Hatch. A date! The kind of outing teenagers and college students went on, and certain preferred single women, like Lisbeth. Good God! Dinah thought for a moment she'd pass out right in the front window of Burger King. But to her amazement she did no such thing. Instead, rather demurely, patting her mouth with a crumpled napkin, she said, "You can follow me in your car."

When left alone in the house, Becky barked the instant a foot connected with the front porch. She yapped herself silly even when it was Dinah or Mikey yelling, "Shut up, it's me!" No voice recognition system existed in the Airedale's brain, and her doggy dementia only calmed when she sighted a familiar face or a known hand clamped down on her head.

"For heaven's sake, Becky, I said it was me," Dinah shouted as, shoving the dog aside, she made room for Joe Connors to enter the house.

"Nice place," he said. "Nice dog, too," he added, though Becky gave him her fishiest look. Do I know you? she seemed to be asking. But when Joe's fingers automatically found the hollows behind her ears and scratched away with vigor, Becky sighed in ecstasy, all doubts forgotten.

"Come on, Beck," Dinah said, holding the door. "Walk time."

"Hey, why don't I take her out and you can cook that doggy dinner you were telling me about. It sounds like a big production."

"Not really," she replied, dubious all of a sudden about Joe Connors's intentions. Had he forced his way in here, sweet-talked her, only to steal her dog? But the silliness of that idea struck her the moment she thought it. "She doesn't like to do her business with strangers," Dinah said. But Becky was fervently licking Joe's hand. She had fallen frantically in love with the man on first sight. *Oh, not you too, Rebecca, ready to go off with somebody else and abandon your first, your truest, friend!*

Joe was already halfway out the door, Becky trailing behind him. "Don't worry, we'll be fine. I'm used to dogs. Honest. For years I had a golden retriever. I'd have a dog now if I weren't away from home most of the time." He waved cheerily and was gone.

Dinah, left standing on one foot in the foyer, could think of nothing to do but go make Becky's dinner and trust that dog and man would eventually return. So recently the victim of a husband abduction, she considered it her right to worry, even if unnecessarily, over those close to her. Sooner or later, if she didn't sink to the welfare rolls, she might recuperate from being a discarded wife, but if Rebecca, or God forbid! Mikey, were taken from her, she'd die.

She had just pressed the microwave timer when there was a clamor at the front door, a machine-gun splatter of nails on the hardwood that signaled a dancing dog, and a gust of laughter, from Joe she supposed. "Back here!" she yelled, and like a genie he appeared along with a blur of Airedale fur. The way Becky was racing around him, she'd turn into butter. Dinah yelled, "Down, Beck! Down!" The dog sank on her hindquarters and somehow slid halfway across the kitchen floor. "Oh, you're impossible, Beast." Dinah rubbed the dog's head and eyeing Joe curiously, asked, "How did you make a friend of Becky so fast?"

He presented that shiny smile, and the gleam against his dark face made Dinah think, *Give the man a sheet, a horse, and some desert to ride across!* "You are the most suspicious woman," he said, shaking his head.

"I'm a woman alone. What do you expect?"

"I'm a man alone, and I trust just about everybody. Which is how come Rebecca and I got to be such great buddies in under five minutes. She's pretty trusting herself."

The timer buzzed before Dinah could patiently spell out the differences between single men who owned their businesses, weren't too heavy in the aft, and hadn't the specter of an uncertain future waving over their heads, as compared to single rejected females, jobless, on the verge of being poorish, and way out of shape. Becky almost knocked her over before Dinah got the dish into the corner and took the water bowl to the sink to refill.

"Ah, I could use a glass of water too, if it's okay," Joe Connors said at her elbow. She turned so quickly she almost spilled Becky's bowl on his coat. The man always caught her unawares, being where she least expected him. Hastily she apologized. "I'm sorry. I should have offered you a drink."

"That's okay. You were busy with the dog food."

Why was he so persistently understanding?

Dinah took a glass out of the cabinet beside the sink. "Would you rather have a soda, or I think I have a beer in the refrigerator somewhere?"

"No, that's fine, really."

His niceness pushed Dinah into trying to please him. "What about a drink drink, like scotch or vodka? Or maybe some wine?"

"Well, if you're having something I will."

"I could drink a glass of wine." Two bottles of Hatch's Beaujolais had been in the kitchen and escaped the massacre in the basement.

"Wine would be great."

"Okay. But you have to open it. I always lose the cork."

"Be glad to," he said, hastily doffing his duffle coat and throwing it over a kitchen chair. Dinah handed Joe one of the bottles and the corkscrew and went to hang her own coat in the hall closet. On the way back to the kitchen, she detoured into the powder room and give herself a quick once-over. Except for the mascara smudges below her eyes that looked, if she squinted, like hollows of weariness such as a sensitive artist ardently laboring over a creation would have, she didn't need too much repair. A brush through her hair, eyebrows smoothed with water on a fingertip, a touch of lipstick, and *There,* she thought, *that's as good as Joe Connors is going to get.* She stepped back and straightened her maroon wool dress which, hanging unbelted from her bust, hid the more prominent of her bulges.

When she came out she found that Joe had wandered into the living room. "Here," he said when he saw her.

She accepted the wineglass. "Thank you."

"It's pretty good by the way, not that I'm much of an expert." She decided against telling him about Hatch's wine cellar. "I like your house too, Dinah," he went on. "It has a comfortable, lived-in look."

Did that mean he noticed the thin layer of dust over everything? Since she'd terminated Mae, the burden of cleaning the colonial rested once again entirely on her shoulders, and now, with Hatch not in residence, she'd less of a reason to do something she hated. But as Joe strolled about, casually glancing at the pictures, the books on the shelves, she wished she'd vacuumed and polished, taken Windex to the glass coffee table, and swept the ashes from the fireplace. Not that he seemed critical, rather the opposite.

Dinah watched him amble around the room until she felt like a security guard in the Grand Union and settled herself on the couch. He hummed and aahed, took a book from the shelf and buried his nose into it, and seemed as at home as if in his own house. She asked, "Where do you live?"

"In one of those apartment houses out by the parkway. Nothing fancy, but I've got a terrace and there's a pretty decent view. One day, though, I'd like to get into a house again." He glanced over his shoulder at her and after another waltz around the room found his way to the couch. Becky, having eaten her dinner in record time, bounded into the room with the humans and under the coffee table. Joe laughed. "She looks like a big fish in an aquarium."

Dinah nodded her head. Hatch never noticed that, he'd just yell for the poor Airedale to get the hell out of the living room. "Doesn't she," Dinah agreed.

After that they descended into another of those deep silences they were always floundering in, during which Dinah wondered if he too flipped through a card catalog of subjects in search of some suitable topic of conversation.

He put the wineglass over Becky's nose and draped his arm along the back of the couch, looking at her with the same attention he'd just given the rest of the room. "You have the greatest eyes," he said.

Surprised with the wine halfway to her mouth, Dinah splashed it on her dress. There was a moment of frantic dabbing up, and then she said, breathlessly, "Me? Oh, come on. My eyes are just old cow brown."

"No they're not!" he cried indignantly. "They're the deepest brown with tiny speckles of gold in them. Really, Dinah, you've got sensational eyes."

He inched forward and suddenly Joe Connors's face swam next to hers. His lips found Dinah's with no effort at all, and she sat like a snowman while he kissed her. *Oh, my God, I don't believe this is happening to me* was all she could think until she realized he'd taken her glass and put it on the table, then directed her arm about his neck.

Oh, this is nice. Dinah practically swooned, Joe's tongue working away inside her mouth. She reciprocated and the sloppy, exciting result overwhelmed the two of them so they fell back on the couch. Somehow Dinah's left breast got jammed under Joe's right hand, and her dress crawled up her thighs. His corduroy shirt came unbuttoned and a dark hairy chest sprang into view. The leprechauns of lust were quickly undoing their clothes as Joe and Dinah rolled about on the couch and almost onto the floor. Becky eyed them with obvious interest and scrambled out of her hiding place to shove a curious nose into the confusion of bodies. Unfortunately it hit Joe's chin and he yelped. Dinah tried pushing Becky away, but she rebounded like a rubber ball.

"Do you think we could go somewhere more private?" Joe groaned.

Dinah stumbled up and off the couch, slapping at her dress and beneath it the half loosened bra and twisted panty hose. Joe struggled after her, and holding on to each other as if alone they'd collapse, they staggered upstairs into Dinah's bedroom. Once there, the door closed and locked with the firm bolt Hatch had installed as soon as Mikey could walk, they tumbled onto the bed and went at one another like sumo wrestlers.

I lost my head. Everything went blank. I didn't know what I was doing! Never again would she disbelieve those proclamations when she heard some criminal swearing them, for in the lurching, tossing melee that was Dinah and Joe Connors making love amid a snare of sheets and quilt, her mind took French leave. She sprouted wings and sailed in a glider pattern; she free-floated in space. With a spastic kicking of uncontrollable legs she tumbled end over end. Her heart stampeded and warm tides splashed in her groin. Then, amazingly, as she groaned, "Oh, no, you don't have to!" Joe Connors's head slipped between her thighs.

"I want to!" he insisted, and threw himself into gobbling at her as if she were an ice cream cone.

The world exploded in a nuclear detonation, pieces of Dinah flying away, and she screamed so loudly the roof must have lifted. Quickly Joe Connors slipped himself, hard, firm, inside her. Another explosion blew what was left of Dinah into fragments, and Joe bellowed too, like a wounded bull. A skiff pitched on stormy waters, they rode each other until, slowly, like a new dawn breaking, the seas calmed and they lay in a pool of sweat tightly glued together.

"That was . . . that was . . ." That was what? Dinah didn't know what she was going to say.

"Wonderful," he breathed in her ear.

"What happened?" Dinah sighed, gripping him fiercely.

She thought he laughed. "We made love."

"I know that! But, oh wow, I felt like a major smack-up on the Merritt."

"You have thunderous orgasms, Dinah, which is just terrific."

Dinah shoved him off and tried to see him better in the fusty light from the lamp lit on the dresser. "That was an orgasm?" she cried, shocked.

He went after her, firmly tethering her next to him once more. "What did you think it was?"

She honestly had no idea. Love maybe. But an orgasm? *Never!* "That wasn't even close to anything I've been through before. I never had a whoosh like going up in the elevator in the twin towers, then that sensation . . . oh," she struggled to describe it. "I guess like the astronauts experience when they're tossed into space. And, the rest of it, oh, I'll never be able to tell you, Joe. But *never,* ever in my life, honestly!" She pushed him gently back again, to stare into liquid eyes that she noticed for the first time were awfully like Becky's.

"Maybe," he said, blinking, "you just never went at it the right way."

"What an understatement!" She giggled. "You're not Jewish by any chance?"

"No, lapsed Catholic. Why?"

Dinah buried her face in the angle between his neck and shoulder. "Because Hatch always told me only Jewish men did, you know, *that!*"

Joe laughed so loudly the bed shook, and as they rolled to the very edge, their hands found, once again, each other's private places. Unbelievably, they were, to Dinah's delight, on a second round of lovemaking.

22

The first storm of the winter struck the Northeast with the ferocity of a wild beast. A light, transient snow dusted New York the day after Thanksgiving, but on December first a blizzard rampaged through the Rockies, picked up force in the central plains states, and slammed the Atlantic coast with gale force winds. The snow began just before dawn.

All during the day the snow fell, fast, faster, until the sanitation crews, out in their giant trucks, cleared the streets only to have them fill up moments later. The schools never opened, and offices sent employees home before midafternoon. The subway trains swooped at their usual rattling breakneck speed underground, but swayed along the unsheltered elevated tracks like high-wire aerialists, barely moving. Buses crept along. Taxis and cars skidded helplessly into each other.

The city came to a halt. By dusk, New York lay inert under a foot of thick drifting snow.

The few vehicles that ventured outside in the premature dusk moved cautiously down the muffled streets. Cars and people were bleached shadows in the falling snow.

It was difficult for the rented Oldsmobile to maintain traction on snow-packed Park Avenue. It fought a labored passage uptown behind the taxi, swirling white sheets keeping visibility to a minimum, so there was no need to fear the cabby's looking back and discovering the ghost car on his tail. Like ragged dancers they journeyed in tandem to Seventy-ninth Street and carefully swung west through the park. Snow mounded on the branches of trees, spun crowns at the tops and skimmed along the bark in lacy dressing gowns. To anyone able to look, the park was a pristine fairyland, but for the driver of the Olds, frozen over the steering wheel, there were only the red twinkling taillights of the cab in front.

With grinding gears both vehicles fought their way out of the transverse and turned north onto Central Park West, where entombed cars hugged the curbs. The streetlamps spilled an unearthly glow. The stone wall bordering the park and the trees beyond it disappeared under the falling snow. The buildings on the west side of the street, with golden windows pitted in their facades, were massive limestone promising refuge.

Traffic was scarce by now and the tire tracks of the few cars still out were covered almost instantly. No walkers strolled the arctic sidewalks, and the doormen remained sequestered in their heated lobbies. The Oldsmobile driver, connected to this snowy outer world by a gauzy inner confusion, was only intent on the twin ruby taillights.

Greg Lamton, huddled in the rear of the taxi, felt a cold coming on. His nose was stuffed up and the back of his throat scratched like an emery board. Tomorrow he'd have blocked nasal passages and a booming bass drum cough. He just knew it. With the cold and the storm he would probably end up staying in bed. Susie could bring him hot tea with a dash of brandy and sit reading in the slipper chair while he slept. When he waked it would be to the sight of her glossy dark hair and the fine curve of her cheek. She'd be soothing and motherly, loving in a way she hadn't been lately. It would be worth being sick to have Susie comfort him. Lying tucked up under the covers, weak and logy, the fumes of Vicks plastered over his chest drifting through his clogged nostrils like faint childhood perfume, would temporarily free Greg from the responsibilities of adulthood. During the drowsy hours he imagined forgetting the problems with Betts, or at least putting them on a mental back burner. Worries about his older daughter, along with the less defined but no less terrifying worries about Susie, could be set aside, excused by illness. How gratifying it would be just to wallow in misery.

The cab skidded to a stop just beyond Eighty-third Street. The driver refused to make a U-turn in the snow to pull up in front of the house, so Greg paid him and stepped out into a dense white world.

To the driver waiting patiently in the Oldsmobile half a block behind, Greg Lamton was a monochromatic shadow in the snow-drenched light. Greg wore a bulky hat pulled low to his eyebrows. He hunched over, tucked in his chin, and shoved against the gale to make his blind way across to the far side of the street.

The taxi shimmied into the next block, and the Olds doused its headlights and sped forward.

It happened so quickly that Greg never knew he was hit. Time squeezed together like an accordion as the future at once became the past, and Susie's husband rose, airborne, light as cellophane, weightless in the current of flying snow, and descended, crumpling in the street. His hat sailed upward, disappearing along the park. The briefcase under his arm spun and slid beneath a snowbound car.

The Oldsmobile's driver took only one hasty glimpse in the rearview mirror before heading north, but Greg, facedown, his legs at odd tortured angles, had a twisted, broken, dead look to him. And a short while later she would learn that that was so.

"I can't believe it," Dinah said for the third time.

At the other end of a line crackling with static, Quinn, high up over East End Avenue, watching the midnight end of the storm trailing its skirts out over the river, sighed. "Why not? It happens every day. It's commonplace, people dying, having accidents."

Dinah sputtered, "But Greg was only forty-five and disgustingly healthy. Besides, we just saw him at Thanksgiving, alive and mad as a hornet."

Quinn rolled her eyes and took a long drink of her scotch and soda before she said, "Sometimes, Dinah, you make me wonder."

"What's that supposed to mean?" Dinah shouted down the wires from Westport, so she could be loudly heard, despite the crackles, in New York.

"Nothing. I'm just out of sorts, worrying about Susie. Don't pay any attention to me."

"How is Suz?"

"Holding in there, I guess. We only talked for a few minutes. She asked me to call you and Lisbeth. And, if the storm stops, if the city digs out from under, to ask the two of you to go there tomorrow. She said there'd be other people, the hideous Lamton parents, I suppose. But I think she needs us." Quinn tucked the receiver between her ear and shoulder and rolled the heavy tumbler in her palms. Though there was ample heat in the apartment, it felt cold this near the window.

Dinah said, "Absolutely, if I can make it down. The trains should be running, or as well as they ever do. What time?"

"I don't know. Afternoon probably. I'd say come over to the lab and we'll go from there, but you won't want to do any extra slogging around the city if you can help it."

"Okay," Dinah said. "And Quinn . . ." Silence filled up the phone. Quinn thought for a moment they'd gotten disconnected, but suddenly Dinah returned. "Are you sure, really sure, Greg's death was an accident?"

"A hit-and-run is what it was. But if you're asking what I think you're asking, how do I know?" Quinn snapped, choosing irritation rather than fright at the question she'd already asked herself. They both hung up quickly after that, and Quinn brooded in the lonely quiet, dissatisfied. She always protested, *I face facts,* but she'd never, she had come so recently to realize, confronted anything head-on, at least not for years now. We are who we *think* we are, Lisbeth had said in some conversation, and Quinn wanted to believe her. But that was a lie. We are who we are, and if we think differently, if we imagine other attributes, even a wholly strange persona, it's all fiction. Lisbeth had always confused make-believe with life, and Quinn, for all her intelligence, wished fervently she could accept this fallacious philosophy. She knew that part of her dodged facts if the reality was beyond enduring, and this depressed her profoundly. Her cowardly responses, as she judged so many of her reactions to be, began with the death of Lily Vaughan.

I'm as bad as Dinah, thinking of Lily, worrying so long after that long-ago winter, she thought, and finished the last of the scotch, the ice cubes rattling like bones in the tumbler. She left the living room, leaving the lights burning. Since the dogs died, she kept all the lamps in the apartment lit, for she could no longer tolerate going to bed in the dark. Out of black nothing something would come to claim her. That was Quinn's fear. But after she undressed, washed her plain face on which she felt the loosening skin, and pulled a cotton nightgown over her head, she dialed Will's Brooklyn number for the hundredth time only to hear the phone ringing eternally in the empty house. She thought, hanging up, no worse terror could attack her than the one with which she was already living.

"He was never good enough for you, Suz, and that's the truth," Lisbeth said, standing before the mirror in Susie's bathroom. She fixed on the reversed Susie in bra and panty hose and black sling-back pumps in the bedroom, pulling on an Anne Klein jersey dress. Susie, donning her widow's garb with her back to Lis, didn't realize that she could watch her. It irked Lisbeth, this impromptu reticence, and sent sharp spikes of pain stabbing behind her eyes. When she wasn't gone in the black periods of time she had a continual headache now. She was learning to endure this presence in her skull, but certain sounds or movements, flashing lights and strident colors, various stresses, and even minor incidents like Susie's reluctance to let her see her un-clothed escalated the pain.

"Don't say I'm better off without him!" Susie cried, rushing to the bathroom. "That's cruel. Greg was a wonderful, loving man, and I wish it had been me instead of him out in the snow."

Lisbeth sorted through the makeup in a cabinet drawer and pulled out a gold tube of lipstick. "Here, use this pale pink. Perfect for funerals."

"What are you doing talking about lipstick? My husband is dead!"

"You're white as a virgin princess. Just a touch." Lisbeth drew faint strokes of color on the wan lips. "There, that's better."

Susie stared at herself with filmy eyes.

"You'll make a gorgeous widow," Lisbeth offered. "Elegant, too, just like my mother." The women watched each other, though to Susie Lisbeth's image glistened in a watery pool. "Girls' love." Lisbeth raised a bony cashmere shoulder in a shrug.

"We're women."

"Girls' love makes it sound silly, something written about in purple prose," said Lisbeth.

"We've put that behind us, like Cabot, like being young, Lis."

"Like Lily?" Susie didn't answer and Lisbeth shrugged again. "We loved one another, Susie, remember?"

"We still do, but not like that. We were experimenting, and we were so drunk with our freedom." Susie was pleading.

"Experimenting. Freedom. God, words are wonderful, but they don't mean a thing. Tiny little spiders crawling across paper. Like the words in *Silver Street*." She laughed and, abandoning the mirror, embraced Susie. "I'm supposed to be comforting you."

"You're keeping me from collapsing on the floor in a shrieking fit, if that's comforting," Susie said. They clung together a moment longer until Susie came away in a stagger.

Lisbeth separated from the dark lake that splashed the edges of her vision and saw Susie with darts of brilliance sparking off her. A pang struck Lisbeth through the heart. She managed even less control over this love than any other. "You think we've made a mess of things," she heard her own voice, rough as the wind, saying, before the descent began again. She struggled to rise back up to the surface.

"It hasn't been so bad, up to now I mean." Susie spun around and walked out of the bathroom. Lisbeth, moving slowly through clouds of water, followed.

When Susie reached the bed she dropped, pounding her fists against the mattress. "What am I saying! Greg's dead. Forty-five and dead. A hit-and-run. Killed, right out there!" She waved a hand toward the window. "I did love him, Lis," she cried with true tears now, "more before than now, but he was a person, good, and he cared so much!"

Lisbeth sank to her knees at the side of the bed. She searched for Susie's eyes, but Susie hid. "When this is over, maybe you'll come out to California. You'll sit in the sun and relax and start putting yourself back together."

"Are you leaving New York?" Susie sat up in surprise.

"Maybe. I might. Now that the play's closed. There's always something happening in the Great Tar Pit, and if I want to do another play, there are theaters galore. Really, I'm not sure why I thought I had to come to Manhattan."

"What about Charlie?"

Lisbeth's forehead crinkled. "Charlie? What about him?"

"He's the first authentic man I can remember you being with, Lis."

"Charlie . . . Charlie's an old toothless bear," Lisbeth said, not wanting to talk about Charlie. She climbed to her feet, smoothed her skirt, and glanced around the room. "If you stay here, redecorate completely. Throw all this stuff out and start from the bare bones. Something softer and more feminine would be right for you," Lisbeth said as somebody knocked on the door. She went to open it.

Mrs. Sloan, all in black herself, stepped inside. "Mrs. Lamton, we better be going soon. The girls are ready. And Mr. and Mrs. Lamton Senior are waiting in the living room for you."

"The car?"

"Downstairs. The doorman called up."

"All right." Susie's lips trembled as Lisbeth gripped her elbow and they walked together out to the foyer, preparing to attend Greg Lamton's funeral.

The sun shone briefly during the graveside service. The funeral preceding it at Campbell's had been antiseptic, with Reverend Ward lamenting Greg's untimely death, his being struck down in the prime of life, leaving behind a beautiful, loving wife and two wonderful daughters, grieving parents suffering the worst of tragedies—the death of an offspring—plus dear friends and admiring co-workers. But the Almighty, in His infinite wisdom, had some larger plan, a grand design mere mortals couldn't comprehend. Susie thought, *What garbage!* She wished, oh how she wished her parents stood beside her, Dr. Bannon gripping her hand and pursing his lips in a gesture of annoyance. She could hear him snort, *Don't give me nonsensical explanations, just the smell of incense, some Latin, a ritual like theater, and a good wake.*

But Susie on Central Park West wouldn't have even the latter. And her parents were in South America somewhere, on a boat trip down the Amazon. Next week they'd arrive in Rio, but that would be too late. Next week was another country in which Susie would journey, as foreign and strange as her parents in Brazil.

Thankfully her friends were here, standing to the right of Betts, Dinah so bundled up only her nose was visible, Quinn, military straight in her fur hat and coat like a Russian general, and Lisbeth, distracted, not paying attention. *Though why should she?* Susie wondered. At the funeral parlor the women intervened between Susie and those, such as the McGraths, whose sympathetic mumblings Susie hated hearing. Claire might not have wished Greg dead, but she was taking an ill-concealed wicked delight in Susie's being a widow. When she bent down from her height, exaggerated by three-inch heels, her eyes positively gleamed as she crooned, "You poor thing, how utterly dreadful for you!" Quinn quickly urged Claire inside, but it wasn't so easy with the elder Lamtons, who felt, not surprisingly, they had proprietary rights with Susie and the girls.

At the Westchester cemetery to which the cortege had proceeded in heavy traffic, the sun slipped through a breach in the cloudy sky and spilled over the snow-covered grounds. It arrived, a strange benediction, just as the coffin was being lowered into the earth. The blinding light elongated the hollows beneath Susie's eyes and splashed on the tears on her ashen cheeks so that the tiny drops sparkled like miniature prisms.

The minister, bareheaded and tall, scrawny as a wading bird, murmured into the wind, his coat flapping about his legs, "From dust thou art, to dust thou returneth. . . ."

Eugenia emitted an ugly crow's cry and lurched as if she would throw herself in the grave, but Jack's tight hand restrained her. Jack Lamton's face was ravaged and he had an air of such utter confusion, as though he'd awakened after one of his drunks in an unfamiliar room, that Susie couldn't help feeling sorry for him. Whatever substance there had been in her father-in-law had long ago been turned to sour mash, and now he had no self to sustain him.

The girls, bundled in heavy coats, anchored themselves at Susie's sides. As she cast a fistful of dirt, throwing it almost angrily into the grave where it splattered upon the mahogany coffin lid, Tia sobbed aloud. Betts might have been crying too, but she'd jammed dark mirrored glasses over her eyes when they left Campbell's.

The small group—only fifteen or twenty people took the long ride out to the cemetery—huddled together and seemed intent on Mr.

Ward's words; but the moment he slapped the Bible closed, they scattered quickly over the treacherous snowy paths between the graves to the cars parked in the narrow lane.

The three women started back to the city in a limousine just behind the family car, but out on the parkway their driver put a heavy foot on the gas and they swung around Susie traveling with her children and in-laws. Their limo sped as though they had a plane to catch.

Quinn said, "I wish he wouldn't drive so fast," and grasped the strap.

"I wonder if Susie has any antihistamines. I think I'm getting a cold," Dinah said. She blew her nose into a crumpled Kleenex.

"Antihistamines won't stop a cold," Quinn announced, as if Dinah should have known that.

Dinah retorted, "They do for me." Quinn always peeved her when she was so know-it-all.

Lisbeth slouched in the corner, appearing half asleep. The only color to her was that tumble of burning hair. "What's the matter with you? A cold too?" Dinah asked. But Lisbeth, her eyes shuttered to slits, hummed tunelessly until Quinn reached over Dinah's lap and jiggled her knee.

"Lis!" Quinn ordered. "Quit it!"

"What?" She glanced at them, confused.

"You're traveling in a different orbit," Dinah told her. Then to Quinn, "She's more out of it than Susie. But Suz always keeps herself together. She's tougher than we think."

Quinn ignored Dinah. "Are you all right, Lis?"

Lis pulled a hand over her face as though she could change the way she looked, as though she might transform herself. But when her hand returned to her lap she was the same Lisbeth. "Anybody have a cigarette?"

"I found a pack from last year in the pocket of this coat. They're stale as ditch water though. But if you're desperate . . ." Dinah wiggled about and dug the crushed pack of Marlboros loose. "Here."

"I wish you hadn't taken up smoking again," Quinn sniffed, sitting stiffly as she gazed out the window at the uninteresting scenery.

Lisbeth lit a cigarette and inhaled a deep lungful of smoke.

They rode quietly, then Dinah said, "How's Will, Quinn, and the family? You should have a big Christmas this year with all those kids." Quinn was stony. "Quinn?" Dinah jiggled her elbow.

"Damn it, stop that!" Quinn flared, jerking away.

"Jesus, what is it with you two?" Dinah cried nervously, glancing from Quinn to Lisbeth, but both women stared out their windows.

Dinah returned, more insistently, to Quinn. "Is there something I don't know about? With Susie? Or . . . or . . . whatever?" She had that plaintive old Dinah tone of voice, sounding as she had on first arriving from Nebraska, before the group formed and she'd been inside.

That must have gotten through to Quinn because, slumping, she dropped back against the seat. "No, nothing like that, Di. It's me."

"Quinnie, what is it?" Dinah asked, wanting to touch Quinn but thinking better of it.

Quinn closed her eyes. "It's Will. He's gone again, with Maria and the children. To Boston."

"Boston? No! Why?"

"He's taking over as the new head of Webster, Inc."

Lisbeth finally came around. "How did that little plot twist happen?"

Quinn explained, her voice a monotone, and as she did so she felt implicated, an accessory to her own betrayal. Had she meant a reconciliation between the dying old man crazed to live on, if only through his corporation, and a tired, impoverished son? And if she had, why? A generous gesture or a masochistic tearing of her heart?

"Why didn't you tell us before?" Dinah asked, again suspecting she'd been left out. She lit a cigarette herself with shaky hands. She sputtered and coughed. "God, these are old argyle socks!"

"So put it out," Quinn snapped.

"Not until I lose fifteen pounds."

Lisbeth said, "So you'll go visit the happy family in Boston. You know there's a shuttle hourly."

"Lis is absolutely right," Dinah agreed sharply. "Boston's not the moon, and at least you know where Will is and what he's doing." She sniffed, thinking of Hatch on the loose in the city.

"You don't understand!" Quinn worked her fingers together. "We had a fight. Worse than a fight."

"A fight! What's a fight?" Dinah said airily. "If you'd ever been married, you'd have learned that people battle nonstop. Why do you think boxing's such a major sport?"

Whatever labyrinth Lisbeth had been roaming in, she'd come fully out into the light, for she told Dinah, "Stop talking garbage, and just shut up. It's not the same thing between siblings."

Dinah, hurt, sucked in her lips. "How would you know? You're an only child, like me."

"He used me and—" Quinn saw her brother's eyes again, flat and, she realized, uncaring.

"Everybody uses you, or makes a stab at it," Lisbeth said. "Seri-

295

ously, money, influence, power—people always come around grabbing. Fistfuls if they can get them.''

Dinah gasped. ''I just thought of it! We're all single again. Just like the old days.''

''The things you think of!'' Lisbeth shook the red cloud of hair.

''Not that I can promise I'll be on the shelf for long.'' Dinah preened, buffing her nails on her woolly knee. ''Because speaking of secrets, there's mine.''

''Hatch has come home?'' Lisbeth asked.

''Oh, Hatch. Fie on Hatch. Not him, Joe Connors.''

''Who's Joe Connors?'' Curiosity jolted Quinn momentarily.

''You remember, Lis. I applied to his ad agency for a job and would have gotten one, too, if you hadn't told me to lie about my volunteer history,'' Dinah replied spitefully. ''Which just goes to show that you don't know everything about everything. On occasion, honesty, the truth, is the best policy.''

''The truth! Oh Dinah, what's that?'' Lisbeth laughed. ''In our experience I think you could say it's whatever we chose it to be at the time. Hmmmm?'' She looked wicked, licking her lips, but she squeezed Dinah's hand, so neither woman could tell if Lisbeth was joking or not.

''Oh, I'm too happy to argue.'' Dinah grinned, hugging Lis, and then, before she could stiffen, Quinn. And on the way from the cemetery and Greg Lamton's funeral, Dinah smiled broadly as a cat who'd just finished off a canary.

23

She hated thinking about Neff. He should have moved in and out of her life with no effect. But she never quite forgot him, except during the blackouts, when she lost all memory. Like the blackness, however, he hovered close by until she'd want him so intensely desire turned frantic. Desire became another kind of pain.

She wanted to hear his gravelly voice, watch the angry scar ride on his face like a snake. She wanted him in her bed, inside her body, so she could close herself around him.

Yet when Neff turned up, his arrival always took Lisbeth by surprise. He stepped out of the void when she least expected him. Was he watching the house, watching her? How else did he appear magically, like a genie?

He rang the doorbell late at night.

"What do you want?" Lisbeth asked. Seeing him on her stoop, hunched up in his trench coat against the light drizzle, she felt arousal and anger equally.

Somehow, before he answered, he managed to get by her. "A drink would be nice." She stayed at the door as he crossed to the credenza and made himself a scotch. "Want something?" He raised his eyebrows. It could have been his apartment rather than hers.

"Make yourself at home," Lisbeth said sarcastically, slamming the door.

"Vodka?" He poured some Stolichnaya into a glass. "Ice cubes." Carrying the two tumblers, he went into the kitchen. Lisbeth heard him empty an ice tray at the sink. He shouldered back through the swinging door and handed her the drink. "Cheers," he said. He drank and sighed. "Good stuff."

"Glad you approve."

Neff pulled off his coat and crouched at the edge of the couch. "Come on, sit." But Lisbeth leaned against the door.

Restless, Neff got up, wandered with quick, jerky motions around the room. He glanced at the titles of the books on the shelves. "A lot of history," he said, then veered and came up on her.

"I like the past tense," Lisbeth said.

His scar seemed more prominent, uglier, tonight. Maybe the cold caused the irregularity to stand out. Again Lisbeth's fingers itched to stroke it, even though she knew so well how it felt.

"The present's better," Neff said with a half smile, one side of his mouth tilting up.

Lisbeth stared straight into his eyes. It was like looking into nowhere, into two dark culverts with no light, only a great emptiness at the other side. His eyes reminded her of something. She thought of her own eyes now and again, but that wasn't it.

Neff leaned over to kiss her, his lips chilly. He tasted like a dead man, and Lisbeth forgot, despite the heat of desire, what it felt like making love with him. Love was the wrong word. No affection, no warmth, existed between them, only fire, only flames.

Lisbeth had trouble focusing and was suddenly afraid. It could go either way now. *I can stay or I can leave.*

Neff stepped back. "You know," he said as he took a circuitous route to the phone on the Empire secretary in the far corner, "we're nowhere on Charlie's case. Not a clue. And suspects—*nada*. The professor's a saint or a fool, maybe you know which." Neff smiled and punched out a number. "It's Neff," he said into the phone, then listened. "No, not yet. Shit!"

Lisbeth finally pushed away from the door and went to the kitchen. She saw on the Mickey Mouse clock that it was midnight. All the hours, since six anyway, were accounted for. She'd been working here in the white-lit kitchen on a treatment, making notes, drawing up character profiles, thinking, watching scenes in her head roll effortlessly. Papers, a half a dozen ballpoints in different colors, were scattered on the oak table. Lisbeth was ready to quit when Neff rang the doorbell. A brandy, maybe a few hits on a joint, then bed. Things seemed almost as they once did—

—*Once, oh once, I remember once how it—*

Lisbeth quickly rubbed at her temples, as if she could scrub off the clear voice sing-songing; but it wasn't outside anywhere, it resonated inside.

The darkness started in a ground swirl, stygian fog seeping from a crack in the earth. Like an anesthetic it crawled up her body, obliterating one at a time feet, ankles, calves, knees, thighs. Waiting to be swallowed in the pitch and toss of nothingness, in that no place she swam through without memory since . . . when? The accident? Neff pushed open the kitchen door.

He wore his trench coat. "I gotta go," he said, swallowing the last of the scotch. "Put something on. I'll take you with me."

The darkness hesitated. The nether land in which she stood like an amputee slowly faded from black to gray to pearl smoke. Lisbeth glanced at the clock. It was 12:08. No-time had escaped into an alien anteroom.

"All right," Lisbeth said. "Wait. I'll put on some boots and a jacket." Neff, with his bag of tricks, surprisingly kept the blackness at bay.

Neff, on the tall stool, smoothly passed a lit cigarette back and forth, back and forth, from one hand to the other, like a conjurer, without paying much attention. He and Lisbeth sat in a SoHo bar with exposed brick walls and plank floors. Viny plants swayed in their wicker baskets on chains from the ceiling. As they talked Neff's gaze shifted right, left, only traveling over Lisbeth, never stopping. Lisbeth hadn't seen him like this before, tense, a wary animal on an open plain. He was watchful, checking the L-shaped room, the gay couple at the other end of the bar, the few late drinkers still at their tables.

"I don't know you," she said.

"I've got more sides than a snowflake," he said, drawing on the cigarette and then stubbing it out. A silky curl of smoke rose up from the ashtray.

"You're acting like a cop."

"What am I supposed to act like, a brain surgeon?"

Lisbeth said again, "I don't know you at all."

"Are we going to have some bullshit psychology now?" Neff growled. "There's nothing to know. I'm just a regular New York cop doing a job. And now I'm waiting to meet a man about a dog, okay?"

All the way to SoHo in the unmarked dark car, Lisbeth felt Neff slipping away from her little by little. Now they passed into another dark angle of their relationship—no, not relationship, Lisbeth thought. Connection. *I am caught by Neff as if he has handcuffs on me.* A cold, clear, steely pain whiplashed around her skull, and she hated this stranger crouched on her flank.

"You want to hear about my kids, or better, my wife? That's usually the thing, isn't it? *What's she like, the little woman home in Bayshore?* And then I get to tell you how Marlene—that's her name, Marlene—how Marlene's a great mother and homemaker. Keeps the house neat as a pin, clean as a whistle, you could eat one of her

299

gourmet meals off the linoleum. And she devotes herself to the kids. Marlene, she's a paragon, right out of *Good Housekeeping*. Yeah, but we've outgrown one another. Nothing in common anymore. I'm sorry about it, but I'm bored. And sex, now Marlene's a practitioner of parochial school sex, mother superior variety. Lay back and spread 'em, babe. Let him do his dirty business. Man's a frigging animal, but it's God's will.''

This tirade of Neff's came steady as water, hot as vomit, while his gaze moved back and forth from one end of the bar to the other. He wasn't obvious about the scrutiny, but he kept at it mechanically.

"So, if you have such a happy home life, what do you want with me?" Lisbeth slapped the bar, sending an empty ashtray skittering to the floor behind it. The bartender heard the crash and turned. The glass hadn't broken. He picked it up and replaced it before her.

"What do I want with you? I want to fuck you, what do you think." Neff sighed. "You're weird. I like weird. We're all kinked, cops, the crap we see. Some guys are boozers, some snort coke or get through the days on speed. Lots of 'em can't get it up at all and they prowl Times Square from one scuzz joint to another hoping. And the ones like me, we handle the disgusting shit we live with day after day by being cock crazy.''

Lisbeth said, "You're the guy who supposedly doesn't screw around, remember?"

Neff shrugged. "So I lied. You should know about lying, writers do it all the time. All made up, everything, even life. You're especially good at tall stories, like being in love with Charlie. The honest, friendly professor.''

"Bastard."

"Yeah, but if it's any consolation, getting it off with just any broad isn't enough for me. She has to be different, peculiar." His glance lingered on Lisbeth for half a heartbeat before, once again, he turned away. "Someone special and strange, out of the ordinary." He lit another cigarette.

His hand dropped down to Lisbeth's leg. Fingers wandered along the seams of her jeans to the crotch where they waited.

"Get off me," she said. Neff's touch should have been unpleasant, stirring disgust not desire. But if anything she wanted him more.

Neff knew. He said, "You love it. That's one of the turn-ons, that you love it as much as I do." Raw longing caught in his voice. "I have nightmares about fucking you; bloody, sick nightmares, until I wake up in a cold sweat.''

Lisbeth picked up the mug of beer she'd been sipping at and spilled a stream in a wavering pattern along Neff's sleeve. "Piss on you," she said, and left the bar with her jacket undone so the cold came at her slapping.

"You walked all the way? From SoHo? It must have taken you hours. Why didn't you get a cab?" Susie asked.

They were in the kitchen, the night light over the double sinks still lit though the first tarnished glow of Saturday's dawn lapped at the window. Susie had the kettle on for tea.

"Here," she said, turning off the gas as the kettle whistled, "you'll drink this in a hot tub." She spoke softly though Mrs. Sloan wasn't in her room off the kitchen but at her sister's and the girls were asleep and would be until late morning. "Honestly, Lis, you could have gotten pneumonia, never mind mugged, raped—" She drew in a hiss of breath. "You know what I mean."

"Mommy," Lisbeth said.

"Goofy." She shook her head. Two heaping spoonfuls of sugar went into the mug and a squeeze of lemon. "Come on, bath time."

Lisbeth, cold only since she entered the apartment, clutched her elbows and trailed after Susie into the master bath. Susie filled up the big tub, throwing in violet crystals until a sweet aroma rose with the steam.

"Well?" Having tested the water Susie got up from kneeling and faced Lisbeth who hadn't moved. "You can't get into the bathtub with your clothes on, Lis. Let's go." But Lisbeth had a vague and vacant glaze to her that disturbed Susie more than anything else since the doorman had rung from downstairs announcing, apologetically, Lisbeth's arrival. Susie was having another of her sleepless nights in which she drowsed fitfully until four in the morning, then lay awake sad and grieving, or she wouldn't have heard the buzzer at all.

Had Lisbeth come all this way—on foot!—to stall, out of energy at last in the bathroom? Susie wondered. She supposed so and pulled off the heavy Italian boots, tugged the wool fisherman's sweater over Lisbeth's head, unsnapped the jeans and slipped them down her legs. Lisbeth wore neither bra nor underpants, she never had, not since Susie knew her at Cabot. Naked, Lisbeth was still lean as a greyhound, her bones jutting under flesh like expensive scaffolding.

"Okay, in the tub." Susie guided her and finally Lisbeth sat in water up to her nipples.

"Oh," Lisbeth sighed, "that feels so good." She leaned back but still gripped Susie's hand.

"Here, let me get your tea." But Lisbeth held her captive, her hold steel.

"Stay with me."

"Lis, for God's sake! I'm only going to the other side of the room."

"No, Suz, please!" A wild, dark light fired in Lisbeth's eyes.

"All right." Susie sank to the floor beside the tub.

Lisbeth smiled. "Get in with me."

"In the bathtub? Oh, Lis, you're cracked. It's seven in the morning. You turn up on the doorstep having walked from SoHo, alive and not frozen solid, which is in itself a miracle—fools and little children! —and now you want me to get in the bathtub."

"Sure, why not?"

Because, Susie almost said, I'm a grown woman, not a college girl. I'm a mother of children, one near the same age I was when we met. And Greg, my husband, is dead.

"More fun with the two of us. Like that time at your house in Baltimore." Lisbeth yanked her hand insistently, like a child. Which she was at times, Susie thought, more than the rest of us. Older and possibly wiser, but younger too. In the steamy bathroom Lisbeth, wet hair plastered in threads to her cheeks, the water's heat raising splotches of color on white skin, was a child again, a young girl, young as she'd been at Cabot. Whatever years she possessed glided away, down the slopes of her bony shoulders into the fragrant water. How easy it would be to succumb to such a nymph as she always had, to Lisbeth.

But she was no longer a girl. She was a woman, a mother, a widow too, and there was Simon waiting beyond the door of the future. Carefully Susie unhooked their hands, the fingers latticed together, and ignoring Lisbeth's splashes of water, crossed the room for the mug of tea. "Here, drink this," she insisted, and held the rim to Lisbeth's lips.

It was the little things she clung to. The small ordinary gestures kept her tethered to the ground since Greg died.

Lisbeth obediently drank when Susie nudged her lip with the mug's rim. "More," Susie said, and Lisbeth sipped again.

When Greg had been hit by that car—a drunk? a speeder?—the superintendent came up to tell her while the doorman was calling the police. Frank was a fat, invariably happy man even when faced with clogged drains and electrical shorts. But his round jowly face when Susie opened the door was pasty as bread dough. Susie never realized until he awkwardly shuffled his bulk in the foyer, sweating, how old the super was. She remembered thinking as Frank whispered, "There's been an accident. Mr. Lamton, Missus," that he should be retiring soon. And she also remembered he had a son in Florida, Jacksonville, she thought, and wanted to ask about him.

Each detail of those few minutes flashed in her memory brilliant as diamonds. How Frank helped her on with her coat, though he tried to persuade her not to go down, and how he then took her elbow and guided her into the elevator. She saw the grain on the wood paneling and the mauve stripe on John's uniform collar during the ride to the lobby. She counted the steps she took to the front door where Frank stopped her, and she recalled the features of each individual face, of the staff and the tenants who had gathered.

How loss makes us notice the inconsequential, she thought. She grasped at the minor details so she wouldn't think of the important one—Greg lying dead outside in the snow.

"I love you best," Lisbeth said, and closed her eyes. Her skin had the unblemished perfection of satin. With a painful awareness Susie sensed that they had passed one another by, that as she had aged, Lisbeth stayed miraculously the same. *What would happen to Lis?* she wondered, frightened, though she knew she needed all her energy now to concentrate on herself, on Betts and Tia, on rising from the treacherous grief that sucked at her like quicksand.

Lisbeth was humming. Sunk in the warm water to the chin, eyes still shut, a thin, unrecognizable tune curled off her lips. "Lily . . . poor Lily," Lisbeth suddenly said.

Susie, surprised, rose to her feet. "Lily? Poor Lily? You hated Lily Vaughan. Don't you remember the terrible things she did to us? Worse, what she threatened to do?"

"Spiteful Lily. She shouldn't have died," Lisbeth said, and opened her eyes. Her green eyes were almost black, glassy, and Susie wasn't sure that Lisbeth saw her, that she was even in present time.

"No," Susie said softly, "nobody deserves to die."

The fear came billowing back bringing memories of Quinn's corgis . . . Charlie Morgan stabbed . . . now Greg dead and buried. Susie hugged herself and watched as Lisbeth seemed to fall asleep again.

Lisbeth slid further down into the water until she went right under. It was a bad joke, Lisbeth teasing her like that, Susie thought and didn't move for a moment. But then she was on her knees, grasping the slippery arm and yanking Lisbeth up. "Stop it, Lis!" she screamed.

Lisbeth blinked, her eyes slitting. She peered out at Susie from some hidden room. Her eyes were dark stars. Her lips quivered.

Susie struggled with the deadweight, pulling Lisbeth out of the water and onto the tile. Quickly she dried her, hugging the cold, dead-feeling Lisbeth whose heart she heard pounding.

After a while Lisbeth whispered in a chilly breath, tracing a trail of terror through Susie's inside, "Where am I?"

24

The amazing thing about another person's death is that life goes on. The hole gets filled up slowly, just like the grave, until the ground is level again, smoothed flat. Memory grows like grass over the remains. None of which Susie expected. She supposed that Greg would have left a much larger emptiness than he did. They'd been together almost twenty years and planned to celebrate their upcoming anniversary with a party at the Plaza. She'd loved Greg in a conventional fashion—*I am supposed to love the man I marry*—and he had fathered her daughters. But only a few days after the funeral life already began to rearrange itself without Greg Lamton. Time promised to pass much as it always had. Greg's lawyer, Clive Pressman, had given her the gist of the will. Susie and the girls needn't change their style of living. In fact, Susie had no worries whatsoever. If anything, Greg dead was worth far more than he had been alive.

The nights, however, were different. Now Susie slept alone in the kingsize bed. She had an acre of space to stretch out in and no other body, no matter how far she reached to touch. The luxury of so much territory made Susie feel guilty.

Lying in the dark she wished she had been kinder to Greg, had loved him more and told him so. Selfishly, at moments, she wished him alive for the physical pleasure he had so often given her.

Alone now it was the girls who frightened her most. Somehow she had to guide them through this time of mourning, to help them come out the other side whole and undamaged. Then there were Betts's problems, all Susie's to handle. If she needed Greg it was precisely so she wouldn't be a single parent, shouldering the pressures and unsure of her decisions. As for the rest, the business of existence, Susie knew there were things she should be doing, responsibilities to be taken up, though she still lacked the energy, but when she finally got through to Rio and her father promised, "We're getting the first plane to New

York. Don't worry, I'll take care of everything," she replied, "No! Don't. I mean yes, come to New York. I want to see you. And the girls need attention. But I'm fine. I can handle whatever." Susie meant it too. For all her worries and the erratic road she knew lay ahead, she refused to have anyone interfering between her and life.

While she longed to see her mother and father, she needed more to see Simon; though when he telephoned, her conscience prickled. It was just a week after Greg had been run down, but a pulse fluttered in her throat as she lay on her bed and listened to the priest.

"I've been waiting to call. I saw the obituary in the paper, but I hesitated to intrude. There must have been lots of people comforting you, and with the funeral . . ." He stumbled to a halt, then rushed: "Susie, I'm so sorry for you."

"Thank you," she whispered, her mouth pressed against the receiver.

The strain between them was tangible, and the silence rolled on dense as ground fog.

"I—"

"Are—"

They both spoke at once. "Go on," Simon said.

"It's nothing. Just, I'll come down to The Good Shepherd as soon as I can. Really. I miss it." *I miss you.*

"That's okay," he said. "Things are a little hectic with Christmas almost on us. We like to give the people as much as we can this time of year. They're so lonely on top of everything else."

"I will come, Simon. I promise. Tomorrow. All right?"

"Susie, no. You have things to do, obligations."

She took a deep breath and launched herself out into space as surely as if she'd stepped from the living room window. "I want to see you."

His pause came to her like a wound, like a bullet spinning at high speed into her chest. She actually touched her breast to see if she bled, but then, far away, in another universe somewhere, the priest whispered, "I want to see you too, God help me. I want to see you more than I can say, Susie." His voice trembled and that sound washed over her in a warm, lapping wave.

"Tomorrow, then. In the afternoon."

"I'll be there."

Finally they hung up and Susie dropped against the pillows of her bed. It was still early, only a little past seven. From down the hall reverberated the pulsing beat of a heavy-metal refrain, the slam of a door, and Tia's voice raised in squeaky protest. "Herman, get out of there!"

Susie was too restless to simply lie and do nothing. She picked up a novel from the bedside table, a mystery someone recommended and that she never got around to reading. This evening, however, the sentences drifted off meaninglessly as air, and Susie had no desire to struggle with what should have diverted her. Putting the book down, she clicked on the TV and switched from channel to channel, searching for some show to hold her interest. Finally she shut the set off and thought vaguely of going to a movie, but Mrs. Sloan, exhausted from the funeral and the constant strangers wandering in and out, had taken a well-earned night off and was over in New Jersey. Susie didn't want to leave the girls, not yet, not this soon, even for a few hours.

Tonight was the first time when they weren't visited by friends, someone bringing casseroles or complete meals from Zabar's or The Silver Palate. Scores of people had come to offer consolation. Many eulogized Greg and mourned his passing while Susie tried with little success to keep from crying. Others behaved as if they'd simply dropped in for a casual visit, as if Susie and the girls weren't bereaved but holding open house. They gossiped, discussed the latest openings, told jokes even, and Susie enjoyed them, though after they'd gone she felt not relieved but guilty. She had no right to such pleasure. She owed poor Greg more than a morsel of grieving, a few tears, a crumpled wad of Kleenex.

Quinn crossed the park each night after she left the lab. Susie said it was too much, all that time spent simply sitting, setting out plates for dinner if Mrs. Sloan needed a hand, talking about hamsters with Tia, trying to find some wedge into Betts's stony silence, answering the phone, performing whatever chore came under her hand.

"You have your own life, Quinnie," Susie protested before she sensed Quinn needed her, needed the three of them, needed to feel as though she had some function.

"I don't have to feed the dogs," Quinn said, pressing her palms together in a manner that suggested a gesture of prayer, "so there's no reason to rush home."

Dinah traveled down from Westport often also, usually during the afternoon to stroll with Susie through the deserted park. A few warm hours melted much of the snow from the paths, but under the barren trees and in the crannies about the rocks it still clung in scattered patches. Occasionally they walked over to Columbus or further, to Broadway, to do errands. The girls were back in school. As Miss Allen, on her proper headmistress call, advised, the sooner they resumed a normal routine the better their subsequent adjustment. Without her daughters, however, Susie possessed hours to fill, and many of them she spent with Dinah. Dinah, steadily losing weight, her old face emerging from that aging plumpness, had also lost much of her agitation. Or perhaps it was, as Susie suspected, Joe Connors who calmed her.

Both women, aware of the similarity of their predicaments, felt closer than they had in years.

As for Lisbeth . . .

That morning Susie dressed her in sweats, wrapped the long red hair in a thick towel, and put her to sleep, unresponsive, in the big bed. Susie, fumbling with Lisbeth, felt as though she were handling a doll. Then Lisbeth slept while Susie curled up wearily on the chaise to drowse. But every little noise, from outside or somewhere in the building, pitched her into wakefulness, and finally she gave up even trying to sleep. She dressed and made coffee, which she drank sitting at her desk.

A neat list of names waiting to be thanked for flowers or donations lay beside a box of engraved stationery. *I should get on with it,* Susie thought, gazing out the wedge of window in the other wall, all the time acutely aware of Lisbeth in the bedroom behind the closed door.

Years and years . . . and so much love!

Of all the many things Susie hated to think about this moment or tomorrow, Lis in the tub seemed the most urgent. Why had Lis come in the early hours? Walking from SoHo? That was craziness even from Lisbeth. And the whispers about Lily Vaughan—if she could simply sweep the episode into some drawer and slam it shut! The peculiar emptiness in Lisbeth, as if she vacated her physical being in the same way a tenant moves from a house. What was wrong with Lisbeth? With all of them? As Dinah moaned, their lives—even after Lily's death—weren't meant to be like this.

Noon came and went; the girls had long before crawled out of bed. Lisbeth still slept. Betts said, "How come Lisbeth's here?"

Susie lied. "Oh, just because she was uptown and too tired to go home."

Tia sniffed. "I used to like Lisbeth best of all the grown-ups, but not anymore."

"Don't be silly!" Susie said.

"It's the truth, Mommy. After Daddy's funeral, when we got back here"—Tia gulped—"Lisbeth told me it was no big deal to be dead, that anybody could do it."

Betts laughed. "Jerko, that was a joke!"

"Well, I didn't think it was funny!"

"It wasn't funny," Susie agreed as Tia ran off to her room.

Around three Susie finally woke Lisbeth. "Enough sleep," she said.

"I'm a bear out for the winter." Lisbeth stretched. "But, oh, that was good. I don't know, Suz, maybe I should move in with you. I haven't slept like this in the last millennium."

Susie was relieved Lisbeth knew where she was. But she couldn't keep the frostiness from her voice. "Glad to hear it."

"What did I do?" Lisbeth asked grimly. She sat up and unwound her damp hair from the towel. "It couldn't have been good because you look mad as sin."

Susie reminded her of what she'd said to Tia the day of the funeral.

"Oh, no, not me! Tia must be mistaken. That's more the kind of drunken remark your father-in-law would make."

"Hardly, considering Greg was his son. Jack can be flippant, even downright cruel, but not about Greg dying. Besides, Tia wouldn't confuse her grandfather with you. That's ridiculous."

"I'm not saying she did—"

"And what's this about, Lis? Walking all over Manhattan in the dead of night, wigged out like some addict or wino?"

"Turning up on your doorstep at two A.M., drunk and disorderly. You've every right to be furious with me, Suz."

"You weren't drunk, though. And it was after six. As far as disorderly, you didn't make any fuss. I put you in a hot tub, and I swear, Lis, if I'd left the room you'd have drowned. You were more of a zombie than anything else."

Lisbeth giggled, knuckles hastily pressed against her teeth. Her laughter was frightening. And death on Susie's mind had her imagining the flesh stripped from Lisbeth's polished bones.

Susie cried, "You didn't know where you were! You asked me!"

"Oh, Suz! Come on. It's been a hard few weeks. I'm worn-out; so are you." Lisbeth was eager for Susie to believe her.

Susie flushed angrily. "Where were you last night, before you beached up here?"

"Out." Lisbeth winced.

"No kidding."

"You're upset. About Greg, I mean. I never thought he meant that much to you, or maybe I did and hated to believe it, but—"

"Stop!" Susie's finger touched Lisbeth's lip.

They stared at one another until Lisbeth finally said, "Suz, I guess maybe I had some dope, or I was drinking too much, but well, after I walked up here . . . That was a stupid thing to do. But"—she hurried— "I just started and kept putting one foot in front of the other. Anyway, I got here, finally, just before dawn, and you made some tea and yelled because I should have taken a cab, and then I got into a hot tub. . . ."

She halted. "I went to sleep, I suppose. That's all there was. I mean, I think so." She bent over, pained, until her head touched Susie's leg. She whispered, "I don't remember, don't don't don't don't. . . ." It became a refrain, and Susie, more worried than ever, smoothed Lisbeth's hair with soft, slow caresses.

They stayed like that for a long while. Tia came to the door and looked in, but neither woman moved. Then Lisbeth said, with a shudder, and so low Susie leaned forward to hear her, "I have such terrible headaches."

Susie reached for the phone. To call Lisbeth, again. Since yesterday she'd called seven, eight times. For no reason, she'd say. Just to touch base. But they both knew that Susie was making sure, though not sure of what. Each conversation grew more strained until in the last one Lisbeth screamed, "What awful thing do you expect me to do?"

Susie still hadn't asked her why it was "poor Lily," why now after so much time, she'd come to say Lily shouldn't have died. She meant to with each call, but the question remained unspoken.

The ringing of the intercom far off in the foyer stopped Susie from lifting the receiver. Another caller to express sympathy; she was both irritated and grateful.

She slipped off the bed, centered the twisted belt of her gray dress, patted her hair, checked the drawn and tired face in the mirror as she passed. Not that it mattered how she appeared. No one expected the usual perfection, rather the opposite. Claire McGrath had scoffed, "You look too good for a woman whose husband's so recently gone. I hope I'm half as fortunate."

Susie savored again her satisfying retort. "What were you supposing, that my hair should turn white and wrinkles spring out on my face? Greg died, darling, I didn't."

Susie went to the front of the apartment and called downstairs, "Who is it?"

"Two men," the doorman answered.

"But who are they?"

The doorman paused before replying, "Policemen." Even the static of the intercom couldn't mask his embarrassment.

"Policemen?" Susie repeated, confused.

"Should I send them up, Mrs. Lamton?"

"Yes, I suppose so." Could she refuse to see them? But why would she?

Tia came out into the foyer carrying Herman as Susie hung up the house phone. "Who's here, Mommy?" Tia, unlike her sister, who considered any visitors an intrusion, who felt she was being stared at like a monkey in the zoo, took an avid interest in the company.

"Nobody, honey. Just some men here on business. Go back to your room, please." Tia slowly scuffed her sneakers along the parquet, a curious glance directed from under her lashes to the door. "Enough, Tia. Go, I said!" Susie raised her voice. Tia pulled up short at her mother's exasperation, for Susie had been soft-spoken for days. She turned and ran. Damn! Susie swore, immediately sorry for the outburst of temper. But she would rather the girls not be around when the police rang the bell. The police, whatever she might think, meant nothing good. They were harbingers of bad tidings, they'd only bring news of some disaster. That was their job after all.

Detectives Sullivan and Oblonski, introduced themselves and showed their IDs. Susie led them into the living room, walking carefully as she used to do in Baltimore with a book on her head. Only now an invisible weight lay across her shoulders.

She sat them on the sofa and secured a less comfortable chair neither close nor too far away.

They had more time than she would have supposed. Both were big men, one in a dark plaid overcoat, the other crowded into a buff-colored down jacket. They should have appeared out of place in Susie's elegant apartment with its costly furniture and the Stella over the sofa, but they didn't.

The older one, who had a neatly trimmed, devilish beard, asked if he could smoke. "Of course," she said, and pointed to a Steuben ashtray on the coffee table.

The lighting of the cigarette was an elaborate ritual. Then Oblonski sighed as if he had just thought of why they were there, and dug a small notebook from the jacket's inside pocket. "Your husband," he stated rather officially, "was Gregory Lamton."

Sullivan interposed with a puff of smoke, "Our sympathies."

Susie nodded and held herself so tightly she could break and shatter. She was glass, delicate, and afraid before these men in her own home. *It's not Quinn's dogs at last,* she thought, *it's Greg.*

". . . struck down right out in front, December tenth, about six P.M." Oblonski read in a bored voice. He sounded no more moved than an announcer reading the weather report. *But why should he? They're policemen; they see death every day. What's one more dead man to them?*

"I don't understand," she said. "Greg was killed by a hit-and-run during that bad snowstorm."

"Why are we here?" Sullivan said as if she'd actually asked, and he was repeating the question.

Oblonski lifted his head. He needed a shave. "We have a witness. In the next building. An old man was looking out the window watching the snow fall. People do that kind of thing." He sighed over such a peculiar pastime.

"There's something soothing about the snow falling. If you're inside," Sullivan said.

"Not for Mr. Levy. He's eighty-nine and feeble. It took him days to come out of his swoon and tell us about what he witnessed," Oblonski went on. He must have been the senior man, since the neater, politer Sullivan eased back when he spoke, as if rebuked. It was Oblonski who'd say whatever the two of them had come to tell her. "Mr. Levy saw your husband hit."

Susie squeezed her elbows. "The car," she said. "The one that ran him down . . ."

"Yeah. Something big. American he thought. Four doors, though he couldn't verify the make. Couldn't even be sure what color it was with the funny light and all the snow."

"So . . . ?"

"The other car. It stopped not that far behind the cab. Then, the moment your husband got out, the driver stepped on the gas. Levy's positive, the car aimed right at him."

"You mean someone deliberately ran down Greg?" Susie cried.

Somehow she had gotten off the chair and was by the window clutching the draperies, staring out at nothing whatsoever. Behind her the policemen stirred uneasily. They were suspicious. Susie bit her tongue to keep from screaming, *Go away! I don't want to know about this! I want Greg dead by accident.* But the men weren't ready to leave, not yet. They intended to stay until she faced them and answered their questions.

"It's not true" was all she could think to say. The silence lengthened.

"Mrs. Lamton," one of them said, she couldn't tell which, "there are a few things we'd like to ask. . . ."

"Yes, I suppose so." Susie, polite to her polished fingernails, once more did what was expected of her. She reclaimed the chair and sat with her legs together. Her voice trembled as she asked, "What can I tell you?"

Oblonski bent forward; his weary eyes, a surprising cornflower blue, were animated for the first time. He asked, wetting his lips, "Do you have any idea why he was murdered?"

All the time the police sat in the living room Susie had trouble keeping in focus. It wasn't the vision of Greg, bundled in his overcoat, clutching his briefcase and hurrying home for dinner, suddenly hurled into the sky, shot upward by the rogue car, that claimed her, however. She actually tried to picture Greg dying, Greg in those last evaporating seconds of life, his face crucified with surprise, Greg shrieking, horrified, *This can't be happening!* What gripped Susie in a mounting panic was the thought of violent death twice in her lifetime, twice death by design and how such things could be coincidence. As the word *murdered* came off Oblonski's tongue and hung in the air, Susie almost told them about Lily and how she'd been stabbed in the snow, the reindeer on her sweater dancing one last time before she was stilled and frozen. Only she didn't, she struck at her offending mouth as if it were someone else's and wept as if the tears had no end to them.

Sullivan lit another cigarette and watched her through the smoke with the intent eye of a predator. Oblonski asked her if he could get her something, a glass of water maybe. Then they both said she should rest, that they'd come again . . . and she should try not to be upset.

When they left Susie shuddered weakly, white as death herself. Even as the door was closing a fit of some sort seized her and she bit down hysterics, knuckles shoved against her teeth.

In the bathroom mirror she saw Medusa, hair standing on end, dark cones triangulated under shrunken eyes. She'd aged years in those few endless minutes. In time she'd actually be that old. . . . *If I live,* she thought, with a sinking feeling like dropping suddenly in an elevator, and she cried, pressing her body against the long glass, against the other Susie, pushing time back, pushing off this Susie for the younger one, spinning up in blurred motion. The present blew apart, exploding, and in a nanosecond she went back to then. . . .

Lisbeth drove the jeep too fast. She often did, but this late afternoon with the ebbing light, the purpling shadows draping off the trees and gulleying through the snow, a heavier foot than usual kept the gas pedal to the floor. The jeep rocketed down the deserted country road, skidding around the curves while they held their breaths. In the back, jammed in together, buffered by the duffles, Quinn, Dinah, and Lily screamed. Lily especially sounded like a crow, her cries harsh and extreme. I'll fix her, Lisbeth had whispered. Susie, in the death seat, heard and shuddered, no! Oh yes! Lisbeth thrust out her chin and drove even faster.

Susie looked back at Lily, and in that small, ambushed animal's face the tiny BB eyes gleamed. She was laughing, laughing as before when she'd caught them in the suite, in Lisbeth's bedroom. Oh, she cried in horrified delight, the laugh like cream on her lips, this is not to be believed! Susie Bannon and Lisbeth Ross! What will people say!

She had crept after them on padded feet, the sneak, the thief in the night, the girl who never fit in, the one they hadn't wanted, and with their fluting cries, in the toss and tumble of loving one another in their girls' way she had caught them. I'll kill you, Lily, Lisbeth had sworn then. Oh no you won't, dear thing! But you will take me with the four of you to that ski house during semester break. And include me in all the other fun things you do . . . forever. The quartet's now a quintet.

She'll tell! She'll tell! Susie's heart broke. Even Lisbeth couldn't comfort her or wash away the fear. We'll be expelled . . . our lives ruined.

We'll take her, then, Lisbeth promised, and so they did.

But why? Both Quinn and Dinah wondered. Lily's dreadful. Lily smells. That was true, for a sour odor like spoiled milk seemed to ooze off her. Her crooked little front teeth looked as though she'd take a bite out of somebody, anybody who'd get near. All the girls avoided Lily. Never! Quinn screamed. Disgusting, Dinah echoed. Lisbeth had been grimly determined. And to Susie, I'll kill her, squeeze the air out of her! Lisbeth, more than once, circled her hands and entwined her fingers until it took little to see Lily's windpipe crushing.

Don't tell, Susie begged.

Never, dear thing. As long as you're good to me.

Susie got so sick she threw up as she'd do again in the snow, when Lily was beyond telling anybody a single secret, even that one . . .

"Mrs. Lamton . . ."

"Mommy . . ."

"Mom . . ."

Susie wound down a long passage as Tia's face burst over her. Tears soothing as oil dripped to her lips.

It wasn't a field, a shore where she lay, but the bathroom floor. The water gushed out of a spigot to soak a cloth that Mrs. Sloan pressed to Susie's forehead. Susie groaned and one of the girls gripped her hand.

"Mrs. Lamton, you fainted. I'm calling the doctor."

"No, no. Don't."

"Mom, are you okay?" It was Betts, kneeling on the tile. Her daughter's intensity caused Susie to struggle up.

Tia closed up to her shoulder, fingertips like moths at Susie's cheek. "Mommy, what's wrong with you?"

"She fainted, dear," Mrs. Sloan said matter-of-factly. "Women often do when they're distressed."

"Do men?" Tia asked.

"Oh, be quiet!" Betts ordered, and to her mother with unexpected authority, "Let's help you up. You'll feel better lying down on the bed, Mom. Come on."

"The doctor now." Mrs. Sloan rose with a whinny of arthritic pain.

"I'm all right. Just a reaction," Susie said, urged upright by her daughters. How strange that they were giving her the ground, though unstable, placing it beneath her feet. The bathroom spun around in leaves like a kaleidoscope. Their images splintered, heads disconnected, arms ran, hair lifted. For a second gravity gave Susie no purchase and she clung to Betts's shoulder. Tia came around at the other side and grasped Susie's waist.

Mrs. Sloan spluttered, "I do think the doctor's warranted."

Betts rebuffed her. "You heard what Mom said."

Together the girls guided her into the bedroom and raised her to the bed like something inanimate. Susie's head found the proper indentation in the pillow. "I'm fine," she protested.

"Get her some camomile," Betts directed the housekeeper. To Susie, "And for once you'll take sugar in it, Mom. You need the stimulant."

Mrs. Sloan scurried. Tia climbed up on the bed and curved into Susie's flank. "What's fainting, anyway? And why did you do it, Mommy?" Her curiosity was sharp and brought Susie further from the seas of oblivion . . . From the dead, she thought.

"It's nothing."

"It's something," Betts insisted.

Susie didn't quite lie when she said, "It's because of your father." The girls, going quiet, looked solemn.

Mrs. Sloan came with the camomile, which Susie drank, propped by pillows and observed by three unwavering pairs of eyes. They kept her on display until Betts said, "That's better. You don't look so much like white bread."

"Yes, indeed, Mrs. Lamton, you've got some color again. Thank God!"

"I still don't understand about fainting." Tia, now cross-legged at Susie's knee, pouted. "Is it like dying?"

"Isn't it past your bedtime, child?" Betts asked disdainfully, and as

Tia scowled, said, "I'll help you get undressed, Mom. Then you can crawl in bed. What you probably need is a good night's sleep."

"Betts is undoubtedly right," Mrs. Sloan said. Together, they maneuvered Susie out of her dress, shoes and stockings, and the silk underwear, and into a nightgown.

"Sleep tight, Mommy, and don't let the bedbugs bite," Tia cried, kissing Susie in a cloud of bubblegum breath. Betts put her hand on her mother's hair.

Mrs. Sloan offered, "Wake me, Mrs. Lamton, do, please, if you need anything. You poor dear!"

Night streamed through the windows, but Susie distrusted sleep. How could she risk dreaming? The dreams might begin at that moment when the jeep plunged from the secondary road onto the snow-packed trail, then in a grinding swerve through the low drifts to the A-frame perched on the hill. Snow soon, somebody had said. It's going to be great skiing if we don't get drifted in.

But they never got to the lifts that year. All too soon Lily was dead and they drove the long way back to town behind the county sander. They wouldn't return to that unlucky house that Quinn's uncle had won on three queens against two pairs—aces and tens. Later he'd sell it to Boston skiers.

Someone cracked the door, and quickly, guiltily, she shut her eyes and feigned sleep. She heard the click of the latch and stared out onto the foreign terrain of her darkened room once again.

In the blackness an ocean of white pooled. Snow smothered the landscape, sculpted the trees, turning them into a ghostly army. The air was crisp. Breath snapped like crackled glass.

Death spread itself in the cold, white world. Lily. Greg, a twisted ruin.

Someone ran him down, deliberately, with malice aforethought. Susie imagined the car, poised like a predator, and then the leap forward.

Susie, under the quilt, knew she couldn't will a state of peace, either dreamless sleep or a lulling restfulness. There was too much snow *out there,* and a dead Greg so recently laughing, alive and loving her, heightened the uneasy fears. *I will go crazy like this,* she kept thinking.

She sat up and switched on the bedside lamp. The hands of the small clock pointed to midnight.

Slipping from between the freshly ironed sheets, she dressed in warm slacks and a wool fisherman's sweater. She pulled on high boots and tugged a brush through her hair.

Susie traveled in a daze, through the slumbering building to the street, picking up a cab at the windswept corner. All the long distance downtown she felt numb, refusing to consider what she was doing, magnetized, with no will to resist, as Simon unknowingly pulled her ever closer to The Good Shepherd.

The old warehouse, squatting on its corner, had a deserted air to it. Except for the dim glow in one upstairs window, it might have been an empty shell. But Susie knew that sixty homeless men and women slept inside on iron cots, Jose, Sven, and Simon too. She threw herself against the metal door and pushed at the bell. In a short while footsteps sounded across the floor and a voice cried out, "Who's there?"

A small panel in one of the doors slid back. "It's Susie, Simon. Let me in, please."

Quickly he opened up for her. "Susie, what's the matter? It's the middle of the night." His hand seized hers and gently he guided her inside. He was carved by shadows, but Susie needed no light to recognize this man. *I've been moving toward him all my life,* she thought, and found her way undirected into his arms.

He held her tightly and she heard his heart. Simon whispered some words into the softness of her hair, endearments or a plaintive prayer, she couldn't tell.

"Oh, Simon, I'm afraid. There's so much I need to tell you. Help me!" she begged, tears scattering on his wool shirt.

Gripping her by the shoulder, he led her to his office, closed the door, and switched on the desk lamp. There was a pool of light on the blotter as she moved blindly against him again.

"Sssh, it's all right now. I'm here," he hushed. Yet he struggled, simultaneously pulled yet thrusting back as she waited, raising wet eyes to him. He stood like a dark wall only a step away. "You must, Simon."

"Try to listen to reason, please," he began, but she flung back her head, frantically keening a long *no*. *I will die without somebody's forgiveness,* she thought wildly. Both Lily Vaughan and Greg clawed at her from their graves, and she'd never sleep again, never draw a restful breath, until she could expiate those signs.

"My fault!" she cried out over the priest's husky protest. "I didn't kill them, but it feels the same."

He wouldn't listen. Settling her onto a chair, he retreated across the room. "Now, what the devil are you talking about, Susie?"

"Listen . . . back at Cabot, when I was a senior, at the winter break . . ." She faltered and slumped against the chair's back. The awful, sudden sensation of losing herself seized Susie, and she imagined she was dead like Lily, tucked into a silk-lined mahogany coffin, only all leathery scraps and long tendrils of hair and nails like a mandarin's. "You have got to offer me forgiveness," she whispered.

"I can't hear your confession. I just can't." His voice shattered like glass fragments under a heavy blow.

"Why not?" she screamed.

He moved even further away until stopped by the door. Susie went after him, stretched out a hand instinctively and touched a fold of wool on his arm.

"Simon, why not?" she asked again, now softly.

"Because I love you, Susie. I love you the way a man, not a priest, loves. I love you as a man loves a woman," he said, tears and hunger both in his eyes.

"Then forgive me that way, Simon," she begged, pulling off her coat and throwing it on the floor. "Absolve me with love. Bring it out of me, Simon, the pain for all the things that went wrong."

Simon had nowhere to retreat when Susie closed in on him. "No, Susie, no!" he cried, shaking his head, thrusting his palms out as if he could restrain her, as if he might halt her flight even as arms Simon barely realized were his own came up automatically and embraced her.

The boundaries between them disintegrated, washed away by desire, though for one further second Simon struggled to contain his wanting. Then the wave that tided up from the center of his being overwhelmed him and he moved with Susie as together they slipped down on the cracked leather couch.

Susie found her way under his shirt and sweater, to the bareness of his hot skin, burning, and she journeyed over his smooth chest, then kissed him frantically from the navel to the neck. "Oh no, Susie, don't. . . ." He groaned deep in his throat. But Susie was beyond listening. She was seized not only with a ravenous hunger, as if this promised to be the first time, as if all these years she'd held off, controlled all true desire until this one man appeared miraculously.

Simon lay alongside her and Susie couldn't stop herself. Shaking hands unzipped his jeans and she fumbled for that maleness pressed toward her, then released him, large and marble hard, into her hand. The pleasure set him shuddering and he ground his mouth into the curve of Susie's neck. When she slowly stroked him he nipped at the soft skin, but there was no pain, only wetness, tears or blood, or maybe both. Susie was beyond caring about anything but the need to love this man, the need finally to lose herself, to die and be born again. *You know about that,* she gasped to Simon, but he didn't answer and she understood she hadn't spoken aloud.

They rushed toward one another, to a joining that cleaved the darkness, brought fire into the world, and she arched as she sought him. He touched her wetness and she guided him into her.

Down, down Susie went, flying through the earth, through the nether regions, into the sea with its shadowy depths, through the coves and caverns of the infinite universe, and the floods swept in to wash her, to wash the two of them, and deep inside her as they rocked in the earthquake of desire, of love itself, she heard the voice. She chose afterwards in the moment of terrified parting when they pushed away from each other, when Simon fell on his knees and Susie dressed herself hastily and ran, she chose then to believe that the word sounding in the plumbed wilderness of her soul was *redemption*. But throwing herself into a taxi and speeding uptown, she knew that hadn't been the word at all. Whatever she wanted to believe or needed to, the word, she couldn't deny it, was *never*.

25

It was Sunday. Sundays were the worst. Even before Quinn found Will and when the dogs were alive, Sunday hours had rubbed against her like a hair shirt. But once she'd gotten into the habit of taxiing out to Brooklyn for long afternoons with the children, one of Maria's elaborate dinners, and then the comforting drive, Quinn and Will alone, back to Manhattan, Sundays became festive occasions she looked forward to the whole week. Now, counting them up, Quinn realized there had been really very few Sundays. The pleasure they gave her were disproportionate to the actual time spent.

This Sunday, awakening at seven, the big apartment empty and silent, the bed chilly except for the immediate area where she had slept, she thought of the poor corgis, who usually made nests of warmth by her thighs and at her feet. She never asked Susie what she'd done with their bodies and wished that at least they had graves she might visit.

She lay in bed purposeless, the hours stretching ahead until tomorrow when she'd go to the lab. Quinn clenched her teeth and turned over, pressing her face into the pillow. Why couldn't she have the flu, a cold, a fever so high she wouldn't be able to think.

She couldn't find a comfortable spot and flung about onto her back, thinking of the money she had given Will, hiding it so as not to wound, when all the while he deceived her. A con game, a fast shuffle, that's what Lisbeth said. "He faked you out and then got you thinking it was your intention in the first place."

The phone rang a few minutes past eight. Quinn shot up on her elbows and stared at the instrument with alarm. No one called this early on a Sunday morning unless there was bad news to relate. Had the old man died at last? Her hand shook as she lifted the receiver. It surprised Quinn that she cared so much.

A strange, croaky voice she did not recognize said, "You promised the other half of that hundred dollars if I called you when somebody came."

The squeezed-up little neighbor of Will's, Quinn remembered. She'd returned to Brooklyn to persuade him with the only thing she had been able to think of, money. "Yes, another fifty dollars," she agreed quickly.

He chewed his gums, making her wait, until he said, "Well, somebody's over there."

"Who?" Hurriedly she got out of bed.

"Can't tell for sure. You coming out here?"

"Right away."

"Just bring my money. And don't you forget," he growled. "I'll be watching."

He would, too, she thought, stuffing extra bills into her wallet as she rushed around the bedroom pulling her clothes on. An alarming pounding in her chest caused her to catch her breath, then stumble, light-headed as though she'd come up too swiftly from doing deep knee bends.

A warm flush suffused her face as she thought—*I'll see the children again, I'll see Sarah.* Ever since they'd gone, with no answer to the ringing phone and no one home, Quinn worried that the children were lost forever.

Only in Boston, Susie reminded her, but Boston existed in another universe. She couldn't go back. Besides, she wasn't sure they were there at all. In Boston. She had called, and neither Earl nor Selma would tell Quinn anything. Her father was incommunicado. As for Edmund Terhune, he was brutally succinct. "It's none of your business now what happens with Webster, Inc." But she didn't care about the corporation, only the children. She saw making a connection with Will's children as a turning around of time, of, in some manner she couldn't explain, bringing back the corgis. *A metaphor only,* she assured herself, and tried not to think of her loneliness. Besides, like the corgis the children—even Carlos, very much the young boy with hard muscles and a chipped front tooth—were fragile. Some instinct in Quinn stirred to protect them. And what about their parents? she kept reminding herself. No matter what Will had done, his lying and conniving, he did love the children and would take care of them. He wouldn't simply abandon the whole family as he once abandoned his own.

If they were in Brooklyn, she thought, running out the door, *I could have them here for Christmas. Or at least the children. With lots of presents and a tree.* The possibility made Quinn smile as she waited behind the doorman for a taxi.

By the time the taxi crossed the bridge, weaving in and out of the sluggish Sunday-morning traffic, Quinn was considering buying Carlos, Isobel, and Sarah a pet. A Siamese would be nice, but a dog would be better. Some breed bigger than the corgis. A dog sturdy enough for the children to roughhouse with. A shepherd or one of the terriers might be the best. Maybe a wirehair or a schnauzer.

Mr. Muldoon was peering out his front window, just as he promised he would, his pointy nose flattened up against the glass. He was out on his front porch before Quinn left the cab.

"Here I am!" he yelled as if she might possibly miss seeing him.

"Have you seen anybody?" she asked as she rushed to his front path to meet Muldoon, who stomped all the way to the gate. The day was raw, but he hadn't bothered to put on a coat. Tiny little white hairs stuck out of his nose, giving him the look of a small, angry boar.

"Nope," he snorted as Quinn fumbled in her shoulder bag for the wallet. "Just that car there when I woke up." He nodded toward Will's small dark compact huddled at the curb like a large bug. "And lights in some of the windows."

"Thank you very much," Quinn said when she passed him the five tens, but he was already stalking off in a pigeon-toed walk to his porch, shoving the bills in the pocket of his maroon cardigan.

Quinn hesitated, but waves of anxiety set her in motion and she ran awkwardly to the door. She knocked and waited impatiently, shifting nervously from one foot to the other. When the door wasn't opened fast enough she twisted the knob. It hadn't been locked.

"Will? Maria?" she called, stepping carefully inside. The house was frigid. It had the dead, closed-in feeling of a long-deserted place. But all the lamps glowed and she heard the hiss of the heat pushing through the floor grates. "Children!" she called again, loudly. "It's Aunt Quinn."

"Aunt Busybody, I'd say," Will said, descending the steps very quietly for such a big man.

Quinn's hand flew to her throat. "Oh! I didn't hear you."

"How could you, making so much noise yourself. Don't decide to take up breaking and entering as a profession, Quinn," he joked sourly.

Maria padded halfway down the steps, but Will sensed she was there and waved her back. Quinn offered up a smile, but Maria disappeared obediently without even saying hello.

"When did you get home?" she asked Will.

"Early, and how did you find out so fast?"

Quinn glanced around and took two baby steps into the room. "How are the children?"

"Why?"

"Oh Will, don't be like that!"

"How should I be?" he asked, scowling.

Quinn remembered, as she hadn't in years, how when they were young Will would throw rocks at the birds, at the gulls and terns along the Vineyard shore. He had an uncanny aim even when the white wings lofted a hawking bird high in the sky.

"Brrr." She shivered, punching her arms. "It's cold in here. It takes a house so long to warm up this time of year. It's almost Christmas, after all."

"What the hell do you want, Quinn?" He stood defiantly at the bottom of the steps, hands on his hips.

Quinn bit her lip, feeling like an awkward child again. *I'll tell Mama* caught on the tip of her tongue. Panic tickled the back of her throat. Carefully she said, "There's no need to shout. And there's no reason whatsoever for you to be angry with me. Rather the reverse." She began to say he played her for a fool, but held back. Quinn, startled though she was by the icy fury inside her, had no desire to rile Will. He held the power; the children were his.

Quinn kept calm. "I simply dropped in to see you all." As if it were a respectable hour rather than nine-thirty in the morning.

"Then you've made a wasted trip."

"What?" Fear fluttered like one of Will's struck birds striving up the blue-washed sky.

"We're not here for long. Just to pick up some things and make arrangements with the moving company to ship what we'll keep to Boston."

As though dismissing her as he had Maria, Will walked off into the kitchen.

She thought to follow him, then stopped, undecided. Where was the assertive woman, the doctor, who made such instant laboratory decisions, the scientist of some repute to whom Stevie and the other assistants all deferred? That person disappeared in Will's cold little house, and in her stead was the girl of the awful snapshots that floated through her memories like the unconnected pages from a loose-leaf notebook.

When Will failed to return, Quinn walked slowly to the kitchen, silently, as if the least vibration would send the pictures crashing off their hooks, and the bric-a-brac that Maria collected—tiny china shepherdesses with pastel smiles and bright Chinese bowls—from the shelves.

Quinn paused in the doorway, feet together, determined not to allow her brother to use love as a weapon.

Will stirred a cup of instant coffee, but he didn't offer her any.

Quinn accepted how naive she was, even innocent, when it came to love, but she knew as well as she'd ever known anything that love shouldn't be bartered or used as a tool of power. She'd realized that at Cabot, and even earlier, when she was a child, for the old man held her mother in thrall during the long torpor of that disastrous marriage. Not money, not family, not children, but the ties of love bound that poor woman to that man. Will thought he could play the same game with Quinn, but he employed, besides his own supposed affection, his wife and his children.

"You think I owe you something, Quinn, but I don't. Webster logic. Bookkeeping. Debits and assets. The red columns and the black. But life isn't fair, and it certainly isn't a matter of accounting."

"You wanted Father and Webster money, not me," she said, as evenly as she was able. "So why didn't you go to him directly? Why make a detour on East End Avenue?"

Will laughed, though his pale eyes darkened like a storm-thrashed sky. "Who knew he was dying and desperate to live on if only through the company and his name? I even had to agree to change Carlos's name to George, the third, of course. Funny, isn't it?"

She felt as though she were wandering the corridors of a maze. "How does Carlos feel about that?"

He quit his hypnotic stirring and raised the mug to his mouth. Before he drank he said, "It's the kids, really, that you're after, isn't it? Hooked on them I'd say, particularly Sarah, who's the one the old man, surprise, surprise, likes the least. She looks too much like Mama." He talked about his children like things. "It was lucky those ratty dogs of yours died, because you got crazier about the kids. I never did figure out what happened to them. Here one day, gone the next. That was a fairly virulent canine pneumonia. And, Quinn, what did you do with them? Do you toss dead dogs down the incinerator, or are you having them stuffed?"

"You're not a nice man" was all she could think to say.

"No one ever said I was." He tucked his denim work shirt into his jeans, tugging the wide leather belt. "Quinnie, you have a first-rate intelligence, but you're a fool nevertheless."

"God damn you!" she cried. "And don't call me Quinnie! You bastard!"

"Sticks and stones, Quinnie." She started to swing toward him, but he held up a hand as if he expected her to stop, and she did. "We can stand around until the cows come home, hurling insults at each other; but that and a buck, as we say. Plus the fact I'm busy. So button your coat and run along back to Manhattan."

Quinn bared her teeth. "Georgie might have been weak and ridiculous, but he was much nicer than you, always," she said without thinking.

"Georgie? Nicer? I suppose so, and a fat lot of good it did him. He's in the ground under that ugly stone angel, nothing but dust and more dust."

Quinn began to retreat. She had no idea how to deal with her brother, whom she knew as little as the old man who had fathered them.

The sun broke through the metallic winter sky, and a shimmer of clear bright light beamed through the kitchen window and feathered down Will's arm. As if the light had substance to it and irritated Will, he shook it off, moving into a smudge of darker space. Quinn thought, *He's never been who I supposed he was,* this brother she brooded over all these years, regretted losing and wondered about. He'd been merely an imagined creature occupying a niche in her memory.

Brother and sister stared at one another, more distant than when they'd met on the street. *Was that, too, arranged?* Quinn wondered but didn't ask. She wished she were clever, that manipulation and dissembling came naturally to her. But trickery was beyond her. Will would see through her clumsy attempt. She could only ask her question outright.

"Can I see the children before I leave?"

"They're busy packing," Will said. She thought he might be laughing, but the brief light faded and Will hid too far back in the shadows for Quinn to see his face.

Quinn slumped, so weary tiny pains shot down her arms and along her shoulder blades. "All right, then." She walked out without another word, carefully carrying her grief as though it would shatter her.

The sky had clouded over again and the Brooklyn street was colorless, dead. The smell of rain was pungent in the cold air. Quinn stepped off the porch uncertainly.

"Aunt Quinn!" Sarah, hatless, her down jacket unzipped, came running around the side of the house. "You were going to go and not say good-bye," she accused.

Quinn apologized. "Oh no! But your father said you were all so busy packing."

Sarah toed the dead grass with her sneaker. "He wants us to hurry up. We got up in the middle of the night, and as soon as our stuff gets packed we're leaving. For Boston," she said. "We're going to live there now."

"Don't you want to?" Quinn asked, her heart pounding.

"I don't know." She looked at Quinn. "It's different. That big house, bigger than Papa Jorge's, it's scary. There's all these things. And we don't have any friends in Boston."

Quinn slowly walked down the sidewalk, along the metal fence with leprous spots of rust, past Muldoon's house, shades drawn, as Sarah kept pace beside her.

"In our new school we have to wear uniforms," Sarah was saying. "And all the other kids just stared and stared at us when we went for the afternoon."

At the end of the block a yellow cab miraculously appeared like an omen. Quinn reached down and took Sarah's hand. The small soft fingers were cold. She gazed up at Quinn as Quinn's other hand, as if it possessed a life of its own, a will not hers but a stranger's, rose and waved down the taxi. "And Daddy says we can't have a dog now, or a kitten either. He says the big house has too many beautiful things in it."

The cab stopped at the curb. Quinn opened the door, refusing to even consider what she was doing. "Would you like to go to the circus?" she asked, helping Sarah scramble inside.

"The circus!"

"Well, they're only here for a little while and we wouldn't want to miss it, would we?" Quinn laughed as the cab sped off.

When they reached Lincoln Center, and after Quinn bought the best tickets available for the noon show, Sarah began to worry that Will and Maria would be angry because she left without finishing her chores. Quinn said she'd call and explain. At the pay phone, however, she dialed the weather report and listened to the latest wintry forecast. Then they both settled back to enjoy the spangled show, which neither had seen before.

They laughed at the clowns with red balloon noses and floppy giant's shoes. They held their breath as the daring high-wire artists danced on the slim, almost invisible thread miles in the air. Screams escaped them as a young girl, slippery as a moonbeam, spun off the trapeze to be caught at the final moment by her muscular partner.

They watched the elephants in their dainty pirouetting, and particularly loved the white, high-stepping horses with braided manes and tails. Quinn bought Sarah a hat, a banner, a clown jiggly on a stick, and a yo-yo that streaked light like streamers of liquid fire.

They ate caramel popcorn, peanuts, and hot dogs and drank gallons of soda. Quinn thought they'd both get sick to their stomachs and didn't care. She had never had such fun in all of her own girlhood, and her pleasure was doubly poignant because Sarah loved everything so.

When the colorful parade ending the extravaganza wound around the ring, they should have been sated but weren't. Quinn was on a roll, understood at last that gambling uncle of hers who could never leave the table as long as luck sat on his shoulder. So they went up to Radio City Music Hall and saw the Christmas show. After that it was dinner at Pearl's, though neither she nor Sarah could eat much of the banquet they'd ordered. Sarah wanted to take the food with her, so the leftovers were boxed in little white cartons and they carried them home to the apartment.

Quinn half expected Will on the doorstep, or even Maria, but nobody waited. Perhaps they decided to leave Sarah with her for a little while. She hoped for such a possibility, though knowing it was the stuff of dreams.

The phone rang seconds after they arrived and Quinn ignored it. "Aren't you going to answer?" Sarah asked.

"Oh, I don't think so." She shrugged, helping Sarah off with her jacket.

"It's probably Daddy wanting me home," Sarah said sadly.

"You can go home tomorrow," Quinn said, sounding firmer than she felt.

"I can stay overnight?"

"Why not?" And tomorrow and the day after that.

Quinn turned down the ringer on the phone, but the soft bleary sound was still audible as she and Sarah lay on Quinn's bed watching *Murder She Wrote*. She intended to put Sarah in the guest room, but the child fell asleep halfway through the program. With shaky hands Quinn took off Sarah's jeans and sneakers and tucked her under the quilt. She was awed and dizzy as she watched Sarah sleeping. Sarah's lustrous hair spread across the pillow like a fisherman's net.

Eventually Quinn fell asleep herself only to be awakened by the shrill sound of the house phone. She sat up abruptly and put an arm over Sarah to protect her. *Will's downstairs,* she thought in agitation. *But I won't answer. Then he'll go away.* The ringing stopped, but after a minute of silence, it started up again. Quinn covered her ears.

Sooner or later she knew Sarah would have to go home, but for this one night Quinn intended to keep her. Oh, but if she could only stay forever! Yet Quinn had no idea how to arrange this. She couldn't just buy the child, though she would have given a large part of her millions for Sarah.

How odd, she thought, leaning on an elbow to stare at Sarah sleeping. *This is what motherhood must feel like.* She tried to imagine her own mother in the shadows observing her as she did Sarah, and for a moment Quinn crossed time, and her heartbeat synchronized with that other woman's long ago.

There was a fierce pounding on the front door. At the furthest reach of the big apartment Quinn heard the thunder of a fist against wood. Will's key was useless because Susie made her change the lock after the dogs.

Sarah stirred, rolled to her back, almost waking. "Hush," Quinn whispered, and smoothed the quilt under her chin. She shut out the knocking as she had the intercom and the phone. Will would give up eventually.

Quinn wasn't at all bothered that she had taken something, someone who didn't belong to her.

Each minute encompassed a whole world. Beyond the boundaries of the next moment, and the one after that, were jagged rocks of the unknown that Quinn elected to disregard. She chose to cling to the ordinary, and after Sarah awoke and showered, with unaccustomed domesticity Quinn prepared a big breakfast.

"What shall we do today?" Quinn asked. Sarah ate a mountain of pancakes as Quinn sipped black coffee and watched her.

"Don't you have to go to the laboratory?"

"Lab-or-a-tory. Bor, like in boring," Quinn explained.

Sarah giggled. "But that's your work, Aunt Quinn."

"So it is," she said.

"And I have to go to Boston." She made a face but kept eating. "I don't want to, like you don't want to go to the lab-or-a-tory, but I guess I will anyway."

"I thought we might take in the Museum of Natural History."

Once again the house phone started its familiar shrilling. Sarah and Quinn sat still, holding their breath, suddenly conspirators. In order to escape Will a little longer they'd have to go down in the service elevator and out through the basement to the rear alley.

"I'm supposed to start school today for real," Sarah said, "Isobel and Carlos too. Isobel says it won't be *that* awful. And Carlos—" She put a hand to her mouth. "Oh, I forgot. Carlos has a new name. We're supposed to call him George. And that's what Daddy told everybody in school his name was."

"Carlos must be angry about that," Quinn said, furious with Will for going to such lengths to please their father.

"He was kind of mad. But Daddy talked to him, and Carlos told me and Isobel his name had to be George or we couldn't live in the big house. Children have to do what they're supposed to, Aunt Quinn." Sarah was solemn. "But Carlos says I can still call him Carlos if I whisper it and don't do it when anybody's around."

The first Quinn knew they'd entered the apartment was when she heard Edmund Terhune's voice ring out with its authoritative Boston twang. "Quinn, where are you?" She jumped up and wanted to tell Sarah to run, to hide.

They came abruptly face to face in the foyer. Behind Terhune's cashmered shoulder the doorman stood shuffling. "I'm sorry, Dr. Webster," he blurted out before Terhune could say anything, "but you haven't been answering the buzzer or the phone, and this gentleman was sure something was wrong."

"How could you, Quinn?" Terhune asked, eyebrows rising.

"If you're okay, Doctor . . . ?"

"Get out," Terhune ordered.

"It's all right," Quinn said, knowing she'd lost the game. The doorman withdrew quietly, closing the outer door.

Sarah slipped from behind Quinn. Terhune stared at her. "So this is the child your brother's fussing about."

"There's no reason to fuss."

"I suppose some parents might if one of their children disappears."

"They knew Sarah was with me," Quinn said.

"And just how would they know that?" Terhune asked, walking around Quinn to the living room. Without an invitation he sat down and made himself quite comfortable.

Sarah came forward. "Aunt Quinn called Mommy and Daddy and said we were going to the circus."

"She did no such thing, little girl."

"Aunt Quinn?" She turned to Quinn and tugged her sleeve.

Quinn was speechless.

"Get your things. Your parents are waiting in a car downstairs." To Quinn, Terhune added, "And you're very lucky the New York City police aren't waiting there with them."

"Don't be absurd, Edmund!" Quinn said, finding her voice.

"Do I have to go?" Sarah asked, still in the foyer.

Terhune answered before Quinn could speak, "Yes, you have to. Now don't be bothersome. Just let's hurry. I have a busy day, which is made all the more hectic by having to fly down here at dawn."

"Just why did you?" Quinn asked.

"Because no one's been able to get you to behave in a rational manner, Quinn. And your brother threatened the old man with the police, with a scandal, newspapers, that sort of thing, unless he forced you to return the child. So I had to come and do the Websters' dirty work . . . as always.''

"How did you get the doorman to let you in?'' Quinn asked as Sarah ran off to the bedroom. She couldn't decide what to do with Terhune in her living room ready to take Sarah away.

Terhune rolled his eyes. "Really, Quinn! A hundred-dollar bill is magic. You should know that.''

"How should I? I never think of money!''

"You should, you certainly should.'' Terhune glared at her, half in anger, half in amusement. "It's only money that's keeping a charge of kidnapping from being filed against you.'' Terhune, so smug, seemed to Quinn a marauder suddenly victorious. Terhune was getting even. Despite his complaints, he was enjoying this trip from Boston much more than the last.

"Don't be silly, Edmund!''

"I'm ready,'' Sarah said. She returned wearing her jacket and clutching the circus treats. Terhune rose. Sarah looked at Quinn. "Thank you, for the circus and Radio City and everything.''

"You're welcome,'' Quinn replied, tears in her eyes.

Sarah's hug was brief as a sigh. Quinn, standing by the door long after it closed behind them, thought she'd just learned a salient fact about happiness; it never does last nearly long enough.

Another loss in a life that had few pleasures to begin with. That's all this is, Quinn consoled herself the following Sunday noon in the breakfast nook, and ate scrambled eggs, bacon, English muffins with blackberry preserves.

Again she'd gone out to Brooklyn. The trip was a foolish gesture, for as she knew, the house was empty. A *For Rent* sign poked up in the front yard like a grave marker. For rent. Will had lied even about owning the little Brooklyn house.

Quinn had walked up onto the porch, the boards squeaking, and peered in the window. The derelict house looked as sad as she felt. The pain of love and of hope gone jackknifed through her heart, and she quickly returned to the sidewalk.

What had she hoped to accomplish?

She had had a long walk from Will's to a better-traveled boulevard before she finally flagged a taxi willing to transport her back across the river. She'd passed a small store with wooden planks nailed up over the windows and a formidable steel door, and heard from deep inside voices raised in song. The singing lifted her flagging spirits and she longed to enter the shabby little storefront church, to sit down with its unseen, joyous parishioners and let the music bathe her like baptismal water. But she'd done no such thing, of course; she'd found a taxi instead. Now she regretted that lack of courage.

Halfway home to Manhattan she realized she was starving. She hadn't even taken her coat off before setting strips of bacon in a fry pan and beating up a froth of eggs. Though the apartment was warm, she sat huddled as she ate and thought that negligible place where people sang and prayed must surely be warmer than here. How strange it was that she who believed in nothing mystical, in no community, in only the seen and scientifically knowable, should have a sudden desire for an unspoken communion. *This will pass too,* she promised herself, as if part of her was parent, part child. As her own beautiful mother, enshrined by death, used to say, *In the morning everything begins again fresh and new.*

That too was a lie.

Quinn cleared the table, but there was still a deep unfillable emptiness in her, and she crouched by the open refrigerator eating spoonfuls of cottage cheese, a hunk of Jarlsberg, a dried-out chicken leg, a slice of rye bread. But the hunger she suffered from wasn't satiable, she realized. She'd only make herself sick.

Moments later, Susie arrived, heralded by the doorman's call from downstairs. "I know you never go far on Sundays," she apologized, untying a dark printed scarf from her head, tossing an old duffle coat on the foyer bench, "which is why I didn't call."

"That's okay," Quinn said, nudged from her preoccupation by a Susie minus makeup and with puffy eyes. In a washed-out sweat suit and Reeboks, Susie no longer looked like a young bride, but had become in the cold winter's light of Quinn's living room one of those older women often seen jogging about the reservoir. Puffing, arms and legs cranking, such women always struck Quinn as grimly determined to steal time, or at the very least hold it outside the gates.

"I wouldn't mind some tea," Susie said, pushing back a wave of hair that fell across her face. Quinn turned for the kitchen. In the dining room Susie stopped, so obviously remembering. "You've changed things."

"As much as I could."

Susie slipped around the table now stretched horizontally and leaving little space behind the high-backed chairs. The sideboard and chest crowded next to each other against one wall. The room resembled a furniture display in a warehouse.

"I suppose it's better," Susie said, dubiously, gliding her hand across the stacks of books Quinn had piled upon the table.

"I'm going to get rid of everything after the holidays," Quinn said. "Though it's not so easy disposing of furniture. I'll probably just call the Salvation Army and let them truck it away."

"They'll give you a tax write-off," Susie offered as she sat down in the kitchen.

Quinn put the kettle on, saying, "What do you know about taxes?"

"I'm not an airhead, Quinnie," Susie protested but without vigor.

"You're right. I apologize."

"Forget it."

"No, Susie, it's true. All of us pretend you wander along a higher plane, never getting your feet dirty in the muck of life."

Susie replied with fervor, "It should only be true!"

"Earl Grey, or I think I have something herbal," Quinn said, rooting about in the cupboard next to the sink. "Yes, here it is. Red Zinger."

"Regular tea's okay."

"I'll brew a pot then." Quinn took out a Rosenthal teapot with a pattern of mauve flowers and a gold stripe. Susie sat silently as Quinn watched the kettle. "How are the girls?"

"Medium to all right I guess. Actually looking forward to Christmas. Besides, my parents arrived last night and they're fussing. They just took them over to the Wollman rink. Exercise, my father maintains, is a curative for much of what ails one in life."

"I've always admired your father," Quinn replied. The kettle whistled and she made busy motions with the ritual of wetting the leaves, waiting, then filling up the pot slowly. "Let it brew for a couple of minutes." Quinn brought the pot to the table, then matching cups, saucers, and a sugar bowl. "I have lemon if you want it, but no milk."

"Just sugar's fine. You know, Quinn," Susie said with a quick smile, "you are the only person I've ever known who uses Rosenthal for every day."

"Why not?" Quinn asked, surprised.

"Never mind, darling," Susie replied, patting Quinn's hand. Quinn didn't spring back, and realized that in these last months, the children had conditioned her to being touched. She had that gift at least to carry with her.

The two women sat quietly, not speaking. After a few minutes Quinn poured the steaming tea. They drank, the only sounds familiar ones. The kitchen became a comfortable cave, homier with Susie at the other side of the table. The tension in Quinn's muscles began to ease, her unhappiness to stir and shift a bit, and weariness overcame her. She nodded sleepily.

"Quinn, I've got to talk to you."

"Hmmmm." Quinn's thoughts ebbed sluggishly.

"Seriously, Quinnie, please!" Susie nudged Quinn's arm.

"What?" Quinn reluctantly raised her head. Her eyes felt puffy, sore.

"The police." The cup shook in Susie's hands and she put it down with a clatter on the saucer.

"The *police*?"

"The police believe that Greg was run down deliberately," Susie said, blurting out the words that were so hard to say. "That someone waited in a car until he got out of the taxi, then drove right at him."

What Susie said woke Quinn right up. Her first impulse, however, was to giggle, and she had to clench her teeth to keep the bubble of mirth inside her mouth. The whole day was filled with the unexpected. Quinn walked through a mirror and stared out from the other side.

"I don't believe it!" Quinn said, but of course she did. She knew somehow that Greg hadn't died by chance.

Susie fished a crumpled pack of Winston Lights and a cheap lighter out of a shirt pocket. "We're all smoking again, every one of us but you," she said, taking a deep, audible drag of smoke into her lungs.

"Why are they so sure about Greg?" She expected tears from Susie, but there were none.

"A witness. An old man watching the storm from his front window in the building next door. He had a ringside seat." Susie did choke then and swallowed hard.

Quinn waited a moment before she asked, "Have they any idea who did it?"

"Isn't it curious how easily we're sitting here and so calmly discussing murder, Greg's murder. No more obvious emotion than we'd give to cocktail party conversation."

"Susie . . ."

"No, Quinn, it's true. We're either jaded New Yorkers, accustomed to anything, muggings, subway strikes, rude taxi drivers, and even murder. Or maybe it's because we've been through this before. I mean it's not our first encounter with—how do they put it on television?—an untimely death!"

Of course Susie was distraught and Quinn had to be patient, understanding, but still she kneaded her hands together and struggled not to shout in anger. "Just how do you know that Greg's death is involved with Lily's?"

"Am I suddenly clairvoyant? Is that what you're asking?"

"Oh, Susie, please," Quinn begged, "let's not argue."

"I'm not. You're right. Sorry." She drank the tea down to the bottom of the cup. "There should be leaves to read," she said, and smiled. She poured some more tea. "How did I know? Just because of your dogs—with the place cards remember—and my flowers, and that mouse in the shoe box you thought the assistant who killed himself sent you."

"Derek Sonderson."

"Yes, Derek Sonderson. As if blowing out his brains wasn't enough to upset you."

"Even if it wasn't Derek, why just the two of us? What about Dinah and Lisbeth? Why haven't they gotten, I don't know, gifts?"

"Somebody did stab Charlie Morgan. Lisbeth's gentleman caller. We can't forget him."

Quinn sighed and rubbed her forehead. "Everyone knows Lisbeth's affections are, to say the least, not reliable. It's Charlie today, God knows whom tomorrow."

Susie agreed. "But for a little bit we all thought, Charlie Morgan, this is it. He's *different*."

"Well, what about Dinah? The only thing that's happened to her is Hatch running off with another woman."

Susie, suddenly urgent, flung herself half across the table. "My husband's dead! Charlie almost died. And the dogs too. They were human for you, Quinn."

Quinn pushed back from the table. "I think I need a brandy. Do you want one?"

"No, thanks. I'm afraid if I start drinking I'll forget to stop. Alcohol kills the pain. Better, it brings a nothingness I can drown in."

At the bar in the living room Quinn filled a brandy snifter almost half full, then returned reluctantly to the kitchen. Susie sat straight in the chair but her shoulders sagged. For one of the few times Quinn remembered, Susie seemed defeated, and she wished comforting came more naturally to her. *But leopards keep the same spots,* she thought, with a shudder of self-loathing. She swallowed a mouthful of the brandy, pleased when it burned her throat.

Susie whispered in the voice of a child afraid of the dark when Quinn sat down, "What are we going to do?"

"Did you tell the police any of—" Quinn shrugged.

"No, but I wanted to. I wanted to tell someone and get it fixed."

"Oh Lord"—Quinn sighed—"just put it back together like a broken-down car."

CONFESSIONS

"That's not what I mean!" Susie cried.

"Drink some tea, swallow, pause for a deep breath, and *think*!" Quinn ordered.

"Damn it, Quinn, you know what I meant!" But Susie drank more tea and let minutes pass before she said, "You realize this isn't the end of it? You do know that, don't you?"

"Now I'm the psychic," Quinn joked.

Susie didn't laugh. "Somebody killed Lily Vaughan in the snow, Quinn. Somebody stabbed her."

"I do remember. That hideous reindeer sweater!" She shuddered. "I can close my eyes and see Lily clear as a picture, just lying there, still as death. Dead, dead, dead. God, how we hated her!"

"And killed her," Susie said.

Quinn seized her wrist. "Stop it! That's hysteria talking! Nobody ever accused us or even thought such a terrible thing, so why should you, Susie, and now at the worst moment possible."

"We knew, we always knew!" Susie screamed, and broke away, sobbing. "One of us killed Lily and one of us ran down Greg!" She ran to the sink and hung over the edge, heaving, making raspy, grating sounds. Quinn thought she'd vomit, but she slowed down and washed her face with cold water.

The clatter of the water on the sink bottom played an irregular tune through Quinn's thoughts until, lulled, she closed her eyes, longing to climb into bed, to sleep for a day, a month, as long as any human was able.

The water stopped and Susie's voice rustled in its place. "Why am I telling you? Why am I sure it wasn't you?"

"A good question," Quinn mumbled.

"Because you'd kill a person, I think, with little or no regrets, but never the dogs. You loved Yin and Yang more than anybody."

Quinn tried opening her eyes, but the strange darkness held her back. In her mind's landscape the ebony surface retreated, until, in ponderous slow motion, the scene gradually formed.

It was the end of the day, the last illumination draining from the sky. The old snow was being dusted by the new as a loose, lazy shower fell, faster and faster. She was gazing out the big picture window at the front of the house. In the drive the jeep whitened until it became a ghost car, a vehicle from a dream. Behind, in the large open room that soared up to the apex of the A-frame, a fire roared in the flagstone fireplace. Invisible arms of warmth widened in an embrace.

Susie spoke in Quinn's twenty-years-later kitchen, though Quinn saw Susie, when she turned from the window, sitting before the fire.

Her hair was longer then, tied back in a thick braid, and she sat with her chin propped on her knees. "You and Dinah never knew why Lily came along," Susie was saying, "what she was doing there that weekend, forever smiling, the original Cheshire cat with that toothy grin." *I don't want to know,* Quinn thought she said, but Susie continued relentlessly. "She made us take her, Lisbeth and me. Lily blackmailed us with something she knew. It doesn't matter what now, but then it would have been devastating if she told."

You too! Quinn cried in that silent, midway place, trapped as though between two rooms, the past and the present. The words formed, *I knew your secret,* but Quinn didn't say them, just as she'd kept still so long ago. Only Lily knew, and she'd found out somehow that Quinn did too. She swore she'd take her tale to President Wellsberg.

"They'll be expelled, and except for Dinah Esterman, what friends will you have left? No more golden girls or magic circle," Lily Vaughan had sneered. "Not unless you take me in."

In that brilliantly lit memory Lisbeth sprawled on the couch as Lily swept by and ran an impudent hand across Lis's hair. Lisbeth cried out, *Don't touch me!* Lily turned mean as death. Ashes filled her mouth. Deliberately she went back and dropped her hand again on that reddish flame of hair. *It's not what you think, E-liz-a-beth!*

Lisbeth rose up, stung, and slapped Lily on the mouth. That was when Dinah came down the steps from the bedroom drinking a beer and said, *We've got cabin fever.*

"You think Lisbeth did it," Quinn found herself saying. "That's why you're so upset." Her eyes flew open as past time vanished.

Susie screamed in the present, "I don't think it's anyone!"

"You just said so." A dull ache spread up the back of Quinn's neck, working its way into her scalp. She recalled Lisbeth's headaches, the brain trauma that never showed up on the CAT scans.

Susie grabbed her hand and held on. "I know I didn't run down my husband, and I'm still not sure where Charlie lives. Your corgis, Quinnie: you can't believe I'd do such awful things to them! And you wouldn't either."

"Which leaves Dinah and Lisbeth," Quinn said hollowly. Somehow the snow swept inside, the cold silvering her bones, none of which was medically possible of course, yet she still felt frozen from the inside out.

"Dinah might shoot Hatch if somebody handed her a loaded gun, or get all agitated by the new neighbor and hit him over the head, but Di's incapable of premeditation. She can't plan a meal, never mind a murder. And she loves dogs too. Remember Rebecca."

Susie had cooled down, striving to make sense, but her bloodshot eyes still had a feverish cast. Susie, like Lisbeth, was capable of blazing, and the thought blundered into Quinn's mind before she could stop it: *What had it been like with them?*

"Yet Di's the only one of us who hasn't suffered some loss, unless you count Hatch, which you can't."

"Which means—"

Susie finished, "If she's innocent, she's next." She released Quinn's numbed hand and sipped the lukewarm tea. "So, if we continue to hide our heads in the sand, something awful will happen to a person Dinah loves. Which means Mikey. There's no one else."

"Oh, really, Susie, that's not possible. Mikey's a child. Who'd even consider hurting him? No"—Quinn shook her head—"I refuse to believe this. You're just overwrought by Greg's death. A few coincidences, awful though they are—" She paused, then said emphatically, "—are not a diabolic scheme of revenge!"

Susie wept. "And if you're wrong? If these *events* aren't isolated incidents? Please, Quinn! For days and days I've been scared, haunted. We've got to do something!"

"What? What do you want us to do?" Quinn realized she was screaming. "Should we gather the four of us together in a locked room and see who goes crazy first?"

"I don't know." She pushed off the chair and paced the kitchen. Quinn could actually feel the temperature rise with Susie's agitation.

"I'm not saying it's one of us, not definitely." Susie stopped by Quinn's chair to give her a dead-eye stare. "Maybe it's someone related to Lily who wants to see justice done, if belatedly. Wants us to turn in whoever killed her. Then that person will leave the rest of us alone."

"Susie, that's stupid."

"All right, so it's stupid. Blame the leprechauns, accuse whoever you want, Quinnie, but please, just drive up to Westport with me. We'll phone Lisbeth to meet us there. And for once we'll really talk about what's happening now, what happened then. We'll stop hiding, pretending."

Quinn sighed, but the sight of tears trickling down Susie's cheeks made her grudgingly agree.

26

Susie called just as Joe was getting ready to leave, and Dinah, off balance with this newly discovered, this entirely unexpected lust and love in her life, failed to notice either the fear or urgency in Susie's voice. "Sure, come on up. Great! Terrific! Mikey's over at the gym practicing his free stroke and Joe's got to go."

Dinah had asked Joe to stay for dinner, but he hadn't wanted Mikey to come home and find him yet again. "He has to get used to me in easy stages. Nothing alarming."

Dinah scrutinized Joe Connors, wondering if he was alarmed himself. Their dates occurred so often now, practically running into one another, with recesses only for work and sleep. Could Joe be having second or even third thoughts?

Dinah had put off searching for gainful employment until after the holidays, devoting herself to romance. Maybe by New Year's she'd be able to pin Joe Connors down to some kind of commitment. True, he could save her from having to earn a living, but she was also gaga about the man, as she exclaimed to anybody who'd listen. She even waxed lyrical to the hairdresser whom she surreptitiously went to—as if Hatch, or worse, her mother, perched on her shoulder—with the monthly installment for MasterCard.

You only buy what you have the money in the bank to pay for: this was the Esterman credo. What would her mother and father think, she asked the woman trailing along the shop windows with her on the way to the car, if they could see her now, hair trimmed and highlighted, all gray roots discreetly shaded brown, and bangs in jagged pickets overhanging her eyebrows, but with a bank balance at the point of no return and bills enough to wallpaper the dining room? *I'll think about that tomorrow*, she thought, parroting Scarlett O'Hara and smiling at the woman who, with eyes outlined a smidge too heavily in black, bore a slight resemblance to a raccoon.

Fluffing up the hairdo that had held its shape admirably since the day before despite Dinah's rough and tumble with Joe Connors, she walked him to his car, a shiny maroon Mercedes. They kissed—a discreet moue, lips to pursed lips—when Joe rolled down the driver's window, and then Dinah watched him drive off.

It was a second before she realized that as she watched the Mercedes until she could no longer see it, somebody had been watching her. The hedges had come undone again, and through a gap like a small porthole a glittery eye inspected her. The eye was almost on a level with her nose, and boldly she marched up to the wall of greenery and stared back owlishly.

"I know it appears as though I'm spying on you," said a smooth, silky voice behind the eye.

Dinah, who stood straighter these days, emboldened by Joe Connors in her life, had been about to snap, *How dare you!* was instantly lulled by the voice, calmed like a cobra by a snake charmer, and found she crooned, "Not at all."

The melodious voice continued, "It's just, you know, that we've never *really* met, except for peeking at each other through the hedges, which I do have to apologize for having barbered with those awful Marine crewcuts, but I mistakenly thought the hedges were mine. Do forgive me."

"Of course!" Dinah cried.

"I mean I really meant to come over the day it happened and even had a foot out the door, but my bouillabaisse boiled over that very second, would you believe. My culinary skills, alas, aren't quite up to my aspirations!"

"Oh boy, do I know what you mean!" Dinah replied with fervor.

A kindred, inept cook hung behind the hedge, though now the eye sidled sideways and the voice drifted toward the front walk. "It's all Julia Child's fault. Those directions seem *très* simple when you read them, but when you're actually in the fray of a teaspoon of this, a tablespoon of that, a pinch here and there, well, it's a whole different kettle of fish."

Dinah wandered along the hedges trying to keep pace with the disembodied voice. "My secret weapon is really *The Joy of Cooking,* which assumes you can't even boil water," she offered.

"Well, maybe that's my problem, that I overreach." He emerged onto the sidewalk, a pixieish little man, much smaller than she thought he would be. He possessed a cupid's face, round and unlined as a Christmas ornament. He had a great mass of curly black hair, artfully threaded with gray, and tinselly strands covered his ears and shagged

339

down his neck. His furry brows curved above luminous brown eyes. *Why, he's cute,* Dinah thought, and returned the smile Mario Ellis beamed out at her.

"So glad to meet you, officially I mean," he said.

"Likewise."

Dinah remembered the day when she was afraid Mario Ellis had run Becky down in his Jaguar. How threatening she considered him then, how frightening! But there was nothing even vaguely dangerous about this short, sunny person. He reminded Dinah of the bronzed boys who occupied the Italian beaches that summer she and Hatch did a month's tour of the Mediterranean.

Dinah also recalled the barrel-chested man with the pointy ears and almost no hair whom she spied once through the hedges. Cautiously, treading with care on the delicate ice of this budding acquaintance, she asked Mario Ellis about him.

"One of my many mistakes," he said with a roll of his eyes and a shudder. "I plan to be much choosier now, given the climate of the times, and after all, this is Westport." There was a definite straightening of his spine and a hint of pride in his voice.

It must be true, the rumors Dinah had heard via Mae and Ruthie Rudolph, that this adorable petite person standing before her, legs apart, hands shoved into pants pockets, and apparently not at all cold in only a crewneck sweater, was a homosexual. For a second Dinah suffered a tinge of real pain because Mario Ellis was so luscious, with skin the shade of crème caramel, that she wanted to eat him up! But immediately she had a vision of Joe Connors athletically cavorting in her kingsize bed less than an hour ago and decided not to be greedy. Besides, the thrill of having this interesting person living next door and possibly becoming her friend overrode her consuming interest these days in heterosex.

To think how she had regretted the Bergers' demise! Of course she wished them alive, in good health, but as warm and nurturing as they were, and how generous when Dinah ran out of sugar or milk, the elderly couple paled against the glamor of Mario Ellis. He was the sort of person she'd never met before. The world, Dinah realized, suddenly struck by a bolt of enlightenment, was filled with so many people not at all like those from Westport or Nebraska, or even the women with whom she attended Cabot, and now, not hamstrung by Hatch—who loathed homosexuals, blacks, Hispanics, American Indians, India Indians, and would have loathed Jews too but hesitated because of the firm's two senior partners—she would meet some.

Dinah, sashaying her hips from side to side with the joy of future, unexpected adventure, unshackled as she'd luckily become from an inhibited, bigoted husband, smiled broadly and cried, "I'd love to have you for dinner one night, if you think you can survive my cooking."

Mario Ellis laughed and his teeth were bright as the whitewashed stones lining the driveway. "I have a better idea. Why don't we make dinner together? That way we have the benefit of both our attempts."

"What a super suggestion!" Dinah cried, clapping her hands with childish glee.

"Marvelous. I'll check my schedule and you check yours and then we'll fix a date."

They both started to backpedal toward their houses.

"I'll call. Or you call me. Though I can slip a note under your door," Dinah said.

"I can slip one under yours."

"So long then." She smiled.

He waved, and sighing, Dinah retreated, her teeth chattering. As the afternoon light began its retreat from the sky on one of the year's shortest Sundays, Dinah skipped up the porch steps and went into the darkening house.

It was dark by the time Susie took the turn off the parkway that would eventually lead her, after a winding, up-and-down country lane, to Delphinium. Dinah, meanwhile, had decided she'd have to feed Susie and Quinn, and emptied two cans of tomato soup into a saucepan. The soup, along with toasted cheese sandwiches and some sliced peaches, should do fine unless Mikey wandered home to eat after practice instead of stopping at a friend's house. Oh well, she thought, it would just be a matter of giving him a frozen pizza to microwave if he balked at the soup and sandwiches.

Mikey, at the moment his mother was considering what to feed him, was wondering if he had enough loose change in his jeans to take a detour to McDonald's after a few more laps. A powerful hunger was building up in his stomach that added another pain to a body already aching with sore arms and legs. Practice had officially terminated almost an hour before and he shouldn't be doing laps alone in the gym. What if you get a cramp, for Christ's sake! the coach yelled at him the last time Moe, the school janitor, caught him churning through the water like a great white. But Mikey possessed a demon's determination to winnow another few seconds off his time, to improve his stroke until his arms sliced through the water like knives through soft butter. Furthermore, his kick lacked punch, and wasn't powerful enough—not

341

for the Olympic trials. So he had hidden in one of the toilet stalls when the coach shepherded everybody out into the night, and Moe, after a dilatory cleaning up of the locker room and a quick swab with a mop around the apron of the pool, turned off the lights and let himself out the big double doors.

Mikey didn't much care for swimming in the murky dark, the slap slap he made in the water echoing against the tile and the glass walls, but a light in the gym could be seen for miles, which was how he got caught last time. The street lamps flung a ghostly illumination against the naked trees, sending shadowy armies marching through the gym windows and into the pool. But he burrowed into the warmish water and put all thoughts of Big Macs, fries, and shakes, as well as the creatures in the horror movies his mother was forever dragging him to, out of his mind as he picked up speed. He felt his body beginning to function with the perfect coordination of a well-disciplined machine as he swam in his element.

Dinah heard the car in the drive and reached the front window just as Susie and Quinn slammed the doors, two rifle shots shattering the Delphinium quiet, and she shivered suddenly. In a second the women were on the front porch and in the house, bringing with them an electric sizzle of tension.

"What's up?" Dinah asked. It had just occurred to her that they might not have come to Westport for a Sunday drive.

"Why don't we try to call Lisbeth again?" Quinn suggested.

"What do you want Lis for?" But Susie didn't answer. She went automatically into Dinah's kitchen and took the receiver off the wall phone. Yet again the only voice that flowed along the wires was the mechanical one from the answering machine. Susie left the message that they were up at Dinah's and to call as soon she got in.

"Do you mind telling me what the hell's going on?" Dinah fairly shouted as she sank down on a chair. The table was laid for dinner, but she forgot all about the soup in the saucepan and the sandwiches lined up waiting to be grilled.

"I wouldn't mind some wine," Susie said. She had hung up the phone, but her fingers danced a silent adagio on the receiver as if she could will it to ring.

"I have some red in the fridge."

"Whatever."

"Quinn?"

"I'd rather have some coffee if you're making it."

"Instant okay?"

"Of course."

Dinah busied herself about the kitchen as Susie and Quinn kept still, but the tension increased until her hair almost stood on end and she was about to scream, *What is it?*

Becky slung through the archway and allowed Quinn to scratch her behind the ears, but the feeling of something not quite right sent the dog crawling into the laundry room and her storebought bed, where she seldom slept or even lay down.

Susie couldn't sit. She walked the floor in quick, nervous, ducklike steps, absentmindedly tugging a strand of hair as she'd done at Cabot when she'd worn it so much longer.

Dinah brought Quinn her coffee and met Susie in the middle of the kitchen to offer her the glass of wine. "Now," she said, when she'd seated herself again, "are you going to tell me what this is all about?"

Susie held the wineglass between her palms and asked, "Where's Mikey?"

Dinah stiffened. "What do you want Mikey for?"

The shadows whipped long, snaky arms across the surface of the pool, then blackened to slithery creatures baring their teeth every time Mikey lifted his head. *Only shadows, nothing spooky. Another two laps,* he promised himself. He concentrated and pushed away the fear that slowed the regulated breathing, the measured inhalation and carefully timed exhalation, and traveled faster through the water in this pool and the next, in the one after that, through as many pools as it would take to the next summer Olympics.

It's all in the head, the coach told him. Winning is only a matter of thinking you'll do it, in being determined to beat off that guy in the next lane chewing up your ass.

As Mikey moved into the shallow end, readying himself for the turn where he could lose or gain precious seconds, he thought of his father sitting in the stands and shouting, *Come on, boy!* just as Hatch did in the den watching football games. His father was basically an armchair jock who, when Mikey was younger, occasionally tossed a softball to him in the backyard and promised skiing trips to Stowe and did once in a while take him out in the boat on the Sound. Hatch swam like a drowning man heading panicked for shore, with a lumbering free stroke, and he couldn't understand Mikey's love affair with the water. What good will it do you? he'd asked once, and Mikey had no answer for that. What good did anything do you in his father's terms? he wondered, coming off the side faster, he thought, than he ever had before, determined not to make this last lap a torturous trip. But then Hatch slid as easily as the currents out of Mikey's mind, for his father had no more substance than the dancing shadows, even when he'd lived in the same house. Less, for the phantasms splintered, and one of them took on weight as it padded on soft cat's paws along the pool's edge.

"I don't believe it!" Dinah was screaming. "You're making it up!"

"Stop it, Di!" Quinn yelled, leaping off the chair and grabbing Dinah by the elbow. "Why should Susie pretend that the police told her somebody killed Greg?"

"Then some business rival did it, or, sorry Susie, maybe a girlfriend. But no one connected to Lily! Fucking damn!" she swore, spinning around on Quinn. "That would be crazy!" She and Quinn hung together in an awkward embrace as Dinah whispered, "Nothing since Labor Day makes any sense! It's been the worst fall of my life!"

She pushed Quinn away and flung herself against the refrigerator, her back to the women. "The worst!" she whispered, thinking of Cabot her freshman year.

She'd been plump with curly hair and wore red lipstick a shade too bright, twin sweater sets topping plaid skirts and pearls at a moment in time when skinniness and straight long hair and no makeup were the fashion. The best girls, the golden ones, all dressed that way, and they all looked like some variation of Lisbeth or Susie. She stuck out, but then Quinn did too, she remembered. Tears prickled her eyes, old tears, and she thought it was a miracle that they'd been tumbled in together, the four of them, and that some magic had taken place. For reasons Dinah never investigated, they'd all become friends. A bonding occurred. Some mysterious glue welded them into a loving relationship, and they became the envy of the campus.

What is it about you, Esterman? Lily asked one morning in the south hall bathroom. How come you're one of them? You're nothing but a hick from Podunk with nothing to recommend you. Spitefully, Lily Vaughan put into words what Dinah often wondered, and taunted her with that worthlessness.

"I hated Lily Vaughan!" Dinah screamed out against the smooth whiteness of the refrigerator.

"Did you kill her?" Susie asked with no emotion.

Quinn emitted a whinnying little cry, but Dinah ignored her as she turned. "I could have," she replied, finishing a glass of wine only to pour another and drink that too before adding, "but I didn't." Dinah opened the last bottle of Beaujolais before wandering about her kitchen as if it were a strange, unfamiliar room. Arriving accidentally at the sink, she washed her hands and patted her cheeks with cold water. A mistake. The chill made her see snow, a blur of color, some bright material through a crack in her forgetfulness. Hastily she drank some wine until a soft buzzing began behind her eyelids.

"It was a tramp, somebody on the road. You've forgotten what the sixties were like, especially in New England. The whole country was on the prowl. Picking apples or growing soybeans or being ski bums or just beaching up in some dinky town and annoying the natives with pot parties. And everyone was into dope. Acid, grass, bennies, uppers and downers, blues, reds, and purples," Quinn lectured in a professorial tone. She added, "And there was evidence for such a person, remember. A path churned to the road."

"I did that," Dinah said. She held the glass to her forehead and looked dreamy.

"What?" Quinn's eyes widened.

"When I saw Lily lying dead out there." Just thinking about Lily tinged the memory snow a winy bloodred. A pulse beat painfully in Dinah's neck. "Mostly that day, day and a half, is a blank. Zippo. A clean slate in my head. At least from somewhere around dinnertime right up to the moment I glanced out the kitchen window and there was Lily like some big dead bird spread-eagled in the snow. Because I'd been drinking. Because of the dope." *Because I needed to forget,* she thought with a shudder. She'd never wanted to know anything that would destroy the magic circle and turn her again into plain old Dinah Esterman.

They shifted around the kitchen in changing patterns, Dinah to sit at the table, Quinn to the window where she could see nothing of the night beyond the glass, and Susie to lean up at the counter.

Dinah went on, slurring her words and in a reflex motion sipping at the wine, "At first I wasn't sure what it was. I mean until I focused I couldn't tell it was a body, Lily's, but then . . ." She thrust a hand in front of her, whether beseechingly, aching for some touch and reassurance, or to hold back Lily's ghostly image, neither Susie nor Quinn could tell. Susie rushed to the table and joined her hand to Dinah's.

"I walked out to the body in an already messed-up path," Dinah continued. "And when I did I saw that clear white crust like birthday cake icing all the way to the road. That part I remember so perfectly, shuffling through the snow in my sneakers, freezing my toes. I shuffled as much of the snow as I could, to stir it up even more, so anybody looking wouldn't find tracks. Lily was already dead, so what did it matter.''

Susie slipped an arm around Dinah's shoulders. "I know."

"Know? Know what?" Quinn asked.

"I saw Di."

"And you never said!" Dinah cried, pulling away from Susie as if some betrayal had just taken place.

"What for?" Susie lowered her head. "You're right. Lily was dead and I hated her so much, as much as I loved the three of you. If one of you killed her . . . I wouldn't, I couldn't tell. It was okay, but of course it wasn't, not for years and years. Lily's death just wouldn't go away."

Dinah stood up. "I have supper if anybody's hungry." Neither of the women replied.

Quinn went to the phone and dialed Lisbeth again, but she hung up without saying a word, so they knew once more there was only the answering machine at the other end.

Susie looked at her watch. "What time's Mikey coming home?"

"I told you, he's at swim practice."

Quinn said, "I just realized, whenever the subject of Lily comes up—"

"Ho, ho, and who's responsible for that ugly business this time," Dinah interrupted. "And just when I was in the loveliest mood, too!"

"Whenever it does," Quinn persisted, "you drink too much and wind up drunk, Di."

Dinah, holding her glass out in a toast first to Quinn, then Susie, drank up all the wine and poured a refill before she answered, "Why shouldn't I? On the old scale of one to ten, that little ski trip gets a minus thirty. What I remember of it. Me, I hate thinking about it . . . Lily . . . snow in Vermont. Think you would too, Quinnie."

"That's not the point," Quinn said.

Dinah screamed, "What *is* the point?" She squeezed her eyes shut. "God, you've given me a headache!"

Susie took the bottle of wine from Dinah and asked her carefully, "What time should Mikey be home?"

Susie, close up, was indistinct, Dinah realized. *Middle-aged, getting farsighted,* she thought with alarm and a cold knot of fear in her stomach. But the fright wasn't over age or the undoubted need at some future moment for bifocals, it was for Mikey. "Why," she said, making a real effort to keep her words smooth and even, not to let them unravel about the edges, "do you keep asking me about Mikey and when he'll get home? Is something wrong, something both of you are keeping tight-lipped about?''

Quinn and Susie exchanged a look, of fear, of complicity too. ''It's late, that's all,'' Quinn commented dryly.

Dinah yelled as if the women were some distance away, ''Mikey always practices until his skin is cottage cheese!''

''Call the gym,'' Susie said, not daring to meet Dinah's gaze.

Dinah, however, already was in motion, rushing for the front door, grabbing her jacket and purse off the bench as she passed. Looking for the keys in the overstuffed hobo bag and loudly muttering, ''Damn, damn, damn,'' she spilled the contents all over the hall, but the keys slid out from under a silk bandanna. Dinah snatched them up and ran, Quinn and Susie following. Becky rushed the door. It slammed right on her nose and she collapsed, whimpering, listening with her head between her paws to Dinah's repeated curses before they were swallowed up by the guttural roar of the car as it drove away.

Mikey kicked off in his last turn, the other end of the water undulating like a nighttime field of corn in the rimy moonlight. Stalking shadows curled over the apron and grew into towering cypresses, Mikey saw, when he raised his head too far out of the water. The valuable second slipped from him and he saw a swimmer in the next lane passing silently in ghostly shimmers, the spitting kick of feet sending up tiny spouts. *Keep your head on the surface; turn only enough to get a mouthful of air,* he reminded himself, and forced his tired body to travel faster to the other end of what seemed, the longer he swam, to be nowhere. His aching arms tried to push him from the water into the air, out of the pool. His arms belonged to somebody else as he gritted his teeth, promising the weary machine he punished for so long now, just one more minute. Less than that on the timekeeper's stopwatch and Mikey would be there. Suddenly he wanted to be rubbing his skin dry and scrambling into his clothes. Forget about a shower until he got home.

The edge of the long pool sped toward him and he experienced an ecstatic high as though this were an actual meet and the coach, hands cupped to his mouth like a megaphone, screamed with the authority of God Himself, *Move, Johnson! Get the lead out!*

Mikey concentrated with the single-minded devotion of an acolyte. Arms at a precise angle. Hands chopping the water. The mechanical scissoring of his legs was perfect as he streaked home ahead of the competition. In this fantasy last race Mikey ran smack into the concrete, grabbing the edge, his heart pounding as he caught his breath. But then something strange took place; his wet head was shoved back into the water. He fought against the pressure, but his head jammed down on his neck and his pedaling legs struck the pool's side as his hands flapped up spumes of froth. The exploding water cascaded over his chin. In his spreading panic Mikey made the bad mistake of opening his mouth and the current slid silkly over his lips. He choked, coughing and spluttering. *Stop!* he screamed, but the plea came with a spray of tiny drops and he swallowed the chlorinated water.

The pressure increased, and he tore at the water, trying to make some inroad in it, but any path he opened up closed immediately on his efforts as he struggled.

Despite his wishes and desires, his young boy's dreams, his determination to rise with the speed of a water sprite from the liquid embrace, Mikey entered the filmy dark. His eyes stared into the drifting, black-green currents. The further down he floated, the hotter the pool water became, until it seemed to boil. Mikey sank, descending easily as a feather. His lungs totally empty of air, fibrous containers already beginning in that first millisecond to rot, graying images wound through his mind before the inside world darkened as deeply as the outer. And Mikey navigated through the longest distance in time, through the gray layers into the absoluteness of nowhere.

27

The revolving red lights spun across the patrol cars, the ambulance, the silent knots of people, and sent a bloody illumination up the wall and windows of the gym. The heavy boots of the uniformed policemen scuffed the pebbles on the open ground in front of the school. A radio from one of the black-and-whites squawked in a garble of static that made no sense to Susie as she stood shivering next to Quinn. But all they really heard was Dinah's voice in discordant agony, screeches, a cadenza of cries without end. Susie wanted to slap her hands over her ears or pull the duffle coat above her head, anything to escape Di's grief that would flow without stopping like Niobe's tears until Dinah too turned into stone.

When Mikey was brought out of the gym on a gurney, Dinah tore back the sheet and threw herself across her dead son's wet body with a scream that silenced the police and paramedics, the gathering crowd, hushed even the wind ruffling through the trees at the edge of the school drive. Susie ran to her and Quinn tried with an arm about Dinah's shoulders to draw her back, but she swung on her friends, howling, "We did this to him!"

They tried to quiet her then, but Dinah beat them off with a windmill of stinging blows and it took two of the burly policemen to restrain her.

"Damn it, isn't there a doctor to give her a shot?" Quinn demanded. She would have injected Dinah with a sedative herself if she had one.

Susie and Quinn were moved none too gently behind the ropes that cordoned off the side of the gym. They watched the police grappling a crazed Dinah as the paramedics attempted to hoist Mikey's lifeless body, shrouded again by the sheet, into the mouth of the ambulance. Somehow mother was separated from child. A shriek of such agony tore through the Connecticut night that Susie blundered into Quinn and pressed her wet face against Quinn's shoulder. Even when Dinah was finally bundled into one of the police cars her screams penetrated glass and steel.

After Dinah was driven away, a cop angled over to Quinn and Susie. His suggestion that they come along to the hospital had the impact of an order. As if they meant to escape him, the cop rode in Susie's car. During the careful trip through the sleeping Westport streets he asked who they were and why they'd all come hurrying to the school gym. What did they know—or if that was too strong a word—*sense* that sent them looking for Mikey Johnson only to discover him drowned in the pool?

Friends of Mrs. Johnson . . . up from Manhattan for Sunday night supper . . . late . . . dark . . . driving over to the high school to give the boy a ride home.

As he lit a cigarette the flame drew a momentary cicatrix on the policeman's cheek. He inhaled and asked, indifferently, what Dinah meant when she cried out, "We did this to him."

Susie's gaze collided in the rearview mirror with Quinn's. Susie said, "I don't know, really."

"Probably just that we were sitting around talking when we should have been thinking of Mikey. Once it got late, I mean," Quinn said.

The detective's jowly, heavily crinkled face smoothed out, and Susie thought, *He doesn't believe us.*

Later, while they waited outside one of the small emergency-room cubicles as the doctor on duty gave Dinah a shot, another policeman, shorter and older but better dressed in a camel's hair coat, arrived to question them. He asked what time they arrived at Dinah's and why they drove up from Manhattan in the first place.

"Why this Sunday afternoon?"

Susie found herself forced into explaining that Greg had died. "I'm lonely, grieving. It's a very hard time for me right now. Dr. Webster and Mrs. Johnson are my oldest friends, from school. "And—" She stumbled into silence.

"How did your husband die, Mrs. Lamton?" he asked, mildly, as if making conversation.

"In a traffic accident." To the side Susie saw the other cop scribble something in a notebook. There was no holding back the information that Greg's death was deliberate. "A hit-and-run, right in front of our building. Someone, on purpose, ran him down." She hunched up, cold, and with a sick feeling of terror. "Which seems impossible," she whispered.

And Mikey, was he killed too, or was his drowning in the unlit pool an accident? Neither woman dared ask, and when they were finally driving back down the parkway, Quinn said, "I'm not sure they can tell. If Mikey has no marks on him and if there's water in his lungs, they'll rule it an accidental death."

Susie clung to the wheel, staring at the straight road unrolling under the glow of the headlights. "Do you think it was?"

"Who knows?" Quinn replied, wearily leaning her head against the window.

"To kill a child," Susie whispered in horror. The car veered in a sympathetic shudder to the shoulder and hastily she straightened it out. A light snow began to trail across the windshield and Susie switched the wipers on. The flakes dusted the hood and wove through the golden beams. Now and then the round-eyed glare of another car going north shone at them from the blackness, then quickly passed by. Susie's foot rested lightly on the gas pedal and the car moved ever slower, almost somnolently.

In the reflected glow from the dash Susie's pale face was pinched and mean. "No one kills a child," she said.

Quinn, eyelids drooping, pulled up against the seat. The tepid gusts of air blowing from the vents, the lulling motion of the car, the clickety-click of the tires on the uneven pavement, had almost put her to sleep. She shook herself guiltily, saying, "People kill children every day. Children are the world's most natural victims. They have so little strength to fight back. Even a fourteen-year-old, if he was tired from swimming. Someone might have pushed him down easily and held his head under water until he drowned."

The car jerked in a wider arc this time, and Susie's hands left the steering wheel. A tire caught the ridge of earth at the edge of the road and they spun off toward the median. Susie fought the skid by giving in to it, and the car careened across a patch of ice. When they straightened at last and continued toward the city in the middle of two lanes, Quinn emitted a pent-up breath that fogged the window in a ragged circle.

"Do you want me to drive?"

"I'm sorry."

"I'll drive, Susie."

"No, I'm okay. It's just that I had an awful vision of Mikey fighting in the swimming pool, in the darkness, trying to escape those hands that killed him." Her voice broke and she nearly wept again.

"We have no proof it wasn't an accident."

"I know, I know! He could have gotten a cramp." Though Susie had the shakes, she kept the car under control. "Oh, my head is killing me!" she said. "An electric drill is grinding into the bone."

"Lisbeth's had bad headaches on and off since the accident. Maybe worse," Quinn observed.

"I know," Susie said, trying to bury her fear.

"Maybe blackouts, though I can't be certain. But she's so forgetful lately, and then, there are those moments. . . . She drifts off."

"Preoccupation!" Which was what Susie wanted to believe.

"No, I think it's more than that. Watch her. She empties, like a bottle turned upside down. All life, or rather consciousness, seems to leave."

Silence settled except for the clatter of the wipers swiping at the snow that thickened the further south they went. Susie realized it was the first storm since Greg died.

"It wasn't Lisbeth, if that's what you're thinking, Quinn," Susie said almost angrily. They were nearing the city and she couldn't let the terrible night end with her own fears unspoken. "To suspect Lis of hurting a child, and Dinah's son, is impossible."

"You thought Lisbeth was guilty of . . . of those other things."

"I didn't!" Susie screamed.

"You did," Quinn said softly. "And where is she? We called repeatedly."

What little traffic there was on the Henry Hudson Parkway moved cautiously. Susie kept to the right, driving well under the speed limit. Only when she slowly swung to the exit and made the wide circle around to the street did she say, striving for reason, "Whatever happened to Lily, whatever one of us did then, if anything, this is today, Quinn. Lily Vaughan alive would want to harm us awfully, doing the worst her nasty little mind could think of. But Lily's dead. And whoever spoke for that poor miserable creature? No one, remember. Even her gay divorcee mother was visibly relieved not to have such an unattractive burden. So why Lisbeth? And why now?"

Charlie Morgan had been looking for her. Chance hadn't placed him on the corner of Sixth Avenue and Tenth Street. He'd gone to her apartment and rung the bell persistently, but she wasn't there.

Lisbeth would have walked right past him if he hadn't grabbed her arm. Stopped, face to face, the snow fell between them. Lisbeth, caught in an inner world, took a while before she recognized him. Charlie's name returned in a painful stab of memory.

"I came to talk to you, Lisbeth," he explained, suspecting she'd drift down the snowy sidewalk and vanish. "Your damn answering machine is still the only voice I get when your phone rings."

Flurries of snow dusted her cheeks, and she was more aware of the soft wetness than of Charlie Morgan or his anger.

"It's been days since I've seen you or even heard from you. What's happening to us, Lisbeth?"

Icicles of frozen light dripped around Charlie's collar. The storm cut him into lucent bits and ebony pieces like a puzzle that needed to be put together.

Behind on the avenue the cars whined, their tires losing traction on the dangerous pavement. Above, the wild wind sizzled around the concrete ledges. A woman tugged a white poodle, almost invisible in the thickly falling snow, toward the corner. Charlie's leather-gloved hands clapped. They reminded her of two reptilian creatures she'd once seen in a taxidermist's window. They dropped, suddenly, upon her shoulders. She felt the pressure returning her to the ground, and below her the patchy sidewalk began splitting in fissures. She cried out, keening, as he called her name. "Lisbeth . . ."

"Let me go!" She struggled with him as his face closed in on her. White beads tatted his lashes.

"What the hell's wrong with you?" he shouted, the pressure of his hands increasing. The weight of Charlie Morgan was terrible. He thrust her down until, legs buckling, the air in her lungs burnt.

With a ferocious burst of energy she reared up, erupting from his grasp, and as she did a small vein burst in her nose. A red spume flashed from her nostrils. Blood splattered her black coat and Charlie's sheepskin jacket.

"What the hell!"

Lisbeth ran, sliding, darting through the gauzy white walls. The snow fell on her like an ashy curtain.

Feet pounded after her as she raced by the fences, the mounded hydrant, the snow-blanketed cars like mummies laid end to end. The high stoops of the brownstones rose in soft ladders.

"Lisbeth!" Charlie shouted.

Her head was being squeezed like a plum, and the pain made her stumble. Charlie closed in on her just as she reached the steps.

"Get away! Get away! I don't want you!" she shrieked. The taste of blood was on her tongue.

"I don't understand," he said, but her cry had stopped him.

Lisbeth crawled up the stoop without bothering to look back. By the time she found the door she forgot Charlie Morgan entirely.

Neff waited wrapped in shadowy darkness by the front window. Mysteriously he managed his way in, through two locked doors. Neff could do things like that.

His collar was unbuttoned, his tie pulled down. The scar angling along the right cheek rose, a reddish delta. She forgot the old wound came originally with Neff, a part of him as known as eyebrows and square chin, and wondered if somehow she had inflicted the raised welt. How angry was Neff, and would he desire vengeance?

A clamorous storm, blustering, rousing winds and shifting sheets of light and dark, blew as harshly in her head as the rampage outside. A tic spasmed at the corner of her left eye and her lids fluttered involuntarily. In her New York apartment she was speeding down the San Diego Freeway at a hundred miles an hour, the ebony car, a beast or demon on her flank. Chasing . . . chasing . . . almost caught me then. She smiled, stepping on the gas.

"What massacre were you in?" Neff asked.

Lisbeth made quick, one-frame cuts and sent Neff into jarring relief.

In the mirror across the room an angular woman flickered, then settled, hanging stapled on the glass. Blood scalloped the chin of this creature who might have been ripping raw flesh with her teeth. She floated nearer the reflection and watched as she touched the damp coat. Fingers came away stained red.

"You hurt anywhere?" Neff had a wet towel and was wiping the image clean. He handed her a glass with colorless liquid in it when he finished, and she drank it standing, dripping puddles on the rug until he stripped her coat off.

"It's nothing, only a bloody nose," he said with a dark smile on his lips. But he had to undress her. As he did she found his name.

"Neff."

"What?"

Her skin burned when he rubbed it. She gazed at the long slope of snowy arm and saw the bruises. He would reach the bones, she thought, as he pressed even harder.

Don't move, someone whispered.

Neff was taking off his clothes. From behind him he drew the large revolver and laid it on the dresser. The gun stared at her with one dark eye.

354

She was naked now. Neff spread the feathery body across the bed and wandered from breasts to groin with the flicking tip of his tongue. "Shit," he complained, "you're as interested as a dead person." And he entered her with a jackhammering shove.

There was no pleasure. The pain in her head took up all feeling in a whirlpool. The body on which he labored was vacant, without life in it.

When he arched, lips drawn back in a grimace, his breath came fluting in a whistle. She thought of trains in old black-and-white movies.

Neff's weight fell on Lisbeth with the finality of a coffin lid. Only then did she struggle, pushing him aside as he weakly snatched at her slipperiness. But he couldn't hold her. She was up and off the bed.

"Jesus Christ, you're crazier tonight than you usually are," he said, rolling onto his back.

She saw Neff coming apart, night tides of blackness washing over him, and spasms seized her. Spiders crawled under her skin.

Someone was screaming.

"Shut up, damn it!"

Neff reached for her, but she could see only half of him. The other side sliced away into nothingness. White and black. . . .

The pale van filled the windshield of memory one fleeting second before the crash, and Lisbeth screamed again.

And yet there was a final moment as she tumbled forward in the colliding Porsche. She flew again over the steering wheel into the shattering windshield, through time, to Vermont, to the February past. Lily Vaughan lay dead in the snow, and Lisbeth, remembering, screamed to Neff, "Did I kill her?"

"Jesus!"

He slapped her hard. She flew back and hit the dresser.

"I don't know who she is, but you sure as shit shoved a knife into Charlie."

"*No!*"

"Bitch!" Neff bared his wolfish teeth. "I just can't figure out why. He's a nice guy, the professor, and supposed to be the love of your life. Right?"

The darkness ebbed, but the pain blew up in her head.

"I should take you in," he growled as she inched back from Neff, groping for firm ground, for an end to the fire incinerating bone.

Her hand found the gun. She lifted it, holding it straight out. A finger curled on the trigger. "It hurts," she whispered.

"Put that down!" Neff yelled.

She saw herself on the screen, one of the good guys twelve feet high. Just as she'd written, a green eye closed and the other, glittery as an emerald, sighted along the barrel.

"I told you to put the gun down!" Neff ordered.

She did, after she pulled the trigger, after a hole, round as a dime, opened in the center of the long, snaky scar.

28

When they reached the heart of the city, Susie could barely see as the wipers fought to clear fans of snow. She had driven at a steady twenty miles an hour down the last hazardous stretch of the West Side Highway, mindful of the wounded cars stalled in both lanes. All the while Quinn had hunched in her corner, stony, and to Susie who kept chancing quick glances at her, plastery as a Segal sculpture.

"Maybe we should wait until tomorrow to see Lisbeth," Susie said, moving steadily south. If she passed through the Village, Little Italy, SoHo, Chinatown, Wall Street, eventually the sidewalks and cramped streets would dead-end and the water flash before her, the river and then the ocean, and beyond that, anywhere. *I can leave here,* she thought, *be someone else, go and never come back,* and she felt the tug as the tires went *skat, skat* on the snow. But her daughters . . . To leave them would be like leaving her arms, going crippled and handicapped. And there was Simon.

Quinn sounded dreamy when she answered, "We can't put it off anymore." Susie started, having forgotten what she had asked.

"Yes, I suppose you're right. And we have to tell her about Dinah. Our poor Di!"

"Poor, poor . . ." Quinn echoed. She was as frozen as the ice floes in the Hudson.

The further south they went the more quilted with snow the streets were, jeweled flakes sparkling under the streetlights. The city lay hushed in a dreamlike world, dissolving and reforming. Nothing was what it appeared to be.

When they came at last to Lisbeth's brownstone, Susie didn't bother searching for a space but double-parked.

"She must be home," Quinn said, glancing at the light-smudged windows.

Susie stepped from the car, lowered her head and butted into the violent wind and snow, flailing a blind passage up the steps. Quinn

357

followed and they stood stomping their feet, waiting for the buzzer that would unlock the outer door. When it didn't sound, Susie leaned inward and the door gave way. They pushed into the common foyer, thankful for the sudden warmth.

"Not safe," Quinn muttered, and anxiously closed the door, making sure the lock caught. Then they rang the bell of Lisbeth's apartment, listening to it echo inside. Just when they were beginning to think she wasn't there after all, the knob turned.

In the narrow space between the edge of the door and the frame, they glimpsed an elongated Lisbeth in a deep green terry bathrobe belted at the waist. Her hair spun in red, dancing flames and curled about the pearly face. Susie gasped and stepped back. She'd never seen Lisbeth so beautiful.

Quinn said sharply, "Are you going to make us stand out here all night?"

Slowly Lisbeth retreated on bare feet, graceful as Markova, almost dancing.

"I could use a drink. A toddy would be perfect, but that's probably too much trouble. A scotch will do." Quinn's words rushed out nervously. She shrugged off her coat and crossed to the fireplace. "A fire would be nice, too, on a night like this. Good"—she nodded with satisfaction—"you have one laid." She knelt in an awkward motion like a much older woman bending to pray, and struck a long match, holding it to the edge of the crushed newspaper.

Lisbeth circled. Susie, hands still shoved in the duffle pockets, watched her warily. "Are you okay? I haven't talked to you in days." Lisbeth hummed and went about the room in circling patterns, her feet arched like a prancing Siva. *All she needs is bells and bangles,* Susie couldn't help thinking. She saw Lis's body through the heavy robe as though she were naked, and knew that at times, like now, she'd be torn in two directions.

The paper blazed. The twigs and slivers of dry wood under the big log burst into feathers of fire. Quinn settled on her haunches. "Mikey drowned in the school's swimming pool," she said without looking around. Lisbeth continued her mysterious dancing.

"Lis, did you hear what Quinn said?" Susie asked.

Quinn rose and poured her own drink. She took it straight without ice and the bitter taste made her grimace. Quinn repeated, "Dinah's son, Mikey, drowned tonight in the Westport High School pool. Maybe by accident, maybe by design."

"Mikey," Lisbeth said, slowly. Her eyes were blank. She pivoted again and glided by the window, barely gazing out. "It's snowing.

Great skiing, don't you know, but we'll have a hard time getting up the mountain. Good thing the lifts are running.''

Susie froze. Quinn ceased the barest movement. They couldn't even glance at one another. They remembered the words as they did each moment of that day and night. The words Lisbeth spoke were Lily's.

"I was a bunny when I went before, but after so many lessons I've probably advanced to intermediate. At least you'd suppose so with all the money my mother spent Christmas at Snow Valley. You know, she had me on the slopes from dawn to dusk until I got the worst cold, and then she would have shoved me out into the snow so she could spend time with Daryl. But I was running a fever and even Daryl said finally it wasn't safe for me to go. Not that my mother cared if I died and they had to bury me in some snowdrift. But whatever little murmur beautiful Daryl makes is law to my mother. So I got to stay in bed, all alone, with only the maid for company when she came in to straighten the room. And later, after they got off the slopes, I heard them through the wall, humping like rabbits."

Lily ran on and on like a waterfall. She talked from morning to night all through the hours as long as there was some other presence, listening or not.

"God," Dinah swore, "she makes me wish I'd go deaf."

And Quinn said, "My sympathies are definitely with her mother and Daryl."

Lily pressed on the four of them like an inflamed wound.

Dinah said, "I could kill her!"

"Why is she here?" Quinn asked again and again.

In the kitchen Lisbeth lit a joint and passed it to Susie, who whispered just as Quinn wandered in, "It won't work. She'll tell anyway."

"Who will tell what?" Quinn asked, taking the joint Susie offered. She rarely smoked and held the joint between her front teeth as she inhaled in a rush of breath.

"Don't eat it, Quinn," Lisbeth complained, and pinched the joint from Quinn's mouth.

Susie leaned against the back door staring out the little window. The snow furrowed the landscape in huge white mounds, crenelated the trees and entombed the jeep.

Lily appeared in the doorway crying with glee, "We're snowbound!" Behind her Dinah made a sour face.

359

―――

"How cozy it is! All snowed in," Lisbeth said in a scratchy soprano not her own. "Great!" She clapped and the sinuous gliding transformed into a shuffling two-step. Eyes wide as half dollars shuttered into narrow slits.

Quinn gagged and dropped the tumbler. Scotch spilled in a puddle on twined star jasmine vines, but nobody noticed.

Susie wore the blank expression of a wax mask. Somehow she found herself on the sofa, pushed against the back as if a hand shoved her in the middle of her chest. She shuddered and saw herself on the sheepskin rug before the dying fire in the A-frame ski house. Outside, in the desolate Vermont fields and woods, another demonic storm raged in furious howling.

Lisbeth outdrank them, finishing a bottle of Gallo red all by herself. She smoked a second joint after the others begged off. Stretched out on the couch, one long, jean-clad leg thrust over the Indian blanket draped back, she slept. Susie touched her mouth, with moth strokes brushing fine wisps of hair.

The others were upstairs, and Susie curled by the hearth, making a game of the pirouetting flames until she too dropped off. She woke to the tickle of breath spiraling in her ear. "No, Lis, don't," she whimpered sleepily. "Not here."

"It's not Lisbeth," the other hissed, and smiled. The slashed mouth came down to bite or to kiss and Susie shrilled, rolling onto her side. "I heard you two call it girls' love. What a giggle! It's this and this and this." The hands scampered everywhere like ferrets in hasty flight. "Doing things to each other, to yourselves."

Susie gagged, a sour taste spuming in her throat. "Let me alone!" she wept, but Lily only laughed.

Lisbeth hit her, a stinging blow to the side of the head that sent Lily sprawling, cartwheeling back.

"You shit!" Lisbeth swore, punching Lily in the stomach. Susie scrambled out from under them as Lily tumbled forward striking Lis in the chin. They fought like two lovers, close in, breathing one another's hot breath, as they wrestled in the cramped space between the couch and the fire. Lily's foot thrust against the charred logs, exploding a shower of sparks. "I'm going to kill you!" Lisbeth snarled, and yanked a hard handful of hair from Lily's head. Lily screamed as Lisbeth slapped her mouth into a cruel twist.

"Stop it! The others will hear you!" Susie begged, grabbing first at one, then the other, but both pulled out of her grasp.

Lily's knee came up and battered Lisbeth between the breasts. Lisbeth gave way and Lily scuttled out onto the hardwood floor. From her knees she leaped up and fled toward the kitchen. Though Susie whispered shrilly, "Let her go!" Lisbeth sprang up and took off in pursuit. Susie followed, running, sliding on the polished floor. She crashed into the doorjamb just as Lily grabbed a carving knife off the drainboard.

"Keep away from me," Lily cried, *"or I'll stick you like a pig!"*

Lisbeth never stopped. She launched herself straight at Lily as Susie screamed. Lily stumbled into the counter and somehow the knife in its flashing arc came into Lisbeth's hand. "Who's going to kill who, bitch!" she yelled, and Lily ran.

Lisbeth was at the window, her face against the pane. "I can see Lily in the snow," she whispered.

"Oh, Lis, don't!" Susie cried, and leaping up, ran to her. She spun Lisbeth around. "You can't see Lily. This isn't Vermont. This is New York. And that, all *that*, was twenty years ago." Susie shook her. Lisbeth was loose as old clothes.

"Suz, where's all the time gone?" Tears sparkled in her eyes.

"Get her a drink, Quinn."

"She's probably had too much already," Quinn said.

Lisbeth blinked and crystal tears trickled down her cheeks. "Suz, my head's killing me. The pain won't let go! Oh!" She screamed and broke loose, pressing her palms to her pounding temples.

"What's wrong with her?" Susie wept.

"The accident. I don't know. God, we better call an ambulance."

"No! No more doctors. No more . . ." Lisbeth shuddered and her voice faltered to a groan. "Oh, the darkness is coming!"

Susie put her hand out to Lisbeth again, but the scream that crashed through Lisbeth sent Susie spinning. Lisbeth dug in the robe pocket and the gun appeared in her hand.

"A gun?" Susie said, disbelieving, as Lisbeth waved the revolver. Light crackled along the shiny blackness in rockets.

"Lis, this is craziness," Quinn said slowly, dragging the words out.

Lisbeth came around in a slow glissade. "Everybody's dead. Lily's dead and nobody was sorry." She cried in great sobbing heaves. "Not me, either. Then I saw the flowers,'' she choked. "My father's dead, too. Did I tell you?'' she asked, now sounding like a little girl.

"I'm calling St. Vincent's,'' Quinn said as Lisbeth swung to her. Susie wouldn't have believed awkward Quinn could move so fast. The poker rose, slicing up through the air to meet Lisbeth's temple just at the hairline.

Everything should have stopped; they should have been frozen in time, Susie thought then and later. But the poker cracked Lisbeth's skull with a terrible crunching sound like somebody stepping on a tin can and flattening it. Lisbeth keeled over in the first ungainly motion Susie had ever seen her make. She stumbled as the red spurt of blood splashed, and fell drunkenly, dropping halfway over the arm of the sofa. The blood flooded in curling riverlets across the beige linen.

When Susie knelt by Lis's side the lustrous green eyes were already dimming.

29

It was another cemetery, another leaden day, but without the promise
of sunlight slicing through the sky. Snow lay hard and crusted over the
uneven ground and banked about the grave markers protruding in stony
wedges. Only the jagged rectangle gaped darkly in the white earth.

A bitter wind blew unbridled. Susie burrowed inside her mink coat,
but the wind stung her cheeks, freezing the tears on her lashes. Quinn
stood at Susie's left side, motionless as a Coldstream Guard, her face
washerwoman red from the cold. They seemed to have nothing more to
say to each other, certainly not now as they hung at the perimeter of the
large gathering that had braved the elements to witness Mikey Johnson's interment.

Dinah's harsh cries drowned out the reedy voice of the minister and
rode on the wind from where she stood at the lip of the grave into
which her son's body would soon be lowered. Hatch was attached to
her with his arm about her shoulders all through the endless ceremony,
as if they were welded together in a bronzed sculpture entitled *Grieving
Parents*. Susie was reminded of Greg's funeral and her in-laws. The
grotesquerie of death, especially a child's, brought at least a momentary peace between combative or distant partners. For the first time in a
long while she watched Hatch Johnson, but then Mikey had been his
son too, and who really knew which of the grief-stricken parents was
actually supporting the other. Stacy Delmonico wasn't present, or at
least no woman who fit Dinah's description of her husband's girlfriend,
and if Joe Connors was in attendance Susie couldn't pick him out
among all the anonymous men in dark overcoats. A whey-faced woman,
beak-nosed and with faded yellow hair, tentatively held Dinah's left elbow. She thought she remembered Mrs. Esterman in that stringy, older
female.

"Then there'll be Lisbeth's funeral to go to," Quinn had said,
riding up in the car from Manhattan, the only time she'd spoken on the

long drive. Quinn had been exonerated by the police for striking the blow that left Lisbeth dead, but the publicity had been brutal. "RE-NOWNED SCIENTIST BEATS OLD FRIEND TO DEATH IN LOVE NEST," "DOC BLUDGEONS COP KILLER," the tabloids had screamed. Reporters and television crews besieged Quinn's building, but the most they'd caught of her was a blurred motion as she hurried into the black limousine old Mr. Webster sent down from Boston. Earl, who came with the car, was more visible on the evening news as he closed the rear door upon Quinn's retreating figure. She stayed these past few days at the Pierre in isolation, not even venturing out to the lab and talking only once to Stevie on the phone.

Susie also suffered from the publicity, though the media were less interested in a witness. But she too spent nightmarish hours being interrogated. It was the naked body in the bedroom that interested the police most avidly and caused the scowling, the angry raised voices. "Why'd she shoot Neff?" they kept asking. But neither Susie nor Quinn even knew the man sprawled cold and dead across Lisbeth's satin sheets. They were as shocked, or more so, than the uniformed patrolmen who discovered the body.

I don't know who he is or how he got there! Susie repeated in a litany until she was hoarse.

Neff, they informed her again and again, was one of them.

How did he come to be in Lisbeth's apartment? And why would she murder him? Why had she then pointed Neff's gun at two of her oldest friends? What did all this have to do with the drowned boy up in Westport? Then a connection was made with Greg's deliberate hit-and-run, after which they hammered at Susie until morning. Just when she thought she should call Clive Pressman, her lawyer, they let her go, along with Quinn. When they finally left Lisbeth's it was dawn, and the storm had blown over.

Lisbeth was mentally deranged, Quinn had pronounced profession-ally to the various detectives. For a while it had seemed the police wouldn't buy that explanation, but in the end they must have, or at least appeared to. There was, of course, the evidence.

Lisbeth died still clasping the gun, and powder burns stained her hands. Later the autopsies revealed that both she and Neff recently had sex. Susie, when she heard this, became physically ill. How could Lisbeth, even believing in her demons—what or whoever they were—murder a man with whom she'd just made love? It hadn't anything to do with love; it was just sex, Quinn said with firm authority, on this subject of which she had no experience, when Susie asked her.

After that night during which both Mikey and Lisbeth died, the women tried repeatedly to contact Dinah. But she wouldn't or couldn't come to the phone. Two days before the funeral they drove to Westport, but a furry little man who identified himself as a neighbor answered the door. After he checked with Dinah, keeping them on the porch beyond the latched storm door, he returned to say she refused to see them.

What did Dinah know? What had she guessed? Quinn and Susie couldn't agree on how much to tell her. Now, hovering in the background like strangers, it appeared as if they'd never have to confide in her at all.

Dinah's voice rose in a heart-shattering cry. The funeral was officially over. Hatch urged her around, almost dragging her, Mrs. Esterman securing her other arm. Together they pulled her down the path opening between the mourners. As they neared the string of cars parked in the road beyond, Susie braced herself and stepped up to the lurching trio. Quinn stayed close behind her.

Whatever words Susie might have offered never got spoken, for Dinah saw them and started screeching, "Your fault! Yours!"

"Dinah, come on. Let's get into the car." Hatch tugged her, but she was immobile as one of the tombstones.

Quinn gasped. "What are you saying?"

Susie knew instinctively what Dinah meant, and tried to retreat. Dinah lurched and Hatch held her off the two women with difficulty. "Stop it! Behave yourself, Dinah!" her mother ordered sternly, but if she heard, Dinah wasn't listening. She struggled like a chained animal.

"If we hadn't stayed together my baby'd be alive today!" she shrilled with a despair colder than the buffeting wind.

"Dinah!" Hatch roared, quivering uncontrollably.

Susie, backed against Quinn, whispered, "Lis never knew what she was doing. That accident in California caused brain damage we didn't know about." Because she killed Lily all those years ago, Susie restrained herself from adding.

Dinah fought against her husband and mother, grief giving her the strength to repulse them. She hurtled at Susie, it seemed, but flew right by her to Quinn. Leather fingers caught Quinn's throat and squeezed. The crowd, which had quieted in horrified curiosity as the women confronted each other, shuffled forward now so as not to miss this scuffling, this indecorous graveyard behavior.

Dinah was screaming. "She never killed Lily, did she, Quinnie?" The old nickname sounded obscene. Dinah growled as she pressed against Quinn's darkening skin cheek to cheek, and Susie thought only she heard Dinah hiss as she fell against the two women,

"You stabbed Lily in the snow that night. I saw you from an up-stairs window."

Afterwards Susie wanted to believe some trick of the wind had transmogrified impotent words into that horrible accusation, for the scuffle was over in a minute. Dark-sleeved arms, Hatch's and several of the other men's, beat down on the three of them, wrenching Quinn free and dragging Dinah off at last to the waiting car. Susie fell to the snowy ground on her knees, tearing her stockings, and an unknown man hoisted her up again. Her black mink hat dropped off and got trampled underfoot. Susie, in her distress, never thought to retrieve it.

All at once the snow that had threatened throughout the burial ceremony began to drift softly downward. The wet flakes kissed Susie's cheeks, but she couldn't differentiate them from the flowing tears. *I won't survive this,* she was thinking, not sure even then which of the blows she meant. As she wandered, dazed, along the cars, a fantasy took shape. She imagined she walked over the shards of her life and ground them with each step into the snow. She envisioned the dead, Greg grim and accusing, Lisbeth with that terrible grimace, Mikey Johnson's drowned face shimmering whitely beneath her boots. Even Simon materialized for a moment as she kept going, a monstrous moan all about her, though she didn't know if it was a sound she made or only the wind.

The familiar dash of the BMW looked as foreign as a space capsule instrument panel, and Susie forgot entirely how to start the car. Not that it mattered. She sat behind the wheel expelling clouds of steamy breath, her hands shaking so she couldn't mate the key with the ignition. *I'll never be able to drive to Manhattan.* Manhattan seemed an impossible distance, a million miles, from here through the galaxy to the next planet. Susie felt stranded.

After a few minutes, Quinn asked, "Do you want me to drive?"

"No, I'll be all right." She put her head down on the steering wheel. The car was cold as a tomb.

The rest of the cortege had left the cemetery. When Susie finally looked up she saw ebony figures etched against a white matt. The gravediggers were shoveling earth into the hole in the ground. Mikey was being covered with darkness.

How could Lisbeth have killed a child?

"Madness," Quinn said, as if reading her mind. "It was a kind of irrationality, that attachment we had to one another, back at Cabot I mean. Afterwards, it was need, a terrible feeling that we had to hold on to one another."

"Because of Lily," Susie said. The snow had stopped. If she ever managed to put the BMW into motion, the roads would be no more treacherous than they'd been earlier. All it took was will and the energy to act, she thought, gripping the shiny key like a talisman. She clenched her teeth and forced her hand to stay steady, remembering that Betts and Tia would be waiting at home. *I have responsibilities and obligations, a life to get on with,* she told herself as the key finally slid into the ignition.

They drove along the narrow cemetery lane, riding in the middle away from the banked-up drifts at the shoulders. As they passed through tall iron gates, she wanted to stop and face Quinn, but her emotions were too churned up.

"Not Lily at all, not really," Quinn said in a voice laden with doom. "It was you, Susie, you and Lisbeth." They drove out onto a secondary road that wound in a riata through a development of boxy houses. "I don't think you have any idea what the two of you were like at Cabot," Quinn went on. Susie stayed in second. She wished her hearing would fail so whatever Quinn said would be soundless. Yet Susie didn't stop her. An icy calm gripped her as she concentrated on not skidding, on keeping the car safe between the two shimmering white lines. She maneuvered over a diagram, a map in her mind. "Both so beautiful. The real golden ones. You with that cloud of wonderful hair and Lis like a flame. Just full of life! Bursting with it!" Quinn exploded, agonized. "Looking at either one of you made the rest of us realize we were second-rate, condemned to be pedestrian no matter what we did. There wasn't a girl in the dorm, in all of Cabot as a matter of fact, who wouldn't have traded places with you or Lis in a flash."

"I wasn't like that at all. Just an ordinary girl from Baltimore," Susie protested, but she lied, for she remembered the power she contained back then, how even the earth had little substance beneath her. She flew, always dancing, forever with a grin of delight. People followed helplessly in her wake. And Lisbeth, Lisbeth was even more special. Lisbeth was tall and lithe, polished marble come to life. Quinn was right; she'd had fire. She had grace, an incandescence, and a mind of sparkling alacrity. Lisbeth's edginess, that intensity and belief in the ultimate triumph of fairy tales, went into making movies where nothing and everything were real at the same time, where truth and the lie fit together precisely.

Susie heard a rustling, Quinn shuffling around on the leather seat. She said, "Who knows what would have happened if the four of us never shared the suite, if we'd all had single rooms, or you and Lisbeth

367

had been alone. But a capricious fate threw Dinah and me in with you, and you accepted us. We thought we were blessed."

They swung off the hills, the parkway below running to two parallel lanes. Susie turned right for the entrance ramp. Soon she'd cross from Connecticut into New York State, and then home wouldn't be so far away. But when she tried to picture the apartment, she brought up only images of Baltimore, her mother's domain. Having started out to imitate her, she'd ultimately done the opposite. Violence and death, so many lies and regrets. She had never mirrored Ivy at all, she finally realized.

"In some insidious fashion Lily would have destroyed us, Susie. Individually as well as together. She schemed for so long, and then she thought she had us. But all she'd gotten was a ticket of admission, won by blackmail, intimidation. She would never have belonged. She must have sensed as much even in those few hours. Lily wasn't stupid, just mean."

"Hungry," Susie interrupted.

"So she got madder and madder, more determined not to be locked out as she always was by her mother and the latest husband."

You didn't have to kill her. Only Susie couldn't say it, for she knew in her heart Lisbeth had always been forgiven as Quinn never would be.

"You and Lis went to bed after that fight in the kitchen. I heard it all from the stairs, then hid when you came up. Lily stayed in a nasty mood, smoking a joint and drinking beer."

"Don't tell me!" Susie cried. The BMW swerved out of control as a horn blared frantically too near her left rear fender. Reflexively she steadied the car again.

Quinn continued relentlessly. "I went down to the kitchen." It was too late to silence Quinn anyway, her need to confess stinging after twenty years. Susie thought of Simon and could have wept. *Why wouldn't he listen to me?* "Lily was mouthing off with all sorts of threats. She even swore to get me expelled, Di too, for knowing about you and Lisbeth. She said that by never saying, or turning you in, we'd condoned that *perverted* lovemaking. Lily's word, not mine," she explained. "I still don't know if Dinah understood about you two. Let's face it, Di's an innocent. She can't see the nose on her face. Look at her marriage to Hatch. Now . . ."

"I never realized you knew," Susie said, but she wasn't surprised, for her youthful arrogance had blinded her to so much.

"It doesn't matter. Didn't. Besides, who was I to judge? I loved you both unthinkingly." They were silent for a while. Then Quinn said, "Maybe this Joe Connors can save Dinah."

"Nobody can save anyone," Susie burst out angrily. "We should have learned that, Quinn. One wrong act, a single mistake, becomes the cornerstone of disaster." She spoke without meaning to and stepped down heavily on the gas. The BMW leaped ahead.

"The carving knife was just there on the sink, and with Lily ranting so foolishly, I picked it up and waved it at her. I guess I must have scared her, because she ran like a frightened rabbit, like the fool she'd always been."

"And you went outside after her."

"Yes."

"You didn't have to stab her," Susie said at last. The words tasted foul. A chasm was opening in the car between her and Quinn, as wide, if not wider, than the crevice Lisbeth's madness created. With one part of her mind Susie comprehended and forgave, instantaneously, Lis's insanity. It wasn't so with Quinn, for here had been the seed that grew and spread its tendrils like a diseased vine through all their lives. What would they have done or been if she hadn't killed Lily? Maybe different, maybe not, she realized, more grieved than horrified.

They were just entering the city, the majestic sweep of the George Washington Bridge on their right holding out some future promise of escape. *If I could only get on it and go west!* Susie thought, passing by the mammoth stone abutments.

Quinn hadn't spoken for miles, but now asked, more defeated than apprehensive, "Are you going to turn me in?"

Susie laughed bitterly. "To whom? The police? What for, Quinn?"

"Conscience, I suppose."

"Come on. All this time I thought it was Lisbeth and I never did a thing about it. So where would I get off suddenly insisting I have a conscience? If I do, it's a small, wiggly thing not worth considering. Besides, as you said, I bear responsibility for what you did. Lis and I both." Silently she asked herself, not Quinn, *How can I be guilty for being only who I was?* The answer came to her immediately. Being inert was as sinful as taking wrongful action. She'd always known that omission as surely as commission damned her.

Susie took Quinn over to the East Side. She intended to drive right to the building, but Quinn asked to be let out a few blocks west. She wanted to walk. Waiting for the light, Susie watched her moving off down the sidewalk, growing smaller and smaller. By the time the signal flashed green Quinn was lost among knots of other people. Would she see her again? Susie thought not. She'd never see Dinah either. It had shattered, the quartet, constructed of glass after all, not steel, and the loss of friendship burned in her, incinerating her heart.

She drove back through the park and at her own apartment building asked the doorman on duty if he'd garage the car.

"Sure, Mrs. Lamton," he replied with a wide smile. "For you, anything."

Upstairs she unlocked the front door and recalled as she stepped into the foyer that Mrs. Sloan had asked for half a day off. Susie called out for her daughters. All of a sudden she needed their warmth, to physically touch them, hold their girlish bodies close to her own.

As she rushed down the bedroom hallway the familiar odor brought her up short. "Betts!" she cried, flinging aside the door. Betts was hastily stubbing out a butt in an ashtray. Tia curled on the bed, a silly grin glued on her lips. "You're smoking grass," Susie accused.

Betts thrust out a strong chin. "What of it?"

"And you gave some to your sister!"

"Just a couple of hits." She shrugged.

Susie's temper ran away with her as she yelled, "Tia is only ten!"

Betts, determined to play hardball with her mother, shrugged again. "So big deal."

"Hi, Mommy." Tia giggled, struggling to sit up. "I feel nice, even better than last time."

Susie grabbed both her daughters, yanking them to their feet. "Let go!" Betts screamed, but Susie held her tightly.

"You're coming with me, both of you."

Tia asked, stumbling weak-kneed, "Where, Mommy?"

"Get!" She threw Betts out into the hallway.

Pushing and slapping at them, she drove the girls like sheep into the foyer. Only at the last minute did she think to grab their jackets from the front closet.

John hadn't had a chance to park the BMW yet. It still waited where she left it before the awning. John leaped ahead of them and pulled open the doors, one with each hand which usually made Tia giggle, though not this time. Susie shoved the girls inside the car unceremoniously and tossed the jackets in after them.

"Don't say a word," Susie advised as she got in the driver's side. "And Betts, if you so much as twitch, I swear I'll—" She drew a deep breath that tasted strangely of dust and ashes. "You'll just be very, very sorry."

They took Susie seriously enough not to speak during the ride down Ninth Avenue. She had never, in their experience, been the parent to lose control and rage. Now she supposed she frightened them like a fire-snorting dragon. Good, she meant to. It was long past the time to do something about Betts. The headmistress's warning rang alarmingly. It wasn't too early either to take a firmer hand to Tia.

The only thought in Susie's head as she swung the BMW in and out of traffic was, *No more mistakes.*

At the shelter she ordered them out of the car. It was nearing supper-time and the homeless were already gathered about the old warehouse in a shuffling formation that extended along the front of the building and around the corner. Accompanied by bulging shopping bags and battered suitcases of belongings, they huddled in shabby jackets and secondhand coats against the cold. Only a few heads lifted up into the wind for weary, red-rimmed eyes to stare uncuriously at the white BMW.

"What's this?" Betts scowled, shrinking against the car.

Susie came around to the sidewalk and hit her, more of a soft clout than a blow, on the side of the head. "Move!"

Simon, in the kitchen helping Jose, glanced through the large pass hole at the slam of the door. For an instant his face hung there like a framed photograph.

Sven, setting up the long serving table, waved a soup ladle in greeting. "Susie!"

Approaching cautiously, Simon said, "Hello."

"Simon, these are my daughters. Betts and Tia." She pushed each girl forward as she spoke her name. "This is Father Simon," she introduced the priest. "He runs this shelter, The Good Shepherd, for all those people you saw outside. He feeds them and gives them a place to sleep. When it's cold like today, there won't be room or food enough. Twenty, thirty, sometimes fifty people will be turned away hungry. They'll sleep tonight on top of a subway grating or in a doorway. Some of them go underground and look for a place in the tunnels. A few of them won't survive until morning. A few more won't make it through tomorrow night. They'll freeze to death or die in accidents or even be killed by some crazy." She rushed on urgently, but the miserable girls standing close to each other might not have been listening. All their attention was focused on Simon.

After one brief intense look at Susie, Simon turned to the girls. "Welcome to The Good Shepherd," he said. Though he wore his familiar flannel shirt and faded jeans, a navy bandanna poking out a hip pocket, he appeared in his solemnity more the priest than usual.

Susie's love barely breathed in the shelter's large main room, the sounds of chairs scraping, plates being stacked for the table, the crash of the soup pot settling upon its iron trivet. She said, "Take them, Simon. Put them to work. Let them help Jose in the kitchen and Sven serving food. Give them mops and have them clean the bathrooms."

"What?" he asked, surprised.

Tia's lips parted and Betts started to say something but quickly changed her mind.

"They've got to learn they're not the only humans on the planet and that there's suffering, hunger, and pain."

"Look, Mom," Betts retorted, "I've seen the news on TV."

"Now you're going to see it close up—broken teeth, ravaged faces, rough shaking hands, wounds and scabs and scars. You'll smell them, too. The homeless smell bad, sour and musty."

Tears filled Tia's voice. "I want to go home."

Involuntarily Susie's hand fluttered down to Tia's head and brushed her hair. For a moment it seemed she could change her mind. Then she whispered, "None of us is special. There are no golden ones."

Jose had come out of the kitchen. Simon called over his shoulder, already widening his arms to gather in the girls, "Jose, we've got two new helpers."

Her daughters would come to love the priest just as she had. She wished she might keep them from that, but there was just so much she could do. Maybe though, if they were lucky, they'd learn in this refuge that love wasn't everything.

"I'll be back to get them later," she said. "But you can expect them tomorrow at the same time. And Saturday all day." If she heard the girls' protests, she never let on. Without another word, and only a last look at Simon already blessing the girls with his smile, she left the shelter for the gathering night outside.

The crowd had grown and the line stretched longer and more ragged. Some stragglers pushed off the sidewalk and into the gutter.

The snow was falling again, now in thick heavy flakes. Susie turned her face up to the soiled, gray city sky and let the snow wet her skin. This storm too would eventually blow over, but there would come another. All through the short cold days and endless nights of winter snow would threaten, fall in scattered flakes or gust with the full force of a blizzard. After a while the earth on its turning would bring them to spring. As Susie got back in the car she thought, *I can wait.*